# Said & Done

Annie Sparrow is in her early thirties, from England and is now living in Dublin. Her background is in sales and marketing and this is her first novel. She is currently working on her second book.

# Said & Done

Annie Sparrow

**POCKET BOOKS**

**TOWNHOUSE**

First published in Great Britain and Ireland by
Pocket/Townhouse, 2001
An imprint of Simon & Schuster UK Ltd and TownHouse and
CountryHouse Ltd, Dublin

Simon & Schuster UK is a Viacom company

3 5 7 9 10 8 6 4 2

Simon & Schuster UK Ltd
Africa House
64-78 Kingsway
London WC2B 6AH

Simon & Schuster Australia
Sydney

TownHouse and CountryHouse Ltd
Trinity House
Charleston Road
Ranelagh
Dublin 6
Ireland

A CIP catalogue record for this book is available from the
British Library

ISBN 1-903650-17-8

Typeset by SX Composing DTP, Rayleigh, Essex
Printed and bound in Great Britain by
Omnia Books Ltd, Glasgow

# Acknowledgements

My sincere thanks go to Rosemary and Sheila for all the cups of tea and support; to my agent Faith O'Grady; and to everyone at TownHouse and Simon & Schuster.

For my parents, Fred and Olive

# Part One

**Mata Hari gets her P45 for renouncing sex,** was highlighted in Emma's e-mail inbox menu. She laughed; it was obviously Jeremy from the London branch. Glancing around the office, she clicked on the title to bring the message up on screen.

```
Darling Emma,

Being my spy at head office, you are
seriously letting me down - lie back,
think of England and get some info. This
is no time for sensitivities.

WHAT IS THE MEETING ABOUT AT MANCHESTER
TOMORROW? AND WHY THE LAST-MINUTE SUMMONS
FOR ALL THE SOLICITORS (BIRMINGHAM AND
LONDON BRANCHES) TO ATTEND?

Unless I receive a suitable answer by
09.30, complete with full gossip, serious
repercussions will follow!

Yours truly,
Jeremy

PS As I will be attending the meeting I
shall stay the evening in Manchester and
*DEMAND* your company for dinner!

PPS Please can you book the hotel for me?
```

```
Richard Hayes wants a room for tomorrow
night also. As it's a Friday, I
understand the others will drive back to
London.
```

Emma was grinning broadly but was confused by the contents. She looked across at Trish, the other legal secretary with whom she shared the small and cluttered office and asked, 'Have you heard about a meeting tomorrow?'

Trish looked up momentarily, shook her head, then carried on applying some red lipstick while staring into a small, hand-held, oyster-shaped mirror.

'That's odd,' said Emma.

'What is?'

'Just got an e-mail from Jeremy. Said there's a meeting here, tomorrow. Everyone's attending.'

'Have we got to go?'

'No. Just the solicitors and clerks.'

'Of course, how silly of me. Thought we were important for a moment.' Trish shot her a look of mock annoyance.

Emma smiled but soon her thoughts turned to the practicalities. 'Conference room's in a right mess, boxes everywhere. Henry hasn't asked me to organise anything.'

'See what he says when he gets in.' Trish put away the mirror and lipstick and started to log on to her computer.

Emma went back into her e-mail system.

```
Jeremy,

At present have no idea what meeting is
about.
```

```
Pretty useless spy, aren't I. I might
need some extra-curricular training!

Henry is in at eleven and I will
hopefully—
```

'Morning, Emma.'

Emma jumped. She turned. Jack Tomkinson, the manager of the London branch, was towering above her.

'Morning, Jack.' She gave a manufactured smile and leant sideways slightly in a pathetic attempt to hide the screen.

'I need to stay another night at the Ramada. You'll organise it, I assume?'

As usual his request sounded more like an order. Emma nodded but was wondering if it would be too obvious if she were to turn and exit out of the programme. Of all the solicitors why did it have to be him, the Pilgrim Father of workaholics? No doubt he'd think it was wasting time and time is money!

'Yes, I'll do that,' she said.

He seemed to hover for a few uncomfortable moments. She watched in horror as his eyes fell downwards towards the screen. Luckily, he turned and marched out. He marched everywhere. Emma dropped her head into her hands. She cringed, screwing her face up. 'This place reminds me of school.'

Trish laughed. 'I agree. The only difference is you're allowed to wear make-up.'

It always amazed Emma how immaculately made up Trish was, every day without exception. It must take her hours. The shoulder-length highlighted blonde hair was obviously curled most mornings. Where did she find the time, or the inclination? Emma would just pull her long brown hair back into the usual ponytail, two strokes of blusher, a quick coating of pinkish lipstick and that was her ready. Then there were the clothes. Trish must have chosen hers for their 'cling' value. Tight-fitting tops, skirts and trousers, all to emphasise her enviable shape.

Emma chose hers for their 'cover' value. Loose fitting to detract from, and hide, her expanding shape. Since reaching her early thirties, her size had slowly crept up. Marks & Spencer sensible skirts and jackets were her usual uniform and they weren't exactly new. It was only since Trish had joined Buckley & Dwyer last year that she had started to realise how her own appearance had somehow become dated and . . . Emma again considered it and struggled to find the right word. Doesn't matter, she thought. I'll do something about it, soon. Maybe.

A few moments later, she continued with the e-mail while cautiously eyeing the entrance to the office.

```
Henry is in at 11 and I will hopefully be
informed then. Love to meet up for
dinner. Haven't seen you in ages. Will
check it with Tony, but he's working, so
it shouldn't be a problem.
Emma.

PS Jack Tomkinson caught me writing this
message. Not sure if he read it. That's
my Christmas bonus gone.
PPS Please delete immediately.
```

Emma pressed the F8 button to send it and quickly exited out of the programme.

Just after eleven, Henry Dwyer the head partner arrived. He was a tall, distinguished-looking man in his mid to late sixties. As usual he popped his head into their office.

'Morning, ladies.'

'Good morning, Henry.'

Emma was about to mention the meeting but quickly stopped herself. Maybe she wasn't supposed to know about it. There was always so much news, confidential information and gossip circulating around the firm. Half the time she got thoroughly confused with how much she was officially supposed to know, who else knew it, who knew she knew it, and who at all costs you were supposed to keep it from. Exhausting! Tony, her husband, referred to Buckley & Dwyer as 'the Asylum', but she knew he had a thing about the law and the legal profession, so his opinion was biased.

She watched Henry leave their office and head off towards his own.

At two-thirty and still with no news of the meeting, Emma took in Henry's afternoon tea.

'Thank you, Emma. Could you sit down for a moment?'

She did so in the leather armchair opposite his solid oak desk. His lined face smiled directly at her. She felt there was a slight sadness in his eyes, unusual for him. Fidgeting with the pen in her hand, she waited.

Henry leant back in his chair and gazed around his impressive office. It was a spacious room with a high, Victorian ceiling and ornate coving. Shelves of old tatty legal reference books covered each wall and cigar smoke lingered in the air.

His eyes rested back on her. 'Would you be so kind as to prepare the Conference room for tomorrow. There's a meeting for all the legal teams. Last count, what, twenty-six people? Unless London's taken on more. Jack's done a tremendous job down there.'

She nodded politely.

'Probably start around ten, finish I suppose, sometime near one. The usual teas and coffees. Also, I know it's short notice, but could you arrange a buffet lunch?'

'Of course. Is there an agenda for typing?'

'No, no. That's not necessary.' He seemed to pause and when he spoke again his tone was more serious. 'I can't really go into anything right now, but there are a few situations that are occurring. *Changes*. They will probably affect your role.' He noted her uneasy expression and quickly added, 'Don't concern yourself yet. Suffice to say, we'll have a good chat next week.'

She gave a worried nod.

'I'll let you get on with it then.'

Emma stood up, smiled and left the room, very intrigued.

The drive home that evening took longer than usual. The incessant rain and slight flooding slowed the traffic down to a crawl; it was always raining in Manchester.

Emma prayed their old Escort wouldn't let her down again, especially in the middle of a junction. It didn't, and eventually, at about quarter past six, she pulled into the cul-de-sac of small Victorian, two up two down terraced houses in Wythenshawe – a suburb about four miles outside the city centre. Cosy, Tony had said to describe the house before they bought it. Cramped and claustrophobic was her first and remaining impression.

She pulled right on to their front garden, now a makeshift parking bay; it avoided the impossible task of finding a space out on the road.

'That you, Em?' Tony shouted from the sitting room.

'Yeah, it's me.'

'You're late. What happened?'

'Traffic.' She took off her coat and went straight upstairs to change.

Not long after, she walked into the sitting room wearing tracksuit bottoms, an old sweatshirt and a pair of Tony's woolly socks. 'Hi.'

'Hi, love,' said Tony, briefly glancing up from watching a re-run of *Star Trek*.

Rob, Tony's younger brother, part-time work colleague and seemingly constant companion, was also there. He was sitting in his adopted armchair and gave Emma a quick nod of his head. Both men were wearing their uniform of black trousers and a black T-shirt with 'Lexson Security' printed in yellow across the front. They were eating their dinner off trays on their laps and each had a bottle of Budweiser by his feet.

Emma continued to stand there for a couple of moments.

Tony looked up at her. 'We're going in early tonight. Some DJ on, so they're expecting a crowd.'

She nodded.

'Would've cooked for you but wasn't sure what time you'd be in.'

'I'm not that late. Always in around six . . .' She said it politely and held back on saying that it had been that way for the last seven and a half years. He was going out soon, so there was no point in creating an atmosphere.

'Only two chicken pies anyway,' he said.

'I know.' She looked over at Rob finishing off her planned dinner, turned and went into the kitchen.

Rob threw a guilty glance towards his brother.

'Doesn't matter,' Tony whispered. 'She can get something later.'


Returning to the lounge with a gin and tonic, Emma went and sat next to Tony on the settee.

'Did you have a good day?' She wasn't sure if he'd heard as several seconds passed before he replied.

'Yeah . . . it was all right.'

She was about to speak further but stopped herself. What was the point? She was obviously disturbing him. After all, television was king!

When *Star Trek* ended, Rob offered to make some coffee. Whilst leaving the room he looked across at Tony and said, 'You gonna mention about Rebecca tonight?'

'Oh yeah, yeah I will.'

'Mention what?' asked Emma.

'Rebecca's calling in the pub tonight. Rob wondered if you wanted to meet her. Seems quite keen on this one. Said you probably wouldn't want to.'

'I'm a bit tired. Just want to relax.'

'That's why people go to pubs, Emma, to relax, to enjoy themselves.' Tony's voice had a slight edge to it.

'I know, I'm sorry. Just fancy staying in. I'm up early tomorrow. There's this meeting at work. It's really *weird*.'

'Why?'

'No one knows what it's about. Henry says it could affect me and what I do.'

Tony looked concerned. 'Your job's safe, isn't it?'

'Expect so.'

'Good. That's the last thing we need.' He got up and stood in front of the mirror above the gas fire. He was at least six-foot tall and, like Emma, his weight had slowly crept up, although he carried it well. He pulled his thinning dark hair back into an elastic band, creating a very small ponytail.

'By the way, Jeremy's up tomorrow night. He's asked me out to dinner,' said Emma.

'Where you going?'

'Not sure yet. He's staying at the Ramada. May end up eating there.'

At that moment Rob entered the room with two mugs of coffee in his hands. 'He's the gay one, isn't he?'

'He *isn't* gay,' she said wearily, fed up of saying it.

The brothers exchanged a funny look.

'If I wasn't convinced he was gay, I wouldn't be happy with you both being so friendly,' said Tony.

'Fine, he's whatever you want to think he is.'

'Well, when was the last time he had a girlfriend? You've know him, what, eight years?'

'Nine.'

'Whatever. I've never heard you mention anyone with him.'

'He's just not into relationships full stop. And who could blame him?' she threw in mockingly.

Tony gave her a dirty look. 'A thirty-five-year-old virgin! Should have been a priest.' Both men laughed loudly.

Even Emma smiled at the thought of Jeremy being a priest.

After gulping down his coffee, Tony leant down and kissed Emma briefly on the lips. 'Bye.' His tired, bloodshot and deep-set, brown eyes studied her. 'Maybe we'll go walking in the Dales on Saturday.

Haven't done that for a while,' he said.

'Definitely. Let's really go.' Inside she suspected that they wouldn't.

'Wake me around eleven.'

She heard the front door slam behind them as they left. Relaxing on the couch she sipped her gin and tonic and considered what the possible changes at work could be. She instinctively smiled when she thought of having dinner with Jeremy. He was many things, but he was never boring.

## 2

At just gone 7pm on Friday night, Emma knocked on the door of room 426 at the Ramada Hotel in central Manchester. The door opened and Jeremy stood there, naked apart from a small towel wrapped around his waist. He was a short, plump man in his mid thirties with balding sandy-coloured hair and a rounded, jolly-looking face. He was grinning and he had a glass in his hand.

'Double gin and tonic all ready for you,' he said.

She laughed, took it and walked in. 'Jeremy, you're a mind reader.'

'Sweetheart, it was hardly difficult. You looked extremely in need of one this morning. I desperately wanted to whisk you away from it all. You were obviously meant for better things.'

'Hardly. Can't even organise a stupid meeting. So annoyed with Paul. He had my key, mislaid his own. And if the ridiculously efficient solicitors hadn't turned up an hour early, there wouldn't have been a problem.' She sat on the bed with a sigh as she remembered the messy and disorganised start of the meeting that morning. Emma hadn't got into the conference room until 9.40, which was when Paul, the caretaker, had turned up with her key. Most of the solicitors had arrived before nine and impatiently stood around the corridors, complaining loudly to Emma. To add insult to injury, Jack Tomkinson had angrily summoned her over the tannoy system, to Henry's office. In front of Harold and Geoff, two other partners, he lectured her, on the importance of basic organisational skills. When she had tried to explain about Paul taking her key, he just dismissed it, explaining the necessity of contingency planning. Inwardly seething, she had listened politely. *Condescending shit*, she'd thought, as she apologised, glad that he worked in the London branch now.

Jeremy poured himself a vodka and tonic from the mini-bar and went and sat next to her. 'Sorry. Didn't mean to turn up early. For some reason there was hardly any traffic on the M6 this morning.'

'Didn't mean you,' she said.

'Oh, so I'm not ridiculously efficient?'

'No. Ridiculous maybe, but definitely not efficient.' She knocked her glass against his. 'Cheers, good to see you.'

'Likewise.' He leant over and kissed her affectionately on the cheek.

'So? What was it all about?'

Jeremy gave her a mysterious smile. His eyes opened wide, gleaming excitedly. 'My darling Emma, fate is dealing you a card. But will you take it or turn away?'

'You're such a bloody drama queen. Just tell me what happened.'

'I'll tell you over dinner.' He got up and took a pair of red corduroy trousers and a yellow shirt out of the wardrobe.

'You sod. Tell me now!'

He shook his head and disappeared into the en-suite bathroom.

Emma sat there drinking her gin and tonic, wondering what Jeremy was going on about. Spotting the full-length mirror, she got up and stood in front of it, turning from side to side, observing herself from various angles. Her hands rested on her stomach, which she stared at for several seconds. Her focus then lifted to her face and she slowly ran her finger underneath her wide, green eyes. I look tired, she thought. Back in her early twenties she was considered quite attractive. She always had the latest hairstyle, clothes, make-up and of course she was tall and slim; ate what she liked and never put on a pound. Now she only had to think of food and her waist seemed to expand. Her clothes were less fashionable and more functional, and her hair was long and had gone back to its natural, mousy-brown colour, which she hated, and worse, there were a few grey hairs running through it.

Grabbing her bag from the floor, she quickly applied some pink lipstick to her full lips. Next, she loosened her ponytail, allowing a few strands to fall around her face, softening her appearance. She took another quick glance at her reflection. Disheartened, she sat back down.

'How do I look?' asked Jeremy, emerging from the bathroom, stinking of after-shave and doing a twirl in front of her.

She thought he looked rather comical dressed in the yellow and red. 'As usual very bright. And of course very nice.'

'*Nice*! How dare you describe my appearance as *nice*! What a cop out of a word,' he said in his theatrical voice.

'You look wonderful, Jeremy. Better than me anyway. I didn't bring a change of clothes so I'm stuck in this navy suit.'

'Yes, very bank clerkish!'

She rolled her eyes at his usual banter.

'Only joking.' He smiled. 'How about going to Dante's?'

'Sounds good.'

He grabbed his jacket and wallet and the two of them left the room. Being five foot eight, she towered at least three inches over him as they walked along the corridor.

Jeremy stopped at the lift and pressed the button to call it. Emma gave him an odd look.

'Stupid of me,' he said.

They went on a little further and came to the staircase. Walking down the four flights of stairs he said, 'At least it's good exercise.'

She knew he was just being kind about her fear of lifts.

Once out of the hotel, they walked for about ten minutes through the back streets of Manchester city centre – mostly shops and office blocks. It was already dark and Emma was glad she wasn't alone; not that Jeremy would be much use.

Around the side of an old factory, now refurbished into offices, they came across a single black door with a small plaque above it, saying 'Dante's Jazz Bar', and in smaller letters, 'MEMBERS ONLY'. They went inside and walked down a cramped staircase into the basement. It led into a plush, red-carpeted reception area with large black and white photographs of early jazz musicians covering each wall.

A mature but glamorous blonde woman greeted them and led them through another door into a darkened room that had no obvious windows. It was lit by brass fitted wall lights and subdued lamps hanging from the ceiling. The room contained about fifteen circular tables spaciously positioned around a small, raised stage area. A 1930s-style oak bar ran the whole length of the back of the room and several people stood around it. Jazz music played through the speakers and a slight smell of cigarette smoke, not unpleasant, lingered in the air.

Emma and Jeremy sat down opposite each other at a

table in a little alcove to the side. Jeremy ordered a bottle of red wine, which arrived immediately.

Once they were alone, Emma said, 'No more excuses. What's going on?'

He took a deep breath, looking her right in the eye. 'Lots.'

She waited, eyes alert.

Jeremy paused, totally thriving on the suspense: he loved any bit of drama. 'Basically, the meeting was about the next three years for the practice. Where we see ourselves, what sort of business we want to attract, opportunities in Europe.'

'And?'

'Well, the first major announcement, and for God's sake keep it to yourself for a week . . . Henry's retiring.'

'Retiring!'

'Ill health. Something to do with his heart. He is sixty-six.'

Emma frowned, confused. 'That's not a complete surprise. But why didn't he tell me himself? Why you lot first?'

Jeremy's mysterious smile appeared again. 'I believe he is waiting on another arrangement being finalised.'

She eyed him dubiously. 'What arrangement?'

'Well, he's retiring by Christmas at the latest. He intends to halve his workload right away. From now on he'll just be looking after the interests of a handful of close clients.' Jeremy drank some of the wine. 'Hmm, this is very good.'

'What arrangement? I presume it involves me. Also, who's the new head partner? Suppose it's Jack Tomkinson? Expect he's on cloud nine. His ultimate dream, our ultimate nightmare.'

Jeremy was grinning and shaking his head erratically. Soon he was practically bouncing up and down in his chair, bursting to tell her. 'No, he's not. Apparently the partners voted last week. It's Harold Ross.'

'Harold! Didn't Jack want it?'

'Of course he did. Partners chose Harold. Surprised us all.'

'God. I bet Jack is totally livid. Bet he leaves.' She gulped at her wine; this was getting interesting.

'I think he considered it, but I don't believe he is.'

'What a kick in the teeth.' Emma couldn't help laughing, especially remembering how he had spoken to her this morning. 'I should feel sorry for him, but I don't.'

Jeremy looked on, amused at her reaction, knowing a bigger shock was to come.

'What about me? Trish is Harold's PA. I expect he'll want to keep her,' she said.

'He does.'

'I'm not out of a job, am I?'

'No. This is kind of point three, which is good and bad.'

Emma sat up straight, concerned at what she was going to hear.

'This is half what I've heard and half my own interpretation. I don't think it is one hundred per cent definite yet, that's why you haven't been spoken to.' He sipped his wine. 'This really is a nice glass of wine. Anyway, over the next few months a new secretarial position is bound to be created. So, the question is, what to do with you until then?'

'Thanks.'

'Don't shoot the messenger, Emma.' He took a small cigar out of his pocket and lit it. 'You don't mind, do you?'

She shook her head.

Jeremy continued. 'You know that there's been talk about opening a Dublin office for ages. A number of our international clients have started operations over there. I understand there's some good tax concessions by having a base there too.'

Emma nodded.

'Well, it looks like it's going ahead. They've got the offices and everything. They need someone on the secretarial side to go over and get it up and running, train new staff et cetera. Only for three to four months, then they come back. Anyway I think that person is you.'

'Me? *Dublin*?' she screamed.

'It's only over the water. Forty-five minutes on a plane. Hardly Hong Kong, Emma.'

'But I've never even been there. Where would I stay?'

'Heard of such a thing as a hotel? Presumably you'll come back at weekends. It'll do you good, a new challenge, a change of scene, a break from Tony.' He said the last bit almost in a whisper, unsure whether he was overstepping the mark again. In their nine-year friendship, the only real argument they had had was over comments Jeremy had made about Tony. Of course he had apologised afterwards, but it had taken a while for their friendship to return to normal.

Emma stared at him but said nothing.

'The only thing is,' his eyes were hiding something, 'the person going to set up and manage the Dublin office for a short while is . . .' he paused.

'Who?'

'It's not definite.'

'*Who*?'

'The delightful Jack Tomkinson.'

Emma screwed her face up and sat back in her chair despondently.

'I know it doesn't sound very good,' he said.

'No it doesn't, so why do I detect an amused glint in your eye?'

Jeremy started to grin. 'You must admit, it is kind of funny.'

'If it was happening to someone else maybe, but it's happening to me.' She pointed to herself for emphasis. She was waving her hands and shaking her head to convince him her answer was a firm no. 'I've worked for him before, remember. Total miracle when he left to set up London. I don't want to work for him again, especially in a strange country. Will he be in the same hotel? He's so tight on expenses, he'll have us sharing a room.'

Jeremy burst into raucous laughter. 'Probably the same bed.'

She started to laugh herself, more at him than the situation.

'He won't allow . . .' Jeremy was literally shaking and couldn't speak for a moment. A few tears fell from his eyes. 'Won't allow . . . hotel meals. Have to send over food parcels,' he shrieked.

He had such a loud laugh that she began to feel a bit embarrassed. She smiled at him but glanced over his shoulder at the customers on the other tables. A few looked over at them.

Eventually when he seemed to calm down a bit she asked, 'When is all this supposed to happen anyway?'

He shrugged his shoulders. 'That is the extent of my knowledge, I'm afraid. For God's sake keep it to yourself.' He drew hard on his cigar. 'Joking aside, if you are asked to go, personally I think you should. How many times have you spoken to me about being in a rut? I can see it in your face, Emma. It would be something different. You'd learn a lot and it would look good on your CV. Yes, Jack is, is . . .' he was looking for the right word, '. . . a pain sometimes, maybe most times. But he's good at his job. Also you're different, more confident. You can handle him.' Jeremy filled up their glasses. 'And just think, I can visit you and we can hit the town over there.'

Emma sipped her wine and was silent.

As the evening progressed, the restaurant area filled up and snippets of conversation, laughter and clinking of glasses could be heard around the room. Halfway through their main course, Jeremy ordered another bottle of wine.

Emma was feeling a lot more relaxed and enjoying her chicken Kiev. 'I'm going to stink of garlic. Tony won't come near me.'

'Quick, eat some more.'

She laughed.

'How is the old man?' he asked.

After some deliberation she replied, 'He's fine.'

'Fine, is he? That doesn't really say much. Is he still working as a, what do you call them, a bouncer?'

She glared at him. He was walking close to the edge. 'Don't try and act a snob. I know you're not.'

'You're mistaken there, I am a snob.'

'Rubbish, you don't look down on the less well off. What about all the free time you give at the Citizens' Advice Bureau? Your politics are so left wing you're positively a communist. You can't be a snobby communist, can you?'

'In theory, yes. However my snobbery is not aimed at those who are materially less well off. Absolutely not! It is aimed at . . . I was going to say the intellectually less well off, but that isn't true either. I am a snob towards the stupid of our society. And stupidity transcends intelligence, material wealth, education, social standing, religion et cetera.' He put a piece of steak in his mouth and chewed it. 'Oh, not that I'm saying Tony is stupid.'

'I *hope* you're not.' Emma's voice had a warning edge.

Jeremy's expression altered to show more concern. 'How is he in himself then?'

Emma looked away and thought about what to say. At times in the past she had really opened up to Jeremy; after all, he was probably her closest friend. But when things then went well with Tony, she always regretted that she'd said anything, feeling almost disloyal. Also, Jeremy never forgot a word and would occasionally remind her of certain things she had said – things she would rather forget. 'He's a lot happier. He's quite busy with various bits of work. When he's busy he's happy.'

'Good. I'm glad . . . honestly.'

'He's still convinced you're gay. It's good in a way 'cause he doesn't mind us going out.'

'Probably just scared of his own sexuality. Most men are.'

She looked him squarely in the eye. 'You would tell me if you were?'

Jeremy looked back at her with a look of astonishment on his face. 'Emma! We have spoken about this. I just can't imagine sharing my life with someone on that level, emotional or physical.' At the word physical he screwed up his face. 'Anyway, you know I'm saving myself for Cliff Richard.'

Emma laughed, but gradually her gaze fell downwards. 'When we first discussed this, years ago, I remember being so appalled and saddened with you basically shutting the door on any relationship. Really thought you were going to miss out on what I then considered was the most important aspect of life . . . love and finding one's so-called soulmate.' She shook her head and laughed at her own romantic notions. 'I used to think that was the main purpose of life.'

'I know you did. Your views were as repugnant and futile to me, as mine were to you.'

'The scary thing is, the older I've got, the less appalling your view is.'

'Is that a compliment? Are you agreeing with me?' he asked.

'No. No way. Not yet anyway.' She smiled. 'It's just that maybe the ground between our opinions is not so wide as it once was. That's sad really.' She sighed wearily. 'I still hope you meet someone, Jeremy. I think deep down you'd really like to.'

'Maybe you will too?'

She glared across at him.

He winked back.

'You shouldn't say things like that. I'm serious, I mean it. You know I have strong views on that sort of thing. No thanks.' She looked away and saw the cabaret was about to start, a four-piece jazz band.

'Sorry. I know I'm a sod. I'll blame it on the wine. I just think . . .'

'I know what you think,' she quickly interrupted him and added very firmly, 'Don't go there tonight, Jeremy.'

He noted the seriousness in her eyes. He sipped his wine and smiled.

## 3

Tony stood, round-shouldered, over the kitchen sink, wearing boxer shorts and a T-shirt. He filled up a pint glass with tap water and drank at least half of it in one go. Emma squeezed past him and placed the four carrier bags of shopping on the floor.

'Hi,' she said.

'Hi,' he replied quietly, rubbing his right eye and yawning.

'Want some lunch?'

He very slowly shook his head, even that was an effort. Drinking the remainder of the water, he filled up the glass again. 'I'll get out of your way,' he mumbled as he ambled back up the stairs carrying the water in his hand.

Emma heard the bedroom door close. She didn't bother asking about the trip to the Dales. It was now one o'clock and so it obviously wasn't going to happen today. Maybe next weekend.

As arranged, she had brought him up a coffee at eleven, but he was dead to the world. She shook him a couple of times, then gave up. For a considerable while she stared despondently out of the window. No one was out. The road was completely still, apart from Mrs McDermott's dog, Tom, who was trying to shelter from the rain under some boxes that had been dumped in his front garden. He looked cold and miserable, half hidden under his wet cardboard cover.

Emma looked back at Tony. He was fast asleep with his mouth wide open. The bedroom smelt slightly musty and damp, so she turned and left, shutting the door quietly behind her.

The day's plan had then changed to doing the washing and taking a trip to Tesco's, undoubtedly the religion of the future. Constantly expanding to meet every conceivable need of their congregation. Our Father, Who art in Tesco's; blasphemous even to joke. Her mother would not be amused.

Apart from the shopping and washing, most of the day was spent doing housework. Emma awarded herself various little tea breaks accompanied each time by a chocolate biscuit or a bag of crisps. A few times she opened up her latest book but she couldn't get into it. Her mind was thinking about what to do next with regard to her job. Eight years of her life had been spent at Buckley & Dwyer. At least Dublin would be somewhere different.

At around two-thirty, Tony got up and had a shower. The water was cold, as Emma had used up the hot to do some hand washing. Wearing an old pair of ripped jeans and a baggy blue jumper, he came down the stairs looking irritated. She kept out of his way and sat at the table in the lounge checking their bank statements. He made himself a bacon sandwich and a large mug of coffee, then followed her into the lounge, switching on the TV and sitting on the sofa.

After about fifteen minutes he said in a despondent voice, 'Sorry about today, Em.'

She looked up.

'Walking in the Dales, maybe next week.'

'That's OK. It's not the best of days to go walking. Got loads of jobs done anyway. How you feeling?' she asked.

'All right.'

'You were back late.'

'Not that late.'

'About three,' she said.

He drank the last of his coffee and said nothing.

'Where'd you go?'

He sniffed loudly a couple of times. 'Just "afters" at the Swan. Phil gave the lads a few free bevvies. Think I had a couple too many.' He put a cushion under his head and lay flat across the sofa, yawning loudly. Conversation was not welcome at this time.

'I had a nice evening,' she said.

'Yeah? Good.'

'Went to Dante's Jazz Bar.'

'Bloody rip-off joint.'

'The band was brilliant. Everyone was dancing.'

'What, you?' he asked, surprised. He was pressing the TV remote control.

'I had a little dance at the end. You should have seen Jeremy, he was dancing with everyone, didn't stop. He did drink two bottles of wine though. This poor waiter couldn't get away from him.' Emma was smiling as she remembered Jeremy trying to get the waiter to dance. He politely declined and must have hidden in the kitchen, as he wasn't seen for ages.

Tony kept pressing the buttons on the remote but nothing happened. 'Did you get those batteries I asked you for? These are completely gone now.'

'Damn, no I didn't.'

'Emma! I asked you last week.'

'I know. Just forgot. I'll get them Monday.'

Looking annoyed, he let the remote slip from his hand and on to the floor. She decided it wasn't the best opportunity to tell him about Dublin. She finished her paperwork and got up to water the plants.

'As you're up, Em, switch over to ITV.'

She was nearly out of the room but went back to the television, switching it over.

'Thanks, love,' he said.

'Are you shooting tomorrow?'

'Expect so, why?'

'Well, let's go somewhere in the afternoon.'

'Make it the evening. Rob's bringing Rebecca down the Swan. We could meet them.'

Emma was silent for a moment, wondering why they always had to meet up with other people, like there wasn't much point in going out alone. 'All right, but let's go out to dinner first and meet them later. I need to talk with you.'

He nodded briefly and continued to watch the television.

The following morning Tony was up and out of the house by eight-thirty. Rob collected him. Emma watched from the window as Tony placed his two licensed rifles in the back of the van. They would usually meet two other mates and the four of them would go off into various woods and farmers' fields, shooting mostly birds, rabbits and other small prey. Emma hated it. She found it barbaric. Tony had started the so-called sport a year into their marriage and it proved to be a major cause of arguments between them. But as the years went by, words became futile and exhausting, so an unspoken and reluctant acceptance emerged. Now the subject was never discussed.

Emma spent most of the morning reading the Sunday newspapers. In the afternoon she felt restless and in need of some fresh air, so she put on her raincoat and went outside. The sky was overcast but at least it was dry. She slowly walked the couple of streets to Grange Park, a group of playing fields. There must have been a football tournament on as it was packed with players, eager supporters and the usual Sunday walkers. The

constant screams and shouts ran through her. She had
to constantly alter her walking pace to avoid collision;
it wasn't enjoyable or relaxing, instead it felt like
walking around a busy shopping centre just before
Christmas. She retreated and went for a walk around
the local roads instead. It was three o'clock and the
weekend was nearing to a close. Already, that Sunday
evening feeling was starting to descend; it seemed to
arrive slightly earlier every weekend. Thoughts of
work, another week and what she considered a wasted
two days, lowered her spirits. Don't think of
tomorrow, stay in the present, enjoy the moment;
hadn't she read all these sayings in various self-help
books? She had her own little library of them under her
bed. In fact they were propping it up, as one of the legs
had broken the year before. At least they were of some
use, she smiled to herself as she continued walking the
damp, grey streets.

That evening, Emma and Tony sat in a busy Pizza Hut
sharing a large deep pan Meat-feast pizza.
    He smiled at her. 'You look nice. Lots of make-up
though.'
    'Not too much, is it?'
    He shook his head and touched her hand briefly.
'What do you wanna speak to me about?'
    'Didn't think that registered with you.'
    ''Course it did.'
    She swallowed the pizza in her mouth and took a sip
of wine, her second glass. 'It's about work.'
    'To do with that meeting on Friday?'
    'Wow, you really do listen.'
    He rolled his eyes. 'Maybe you don't listen to me.'
    'I *do*. Every word.'

'Batteries.' He said it forcefully but then laughed. His face completely changed when he laughed; his heavy features lifted and the deep-set brown eyes came alive.

She smiled, pleased to see him so relaxed; he must have had a good day shooting.

'What's happening at the Asylum then? Who's screwing who? Let me guess, it's either about someone leaving, joining or getting pregnant,' he said.

She nodded, grinning broadly.

'Told you. Which one is it then?'

'Well, it's a bit more than that.' She perched forward on her seat. 'Firstly, Henry's retiring, ill health. Harold Ross, not Jack Tomkinson, is to be the new senior partner, and lastly, although probably the most important with regard to us, they may want me to go to Dublin for three months to help set up a new branch. Wait for it . . .' she raised her hands. 'With Jack Tomkinson.'

Tony drank some of his beer. 'Always wanted to go to Dublin. Supposed to have a great night life.'

She screwed her face up in shock. 'Hang on a minute, I'm not sure I'm even going.'

'No?'

'No! I mean, I *may*! I just don't know yet. It's not definite,' she insisted.

'Whatever. Calm down.'

'Didn't think you'd want me going.'

He shrugged his shoulders. 'You'd be back at weekends, wouldn't you?'

'Expect so.'

'I don't mind then.'

She stared at him with narrowed eyes, took another bite of her pizza and continued looking at him as she chewed it.

'You going to be working for Harold then?' he asked.

'No, he's keeping Trish. Probably end up working for a new member of staff.'

'What about money? You got more working for the head partner. They'd better not try and take that away.' He instantly looked more serious. The brightness in his eyes retreating.

'They won't.'

'That's all right then, less responsibility for the same money. You should be celebrating.' He raised his beer glass to toast her.

She threw him an annoyed look. 'It's not just about that. I'm thinking about moving on. Should've done it years ago.'

'To do what?'

'Don't know yet. I just don't want to spend the next ten years doing what I've done for the last ten. There's more to me than this.'

'Like what?'

She glared at him. He smiled back, unsure what he'd said wrong. Her gaze dropped. 'I need something new, that's all.'

'Fine. Just be careful. Your job pays more than most secretaries earn. Legal secretary's a good job.'

Tony was trying to pick a piece of onion out of his teeth as he spoke.

Emma pushed her plate away in frustration.

'Maybe I don't want to be a secretary any more. Maybe I want to be a solicitor, with a secretary working for *me*, a male secretary, who *I* can flirt with. *They* can run around making *me* cups of tea. I'd be far too important to stick a tea bag in a cup. Maybe I want to prepare the defence or draw up contracts instead of just typing them like some robot, having no input whatsoever.' Her fists were clenched on the table. 'Sometimes I feel like an eighteenth-century housemaid, but instead of dusters, we now have keyboards.' She grabbed her glass of wine and gulped some down.

Tony had an odd look on his face. 'Henry didn't flirt with you, did he?'

She screwed her face up.

'Well, did he?' he repeated.

Emma slowly shook her head at the absurdity of it. 'No, Tony. That wasn't the point I was making.' Exasperated, she looked out of the window.

'I get the point, Emma. You're pissed off and want a change – so does half the population. But we have to be practical. At the moment we need your salary. You have to get a job that pays the same, if not better. Those sorts of jobs don't grow on trees, Em.'

She gazed out of the window at the passing cars; his words echoed in the background.

'I only said "at the moment". Things'll change. I get pissed off too. Shit, tell me about it. You know the crap I've had with work. Been a bloody nightmare since leaving the army.' Tony looked down at his pizza but stopped eating.

After several moments of silence, she turned and spotted the heaviness back in his face. Over the eight years of their marriage she had heard the same regrets numerous times. Hadn't she spent hours encouraging him to do whatever he wanted, even re-enlisting! But he never did. Emma reached over and held his hand in hers.

He didn't look up but he held on to it tightly, with a degree of neediness.

'Cheer up you,' she said.

'And you,' he replied. He stared at her with an expression she couldn't make out. 'Don't really want to go to the pub any more. Shall we just go home?'

She nodded, relieved; evenings at the Swan were endured, not enjoyed.

They walked the short distance home hand in hand. Halfway there, Tony placed his arm around her and hugged her close as they continued on their way. Arriving back by nine o'clock, they went straight into the lounge and sat on the settee.

'Want a coffee?' she asked.

He shook his head and smiled. He carried on staring at her.

'What?'

His smiled remained, if somewhat faded. With a warm, concerned expression on his face he took hold of both her hands and whispered, 'Don't know what I'd do without you.'

She squeezed his hands in hers.

'Things will change,' he said, as he kissed her gently on the lips. 'I've still got plans.'

She nodded.

He kissed her again, this time for longer. Soon they were fully embraced, with her lying across the settee and Tony on top of her. His hands ran all over her, undoing her shirt within seconds. It was too fast, too mechanical. She wanted to kiss him more and tried desperately to keep him occupied with it. But he pulled back. 'Let's go upstairs,' he said eagerly.

She stared into his eyes, saying nothing. Gradually her eyelids lowered. Jumping off her, Tony grabbed her hand and led her away.


A little while later, Emma lay in bed with Tony moving inside her. Now and again they kissed. She noticed his breathing become heavy and quick. She calmly observed the contortions in his face and wrapped her legs around him, she guessed he liked that. The kissing had all but ceased, a distraction for him, hardly necessary. She tried to move her body in time with his. And as he came closer to that moment, she matched his intensity, like for like, watched and waited, seconds passing, hoping, trying. A car pulled up next door. A couple of dogs were barking outside. Tony let out a huge sigh. It was over.

He collapsed on top of her, his heart racing, skin hot and clammy. She felt the full weight of him above her and strangely, took a certain amount of pleasure that he appeared content, kissing his forehead, stroking his back. Yet he rolled off her, on to his side, giving her a brief smile. She smiled back, but started to feel the cold draught in the bedroom.

Emma lay there, next to him, together, alone, feeling his immediate restlessness beside her. She cuddled up close to him and kissed him on the lips. Gently easing himself free, he lay on his back, closing his eyes. For what seemed like ages, she just gazed trance-like at him. Her face was blank, distant and removed, as though she was examining everything and nothing. A little while later, as if suddenly waking, she sat up; it was too early to sleep.

Tony opened his eyes and looked up at her. 'Shall we have that coffee now?'

Motionless and silent, she stared ahead.

'Wait there, I'll make you one.' He put on his dressing gown and went downstairs.

Emma lay there, wrestling with a feeling of sadness that was fighting to come up and be noticed. It would have to wait. She couldn't acknowledge it now for fear of falling into it, spiralling downwards, twisting, winding, plunging further down. She forced herself not to think, instead she stared intently at her body, touching her stomach, soothing it and almost caressing it. A shiver ran through her, blamed on the cold bedroom.

She pulled the covers across. Her eyes travelled around the narrow, rectangular room, with its low ceiling and two small sash windows that rattled in the wind. She was convinced the walls encroached inwards a little further every year, like a ready-made coffin. Shaking her head, she forced herself to smile.

## 4

Emma checked her watch. Only another five minutes before her meeting. She dried her hands with a paper towel and came out of the ladies toilet for the third time that afternoon.

Walking back along the corridor, she spotted Trish and Steve Ingrams, a solicitor from the Birmingham branch, talking in Harold's office. They were standing quite close together and were deep in conversation. For some time, Emma had been convinced that something was going on between them. They were forever having discreet little chats that would suddenly stop if you approached them. Trish had never said anything and she would never ask, probably because Steve was married, with a two-year-old son. Also, Emma liked his wife, Sarah, and wanted to stay well out of it.

She went back into her own office and sat down at her desk. Her stomach began to ache again. Wednesday, three o'clock had finally arrived, the time Henry had asked her to attend a meeting with himself and Jack.

At that moment, her terminal bleeped indicating an incoming e-mail. She opened it up.

My darling Emma,

Just wanted to wish you good luck for
3pm. Remember what we discussed last
night:
1. Don't be bulldozed by Jack! Stand your
ground.
2. Don't agree to anything there and

```
then. Get all the facts, more money, and
have a think tonight. (I'll be home by 8,
call me).
3. For God's sake, ACT SURPRISED! You
aren't supposed to know anything.

Speak to you later,
Jeremy

PS I bet I can guess what you're wearing
. . . Your navy suit? So predictable ;-)
```

Emma's face dropped, along with her confidence. She looked down at her outfit, her navy suit. Biting her bottom lip she deleted the message. Jeremy meant well, she reminded herself.

Her telephone rang. She hesitated, sat up straight, then picked it up. 'Hello.'

'We're ready if you are,' said Henry.

'Yes, that's fine, I'll come straight in.' She replaced the handset but continued staring at it for a few seconds. Slowly, she stood up, took a few deep breaths, then walked towards Henry's office.

'Please take a seat, Emma.' Henry pointed politely to the chair opposite his desk as she shut the door.

She sat down and had to stop herself fidgeting with her bracelet. Jack sat in an armchair, slightly apart from them, facing Emma on her right. He was sitting well back in the chair with his legs loosely crossed, his hands resting gently in his lap, the picture of confidence – or arrogance, she wasn't sure. Jack wasn't that tall, maybe five foot ten, but his presence and stature gave the impression of a much larger man than he in fact was. He was in his early forties with short, dark, slightly-greying hair, parted on one side. His suits were well-tailored, some expensive designer name which meant nothing to Emma. He kept himself trim by jogging every morning, whatever the weather, his routine was never broken: marriages, births, funerals and divorces, he still jogged first thing. Some people would call him distinguished-looking – quite attractive, some of the girls in the office thought. Emma just saw him as a pompous head teacher and felt on edge around him.

She looked in Henry's direction, one friendly face at least.

'Emma, as I mentioned to you last week, there are a number of changes happening here. One situation involves Jack, hence his presence.' Henry pulled a look of annoyance. 'Unfortunately I don't have much time . . .'

Emma instinctively put her hand across her mouth, she hadn't realised his condition was so dire.

'Just heard about a last-minute appointment in Altrincham. I have to be out of here in fifteen minutes,' he added.

She quickly placed her hand back on her thigh. How stupid! She glanced at Jack. He was staring directly at her, his expression blank. Her face began to flush.

Henry continued. 'My apologies if it feels like I'm skirting across important issues, it wasn't intentional. I'll have to leave you in Jack's capable hands.' He coughed a couple of times. 'Well, firstly I am retiring. Damned health, you see.'

'I'm sorry to hear that, Henry. Is it serious?' Shit, why ask that. She shifted uncomfortably in her chair.

'Serious in the sense that my wife thinks so, and she's threatening to divorce me if I don't take things a bit easier, and I can't afford a divorce.' He laughed. 'Ah, Jack.'

Emma felt embarrassed. She thought it a bit close to the mark.

Jack smiled however, and nodded at Henry, knowing no offence was intended.

'I would, of course, like to thank you for all your hard work, Emma. You've done a splendid job, most impressive,' said Henry.

'Thank you, too. I've enjoyed working for you. I'm very sorry you're going.'

'I'm sure you'll see me around occasionally. However, Harold Ross will be taking over as senior partner, closely assisted, I am sure, by Jack.'

Emma looked over at Jack. Again his expression gave nothing away.

'I've written out a memo that I'd like you to type and circulate to all staff as soon as possible. I'm sure some rumours have already started,' said Henry.

Emma shook her head innocently. 'None that I've heard.'

'Oh good. But now to you, Emma. It's understandable that Harold would wish to keep Trish, lovely girl, always so jolly. However, an opportunity has arisen which we would like you to consider. We're opening a branch in Dublin, hopefully by March next year. In addition to looking after London, I have asked Jack to get the Dublin office up and running, and manage it for the first year. He has great expertise in this field.'

She again glanced at Jack but quickly looked away. She felt his eyes observing her.

'Jack needs an assistant to go over for maybe three or four months, and help sort out the administration side of things, until the right staff are recruited in Ireland. We both feel you would be an ideal candidate.'

Both men waited in silence for her reaction.

She opened her eyes wide and pulled a look of surprise. 'Well, it's all quite a shock,' she said, touching the back of her neck and moving in her chair. 'I'll have to give it some thought.'

'Of course, of course,' said Henry. 'We don't expect an answer right now. No doubt you have numerous questions that you want to ask. I should add that no expense would be spared. You'd be staying in a first-rate hotel. All fares would be paid for you to travel back at weekends or, if you wish, Tony could travel to Dublin. There's also a generous bonus, a lump sum paid to you once your services are completed there. Jack is working out the particulars. And after you return, you'll start working for someone else here.'

'It sounds very interesting,' she said.

'I want to add that you don't have to go, it's your choice. If you decide not to, we'll understand. I'm sure we can find you something to do here. Let us know your decision next week.' Henry stood up. 'Forgive me, I must be off.'

Jack stood up also and shook Henry's hand. Emma stood up but felt in the way. She sat back down.

'I'll see you Friday, Emma. Here's that memo.' Henry handed her a piece of paper. 'Ensure the other branches circulate it also.'

She took the paper, thanked him, then Henry left the office.

The door closed. Like a flick of a switch the atmosphere changed. Jack immediately went and sat in Henry's chair and stared directly at her, slightly longer than would be deemed polite. Neither spoke. She fidgeted with the paper in her hand. He checked his watch, then laid his arms on the chair rests and glanced around the room. His piercing eyes gradually focused back on her again. Emma braced herself.

'It's not exactly the rosy picture Henry described,' he stated, in his well-spoken yet off-handed manner. 'In fact, it came across as if it was totally your choice . . .' He leant forward. 'The question isn't just whether you want it . . . but whether you are the right person for the position.' A short silence ensued. His eyes narrowed slightly.

Emma swallowed.

Jack continued. 'I'd like to describe the type of duties involved and the sort of person I need.'

It occurred to her that it was a bit like a good cop, bad cop scenario. She was now in the hands of the bad cop, and she prepared herself for the verbal punches.

Jack began, 'I don't need a secretary, I want a right-hand man. Woman, if we want to be politically correct. I need an organiser, someone who can *implement* ideas, not just *follow* them. The office may be opening in March, but if that's to happen, the work needs to start right now. You'll need to organise equipment, furniture, e-mail links, phone systems, the layout of the offices, headed stationery.' He paused; his eyes seeming to penetrate deep within her.

She stared defiantly back at him but soon felt compelled to glance away.

'Recruitment of staff, placing adverts, liaising with agencies, planning office procedures, arranging an office launch party, greeting and socialising with potential clients, producing and keeping to strict budgets, et cetera, et cetera. This is just off the top of my head. I need *you* to tell *me* what is needed, how it's going to be done and by what date.' Again he paused for several seconds before continuing. 'I won't have time to get too involved in any of these issues. My role is to generate new business, work on cases, recruit a couple of decent solicitors and manage London. It'll be long hours and a pressurised environment.' He got up and started to walk around the office.

Emma's head was spinning but she hid it well. It all came back to her why she had hated working for him before. He was like some fascist dictator. Seven years ago she had had enough and was about to hand in her notice when he got transferred down to London to set up and manage a new branch. That day she went home and shared a bottle of champagne with Tony to celebrate.

'You'll have to come to London and have regular meetings with me. There'll probably be a couple of trips to Dublin before March and full-time from then.' He stared out of the window. 'In recognition of the additional skills and workload required, there would be a bonus. I'm thinking in the region of two to three thousand pounds, paid in one lump sum to be included with your May salary.'

Emma's eyes widened.

He turned, but remained standing by the window. 'You'll have earned it. So no beating around the bush. Question one: are you up to it?'

She stared towards Henry's empty chair, thinking. What could she say? No, and look a complete fool: yes, but she wasn't really sure? Could she think about it? He'd interpret that as a no. How he irritated her. She looked up at him and said in a deliberately confident manner, 'The answer to question one is: yes.'

Jack was silent for a moment. He looked slightly taken aback. 'Question two then.' He came and sat back down. 'Do you want it?'

'I thought I had a week to decide.'

'You've already had a week. Your acting won't win an Oscar.'

She gave a nervous smile, but felt a bit embarrassed.

Did he look amused? It was difficult to tell.

He leant back in Henry's chair, calmly crossing his legs, all the while staring at her intently. He was so controlled, never once letting his guard down. 'Of course, I'll offer guidance. But I can't carry anyone,' he said.

'I don't want to be carried,' Emma retorted icily.

'Glad to hear it.'

'I'm different now. I was a lot younger, less experienced when I worked for you before,' she said.

He leant forward and said in a somewhat softer manner, 'Maybe I'm different too . . . or isn't that allowed? A lot can happen in seven years. A lot *has* happened.'

She wasn't sure what to say. She smiled uneasily, uncomfortable with the direction of the conversation. Almost immediately Jack reverted back to his forceful approach. 'So. What's your answer?'

'Could I let you know tomorrow?'

'Why?'

'Because . . . because it's a big step for me.'

'And you don't like big steps? You like nice, safe, familiar little steps, is that it?'

His words surprised her. 'No, that's not it,' she said defensively.

'Then what?'

'I . . . well, there's Tony, for a start. I have to talk to him.'

Jack looked down at his watch before swirling his pen around his fingers. Silence descended for a few moments.

'Surely a day won't make much difference,' she said.

There was a knock at the door.

'I did ask not to be disturbed,' Jack shouted loudly.

The door opened anyway and Trish was standing

there. 'John Collins is on the phone for you. He said it was urgent.'

'He'll have to wait.'

Trish, unfazed, winked at Emma then left. Emma hoped Jack hadn't seen it.

'So where were we?' he asked. 'Oh yes, I was asking you to make a decision and you were giving me reasons why you couldn't.' Jack sat back in his chair. He stroked his right eyebrow a few times. When he finally spoke, his voice was slow and more relaxed. 'I have such a crazy diary right now . . . Dublin wasn't something I was expecting to do. However, situations planned don't always materialise. Other, unexpected ones do. Steps, big or small, sometimes just have to be taken. I also believe that deep down you already know what your decision is. I would appreciate an answer, yes or no, so I can just get on with it all. Hate loose ends,' he said, screwing up his face.

She stared at him. 'You really think I can do it?'

'You just told *me* that you were up to it. The question remains: do you want it?'

Emma thought for a moment. It would be a challenge, a change. What else was there, continuous typing? Two to three thousand pounds, they could really do with that. Oh hell! 'Yes . . . I'd like to do it.'

He leapt up and grabbed his briefcase, preparing to go. 'The first step is to produce a working document. You've done that before, I presume?'

She looked worried. 'No.'

He shot her an irritated glance. 'Come to London next week. I'll e-mail you with a date and time. I've got some examples. Have to catch my train now.' As he neared the office door, he turned and said gravely, 'I hope you *are* up to it.' With that he marched off.

Emma sat there. She had a string of unanswered

questions. For five minutes she didn't move; excitement
and fear consumed her in equal measures. She tried to
remember some of the list of duties Jack had flung at
her – recruitment of staff, office equipment, phone
system, headed stationery, cuddly toy. She felt like a
contestant in *The Generation Game*.

Eventually she returned to her own desk, relieved to
see that Trish wasn't there – she didn't really want to
discuss it right now. Jeremy had said he would be
telephoning tonight. She'd e-mail him now instead.

```
Dear Jeremy,

Meeting went OK.
1. Stood up to bulldozing - I think -
maybe not :-(
2. Agreed to go to Dublin - I'm happy with
decision - I think. (Maybe not . . . )
3. Acted surprised - Henry fooled - Jack
not!
4. Have murderous thoughts towards Jack
already - as my solicitor, please advise
how many years I'd get if I actually went
through with it.

Can't talk tonight. I'll give you a call
in the next few days.
Emma
```

Hopefully that would stop Jeremy ringing tonight.
He was a great friend but she didn't need him going on
at her right now. He was always going on at her about
something or other. She knew it was only because he
cared about her – and she him.

Since answering his advertisement for a flatshare nine

years ago, they had become the best of friends, hitting it off immediately. She was never sure why this was, because they were complete opposites in everything. At the time, he was a junior solicitor at Buckley & Dwyer in Manchester and it was he who had mentioned the secretarial vacancy to her. However six months later, he was transferred down to the new London office. It was around the same time that she met Tony.

Her thoughts returned to Dublin. Suddenly, she found herself smiling. At least it was something new.


The rest of the week flew by. Henry's workload was being distributed between Harold Ross and two other solicitors at the Manchester branch, so Emma had to work closely with their secretaries to hand over and explain the situation with each client and case. Henry did the same to the relevant solicitor. He also produced masses of typing; it was as if he was going for a promotion, not retirement. Emma had little time to dwell on Dublin.

On Friday afternoon at two-thirty, she received an e-mail.

Emma,

Can see you either Monday 5th December at 08.30 hrs for approximately one hour, or Wednesday 7th December at 18.00 hrs. (Both in London office.)

Confirm this afternoon which time you would like.

Regards,
Jack

Emma glared at the dates. The 5th was this Monday coming, hardly much notice. And the times! She'd either be travelling on the train very early or very late. She'd have to stay the night at Jeremy's.

After brief telephone calls with both Tony and Jeremy, Monday morning was chosen, which meant her having to travel down to London on Sunday evening. Jeremy arranged to meet her at Euston and drive her back to his flat in Richmond, where he'd cook her a celebratory dinner. Tony was pleased because it meant they'd have to cancel Sunday lunch with her parents in Chester. Emma e-mailed Jack with her confirmation.

```
Dear Jack
```

She paused before deleting the 'Dear'.

```
Jack,

I would like to confirm Monday 5th
December at 08.30 hrs for our meeting.

Regards,
Emma
```

She read it twice, then sent it.

On Saturday morning Emma had the task of telephoning her mother, Charlotte, to cancel the lunch. She stood by the telephone for some moments preparing herself. It will be great when everyone has e-mail, she thought. You can just write the message, send it and walk away. Mothers won't be able to moan back at you and make you feel guilty.

She picked up the handset and dialled the number. After two rings she heard, 'Hello.'

'Hi Mum. How are you?'

Her mother hesitated before saying in a courteous, almost professional manner, 'Splendid. So looking forward to seeing you both tomorrow.'

'Actually, that's why I'm ringing,' said Emma sheepishly.

'I've spent the morning shopping,' her mother enthused, as if oblivious to Emma's comment.

'I'm really sorry, Mum, but—'

'Up and out early. Planned a lovely dinner. Can't wait. Feels like ages since we've seen you both.'

'Three weeks.'

'Surely it's longer.'

'No. Three weeks,' said Emma.

'Well, who's counting anyway.'

'The thing is—'

'You can't possibly be letting us down can you, not at this late stage? Tell me you're not.' Charlotte's voice was still exceptionally polite, yet somehow cold, insincere.

'I am. Sorry. Can't be helped. I've got to go to London.'

'Why?'

'Work. I've—'

'On a Sunday!' she interrupted again.

'I have to attend an early meeting on Monday so I'm travelling down Sunday and staying at Jeremy's.'

Her mother was silent. Emma added, 'Hope you haven't gone to too much trouble.'

Again no response came.

'I only found out yesterday.'

'Yesterday,' her mother repeated. 'At least that

would have saved me my morning's shop. It's only money, I suppose.'

'Sorry. We're only postponing it. How about next weekend?' asked Emma, frowning at the words that had just come out of her mouth.

Tony was walking up the stairs and was vigorously shaking his head. She ignored him. At times like this she wished her brother Richard wasn't living in Canada – he could have taken some of the heat; yet he had moved away seven years ago and rarely kept in touch.

'That's not too bad. Next weekend will be fine. Your father and I will look forward to it.'

'Good.'

'I'd call your father, but he's out filling the car up with petrol. He had planned to drive us all to Colwyn Bay tomorrow.'

Emma closed her eyes and said through gritted teeth, 'You two can still go, can't you?'

'It's not really the same, is it? But who knows, maybe we will. He'll be back in about twenty minutes if you want to call him then.'

'I can't today, I'm afraid.'

'What's the big meeting about in London?'

'Nothing very exciting. Admin procedures.' Emma wasn't going to mention Dublin at this point.

'No, not very exciting, all right. I'll send your love to your father. He'll be so sorry he missed you. You might consider phoning later.'

Emma hesitated. 'I'll see, but it's a bit mad today.'

'Everything is always mad with you. Anyway I must be off. There's a committee meeting at Roger and Jill's. Take care in London. Don't forget to call your father later.'

'I did say I might not be able to,' said Emma, her voice agitated and raised somewhat.

There was a moment's silence.

'Well, only if you can fit it in,' said her mother.

'As I said, it's mad today. In fact I shouldn't have committed to next weekend. Something's happening at work. Can't go into it now. I'll call you in the week.'

Her mother let out a strange laugh. 'Whatever suits you. I have to be going. Meeting starts in ten minutes and I don't like letting people down. Lovely to hear from you. Take care.'

'Sorry about tomorrow,' said Emma.

'Goodbye, Emma.'

''Bye Mum.' Emma slammed down the phone and let out a loud sigh. Tony was sitting at the top of the stairs watching her. She looked up at him and shook her head.

'How's Cruella then?' he asked, pulling a funny face.

'Splendid,' she mocked in an enthusiastic voice. 'Just splendid.'

He laughed. 'Come on, I'll take you out to lunch.'

'Splendid idea. A lovely lunch. Wonderful,' she ranted as she went in search of her handbag.

Tony stood smiling at the front door, amused by Emma's impersonation of her mother.

Emma returned to the hall, leant against the wall and screwed her face up.

'If I ever show signs of turning into my mother, you will get me to the best doctors, won't you? Have me sectioned. Anything.'

Tony nodded sympathetically.

'She's a very good argument for not having children. The defunct genes can die out with me.' Emma laughed loudly.

Tony watched her. He smiled but that was all.

Noticing his reticence, she appeared more serious

and said, 'So, where are you taking me for lunch, then?'

'A la carte McDonald's.' He took her hand and led her outside.

## 5

'Excuse me, are these seats taken?'

'No, they're free,' said Emma.

The man, dressed smartly in a brown suit, sat down in the window seat exactly opposite her and placed his briefcase on the seat next to him. They smiled politely at each other. Emma had hoped to stretch her legs out under the table, but not now. There was still another hour and a half to go. She stared out of the window as the Intercity train pulled out of Crewe station on its way to London, Euston. Jeremy said he'd be waiting there at six-thirty. Surprisingly, the train wasn't all that busy, only half full with various weekend travellers. She'd managed to have the set of four seats to herself so far.

As the train picked up speed she glanced around the carriage again. Sitting across the aisle in the set of four seats to her left, were two large American ladies. They had spent the journey chatting loudly, mostly about books they'd read and their authors. Emma hadn't heard of most of them and she doubted the rest of the people in the carriage were interested either.

Aimlessly looking around, her eyes suddenly met with the man's opposite. Instinctively, she looked away. She picked up her book on the Hay Diet and started to read. After a while, she felt restless again and glanced up. Once more, her eyes accidentally met with the man's. She gave a glimpse of an awkward smile before returning to her book. When it happened a third time, she grew curious. After five minutes of staring out of the window, she quickly and casually, without turning her head, looked across at him. He was staring right at her!

Her eyes darted back to the window. Why was he staring at her? Maybe it was a coincidence. He might be asking the same question of her. He was well-dressed, short brown hair, didn't look odd or anything, probably in his early fifties. She was trying to look at him out of the corner of her eye. He appeared to be staring at her still, but it was difficult to be sure.

For the next ten minutes, she closed her eyes and thought about the next day's meeting. The day before, she had written down a list of tasks that she remembered from Jack, plus a few ideas of her own. She had reconciled the fact that she would do whatever necessary to ensure the branch opening went well. If it didn't, it would not be down to her. Yet all the time she was thinking about work, she felt as if the man's eyes were upon her. She really had to fight the temptation to look at him and check.

The train stopped at Wolverhampton and a few more people got on. Emma moved her handbag in case anyone wanted to sit there; she was hoping someone would, or that the man opposite would get off, but neither happened. The train continued on its journey, with no more stops scheduled until Milton Keynes.

As the train entered a long tunnel, Emma could see quite clearly, in the now mirror-like window, that the man was still staring directly at her. What a weirdo! She was biting her thumbnail, wondering if she should say something or just get up and move seats.

Suddenly, under the table, his leg brushed against hers. She jerked her leg away in surprise. Had it been deliberate? Her heart started to beat faster. She convinced herself it was an accident; happens all the time on trains. Oh God! There it was again. His leg seemed to rest against hers. Jerking her leg even further away, she stared directly at him.

He stared back, cool as can be, not even blinking. Emma looked across at the Americans; they were now reading. She grabbed her own book, opened it anywhere, and pretended to read. Her palms felt clammy. Her breaths were short, stilted. She was starting to feel quite scared. She closed her eyes, feigning sleep. But if anything, felt more vulnerable with her eyes shut. Her whole body tensed in case he touched her again. *This is getting ridiculous, I'm just overreacting*, she told herself. Yet within another minute, she felt his leg rub slowly up against hers. Annoyed now, she glared across at him.

As if pleased that he had her attention, he developed a smug expression. The focus of his eyes fell downwards towards her chest then back up to meet her eyes. He opened his mouth, but was silent.

Emma sat motionless for a couple of moments, her face blank, in total shock. 'Is there something wrong?' she finally said, very quietly, so as not to make a scene.

He didn't speak. Instead he shook his head from side to side, slowly, rhythmically, with the smug expression remaining. Almost in slow motion he took his right hand off the table and very deliberately, almost gracefully, placed it somewhere under the table, out of her sight. She watched his elbow start to move up and down. She couldn't believe it. Here, in the train! She looked towards the Americans, towards her handbag, back out the window, anywhere but at him. Maybe he wasn't doing what she thought. But out of the corner of her eye she could see his arm jerking up and down, as he touched himself. Should she outstare the creep? But she couldn't. Her heart was pounding. She glared at the Americans; why couldn't they see what he was up to?

Finally, Emma jumped up. She grabbed her handbag, and tugged her overnight bag off the rack above. The man was grinning broadly. Emma walked out of the carriage, still trying to act calm; just in case she'd got it wrong. A few people looked up, as she walked through the next two carriages, her stomach sick inside. Three times she looked behind her, dreading he'd be following. He wasn't. At last, she sat down opposite an elderly couple. They looked at her enquiringly as if wondering where she had come from. She leant her head against the window and tried to slow her breathing. She actually felt physically sick. She should tell someone, but who?

The train eventually pulled into Milton Keynes station. Emma prayed the elderly couple wouldn't get off. Suddenly she saw him. The creep! He was walking down the platform, carrying his briefcase; the picture of respectability. She pulled back slightly from the window so he wouldn't see her. Oblivious to her presence, he walked straight up to a woman dressed in a green jacket and tan trousers, and kissed her. She embraced him and kissed her back.

Emma watched, horrified, as the two stood there chatting, smiling, laughing together. Emma's face showed the disgust she felt inside. She didn't move, nor even blink, as she stared transfixed at the couple until the train began to slowly pull away and they disappeared from view.

Numb, Emma sat, gazing into space. Had anything really happened or had she imagined it? She was sure it had, and at that moment immense anger filled her. *How fucking dare he?* Fury descended on her. *I should have done something, hit him, screamed, anything.* Her head fell into her hands. The elderly couple looked at her but said nothing. The overwhelming anger continued to build – an inner rage at herself, with no outlet to vent it. Her fists were tightly clenched. If he was still

on the train she'd go and punch him. *You fool, Emma.*
*You stupid fool.*

The smell of exhaust fumes and diesel immediately hit
Emma as she walked down the station platform at
Euston. Nearing the main concourse, she spotted Jeremy
waving frantically. He made a beeline for her, kissed her
on both cheeks and automatically grabbed her overnight
bag. She stood still, offering no affection in return.

Stepping back he asked, 'You OK?'

'Not really.'

'My God, what's happened?'

'Just get me to the car, I'll explain then.'

'Darling, you've got me all worried.'

'Please, Jeremy! The car.'

Jeremy took her hand and led her down to the
underground car park. Whilst walking he kept looking
across at her, both concerned and intrigued at what
might have happened. Once on their way, safely inside
his red Peugeot 205, she told him about the man on the
train, leaving nothing out.

'In heaven's name, why didn't you call the guard?' he
asked, sounding annoyed.

'What guard? Never saw one.'

'There must have been someone.'

'A pubescent teenage boy working the buffet. What
would he have done?'

'Oh Emma, the Americans, surely they could have
helped. You should have called over.'

'I know, I know. It's crazy. Can't believe I didn't. I
didn't want to make a fuss. What if I was wrong?' She
shook her head in disbelief.

'Absolutely not! You weren't wrong. The pervert
obviously chose well.'

'What's that supposed to mean?' she asked angrily.

'You've got "I don't want to make a fuss", written across your forehead. That's what they bank on.'

'*What?*' she screamed. 'I don't believe you said that. You're acting like it's my fault. Jesus! You'd be a great rape counsellor.' She bent forward, dropping her head into her hands.

'Shit! I didn't mean that. Sorry. Of course it's not your fault. It's just that . . . It doesn't matter.' His voice trailed off. He looked down at her. Her hands were shaking. 'Emma, talk to me. Are you all right?'

For a few moments she didn't move.

'Emma.'

She sat bolt upright, incensed. 'Right now I'm just so angry, not only with him, but with *me*. Yes, I should have done something, but I didn't, couldn't. I felt awkward, embarrassed, scared, sick, all the things he probably meant me to feel. I just wanted to get away from him.' She looked down towards her feet. 'He's probably at home having tea with a devoted wife and kids.'

Jeremy drove the car into a side street. He parked up, leant across and hugged her, a warm, protective hug. As he drew back, he noticed tears in her eyes. He looked really concerned.

'I'm OK,' she whispered.

'We should go back and report it.'

'No. Not now. Couldn't face it. I just want to get to yours and relax. They're not going to catch him now.'

He squeezed her hand. 'I've prepared an Indian meal for us tonight. Most impressed with myself. I guarantee to have you laughing within the hour.'

She stared at his smiling face. 'We'll see.'

Jeremy started the car again and drove off towards Richmond.

Emma spent a lot of the journey quietly gazing out of the window at the hubbub of life on the streets. She thought about what had happened, her reaction and how she must come across to people. *It'll never happen again*, she told herself. *Never!*

'I need to toughen up,' she said aloud, staring ahead.

Jeremy considered how best to answer.

'With everyone,' she added firmly.

## 6

The next morning, at five past eight, Jeremy and Emma arrived at the Buckley & Dwyer offices in Blackfriars. The company occupied the fifth and sixth floors of a twelve-storey building, but Emma walked all the way up the stairs to the fifth floor while Jeremy, who had taken the lift with her bags, waited for her in reception.

'What kept you? Did you stop for tea on the third?' he grinned as she appeared, pink-faced from the exertion. 'I nearly organised a search party.'

Emma walked past him and practically collapsed on to the sofa by the reception desk. Her breathing was heavy. She held her hand up to silence him. 'A couple of minutes . . . give me . . . two minutes.' She was desperately trying to catch her breath.

'Oh please. And you have the nerve to go on about my fitness! Another floor up and you'd be in need of oxygen.'

She didn't answer him.

'Cup of tea?' he asked.

'Love some . . . water.'

Jeremy obliged and went off to the water machine. Emma, still breathing heavily, looked around the newly decorated offices. In total contrast to Manchester, the place appeared very modern and plush. Wooden floors ran throughout the various corridors surrounded by glass partitioned offices. Venetian blinds were the only source of privacy. A selection of rich green plants were positioned sporadically along the walls, interspersed with numerous abstract paintings hanging in large metal frames.

Jeremy returned with the water and Emma soon

recovered her composure. She hadn't been to the London office for over two years, so Jeremy walked around and introduced her to a number of new secretaries and admin staff. She knew most of the solicitors as, at some time or other, they had visited Manchester. She finally got to meet Julia, Jack's secretary for the past year. They had spoken at various times on the telephone and communicated by e-mail, but had never actually met.

'At last we meet. How are you?' asked Julia, shaking Emma's hand and oozing confidence. She was an attractive and petite young woman in her late twenties, wearing a ruby-red trouser suit. Her dark hair was cut into a stylish bob, her lips a deep red to match the outfit. Her blue oval eyes, a touch oriental-looking, looked Emma up and down.

Emma instantly felt frumpy by comparison. She was wearing her black, below-the-knee skirt, honeycomb jumper and black jacket; the navy suit had been banished to the back of the wardrobe for a while. Her hair was tied back in a plait. At Jeremy's persuasion, she had put on more make-up than usual. 'Hi. I'm fine. Nice to put a face to the voice finally.'

'I know. You're not a bit like I expected.'

'Aren't I?' asked Emma, self-consciously.

'No. But then no one ever is, are they? You must have been up at the crack of dawn.'

'No. I stayed at Jeremy's.'

'That was handy. His lordship does have meetings at the strangest of times.' Julia rolled her eyes over in the direction of Jack's office behind her.

'I remember,' said Emma.

Both women smiled at each other in mutual understanding. Jeremy made some flippant comment about feeling like a gooseberry then went up to his own office on the sixth floor.

'I'll let Jack know you're here, but I know he won't see you until eight-thirty.'

'I know that too.' Again, both of them smiled.

Julia telephoned Jack and informed him of Emma's arrival. She replaced the handset.

'As expected, he said "fine". That's all. Just "fine".' She stood up. 'Coffee, tea?'

'Tea would be great.'

'How do you have it? Actually, come with me, we can have a chat.'

Both women walked along the corridor to the kitchen and staff lounge, and were greeted by the smell of freshly ground coffee. No one was there, so they sat down and started discussing the company, Jack, and, of course, Dublin.

'I would have liked to have gone,' said Julia in a matter-of-fact way, pulling her hair behind her ear for the umpteenth time. It immediately fell back around her face.

'Really?'

'Of course. Who wouldn't?'

'Did you tell him that?'

'Yes. I approached him. He said you'd been chosen.'

'You don't mind, do you?' asked Emma, feeling guilty at initially not even wanting the position.

'I'm annoyed, but not against you. I'm not like that. But I did think I was the most obvious choice.' Julia spoke more quietly. 'I want to move into event management or hospitality, much more exciting. Get to travel a lot. Meet more interesting people than you do around here. Setting up Dublin could have helped me get my foot in the door somewhere.' She shrugged her shoulders. 'C'est la vie.'

Emma felt compelled to say, 'I suppose with Henry retiring, I was free, that's why they asked me.'

'Yes, I expect that's the case,' said Julia, a slight edge to her voice.

There was a moment of silence. Emma wasn't sure what to say. 'Anyway, I expect it's going to be really long hours over there. We both know what Jack's like.'

'In what sense?' asked Julia.

'Well . . .' Emma hesitated, unsure why Julia even needed to ask such a question. 'He's always working, of course. No wonder his wife left him.'

'Very driven all right. Works a hundred miles an hour. Not everyone could cope.'

'Or would want to.'

'I enjoy the pace. Makes the day go quicker. Keeps me alert.'

Emma just smiled in reply. She drank some tea.

'He's been strange this week though,' said Julia, delicately stirring her coffee for the fourth time. Again she pulled her hair behind her ear, revealing pearl earrings set in a gold surround. On her wrist was a solid gold bracelet.

'How?' asked Emma. In her opinion Jack was always strange.

'Difficult to explain. Almost subdued. Most people wouldn't notice. I think he's very disappointed about not being made senior partner.'

'Disappointed? More like livid.'

'Well, who can blame him. I understand it's down to Jack that the practice expanded. It's no longer some parochial back-street operation. He should have been given it.'

Emma nodded politely. She was aware of Julia's changing stance, now loyally praising Jack, like some devoted Oliver North secretary. 'I better get back,' she said.

Both women took their cups into the kitchen. Julia

emptied the contents of hers down the sink. She hadn't drunk any.

Emma went to sit outside Jack's office, reading through her notes. Knowing she had been chosen for the Dublin position, in spite of the competition, should have made her feel more confident. Instead, she felt surprised, intrigued. The usual butterflies were building in her stomach. She was never nervous before her meetings with Henry, but with Jack it was different. Sometimes it was like going four rounds with Lennox Lewis. She wondered if Julia, who was typing away at impressive speeds, ever got nervous with him. She doubted it. She looked like she could handle most things.

Julia's telephone rang. Emma jumped.

'I'll let her know.' Julia looked over at her. 'He's ready.'

'Thanks.'

'Let me know how it goes, what he says to you.'

'Right,' said Emma. She stood up, took a deep breath and walked in.

Jack Tomkinson's office was massive, easily as big as the conference room in Manchester. It was on the corner of the building and Emma immediately noted that the two external walls were pure glass, reinforced hopefully. You could see right across London. The second thing that struck her was how tidy it was. His desk was completely free apart from a telephone, a pc monitor, and some bizarre object in a glass tube, probably some executive toy – he'd hardly bring a sex aid to work!

'Good morning,' Jack said.

'Hello.'

He was sitting at the head of a large oval table, a little distance away from his desk. Three files were piled neatly to his left. He observed her entrance and pointed with his index finger to the chair on his right. She politely sat down where he indicated, placing her notes and writing pad on the table.

'You've been busy scribbling, I see. You can kick off then,' he said, glancing at his watch.

Emma froze. She sat totally still and stared at him. He'd taken her off guard; she'd been admiring the view over the Thames. Where were the pleasantries? Her pulse quickened. What to say? Where to start?

Maybe he read her mind because, as if ignoring his previous statement, he picked up the first file next to him and carefully placed it in front of her, leaving his hand on it. With eyes narrowed, he said very seriously, as if her life might depend on it, 'For the next four months this will be your bible.'

For a dreadful instant she almost laughed. She pressed her lips tight together and looked down towards the file. He had some dirt under his fingernails. That wasn't like Jack. She looked back up at him. *Hardly Jesus*, she thought, although his eyes really were a piercing blue. But was that like Jesus or just the actor, Robert Powell?

'Of course, I don't mean this particular document,' he said. 'I used this working document when setting up London. But it'll show you the layout and type of activities needing to be logged.' He appeared to move up a gear suddenly as he quickly opened the file and started speaking very fast. 'Example: in June I had to ensure all of these tasks were actioned i.e. sign office lease, submit new profit forecasts et cetera et cetera. You can see there are about twenty points there. Then,' he flicked on a few pages, 'when you get nearer to opening, it becomes a daily reminder i.e. August 5th, installation of telephone system, laying of computer cabling, delivery of desks and office furniture.' He continued to read: 'Emergency exits must be open for delivery, and so on. You get the idea?'

Emma stared at the file. He'd spoken so fast. 'I believe so.' She could work it out later at home.

'This was the last draft for London so it's fairly complete. The working document for Dublin will be updated every time more information is confirmed or actioned.'

She looked him right in the eye and smiled. 'I understand,' she said.

'We'll be meeting next Monday. You'll need to produce a first draft for Dublin. At this stage it'll be one big action plan with estimated dates of implementation. It's important we have some direction to work to.'

He took the second file and placed it in front of her. She looked down. She couldn't believe he had dirt under his fingernails. He was always so pristine looking. Even today he wore a stylish dark suit with a blue shirt. His hair was always cut short, so exact. But then again, it looked slightly longer today with a bit of a flick to it.

Jack opened up the second file and removed some computer printouts. 'Familiar with Excel?' he asked.

'A basic knowledge.'

He sighed loudly. 'That won't suffice.'

'I can learn.'

'Fast, I hope.' He left her no time to answer and continued talking at speed. 'Budget forecasts. You'll need to set up a spreadsheet and enter a costing for every item, broken down fully: salaries, expenses, equipment, launch party et cetera. Example, recruitment of staff, broken down into categories, agency fees, four thousand pounds, advertising one thousand pounds and so on.'

Though relieved that she understood the concept, Emma was nonetheless daunted by the amount of work involved in producing accurate costings. Jack noted her anguished expression.

'In this third file are various items.' He opened it in front of her. 'It contains a copy of my three-year business plan for Dublin and has various estimated costs. Work on those initially, but quite quickly I'll need actual costs inserted.'

Emma nodded, as he continued. 'There are also various details on the new office, I believe. Yes, here it is, an internal drawing showing the space available. Use this to design the office layout. With reference to suppliers, a few companies are listed here. Approach them first. Apart from that it's a case of getting hold of an Irish directory and phoning around. Three quotes required on each area.'

Jack showed her various other documents from the file, the office lease, more computer printouts, a map of Dublin. Emma sat surrounded by the three files and an increasing mass of paperwork. Jack was speaking at such speed and pointing to so many different bits of paper, she was utterly confused. *The pig is doing it deliberately*, she thought.

Suddenly, Jack stopped. He moved back in his seat, glanced at his watch then stared at her for several seconds with an anxious look on his face. 'Is this all making sense?'

Emma looked at the files and numerous papers on the desk and started rubbing the back of her neck. 'Mostly,' she said, uneasily.

He frowned. 'Only mostly? What don't you understand?'

His attacking manner unsettled her. It wasn't so much that she didn't understand, she just needed some time to read through all the papers quietly on her own.

Impatient for an answer he said, *'Well?'*

'It's just . . .'

'What?'

'I just need some time.'

'How much?'

She shook her head, becoming increasingly flustered. 'A few hours . . .'

His eyes locked on to hers. He leant forward and started stroking his right eyebrow. 'Just a few hours?' he said. 'I believe we've already identified several gaps in your knowledge.'

Emma swallowed hard. She was instantly filled with self-doubts about her own ability to do the job. Defensively she said, 'Why choose me for the position then?'

He hesitated. 'I didn't choose you . . . I was given you. I might as well admit that I accepted under protest.'

Emma glared at him, silently. So he didn't even want her going to Dublin. *Probably thinks me useless*, she thought. She felt like pulling out there and then but she would never give him the satisfaction.

'We'll meet in Manchester on Monday, at five-thirty. You can present drafts of both the working document and budgets. Let's see how you get on then.' He searched her face for a reaction. None came. He glanced at his watch. 'Any questions?'

Emma picked up some papers and tried to find something intelligent to ask, but at that moment her mind went completely blank.

'It's good to have a challenge, Emma. Keeps us from going stale.'

*I'm not some loaf of bread*, she thought, yet she felt obliged to nod.

He jumped up. 'We're finished for this week then.'

*Was that it?* she thought, unconsciously frowning.

'See you next Monday,' he said, waiting for her to get up.

Still dumbfounded, she remained seated.

'Was there something else?'

Slowly, Emma shook her head, before coming to and hurriedly gathering all the papers and files together.

Walking over to the door, he held it open for her. 'Goodbye.'

'Bye,' she said, giving a slight nod of her head. She walked out and heard the door close firmly behind her.

'That was quick,' said Julia, looking up from her desk.

Emma nodded.

'Is everything OK?'

'Fine.'

Julia's telephone rang and soon she was deep in conversation. Emma stood in the corridor as a surge of anger swept through her. *Bulldozed again! How dare he treat me like that? Why did I let him? What's wrong with me?* She was furious with her own pathetic reaction. She felt like going back in and telling him what an insulting, rude and obnoxious pig he was. Julia had said he was subdued, that was a laugh! She looked at her watch. Twenty minutes! All this way, for a twenty-minute meeting! She wondered what he was like at sex. No doubt it was scheduled and timed. God forbid it should over-run, even by thirty seconds! She huffed furiously. *Never, ever again will you treat me like that. You just wait, Jack Tomkinson. You'll have a different Emma to deal with in future.*

She put the files in her overnight bag, mouthed 'Goodbye' to Julia and left.

*

Thankfully, the train journey back to Manchester was

less eventful than the journey down. However there was a tiny part of her that was secretly hoping that she'd see the pervert again, just so she could give him what for. He'd be dealing with a different Emma today, as well. Her anger was making her feel very brave.

With only fifteen minutes of the journey left, she put away the files she'd been studying and picked up her book on the Hay Diet. Not that it was exactly a diet, more a change in eating patterns. It explained how not to mix proteins and carbohydrates in the same meal, to aid digestion and therefore help the body lose weight. Emma read it with interest. She promised there and then to try it out for a couple of months. Why not? She was fed up with feeling frumpy.

She arrived back at the office far earlier than she had expected to and spent the day drafting the working document and learning Excel. It turned out to be much easier than she had feared. Jack had made it sound so complicated.

That evening, as she arrived home, Emma immediately heard the television coming from the sitting room. It was very loud. She walked in and hoped Rob wouldn't be there.

'Hi,' she said.

Tony lay flat out across the sofa, watching some action video. 'Hi,' he replied, sitting up and smiling. He looked tired, drained and obviously hadn't shaved, but at least he was on his own.

She went and sat by him and gave him a brief peck on the lips. He held on to one of her hands.

'How'd London go?' he asked.

'Awful . . . I hate him, the pig. He was so rude again, our meeting only lasted twenty minutes.'

'Wasn't worth going,' Tony stated.

'He's obsessed with time. He even admitted he didn't

want me for the job.'

'You're definitely going to Dublin, though, aren't you? Think of the bonus.'

'Oh, I'm going all right. But I'm not going to take any more crap from him.'

Tony nodded then flicked off the television with the remote. 'Missed you last night,' he said.

'That's nice.' She squeezed his hand. 'You look tired.'

As if on cue, he yawned. 'Ended up going out.'

'Oh . . . Where?'

'Swan, with Rob and Becky.'

'Rebecca, or is this yet another girl?'

He smiled. 'Same girl.'

She ran her finger slowly down the side of his face, then touched the dark circles under his eyes. 'Have you eaten?'

'Thought we'd get a takeaway. Save you cooking.'

Emma stared down at her hand in his. Eventually, she shook her head. 'I'll just make something.'

'Aren't you tired?'

'A bit.'

'Let's get an Indian then,' he said.

'No. Really, I'll just cook. I'm starting this diet.'

'Another bloody diet.'

'Thanks for your support.'

'Sorry, but I don't know why you bother . . . You look great to me.'

She raised an eyebrow. He pulled her to him, embracing her tightly and kissing her on the cheek. 'How about you decide what you want to eat and I'll cook it?'

She smiled at him. 'It's good to be home.'

## 7

Jeremy sat back against the leather sofa, sipping his champagne and noting with approval the heavy, crystal glass. In the spacious yet darkened room, he looked discreetly around at the impressive collection of sculptures, erotic oil paintings and tapestries that lined the walls. Blatant yet tasteful, he thought.

Underneath the dimly lit chandeliers that hung high above them, bemused he observed the attentive gentlemen watching the supposed entertainment from their assortment of booths and private alcoves. Each high-backed booth had its own circular sofa, which surrounded a solid marble table, and was carefully positioned on a slightly different level to the next, ensuring a certain amount of privacy. A deep emerald-coloured carpet ran throughout and the rich smell of cigars filled the air. Several lone, professionally sociable women sat amongst the men, all beautifully made up, lightly tanned, slender, and wearing expensive low-cut cocktail dresses in various colours – magenta, sapphire, silver, ruby. Over half the men appeared to be of Arab extraction, but this being Mayfair, it was hardly surprising.

Jeremy glanced at the female dancers, then back at the three gentlemen he was with. He smiled to himself; men were so easy to please. These men, who two hours earlier had sat across the boardroom table, stern, serious and sitting erect as though they had iron rods up their backsides, were now smiling and drinking, occasionally laughing, a sparkle in their appreciative eyes.

Coming to this place had been their idea. One of

them knew someone here, otherwise they wouldn't have known the place existed. From the outside, it was just a row of large, Georgian mansions at the back of Grosvenor Square.

They were seated at the front, a few feet from the raised stage area where three young female dancers were performing a slick, choreographed routine to a reworked, up-tempo version of Marvin Gaye's 'Sexual Healing'. Each wore a variation of a similar outfit – one danced in a black leather basque, another in a tiny, black leather G-string and bra. The third wore a leather mini-skirt with slits up the back and front and a see-through lace top, legs clad in thigh-high boots.

The dancer in the G-string stepped closer, as if dancing especially for them. She had a full and curvy figure and stared directly, defiantly, into each of the men's faces while she slid her hips and groin from side to side, backward, forward, round and round in time to the heavy, repetitive drumbeat. The three men sat completely still, entranced by her.

Jeremy glanced away, lit a cigar and drank more champagne. He picked up the bottle and diligently read the label – twice.

The dancer's long blonde hair fell around her heavily made-up face as she swayed her head, but always her eyes returned to the men, like the eyes of a painting that follow you around a room. She turned her back to them, appearing almost naked from that angle. Bending down she ran her hands slowly up the backs of her bare legs, reaching the top and teasingly touching herself as part of the dance.

Turning again towards them, she deliberately fell on all fours, remaining completely still and smiling provocatively. The music continued but she didn't move a muscle. She was so close that if they had reached out, they could have touched her – but they all knew not to. Leaping up she began to dance more wildly, less controlled, cavorting up and down with the quickening beat of the music.

At that moment, Jeremy glanced up and got an eye full of the large bouncing cleavage in front of him. He grimaced. What an absurdly overrated thing, he thought. It has become the commodity of the millennium; staring down from every billboard, peering out from every magazine and newspaper, on the telly selling everything from ice-cream to mobile phones – totally irrelevant! There was no escaping breasts these days. He was forever having them pressed up against him – in a crowded lift, sitting opposite him on the tube directly in his eyesight; even some of the secretaries in the office proudly displayed their cleavage, every day without fail, like the plumage of a peacock. He felt stalked by the damn things – they lurked around every corner. He puffed his cigar and looked across at his clients. At least they were enjoying it, and that was the purpose of the night. Their litigation work brought in five per cent of the London office turnover – so the twice-yearly night out on Buckley & Dwyer was expected.

Jeremy's gaze wandered around the room again. At the back was a large spiral staircase next to one of the bars. He'd been told it led to a small casino upstairs which he was intent on trying his hand at later, depending on what the minimum stake was, of course. In this place it could be anything. If money had a smell, it smelt like this.

'Another bottle, gentlemen?' A very attractive lady in her early twenties, dressed in a clinging blue, off-the-shoulder embroidered dress – ample cleavage showing, of course – stood in front of them carrying an already opened bottle of champagne and an empty glass. Her shiny, long dark hair was neatly piled on top of her head with a few selected strands hanging down around her delicate, pretty face. She had a warm, welcoming smile.

'Why not,' beamed Richard. The other two men nodded in agreement.

The girl leant slowly over the table, topping up each of their glasses. Jeremy noted the perfectly manicured nails with understated, beige varnish. On both her wrists, she wore thick, solid gold bracelets, and of course, like the others, no watch; time was of no importance here.

Placing the empty glass on the table, she said in a well-spoken voice, 'Would you like me to join you?'

The silence lasted all of a second, before a chorus of 'Of course,' and 'Please do.' The men eagerly moved up along the sofa to make room for her, nearly pushing Jeremy off the other end. Sitting down, she filled her own glass.

'My name's Francesca. I don't believe we've met before.'

'Er, no. I'm Richard, this is Derek, Philip and that's Jeremy on the end there.'

Jeremy nodded and offered a smile, surprised it had taken so long for her to approach. He was happy to sit as a spectator, admiring her seamless, expert manner. She subtly plied them with equal amounts of compliments and champagne, listened intently to every word, agreeing of course, laughing at their silly, unfunny jokes, telling them what they wanted to hear and luring them out of themselves. What happy clients he had. At least she took the onus off him having to talk any more. It had become a drag. Apart from female anatomy, all they were interested in was the value of their shares and pension schemes. Other clients were fun to take out, but he always felt he could never be himself around these three. Once he became a partner in the firm he'd be able to pick and choose his clients. Mind you, no one had mentioned him becoming a partner in ages.

As the evening progressed, constant bottles of champagne found their way to their table, the cost of which was still unknown. Cash was immaterial in a place like this. How quaint to carry currency!

Different dancers came and went. A young woman who was dressed like Shirley Bassey sang covers of her songs – surprisingly very well. Another hostess approached them and was warmly welcomed, squeezing in between them.

Jeremy saw this as an opportunity to go for a wander. He doubted he'd be missed now. 'I'll be back in a little while,' he said as he stood up. He waited for a response but none came. Walking down the central aisle towards the bar at the back of the room he wondered how he was going to get Jack to approve such a high amount on expenses. He could say they'd brought their wives – that would account for some of it.

Reaching the bar, he saw an empty stool but stood instead by the counter. 'Brandy, please.'

A smartly dressed barman poured it in front of him into a glass. Jeremy watched him but became aware of a lone woman on his right turning towards him. He quickly turned to the left hoping she'd approach someone else. Luckily she stood up and left. As he looked up, his eyes met with the eyes of a young man in his early twenties, dressed in a conservative business suit, standing further along the bar. They nodded at each other politely before glancing away. When the barman departed, Jeremy picked up his glass and sipped the fine brandy with pleasure.

'Interesting place.'

Jeremy looked up again. It was the young man who was now standing a few feet from him – short blond hair, blue eyes with small rimmed glasses and surprisingly fresh faced, especially for a place like this. Jeremy raised an eyebrow. 'An *expensive*, interesting place.'

'Fortunately, I'm not picking up the bill.'

'Unfortunately I am . . . well, my company is. I'm entertaining clients.'

'And are they?'

'Entertained? Oh, very. They're most impressed.' He raised his glass as a toast to the evening. 'The night has been a great success.'

'Well, I'm glad someone's enjoying it. It's not really my scene,' said the young man.

Jeremy guessed it was all a bit much for him. He looked more suited to Sunday bowls. 'Mine neither . . . all this flesh flying around, I feel positively queasy.'

The young man smiled, amused by Jeremy's jolly manner. 'So, what business are you in to warrant entertaining here? Oil? Arms? Finance?'

Jeremy laughed aloud. 'The legal profession, I'm a solicitor.'

'And this is a usual way to win business?'

'Clients get what clients want.'

'Ah yes . . . A great motto for capitalism. "Clients get what clients want", he said with a considerable level of disdain in his voice.

Jeremy went to respond, but decided against getting into a political discussion at that time of night. He sipped his brandy, intrigued by the young man before him. 'How come you're here then?'

'I've been asking myself the same question – met up with a few old school chums and they ended up dragging me along. I was about to leave.' He was softly spoken with a precise, public school accent.

'Where are they now?'

He shrugged his shoulders. 'Being mauled by hostesses or losing money in the casino.'

'Don't be too harsh on them . . . It's the genetic make-up of men. Expect this place is a bit over the top for you?'

'Actually I find it sterile and conservatively tame.'

Jeremy pulled a look of surprise.

'Well, there's hardly a great buzz here, just some boring, middle-aged, wealthy business types getting off on some forbidden fanny . . . How clichéd!' The strength of his words wasn't reflected by his calm, polite delivery.

'I hope you don't include me in that.'

'No, it doesn't look like your kind of thing.'

Jeremy put his hands on his hips, feigning offence. 'I meant middle-aged.'

The man laughed. 'I'm Thomas by the way.'

'Jeremy.'

They shook hands.

Although Jeremy had initially wanted to avoid politics, the continued conversation with Thomas spiralled into a heated debate about world trade and globalisation. Jeremy had always considered himself to be fairly left wing, but compared to Thomas he was a fascist. The world, according to Thomas, would soon be controlled by a handful of powerful conglomerates, with puppet governments creating the façade of living in a democracy for the masses. He was a driven man with a mission and belonged to various political groups, most of which Jeremy hadn't even heard of. He was passionate about his beliefs and untainted by the cynicism that too often besets an older person.

'So you're out to save the world?'

Thomas smiled. 'I'll give it a go.'

'What do you do as a job . . . presumably you have one?'

'I have to pay the bills like everyone else. I work in the archives at the BBC.'

'Interesting. Or is it?'

'Very.'

Conversation continued until Jeremy managed to persuade Thomas to accompany him upstairs to the casino. However, after five minutes Thomas left saying he'd meet up with him later in the bar; he couldn't approve of such blatant misuse of wealth.

Jeremy nodded sympathetically at him, inside completely approving; wealth is meant to be misused. This was the best part of the night. Unfortunately, the average stake was a bit out of Jeremy's range, so he stood by the roulette table and watched. It turned out to be just as addictive – more for the amounts people were losing than winning.

Nearly an hour passed before Jeremy suddenly remembered Thomas and his clients. He hoped Thomas hadn't left; he'd enjoyed talking with him. He hurried down a different set of stairs and accidentally ended up in another part of the club, a fairly quiet and relaxed lounge. A new dancer was just emerging from behind a curtain, wearing a red lace mini-dress, deliberately revealing red knickers and bra. She made her way to the small stage at the side.

Jeremy turned to leave, but stopped; there was something about her . . . he stood and stared. She had a ridiculous amount of make-up on and her blonde curly hair obscured part of her face. She began a slow, seductive dance to the Prince song, 'If I Was Your Girlfriend'. He stared intently at her for ages, trying to get a better look. What was it? Did he know her? No. *Ridiculous*, he thought, and he finally left the room walking back up the stairs from which he'd come.

Nearing the top, he stopped. He gazed into space for ages thinking, recalling; it was playing on his mind. Screwing up his face, he felt compelled to go back down.

Standing in the doorway at the back, Jeremy watched the woman. She had a petite figure and twirled around on the spot like a trained dancer. *Those eyes*, he thought. The song ended and she held her last pose for a few seconds.

Then he gasped. Oh my God, it couldn't be! He grinned broadly. It was. It really was. He shook his head in disbelief. Why would she work here? He darted into the corridor, not wanting her to see him. Falling back against the wall for support, he burst out laughing, cradling his stomach and shaking his head. Underneath that blonde wig he knew it was her – the double life of Little Miss Home Counties. Another burst of laughter erupted from him. What delightful fun he would have with this knowledge.

## 8

Jack was five minutes late. Emma wondered if she'd got the date wrong. He was never late. *He'd better turn up*, she thought. She had spent hours, including evenings and all weekend, working on the two documents. She sat at the head of the table in the boardroom at Manchester, wearing her beige trouser suit, which hadn't been worn for ages as the waistband was too tight. Not that she'd lost much weight in a week, only three pounds but, as a temporary measure, the button had been moved half an inch to the left. Feeling confident with her work, she was determined to run the meeting herself. Jack Tomkinson would not get the better of her again. No more bulldozing from him, or anyone else.

She checked her watch, it was nearly 5.40. At that moment, Jack appeared at the door, his hair slightly ruffled. He marched over to the chair next to her and placed his briefcase down on the table.

'Good evening, Jack,' Emma said warmly, deliberately smiling at him.

'God awful traffic. Hello.' He took some papers from his case.

'Would you like some tea or coffee?' she asked.

'No. No. Let's make a start.' Within a second he had removed his coat and was sitting down staring at her, waiting for the documents.

Emma ignored his impatient posture. She slowly reached over for the first file next to her and opened it. She coughed a couple of times but spoke confidently. 'Right, then. I believe we should tackle this meeting by going over the working document in detail initially.

Understandably, I have numerous questions, everything from telephone systems to the number of PCs. After that, I suggest we go over the budgets. I need your authority to press ahead with certain purchases; some companies have long lead times.' She looked him straight in the eye.

His unblinking, intense eyes stared back.

She gave a slight smile. 'Obviously, I've only had a week, so I've taken a lot of the costs from your business plan. That'll change over the next two weeks.'

He nodded.

She handed him a copy of the twenty-page working document, which he immediately opened and started reading.

'I'd like to go over each item together if that's OK,' she said.

'I'd prefer to read it fully myself first. At the end you can go over your queries. It'll save on time.'

'I had planned to talk you through it,' she said with some insistence.

'It's easier this way.' Without waiting for a reply, he looked back down and started reading the document again.

'You might not understand certain entries.'

Jack looked up at her. 'I'll ask,' he said, then added with a smile, 'You mentioned some coffee.'

With his head back in the document he couldn't see the annoyance across her face, her lips tight and pinched. Two, maybe three thousand pounds, she reminded herself. She stood up and luckily, caught hold of Tracey, the office junior, in the hall and asked her to organise the coffee. Returning to the boardroom, she sat back down and watched Jack examining her work. He didn't look up once. Occasionally, he wrote something across the page. He even crossed out a couple of entries. All of it in absolute silence.

Shortly, Tracey entered the room with their coffee then left. Feeling redundant, Emma sipped her coffee and continued to observe Jack, hard at work, but glancing at his watch every so often. The sound of cars being started in the car park below could be heard, as the other staff departed for the day. She was alone in the boardroom, maybe the whole building, with Jack Tomkinson. As time went on, her mind started to wander off with mad, surreal thoughts. She imagined suddenly jumping up on the table, ripping off her clothes and singing 'Bohemian Rhapsody', just to see his reaction, to shake him from his controlled stance. He'd probably just tell her to stop wasting time.

After about twenty minutes, Jack eventually turned over the last page and looked up at her. Emma was still miles away, imagining herself being interviewed on *Oprah*, promoting her book entitled *Men and Dishcloths*, and discussing her phenomenal success and inspiration to women all over the world.

'Emma,' he said.

She jerked forward, startled by the sudden interruption.

'I've finished reading.'

'Right.' She waited for some comment.

'Before we go over this, I'll take a look at the budgets you've produced,' he said.

Emma politely surrendered to his request and passed over the second file containing the spreadsheets. He looked at his watch again. Taking out a copy of his initial business plan, he compared each item on her list against his own.

'You need to build in something for currency fluctuations. I suggest four per cent.' His eyes never left the page.

Emma was silent. After a moment he glanced up at her. 'This figure for airline travel is too high.'

'I took it literally from your business plan.'

'I was working on three people travelling back and forward. It's now only two, you and me.'

'Then when I come to insert all my own figures, I'll amend it,' she said defensively.

Jack ran his hand through his hair. 'That's fine, Emma, I was just pointing it out.' He continued reading.

Emma closed her eyes for a moment and breathed heavily.

'Of course there's the launch party still to budget for,' he said.

She glared at him. Maybe he was unaware how accusing his voice could be. She said determinedly, 'I have no details whatsoever of what you've got in mind for this party, how many people, what sort of food. It was one of the numerous questions I had planned to ask when going over the working document. I really would have liked to have started there. This way feels more hostile than productive.'

Jack's eyes opened wide. He sat quite still staring at her and was silent, surprised by her words. Emma's heartbeat quickened.

He put down his pen and sat back in his chair. Glancing at his watch again, his eyes then rested on Emma. 'Is something wrong?' he asked, a confused expression on his face.

She cleared her throat and said quietly, 'Um. . . yes, I suppose there is.'

Jack looked concerned. He sat upright, ready to listen.

'It's difficult to explain,' she said.

'Try. I'm not a complete fool. Best we sort this now.

I don't want any problems in Dublin.'

'Of course not. That's exactly what I want to avoid, too.'

'Then what?'

Emma took a deep breath and said in a deliberately friendly voice, 'We're going to be working very closely for the next few months. Don't you think we need to develop a good working relationship?'

'Absolutely,' he said.

'You may not have chosen me for this position, however I know that I am more than capable of doing it. I am addressing any so-called gaps in my knowledge and the bottom line is . . . we're stuck with each other. Therefore I believe we need to look at the way we're going to work together, because I don't work the way you do.'

His eyes narrowed. 'In what sense?'

She shook her head. 'I might as well say it.' She paused nervously. 'Everything feels so rushed. It's efficient to the point of being uncomfortable. I feel on edge, thinking that I may be wasting your time. You're constantly glancing at your watch as if you're ready to dash off at any minute. We're going to be living out of each other's pocket soon. I'll need to contact you on a regular basis and I don't want to think, Will Jack think me stupid for asking this or that question? I kind of think that now.' She stared at him, waiting for his response.

Jack was swirling his pen around his fingers.

'Am I making any sense?' she asked. 'I don't wish to sound rude or inefficient. I like to think I'm neither of those things. I am aware of and hopefully practise the wonders of time management but even a little chat over a cup of tea now and again would just lighten things up.'

For several moments Jack just stared at the pen which he continued to swirl around his fingers. Then, putting it down, he said in his official-sounding voice, 'Maybe a social drink is called for.'

She stared at him in surprise. 'A drink?'

'Yes.'

'When?'

'Now.'

She lowered her eyes. 'What about the meeting, all this?' She gestured at the files.

'I'm up for two days, we'll grab another hour tomorrow. You're right. If you were a client we would have had a lunch by now. I've just had a lot on my mind. I'm sure you can guess what.'

She looked up at him but said nothing.

'We should clear the air. Find some mutual ground.'

*Mutual ground!* She wasn't sure there'd be any. He was waiting for a response.

'OK.'

'We'll walk over to the Barge.' Jack stood up and placed all his papers back in his briefcase. 'Is anyone using the boardroom tomorrow?'

'Not until after lunch.'

'I'll leave all this here then.' He touched his back pocket checking for his wallet. 'Meet you in reception,' he said, as he left the room.

Emma sat, glaring at his briefcase, reluctant to move. Why had she said anything? Now she had to go for a drink alone with Jack Tomkinson. What would they talk about? Hopefully there wouldn't be lots of long, awkward silences. *How awful!* She cringed inside and shook her head. *Wait till I tell Trish*, she thought.

They met in reception a few minutes later, then left, locking the door behind them. Walking the short distance, Emma felt embarrassed at the silence and was searching her mind for topics to discuss. Thankfully, they soon arrived at the Barge, a refurbished pub on the street lining Salford Quays. Inside, it was modern. Long but very narrow, windows ran the length of one side overlooking a small dock encircled by newly built apartment blocks.

Emma sat down at a table while Jack went to the bar, returning with a bottle of Californian Chardonnay and two glasses, which he put on the table. He poured wine into the two glasses, and handed her one. She smiled awkwardly. He sort of smiled back.

'Cheers.'

'Cheers.'

They sipped their wine. Jack moved his seat slightly. He looked around the bar, which was nearly empty apart from a few lone drinkers sitting along the counter. 'Quiet here tonight,' he said.

'I suppose 'cause it's Monday.'

They drank more wine. Jack scratched his forearm. Emma crossed her legs over.

'Nice wine,' she said.

'Yes, not bad.'

Jack picked up his beer mat as if to read the back of it. An uncomfortable silence descended. Emma thought about disappearing into the ladies toilet but considered it a bit too soon.

'Christmas party next week,' she quickly threw in.

'Oh yes . . . yet another one.'

'Scary how fast the years fly.'

'You must have been with the practice for what, eight years now?' he said.

'Nine in June.'

'Almost as long as I have.'

'Long time all right,' she observed.

'Surprising.'

'Why?' she asked.

'I thought you would have left by now.'

'I may have appeared more ambitious than I was.'

Jack took a sip of wine. 'Actually I thought you would have had a family.'

'Oh, I see.'

He looked worried. 'I didn't mean anything by that.'

She smiled briefly to reassure him.

'Then there was talk of emigrating.' He touched his forehead. 'Canada, wasn't it?'

She nodded, then shrugged her shoulders. 'Tony and I spoke about it, but it was never definite.'

'I got the impression it was. Didn't I write you a reference for the embassy?'

'We decided not to proceed.'

'Really? Why not?'

She sipped her wine thinking what to say. She couldn't tell him the truth. 'When it came to it . . .' she trailed off. 'We just decided against it.'

He nodded and topped up her wine.

*What next?* Emma thought. 'I think we're on the same table,' she said.

He looked confused.

'Christmas party.'

'Oh.'

'Harold's idea,' she added. 'He wants the branches to get to know each other better. There'll be someone from Birmingham and, of course, Henry.'

Jack nodded but she guessed he wasn't too interested in the seating arrangements. Emma desperately racked her brains for the next topic. To her relief Jack started a lengthy conversation about work, elaborating on his plans for the Dublin office.

'It'll mostly be corporate business, not criminal . . . European Law consultations, devising contracts, that sort of thing. That's where the money is.'

His intention was to spend three days a week in Dublin and two back in London. After a year, once everything was up and running, he'd hand over the reins in Dublin to someone else. He spoke about purchasing a property over there, part home, part investment. Emma started to convey her own ideas for the administration side of the office and recruitment of staff. It turned out to be a fairly relaxed discussion, which made the evening pass quickly.

Some time later, midway through one of her sentences, she caught him checking his watch again. Instinctively, she ceased talking.

He looked up. 'Just a habit,' he said, as if defending himself.

She nodded, amused.

'By the way, I thought your working document was very comprehensive and concise,' he added.

Maybe it was the two glasses of wine on an empty stomach because at that moment she found him rather comical. 'I take it comprehensive and concise are good things, a compliment.'

'Damn, a compliment. I must be slipping.'

Emma looked away to hide a growing smile.

'So you feel rushed by me,' he said out of the blue.

Emma stared at him, examining his expression for an indication of how the comment was meant. As usual he gave nothing away. 'At times,' she answered, determined to stand her ground.

His gaze travelled around the bar before looking back at her. He stroked his eyebrow as if considering what to say, but he said nothing.

'I suppose we just have to get used to working together again, understanding each other's odd ways,' she said cheerfully, hoping he'd laugh.

He gave a brief nod of his head but said with a degree of seriousness, 'I'm not into tiptoeing around people's personalities. We are who we are. Once the working document has been fully drafted, you'll be pretty much your own boss anyway. As long as every deadline is met, work however you wish.' He sipped his wine and stared out across the water.

Emma gazed down at the glass in her hand, slightly offended and embarrassed at his apparent non-chalance. She said firmly, resolutely, 'There shouldn't be a problem then.'

He looked back at her. After a moment's pause, he stated, 'None whatsoever.'

Now it was Emma who checked her watch, wanting to leave.

It was a busy week. Emma hardly saw Tony. Both of them were working long hours, she at the solicitors', he with his two jobs, days as a courier and nights as a doorman at the Swan. In the evenings they crossed paths in the hall, she arriving home and he just leaving. A quick kiss would pass between them. One evening, he appeared in the hallway with bruising around his left eye; there had been trouble at the pub, a vicious fight between two guys. Both he and Rob had piled in and eventually broken it up.

Emma gasped and gently held his face in both her hands, worried at what could have happened. He shrugged it off, but looked drained, exhausted, his skin sallow and pale, the late nights and early mornings a shock to his system.

In contrast, Tony noticed Emma's beaming face as she'd bound into the hall, kicking off her shoes. He'd get a two-minute summary of the day's events and what Jack had done now. Sometimes she complained ardently, other times she laughed, relaying her responses to his e-mails.

'I gave *him* a deadline today,' she said, pleasantly entertained by it.

Tony nodded, wondering what the big deal was. She too said she was tired, but she didn't appear it to him.

The morning of the Christmas party, Tony dropped his bombshell.

'We need the money,' he said, justifying his plan to work that evening and not attend the party.

'You've known about this date for three months.'

Tony was pulling on his jeans in the bedroom. 'The

Swan's been packed all week. They need help . . . said they'd make it worth my while. Could be double pay.'

'No,' said Emma, still remaining calm. 'I can't go on my own. It's partners.'

'What about Jeremy?'

'He's been paired up with Julia for the night, Jack's other secretary.'

'Don't go then. Stuffy lot! Ain't much fun.' He didn't like the people she worked with, thought them boring, snobby; *they're talking about me*, he had whispered in her ear last year. She told him not to be so silly, but he was convinced they were. Emma knew it wasn't his favourite event, but she rarely asked him to do anything that he didn't want to, a monthly lunch with her parents and once a year the Christmas party. That was all!

'I'm late. I'm leaving. Don't let me down, Tony – *please!*'

'Didn't you hear? What about work?'

'*Please*,' she begged. 'I'll see you tonight.' She walked down the stairs already planning to telephone him that afternoon. Even if he did come, she wondered about the sort of mood he'd be in.


That evening, Jeremy, smartly dressed in his black dinner suit, spotted Emma from across the crowded hotel lobby and made an instant beeline for her. 'Your hair. It's lovely, positively wonderful. You never told me.' He touched it and ordered her to do a twirl.

She smiled, slightly embarrassed at the loudness of his voice. 'Had it done this afternoon.'

'Love it!'

It was now shoulder length and auburn-tinted, with various layers cut in and a lightly feathered fringe. She was wearing her long and loose-fitting black velvet dress; hopefully no one would remember she'd worn it the year before last.

'You look so different. Softer . . . *sexy*, my dear. You'll be fighting the bastards off. Where's Tony . . .?' He stepped back and opened his mouth wide to mimic a shocked expression. 'Not that I was implying . . .'

'He'll be here shortly. Said half seven.' She checked her watch.

'Let's get a drink.'

'I said I'd meet here.'

'We're only in the next room, surely he'll find you.'

She was shaking her head. 'No, I'll wait.'

'You're a lousy feminist.'

She gave him a dirty look then continued inspecting the packed foyer for Tony's familiar face.

'Wait here then. I'll fetch a couple of glasses.' He turned and soon disappeared into the crowd.

The Albert Hotel was the largest in Manchester, with over two hundred bedrooms and four large function rooms. Built in 1895, it still retained a lot of original Victorian features; the high ceilings with ornate coving and the exceptionally large circular lobby area with a cherub fountain in the middle – still working. Small groups of merry people surrounded it, chatting, laughing. A couple of guys were singing, worse the wear from their Christmas lunch.

Emma stood by the main entrance, observing everyone who entered. All the different dresses, colours, materials, styles; she noticed them all. New outfits bought for the annual night out. Most of the Buckley & Dwyer party were already in the Prince Regent Room having their buck's fizz reception. Dinner was at eight, so there was still time for Tony to arrive. After considerable persuasion that afternoon, he had finally agreed to come, although he made it quite clear that he didn't want to, he wouldn't enjoy it and it was only as a massive favour to her. She thanked him. He'd go and borrow his dad's suit and come straight from there.

At that moment, descending down the main staircase she spotted Jack, hand in hand with a tall slim lady, wearing a long clinging red dress with a slit right up the middle. Even from across the lobby Emma expected to see her knickers. But no, an inch of material enabled a certain standard of decency to be kept. She glided down the stairs like a swan, confident and proud. She had short dark hair, but Emma couldn't really see her face, just the graceful silhouette descending each step. Soon they were lost in the crowd.

'Get that down you,' said Jeremy, back with two flutes of champagne. 'Persuaded the waitress to hold off on the orange. Sacrilege adding it to such a fine drink.'

'Always goes straight to my head,' Emma replied, taking the glass.

'Mine also.'

'Cheers. Happy Christmas. How's the party going?' she asked.

'Rather reserved at the moment, casual small talk.'

'I see Jack's honoured us with his presence this year. Who's the woman with him?'

'The name's Rachel, I believe.'

'News to me. How long's that been going on?'

Jeremy's eyes gleamed maliciously. 'News to everyone! No one's heard of her before tonight. Greg and I conclude she's an escort, maybe a high-class call girl. He'll probably claim for her on expenses.'

Emma laughed but shook her head. 'You love it, don't you. Any bit of gossip and you're in your element.'

'Moi?' he asked, innocently, pointing to himself. 'You're on their table so I expect half hourly reports. Start with "Have you known Jack long?" Note the expression, not just the reply.'

'No way! Find out yourself.'

'Don't claim the moral high ground on me. You're as intrigued as me.'

'Oh, sure I am,' she said, glancing around the lobby. It seemed to be clearing as people started to enter their appropriate rooms.

'What if he doesn't show by eight?' Jeremy asked.

She didn't respond initially, just kept looking around, praying he'd turn up. 'He *promised* he'd be here.'

Jeremy couldn't think of anything reassuring to say. After a little while he gently took hold of her hand, squeezing it in his and said in a serious manner, 'You do look lovely tonight, Emma. Your hair really suits you.'

She leant over and pecked him on the cheek. 'Thank you. You really are the best, Jeremy.'

His face lit up. Her thumb was rubbing off the lipstick mark she'd made when she noticed his eyes focus on something behind her.

'Hello,' said Jeremy, a faint, put-on smile appearing. Emma turned. 'Thank God you're here!'

'Don't panic, said I would, didn't I?' Tony stood fiddling with his shirt collar. 'Too tight,' he said.

The rest of the dinner suit wasn't the best fit either, the arms were slightly too short for him. But he'd shaved, tied his hair back neatly and smelt of the after-shave she'd bought him for his birthday.

'All right, Jeremy? How you been?'

'Oh, I get by. How are you?'

'Busy. Damn busy.' He pointed at Emma's head, looking perplexed.

'Last-minute thing. Like it?' she asked.

A noticeable pause followed. 'Yeah, course I do. Surprised, that's all.'

Emma just smiled, relieved and happy he was there.

By the time they entered the Prince Regent Room, the buck's fizz reception was over. Most guests were already seated. There were ten tables of eight, nicely spaced out, filling up one half of the room, with a dance floor and DJ accounting for the other half. The ceiling was covered in streamers and different coloured tinsel. An over-decorated Christmas tree stood in the corner by the DJ. Emma and Tony arrived at their table and introductions were carried out, followed by polite handshakes. The table consisted of Henry and his wife Elizabeth, Steve Ingrams and wife Sarah – Emma wondered how Trish would be coping – plus Jack and the mysterious Rachel woman. Emma had Tony to her left and Steve to her right.

'Red or white?' asked Henry.

'Red please,' replied Emma.

'Yeah, red'll do for me too,' added Tony.

All eight occupants sat in silence watching Henry pour. Everyone proceeded to sip wine, a few uncomfortable smiles followed. The other tables emitted much more noise with regular bursts of laughter. Tony cast a discreet glance in Emma's direction; its message was received loud and clear.

'Is that a new hairstyle, Emma?' Henry bellowed loudly across the table.

Everyone stared at her. She blushed. 'Yes. Yes it is.'

'Marvellous, isn't it, Elizabeth?'

Elizabeth, grey-haired with spectacles and in her early sixties, had the no-nonsense character of Barbara Woodhouse, but instead of dogs her passion was horses.

'It's hair, Henry. No doubt it's fashionable, but marvellous is hardly an apt word for a hairstyle,' she retorted, forcefully.

Henry laughed out loud. Most of the table politely smiled. Emma hoped her face wasn't as red as it felt.

'Not that I saw it before, but *I* like it.' It was Rachel, sitting the other side of Tony.

'Thank you.' Emma smiled, at last getting a good look at her face. It was smallish like an elf's, her short brown hair almost cropped. Her eyes were large and hazel, lips full and protruding, painted deep red and surrounding a set of amazingly white teeth. She wasn't exactly beautiful but she definitely had something that made you want to stare a little longer. Emma's eyes met Jack's. He briefly nodded, then turned towards Henry.

'Melon or soup?' asked a waitress, appearing at her elbow.

Soon they were all eating and conversation became a little easier, mostly with people chatting to their immediate neighbours. Emma overheard Rachel starting up a conversation with Tony.

'I take it you're not a solicitor then, Tony?' She had a distinctive low, throaty-sounding voice.

'No. No way. Not me.'

'Such a definite and forceful reply. Do I take it the law doesn't interest you?'

'You could say that. Some laws are needed.'

'Only some?' Her eyes, deep and cryptic, were fixed tightly on to his.

He held her gaze. 'Yes, only some.'

'How interesting! Are you an anarchist?'

'No,' he laughed.

'Then what? I'm intrigued.' She leant further towards him, one hand leaning on the table, slowly sipping her wine at intervals.

'I just think laws are supposed to be there to protect the average man in the street. Nowadays, they're used to beat him around the head. It's big business and who's getting rich . . . solicitors.' He gulped his wine almost emptying the glass.

Emma coughed. *Oh God, not here*, she thought.

Rachel smiled at him for some moments. She was sucking the tip of her index finger. After a long and deliberate pause, her stare unbroken, she whispered loudly, 'You won't be impressed by *my* occupation.' Her eyes narrowed slightly. Tony grinned.

'Go on, do your damage, what are you?'

Sarah was talking to Emma about the wonders of her two-year-old son James. Emma nodded politely but was secretly straining to catch the conversation to her left. Out of the corner of her eye, she saw Rachel practically leaning against Tony, touching his ear and whispering into it. She seemed to be perched there for ages. The two of them then chuckled together like kids with a naughty secret. Tony topped up both his and Rachel's glass. Emma's was nearly empty but it was left untouched.

Out of nowhere, Jack asked, 'If only some of the laws are needed, Tony, and the rest are just to make solicitors rich, in your opinion, which laws aren't required?'

Tony glanced at him only briefly, then looked back at Rachel. There was a strange smile across her face. Anticipation? Amusement? Emma, still politely nodding and half listening to Sarah, waited nervously for Tony's reply.

'Prostitution,' he said. 'Why's that illegal? Judges and other legal types are the best customers, I'm told.'

Jack appeared unmoved. 'There's no money in either defending or prosecuting prostitutes. Prostitution is unofficially tolerated. The law's a safety net.

Prosecutions are mostly sought for secondary reasons, for example, to ensure antisocial behaviour isn't a complete nuisance to other residents.' He was sitting upright and talking as if conducting a meeting. 'Which other laws do you deem unnecessary?'

Tony stared at him coldly. 'It's really about why people commit crimes, and whether locking them up is going to solve anything.'

'A politician's answer there. The question was about which specific laws you find unacceptable.'

'What do you want, a list? Can't do that . . . You're the solicitor.'

'I was just defending the fact that I believe most laws, with of course the odd exception, are needed, at least to be in place. Why people—'

'Obviously,' Tony interrupted. 'It's how you make your living.'

'Why people break them is a long and complicated discussion. A separate matter. It doesn't make the particular law less valid.'

Tony was shaking his head, annoyance building. Emma dreaded what he'd say next.

Rachel interjected, 'Yes, long and complicated, not entirely suitable for this evening. I started this, so I claim the right to end it. The law and crime, be it one subject or two, shall for the remainder of the evening be taboo.' She toasted both gentlemen with her glass.

Tony sat completely still, his face taut. Jack glanced at Emma and noticed her discomfort. His stare fell away. Emma was about to touch Tony's hand when Rachel whispered to him, 'So, how do you make *your* living, Tony?'

He focused back on her, hesitating, then said, ' I'm a doorman at a pub. I throw out drunks.'

She looked serious, stern. 'Promise not to throw me

out tonight. I intend to drink quite a lot.' She flashed him a wicked grin. Tony grinned back.

'Drink away. I'll join you.'

The waitresses came and cleared the plates. The main course was served, a traditional Christmas dinner of turkey, roast potatoes, sprouts, the lot. As the wine flowed, the conversation started to flow also. Crackers were pulled and everyone wore their paper hats and read their nonsense jokes out; at this point they sounded quite funny.

Emma kept a watchful eye on Trish who was seated at the table to her right. Several times she had caught her staring at Steve and Sarah with a sad, vacant expression across her face.

Table four was the loudest, which of course had Jeremy, Greg and Richard on it, the jokers from each branch. Jeremy winked across at her a few times and made funny eyes towards the back of Rachel, as if to enquire what she'd found out. Nothing so far, other than that she was a massive flirt. Julia was sitting next to Jeremy and nodded at Emma, as if to say hello. Emma nodded back.

At one point, a large sprout flew out of the sky and ended up floating in Elizabeth's wineglass. Not that it fazed her. 'I've heard of it raining cats and dogs before, but never sprouts,' she shouted out, laughing heartily, so everyone else laughed too. Emma guessed which table it had come from; its target had probably been Jack. Halfway through the main course, Trish disappeared off towards the ladies. She was gone for ages. Emma was about to go and find her when she re-emerged, silver lycra dress shining, her face smiling, making quick retorts to all in her path. But on returning to her seat she slumped back down, shoulders curved and eyelids lowered.

'Your husband's been telling me he's about to be a bachelor again for three months,' ventured Rachel, glass in hand, her elegant painted fingers delicately tracing around the rim of the glass. Her eyes were now wide and innocent.

Emma turned towards Tony. 'For the week nights. I'll be back at weekends.'

'How very trusting of you,' Rachel beamed, amused.

That was it, Emma thought. 'So, how long have you known Jack?' she blurted out.

Jack, ears like radar, stopped what he was saying to Henry mid-sentence. He stared across at Emma, eyebrows raised. She cringed, quickly averting her eyes and pinning her gaze back on Rachel.

Rachel smiled at Jack and touched his shoulder. 'You answer, darling.'

At that moment, the rest of the table ceased talking and looked at him, waiting. He put down his knife and fork. 'Two months,' he said reluctantly.

Elizabeth asked in her usual brusque manner, 'Yes, and how did you meet? Tell all, my boy.'

'Now Elizabeth, stop prying,' said Henry.

'Rubbish, don't be such a bore. Go on Jack, we ladies are waiting for all the romantic details.'

Jack spoke unusually quietly for him. 'Rachel works for the Inland Revenue as a tax inspector. She was looking into another small concern I run.'

Emma glared at Rachel who was smiling sweetly at Jack. A tax inspector! Inland Revenue! A civil servant! What an anticlimax! He had fallen for her over balance sheets and profit margins! Maybe it wasn't true. She'd ask Tony what Rachel had said earlier to ensure their stories matched up.

Jack picked up his knife and fork and continued eating.

A while later, the DJ, large and bearded, made an announcement. 'It's time to work off that dinner. It's Christmas, we're having fun, the drink's free, let's dance,' he shouted. At that, Showaddywaddy's 'Let's Party', came blaring out. Immediately, at least ten people, the most confident or most drunk, jumped up and on to the dance floor. Soon another twenty or so joined them, dancing away. Limbs were moving in very odd ways, but no one seemed to care. As usual, Jeremy was one of the first ones up, shaking his bits. He waved for Emma to join him but she shook her head, mouthing 'later.' More tunes came on: 'Hi Ho Silver Lining', 'The Locomotion', all the old favourites. At one point, Jeremy and Elizabeth entertained everyone by doing a version of the twist together. Hopefully, Elizabeth's heart was in better condition than Henry's.

After about an hour, Emma and Jack were the only two left seated at the table as the others were either dancing or mingling with people elsewhere. At least Tony was enjoying himself this year, bopping around with Rachel and Sarah. She hoped he wouldn't drink any more though. Jack took off his blue paper hat and scrunched it up. He looked across at Emma, both smiled politely. The music was so loud it was difficult to hold a conversation, so they just sat, silent, observing the dancing and sipping their wine.

Surprised by how awkward she was feeling, Emma got up and went to the ladies. While she was washing her hands, Trish walked in, eyes glazed with unwanted tears. She rushed into a cubicle and locked the door. The sound of muffled crying started. Emma went over to the door.

'Trish, you OK?'

There was no reply.

'Trish, it's me, Emma.'

The sobs got louder.

'Please. I'm worried.'

The door opened slowly and Trish walked out, streaks of mascara across her face, eyes bloodshot and nose running.

'Oh, Trish.' Emma instantly put her arm around her and led her to a small sofa just past the sinks. They sat while Trish continued to cry. Occasionally, she'd almost collect herself, before a new bout of crying took hold. Emma kept getting up to fetch loo roll. Women would enter and stare in their direction, but Emma assured them everything was all right.

When they were finally alone, Trish spoke, initially sounding quite calm. 'I know you know.'

Emma nodded. 'I suspected, I wasn't sure.'

Trish rubbed her eyes. 'He's ignored me . . . tonight . . . It's been . . .' she bit her lip '. . . *awful* seeing them together.'

'I can imagine.'

'Followed him to the lobby. He told me to stop staring . . . too obvious. Told me to go away . . . too risky.'

Emma squeezed Trish's hand. 'It was always going to be difficult tonight. I'm surprised you came.'

'Wish I hadn't now. Felt I had to, wanted to. I don't know any more . . . What's she like?'

Emma frowned, unsure what to say. 'You don't really want to know that.'

'I do. Tell me. Is she nice? He says she's cold.'

'She's . . .' Emma hesitated. 'I'm sorry, but what can I say? Don't ask me things like that.'

Trish shook her head. 'Knew you wouldn't approve. That's why I didn't tell you. It's not some dirty fling, you know. It's serious! I love him, Emma. He loves me.'

Emma looked away. She'd spent a lot of the evening

listening to Sarah and her plans for her son James, possibly a little brother or sister. Yes, Steve had appeared tense at that moment, he'd been extremely quiet all night, but they appeared to be a happy young couple. Did Sarah have any idea? For a second she wondered about Tony. He was always out without her, plenty of opportunities. Even when they went to the Swan together, there were always young girls that he knew by name, coming up to talk with him. It was obvious he enjoyed the attention. Innocent flirting to boost his damaged ego, she told herself. An understandable result of his loss of direction since leaving the army, the numerous dead-end jobs and the fact that she earned more than him, which he said he hated.

'No, I can't approve, but I still feel for you. I know you're hurting. I know what that's like,' said Emma.

Trish dropped her head into her hands. 'It wasn't meant to happen, just did. I tried so hard to fight it. We both did. Just happened.'

'Where's it all going to end? Have you spoken about that?'

'If it wasn't for James, he'd leave. He loves him so much. It's so *unfair*.' Trish's tears began again.

'Oh God, I hate seeing you so upset. This is going to sound really hard but is there any way you'd end it now before it gets even harder, more hurtful?'

'*What?*' Trish gasped, her eyes almost bursting with anger. 'How can you ask that? Haven't you listened? I couldn't. Don't you see? I *love* him. It's gone too far already. He loves me. Just needs time to sort things out.'

Her body seemed to jerk from side to side as if gripped by panic. 'How could I end it? This is real. I knew you wouldn't understand. Your life's neat, *packaged*.' Her voice rose to a shriek. 'You have *no* idea. It's gone past all reason.'

An instant later, almost in a whisper, she added, 'No one understands, just me and Steve.' Her head dropped into her hands again. 'I should go.'

'I'm sorry,' said Emma, shocked at the force of her outburst. 'I'm sorry. I'm just worried for you, that's all. I'm really sorry.'

Trish was quiet for a moment then said, 'I want to go home.'

'I'll walk with you to get a taxi,' Emma offered.

Trish nodded but spoke no more. They walked together in silence through the hotel lobby and out the main door down the steps to where a couple of taxis were waiting. Emma opened the door for Trish. 'You going to be OK? Ring me later if you want.'

Trish gave a quick nod and got into the car, pulling the door shut. The cab pulled away and Emma walked solemnly back up the steps, annoyed at herself for the way she'd handled the situation. She wondered what else she could have done. Trish's words 'neat' and 'packaged' flew around in her head.

'Is she all right?'

Emma looked up. It was Jack. He was standing just outside the main entrance watching her.

'A headache,' said Emma.

He looked at her suspiciously. 'The headache being the wife, I presume.'

She stared at him. 'How did you know?'

'A guess.'

'You seem to know a lot of what goes on,' she said accusingly.

'Observant, I suppose.'

'No hidden cameras back at the office then?' she joked.

Jack smiled. 'Only in the ladies toilets.'

Emma looked back down the steps. 'I think we're the only ones who know about Trish and . . . Steve. It's probably best kept that way.'

'Of course! Gossip isn't a pastime of mine.'

She nodded, knowing it to be true.

'So she's OK?' he asked again, seeming genuinely concerned.

'As much as she can be, on her road to nowhere.'

'No one knows that for certain.'

'You approve?' she asked, surprised.

'Not my business, unless it involves the practice.'

'Oh, absolutely,' she spoke loudly, angrily. 'If it doesn't affect profit margins it doesn't matter.'

'I didn't say that.'

'No?'

'No. I said it wasn't my business. They're adults. Whether I approve or disapprove is irrelevant. Why are you so annoyed? I take it you don't approve.'

'No way. Another man screwing around. He won't leave his wife, children, house, pensions.' She was shaking her head. 'It's wrong. You met Sarah. She doesn't have a clue.'

'Of course it's always the man's fault. Women don't do these sorts of things, is that what you're saying?'

'Maybe.'

'Ridiculous,' he stated.

She suddenly remembered. 'Oh God, not always . . . sorry,' she mumbled, looking away.

'Seems you know a lot that goes on too.' He kicked a stone off the step, his eyes following its flight.

'No, I don't really know, as such . . . Offices, people talk, you know,' she tried to reassure him. *What a night*, she thought.

He leant against one of the pillars, gazing upwards towards the sky, his face blank. She traced his stare upwards, only clouds and lights from tall buildings. He stood silent and still, supported by the pillar. For an instant she almost felt a tinge of sadness for him. But suddenly he stood up, tall and erect. Staring slightly beyond her, he said, 'I think Henry's going to make his speech soon.'

She nodded and walked beside him back into the hotel.

## 10

The following day at the office, no one seemed to be doing much work. Everyone was tired and hung over from the previous night's party, considered a success by most people. Even Tony, sipping black coffee in bed that morning had mumbled that it had been an 'all right' night; two headache tablets proved it. Of course, Emma had asked him about Rachel's occupation. Still half asleep, he yawned, drank some coffee then screwed up his face. After another wait he'd finally said, 'Tax inspector,' and sniffed loudly, adding, 'Surprising. Didn't seem the sort.' Emma had frowned, disappointed.

Trish arrived at work looking her usual radiant self, wearing a lime-green knitted dress, curled hair and bright eyes. She chatted and laughed with the others who were relaying the evening's events; who had become over-familiar with whom. Once alone, she assured an inquisitive Emma that she was fine and felt it best not to talk about Steve at work.

Emma agreed, but added, 'I know I said all the wrong things last night. I'm sorry, I really am. But if there's anything I can ever do, just ask.'

Trish nodded and smiled, before changing the subject.


Jeremy pulled on to the M6 heading back to London at just gone eleven that morning. Apart from Julia, who was sitting cross-legged in the front seat next to him, most of the others had caught the train or left the hotel well before nine. She'd overslept; neither phone calls to her room or banging on her door had awakened her. Pleased by the opportunity that presented itself, Jeremy said he'd wait and insisted the others head off.

Julia was resting her head against the car window, tired and hung over. In a sleepy, yet eloquent and precise voice she asked, 'What time did His Highness leave?'

'Around seven, I think.'

'He'll be in the office by now, annoyed I'm not there.'

'He'll cope.'

'Jack always copes. He'll still be annoyed.'

'Ignore him. It's Christmas.'

'It was wrong of me to oversleep.' She let her heavy eyelids close and immediately started to drift off while listening to the repetitive, hypnotic sound of the tyres speeding over the motorway surface.

Jeremy glanced over at her. She was always so stylishly dressed, he thought. Even today, a little worse for wear, she was wearing a maroon, v-necked, fitted dress, with a pearl necklace and drop earrings and a new pair of black strappy sandals. Hanging up on a peg in the back was a pure silk, maroon jacket that completed the outfit. Her dark bobbed hair gave off a healthy shine and her full lips were perfectly painted a reddish, bronze colour.

He smiled to himself, but deliberately assumed an expression of innocence. 'Great night last night.'

Julia mumbled something resembling agreement.

'You're a very talented dancer.' His words sounded faint in the distance. 'I was watching you last night. You're a very talented dancer,' he repeated.

After a moment, she opened her eyes and smiled. 'You seemed to be having a good time yourself doing your thing.'

'I was just having a laugh, but you? I was impressed.'

No response.

'Did you go to dance school?'

'Oh *please*.'

'But you're so good.'

Her eyes narrowed. 'Calm down, Jeremy, I'm nothing special.'

'I disagree. You could earn a living at it.'

Julia stared across at him with a sceptical look on her face. Jeremy kept his eyes fixed firmly on the road, his hands gripping the steering wheel. Julia continued to look at him for a few moments longer, before turning up the radio. Some slushy Christmas pop song was playing.

'What an awful song. There're some CDs in there. How about Prince?' he asked.

She opened the glove compartment. 'I'd prefer something else.'

'But I love Prince . . . thought you would, too.'

Julia hesitated but slowly picked up the Prince CD and held it loosely in her hand. Several seconds passed before she finally placed it in the stereo and the first track, 'When Doves Cry', immediately blasted out, filling the car with a heavy drum and bass rhythm.

'This is great to dance to. Something very seductive about his work,' said Jeremy.

Julia didn't comment.

'Very sensual.'

Her eyes sharpened their focus on him. 'I didn't realise you were such an obsessive fan. Somehow doesn't quite fit with you.'

He laughed. 'Life is full of surprises, Julia. People are full of surprises . . . don't you think?'

'Are they? Most are boringly unsurprising to me.'

'But then there are others who aren't quite what they appear to be.' Out of the corner of his eye Jeremy saw her staring out of the window, shaking her head. A tinge of guilt ran through him but he asked innocently, 'What? Is something wrong?'

Strangely, her whole stature and demeanour seemed to increase as she gracefully uncrossed her legs and sat up straight. A brief, nonchalant laugh came from her.

'What? What's funny?'

Eyes wide, now fully awake she said, 'Did you go yourself, or did someone else inform you?'

'What *do* you mean?'

'I'm surprised they let you in. It's usually members only.'

'Where?'

'Entertaining clients, were you? Can't imagine it being your scene. Bet they stung you for a big bill – a different league, you see.'

'For the life of me, I'm at a loss. What *are* you talking about?'

Unperturbed, she said in a strong, commanding voice, 'Don't think I'm the remotest bit embarrassed . . . I'm oblivious to such delicacy.'

Conversation ceased. All that was heard was Prince, who was singing in an increasingly high-pitched, frenzied manner. Jeremy turned to her. Her glaring, blue oval eyes had a hardened and somewhat distant look to them. This wasn't going to plan, he thought. He smiled and gave her a cheeky wink.

For a moment she continued to stare at him, before calmly, defiantly, smiling back.

Jeremy concentrated on the road ahead, amazed at her cool reaction. A huge grin spread across his face. The next moment he burst out laughing, while desperately trying to remain focused on the road. Julia watched his reaction with amusement; there was nothing subtle about Jeremy.

'Julia, Julia,' he bellowed excitedly. 'What an intriguing person you've turned out to be. I'm in shock! Thought you'd deny it. When I realised it was actually *you* up there, you can imagine. I nearly *died*,' he squealed. 'You of all people, Little Miss Home Counties, Jack's secretary! How in the world did you end up in a place like that?'

'A place like *that*,' she repeated – a sudden edge to her voice. 'I dislike being judged, Jeremy.'

'Of course. Presumably you have your reasons.'

She opened her handbag and pulled out a pack of cigarettes. 'You don't mind, do you?'

'I'll make an exception.'

With a solid gold lighter she lit one, drawing hard on it and exhaling a long line of smoke in front of her. Jeremy waited for her to add something else, to explain, say anything. But she seemed content to gaze out of the window, smoking her cigarette so elegantly, holding it between two perfectly manicured fingers.

'My God Julia, don't leave me dangling in suspense. I have to ask why. Why do it?'

'Why do anything? Money of course.'

'So it's well paid?'

'Very . . . cash in hand. It's just a couple of nights a week. I could never have afforded to buy my apartment in London on what I get from Buckley & Dwyer.'

Jeremy seemed to hesitate, his mind in over-drive. 'Not bad just for dancing.' The 'just' had been subtly emphasised.

Her response was adamant. '*Just* dancing or talking, *nothing* else. Some of the other girls go further . . . I don't.'

'Didn't think otherwise.'

'Does anyone else know I work there?'

'Haven't told a soul, not even Emma.'

'Don't tell her, little Snow White. Although I have no problem with my part-time job, I would appreciate it if you kept it to yourself. In this world of double standards, it's acceptable to be entertained there, but not to be the entertainer.'

He nodded, knowing it to be true. 'I still can't believe it, not that I'm judging you. It's fine by me. In fact,' he paused, then said in an exaggerated whisper, 'I'm secretly impressed.'

'Don't be, it's no big deal. Well, it was at first, but not now. It's just a job.'

'Doesn't it bother you?'

She drew hard on her cigarette and shook her head. Jeremy pulled out of the fast lane and into the centre.

Sounding more serious he said, 'But all those men gaping at you.'

She closed her eyes and was silent for what seemed like ages before sighing loudly. 'Jeremy, you're very sweet but I doubt you'd understand.'

'Understand what?'

'I don't come from the nice cushy little world you come from.'

As she was speaking, he noticed a slight London twang creep into her accent. 'What's the point in asking myself if something bothers me? That's a luxury for those who come from privileged backgrounds. It's a totally different way of life. Maybe it's the same planet, but if you ask me, it's more like a parallel universe – same surroundings, different worlds. At the end of the day if a person, any person, wants a better life, they need money. I figure I have two choices, earn it or marry it. All the guys I've liked never had a penny. So until I marry it, dancing around in some skimpy outfit is a bloody easy way to earn it.'

Jeremy looked perplexed. Who was this woman

beside him? He thought she'd be dying from embarrassment. Instead she was sitting there, poised and relaxed,
talking about different worlds. Certainly a case for *The
'X' Files.*

'Why not dance full time?' he asked.

'*Never*. No! Definitely not.' For the first time Julia
sounded offended. 'That's how I earn extra money. But
I want a proper job, a career, a husband – as long as he
has money – I want it all.'

'The cushy life you accuse me of coming from.'

'Damn right.'

'But you may miss your parallel universe.'

She grinned. 'I could always pop back for the odd
night, tell hubby I'm at a pottery class.'

They both laughed.

For the next hour and a half they drove at speed
down the M6 and eventually on to the M1. Julia
removed the Prince CD before it had finished and put
on ELO's Greatest Hits; it was the best she could find.
All the while, Jeremy fired a constant stream of
questions at her about herself, her background and her
evening job. She'd had quite a tough upbringing, as her
father had walked out on her mother, leaving her with
four children, Julia being the youngest at four years old.
Money had obviously been very tight, which Jeremy
guessed accounted for her approach to it now. She
spoke about it as though it was a medicine that would
cure all ills.

He found himself totally intrigued by her unconventional opinions and ideas. She was intent on finding
a man with money; it was her project for the next two
years. Jeremy delighted in offering his help but she
declined, reminding him it wasn't a game and subtlety
was required. Still, he racked his brains for suitable
candidates and invited her out for a drink the following

week. He had a feeling they were going to become friends.

With only a quick stop for a coffee, four hours after setting off, Jeremy parked up in the underground car park beneath the Buckley & Dwyer office in Blackfriars. Julia checked her make-up in the visor mirror and reapplied some lipstick.

'Hardly worth coming in,' he said, glancing at his watch, which showed ten past three.

'No choice for me. Expect I'll have to work late, no doubt Jack will have a pile of things for me to do.' She got out of the car and gently put on her silk jacket, before picking up her handbag and small overnight case.

Jeremy got out too and said across the car roof, with a cheeky grin, 'No time for moonlighting tonight.'

In a calm yet uncompromising voice she stated, 'Please don't mention that here . . . *Never*.' Turning sharply, she walked towards the lift, looking every bit the efficient secretary that she was.

He smiled to himself; yes, they were definitely going to be friends.

## 11

That evening, as Emma walked down her road, she spotted a man standing outside her door. Drawing closer, she saw it was her father, William. He stood still, watching her hurried approach.

'Dad, this is a surprise!'

'Hello Emma, where's your car?'

'The garage. It's—'

'Has it let you down again?' he asked in an accusing sort of voice.

'No. Nothing like that. Just some minor work to get it through the MOT. Tony's got it.' She looked back down the street. 'Where's yours?'

'Fed up of getting blocked in down here. Amazes me people would do that. Parked around the corner. Just hope it's safe. Shan't be staying long.'

'Is everything OK?'

'Yes, yes. Do hurry and open up. Absolutely freezing out here. Nearly decided to head off home.'

Emma opened the door and walked straight into the kitchen, flicking on the heating and automatically putting on the kettle.

'Not for me,' her father said, walking into the lounge.

Emma followed him and sat down on the sofa. He stood for a moment looking around and then went over to the back windows, tapping them and their wooden frames in various places. Emma watched him, but said nothing.

Eventually, he walked over to stand by the mantelpiece above the gas fire. William was a tall slim man, a retired civil servant, sixty-seven last birthday, still with a full head of hair, though grey now. 'Where's Tony?' he asked.

'Swan.'

'Early, isn't it?'

'It's Christmas,' she replied, getting up. 'Are you sure you don't want some tea?'

He shook his head but followed her back out to the kitchen.

'I'm surprised to see you,' she said again.

'Didn't your mother say I had a day's golfing in Altrincham?'

'Oh, that's right. How was it?'

'Pretty awful actually. Damn shoulder's been playing me up again. Anyway, thought I'd pop in. How are you?'

'Great. Everything's going really well.' It was her usual response.

'Tony?'

'He's good too. Working hard. He has two jobs at the moment. Poor thing's totally exhausted.'

Her father gave no sign of acknowledgement, but stood watching her, then his eyes inspected the kitchen. Suddenly clearing his throat he said, 'Your mother and I were talking and she's very kindly offered to have Christmas at our house again.'

Emma gently put down the kettle and turned towards him. 'But it's all arranged for here,' she said calmly.

'We'll just change it.'

'But I've already bought most things. The turkey comes tomorrow.'

'Bring everything with you.'

Her eyes narrowed. 'Why? What's wrong with here? Has something happened?'

'We know how busy you've been, what with this

Irish trip coming up. Thought you'd be pleased.'

'It's just, well . . .' She hesitated, suspicious of their reasons. 'Thanks for thinking of me. But really, I've arranged it all. It's not a problem.' She carried on filling her mug with water.

Her father's thin, gaunt face tightened. 'What's the problem with changing to ours? You could still prepare most of it.'

'You know Rob and Norman are coming.'

'Yes. Your mother has kindly invited them also. She's telephoning them this evening.'

'*What!*' Emma shook her head in disbelief. 'Why is she doing this?'

'Calm down, Emma. Hardly the end of the world. There'll be so much more room at ours. It's very cramped here, especially for six. Just take a few moments to think about it.' He walked into the lounge, displeased by her manner.

Emma took a couple of deep breaths and reminded herself not to get angry this time. She continued making her tea in complete silence and considered the practicalities. Tony wouldn't want to go. Rob definitely wouldn't want to, he was spending Christmas evening with Becky's parents. The thought of her mother phoning him made her furious. Norman, their dad, would go anywhere as long as there was a bottle of whiskey at the other end. He was usually asleep by the afternoon, if you were lucky.

Taking another deep breath, she went into the lounge and sat down at the table with her cup of tea in hand.

Her father was back standing by the mantelpiece and said confidently, 'So, can I tell your mother everything is agreed?'

'But why? Yes it's small here, but I've held it before.' Her father looked away, changing his weight from one leg to another, before coming over to sit in the chair next to her. His manner appeared friendlier, more relaxed. 'Well, we wouldn't be able to get here until at least three. The day's nearly gone by then, hardly worth it.'

She looked puzzled. 'Why? Where will you be?'

'Only found out yesterday. We've been invited to the Vaughans' for Christmas morning drinks. Quite a relief really. Everyone's been invited, the Haywards, Lawrences, John Mills MP. We thought we'd been deliberately left out. Thought we'd accidentally offended them and have been racking our brains to think how. Turns out it was an oversight. Richard thought Jean had invited your mother, she thought he had mentioned it to me.' He laughed out loud for several moments, totally oblivious to his daughter's complete silence.

'Thank God it's come to light now. What a mix up.' He laughed again.

Emma's face fell.

'Anyway. You can come down early Christmas morning and organise things as planned. Of course, your mother will help. Should arrive home around two, open pressies, then sit down to lunch.' He smiled, pleased that everything would work out so well.

Emma was biting her thumbnail.

'Would it be a help if I took any food with me now? There's bags of room in our freezer.'

She shook her head.

'Whatever. The offer's there.' He jumped up as if to go.

Looking up at him, she said quietly, but deter-minedly, 'No. I don't want to alter the arrangements. I mean . . . if you can't come here, maybe we should spend it apart.'

He stared at her amazed. After a while he let out an uncomfortable laugh. 'Don't tell me you're serious. We always spend it together. What's got into you lately? Is it this Irish trip?'

She replied, 'Rob won't be able to go to Chester. And to be honest, as you said, I've been busy. I don't really want to be driving on Christmas Day.' She wondered if their car would even make it. 'I just fancy a quiet one this year.'

William opened his mouth, paused, then closed it. His stern face observed her. After several moments of silence he suddenly smiled. 'I think I'll let your mother take up the conversation from here. I've done my bit.' He leant down and kissed her on the cheek. 'Take care, darling. I must be going, sorry it's so brief. Don't want to be travelling back late. We'll talk soon. I'll see myself out.' With that he was gone.

Emma heard the front door close behind him. She didn't move from the table. She was expecting the usual waves of anger and rage to descend on her, possibly followed by tears of frustration. She waited, bracing herself, but nothing happened. Her mind was surprisingly still, cut off, remote from the situation, a substitute for calm. The minutes passed. Emma sat on, her tea now cold. Then, as if waking from a daydream, she stared around the small living room. There was a slight irritation tugging at the back of her mind, but nothing else. It was as if she didn't care any more. Pleased by her lack of reaction, a slight euphoric feeling developed. *I don't care*, she thought. *I don't care. It doesn't matter. I refuse to let them get to me. I refuse to let* anyone *get to me. That can be my New Year's resolution – not to care so much*. And to toughen up.

She smiled, confident and determined that things were going to change.

# Part Two

## 12

Emma's hotel room was spacious and bright, giving a good view across Dublin. Gazing out of the window she lost herself listening to the sounds from the unfamiliar city: church bells, pub music, an array of accents, a boat travelling down the nearby River Liffey, sounding its horn. She felt so content to be there, excited about being somewhere different, a change. Everything was new, waiting to be seen and experienced, every street full of character, its buildings, the people, even the smells.

There was a knock on her door.

'One second,' she shouted, quickly pulling on her dress. She opened the door to find. Jack was standing there. He glanced at her bare feet.

'Sorry. Another ten minutes,' she said.

'Meet you in reception.' He was already walking down the corridor.

Emma gulped down her gin and tonic from the mini-bar; a little aid for the evening ahead. She hurriedly finished getting ready and headed out to the lift. Pressing the ground-floor button, she looked at herself in the mirrored walls. It took her mind off where she was, third lift journey in a month. She tried to stay focused on her clothes, a knee-length wine-coloured fitted dress and matching short jacket, bought especially for the three-day preliminary trip to Dublin, where they were checking on the offices and inter-viewing potential staff. Her new outfit was a treat for losing twelve pounds in eight weeks without even starving herself. A slight smile appeared on her face.

Suddenly the lift stopped and Emma's heart leapt.

Three seconds passed, an eternity before the doors opened. *Thank God*, it was the ground floor. There was a buzz to her step as she walked out.

Jack watched her spring from the lift and walk through the reception area in the opposite direction. He was sitting in a chair to the side and observed her as she wandered around. Eventually, she turned and spotted him, and he stood up to walk over to her. He was wearing a light blue sports shirt and tan trousers and was carrying a raincoat. It was the first time she'd seen him out of a suit. It was also the first time she was having dinner with him, although they had shared a couple of pub lunches, the conversation mostly limited to work; it was easier that way.

In the six weeks since the New Year, they had met up on a weekly basis, usually in London. Whilst there she'd bumped into Rachel a couple of times. Late one Friday afternoon, Emma was sitting outside Jack's office waiting for him, when his door had opened and out she breezed – full lips pouting, hips gently swaying. She was wearing a fitted, sapphire-coloured suit with an incredibly short skirt which drew your eyes to her slender legs and stiletto shoes.

'Hello Rachel,' said Emma.

Rachel stopped and squinted her eyes as if not recognising Emma. Emma knew full well that she did.

'Oh yes. Jack's other secretary.'

'It's Emma.'

'Of course. Actually I've named you Northern Secretary and Southern Secretary. Saves any confusion,' said Rachel in her low, throaty voice, glancing towards Julia.

Julia's eyes shot up from her computer screen. 'And we've named you, Southern Girlfriend and Northern . . .' She deliberately stopped mid-track and mockingly placed her hand across her mouth.

Emma grinned. She felt like she was witnessing the clash of the Titans.

Strangely, Rachel just beamed one of her exuberant smiles at Julia, so sweet – so insincere. Her eyes rested back on Emma. Easier prey? 'How's that cheeky husband of yours? Started his revolution yet?' She winked and continued on her way, gliding down the corridor, shouting back, 'Expect I'll see you in Dublin. Bring Tony. Maybe I'll join his band of revolutionaries.'

Emma and Julia exchanged disapproving glances – for once, united.

The nice thing about Emma's visits to London was that, for convenience and fun, she had become a regular visitor at Jeremy's, which they both enjoyed and looked forward to, especially their nights out. She met up with many of his friends, old and new, some she hadn't seen in years. There had been dinners, visits to the theatre and cinema, and also a trip to a very dubious club in Vauxhall where everyone seemed to know Jeremy by name, including the cabaret, mostly drag acts. The party atmosphere was great and Emma surprised herself by dancing for hours, a great way to burn off calories.

Late one night, slightly the worse for wear, they were walking up the stairs to his apartment when Jeremy shouted out, 'My God, Emma.'

'What?' she cried, looking alarmed.

'If this goes on much longer, you'll be in danger of developing a social life.' He fell about laughing. She almost pushed him down the stairs.

She wondered what tonight would be like with Jack.

'Table's booked for eight,' he said, checking his watch. He put on his coat and she followed him outside into the busy Dublin street.

Their hotel was very central – within walking distance of the business district, main shopping areas and tourist attractions. For a February evening it was quite mild and Emma breathed in deeply, looking up and down the street at the large Georgian buildings, wanting to take everything in.

Jack opened his Dublin Street-Finder map and, as if on a military exercise, planned the most efficient route; their destination, a restaurant in Baggot Street that a colleague had recommended.

'This way,' he said, marching off at a fast pace.

Emma was almost jogging to keep up with him and had barely any time to look around. However she did glance at a large-gated mansion with its entrance guarded by two policemen. She knew it was Leinster House, the Irish Parliament buildings and next to it stood the National Museum. She would have pointed them out to Jack but he was at least three paces ahead of her and seemingly only interested in street names, to check he was going the right way.

They arrived at the edge of St Stephen's Green, a large, enclosed park area right in the centre of the city that was encircled by magnificent eighteenth- and nineteenth-century buildings. But again there was no time to stop and stare.

Baggot Street started at one end of the park and was a hive of activity; wine bars, pubs and cafes lined each side. The smell of beer, coffee and food filled the air. The pavement was packed with people, business types, tourists, locals, all age ranges. Some were just milling around, laughing and chatting. A small crowd had gathered around a couple of mime artists who were performing on one of the street corners.

Jack glanced at his watch then immediately stopped. He turned and saw Emma someway behind looking in all the windows that she passed. When she finally caught up with him he pointed to a pub appropriately named the Baggot Inn and said, 'Time for a quick drink.'

She nodded, slightly breathless from their race through Dublin. He held the door open and she walked inside. It was a dark, smoky, old-style pub with wooden tables and benches, teeming with people, merrily drinking away. The sound of Irish music was coming from another part of the pub. It sounded like a live band but it was too packed to see anything. Emma saw two seats by the window, which she grabbed, while Jack went up to the bar.

When he returned he was carrying a gin and tonic for her and a pint of Guinness for himself.

'When in Rome,' he said, raising his glass.

'Cheers,' she said.

Thirstily he drank a few mouthfuls in one go, before asking, 'So who impressed you the most?'

'Rosemary,' she answered, slightly irritated. Was tonight going to be all about work too?

'Thought so.'

'You agree?'

He shrugged slightly. 'She's got all the skills, the experience, initiative.'

'I feel a but coming.'

'I'm concerned as to why she's leaving her present company. After all, it's essentially the same job – legal secretary, same money, same prospects.'

'But she explained. She wants a change. Three years is a long time for a young girl.'

He shrugged his shoulders again. 'See what the others are like tomorrow. It's your choice though.'

Emma felt tomorrow's candidates would have to be very good to match Rosemary. She sipped her gin and tonic, already feeling the effects of the first one gulped down back in her room.

Jack relaxed back against the wooden side of the alcove and looked around. An old, wrinkled man sitting in the corner poured some of his Guinness into a saucer and placed it on the floor for his dog, who eagerly lapped it up, tail wagging. He looked back towards Emma. 'You know, I'm quite looking forward to spending some time here. So much more relaxed than London.'

Emma smiled, and Jack glanced at his watch.

'I was impressed by the offices,' she said. They had the whole of the second floor of a modern four-storey building, next to the Grand Canal Docks in central Dublin, which were being renovated into offices and apartment blocks. Their section was large enough to accommodate at least fifteen staff. There would only be four or five initially. Room for growth, Jack had said.

'Reception area needs jazzing up some. Don't like the blinds, acceptable for the offices but not reception. Need a few paintings. How are you on art?' he asked.

She thought hard. He waited.

'Well . . . I know what *I* like.'

'Which is?'

'Um . . . I like large, modern paintings, but not so modern that you think a two-year-old painted them. I also like old paintings in beautiful frames, Victorian, not really scenes, more people. Not old-fashioned ones.'

Jack opened his eyes wide. 'So you like modern, but not too modern. Old, but not old-fashioned. That says a lot.'

Emma laughed. 'Well, it's difficult to describe. I need to be in front of the picture.'

'So if I sent you out tomorrow to some galleries,

you'd be happy to buy four paintings for the firm?'

'How much money are we talking?' she asked, concerned.

'About five hundred each. Hardly Picasso's. Just something interesting and modern, by a local artist.'

Her eyelids lowered and her fingers tapped the table. 'What if you hate them?'

Jack drank some more Guinness, observing her. 'So you don't want the responsibility?' It was more an accusation than a question.

'I'd just be worried you . . . or others, wouldn't like them. I should add, they're not in the budget.'

'Enter it under office furniture. Make up the deficit elsewhere. As for whether I like them, why does that matter? Don't you have confidence in your own opinions?'

Slightly taken aback, she blustered, 'Well . . . maybe. But . . . they're going to be hanging on display for everyone to see, to judge.'

'And?'

'Fine, I'll buy the paintings. If you hate them it's tough,' she said.

'Of course. It should always be like that. You worry too much what people think.' Allowing her no time to answer he stood up. 'Another one?'

'Still have this.'

'That's OK.' He walked off.

Irritated, she watched him walk to the bar, sipping her drink and thinking about his comments. When he turned to come back, she quickly glanced out of the window.

Jack sat down with another gin and tonic and a pint of Guinness in his hands. 'Anyway,' he said forcefully, 'if they really are hideous, we'll put a plaque underneath them saying "chosen by Emma Hughes".'

She gave him the ghost of a smile. 'It's quite natural to be concerned what others will think. Lots of people are. Aren't you?'

He took a moment to decide. 'To a point. Fortunately I'm not over-burdened by it like some.'

They stayed for another ten minutes, finishing their drinks and chatting. Realising it was just after eight, he leapt up. Emma was going to leave the remainder of her drink but he said he'd wait. Considering his obsession with time, she thought it a major concession. She obligingly gulped it down in two swigs then jumped up too, and had to grab the corner of the table for support. Her head felt woozy. It wouldn't be until the next day that she found out Irish measures were larger than English ones.

Carefully, she followed Jack outside, marching down the street, matching his stride, step by step, like soldiers on parade. He would have been good in the army, she thought, or as an RAF bomber commander, Lawrence of Arabia, Genghis Khan. It suddenly struck her: the trouble with Jack was he was born a few centuries too late. He'd have been quite a catch in the sixteenth or seventeenth century. Maybe she'd tell him that later.

They went into Passario's and immediately took their seats in the large, spacious restaurant. It was a totally different atmosphere to the pub, much quieter, only half full, with a woman pianist in the corner singing popular melodies. They looked over the menu.

'Shall I order the wine?' asked Jack.

'None for me,' she said quickly.

'Not even a glass?'

She hesitated, assuring herself that she would soon be eating. 'Maybe just one, then.'

A little while later their starters arrived. Emma had vegetable soup, while Jack had oysters. She sipped her wine and watched him empty the slippery creatures from their shells and swallow them. She couldn't help screwing her face up.

Seeing her disdain, he said, 'They're delicious. Want to try one?'

'Only for prize money in a Japanese endurance test.'

He looked surprised.

'Joke,' she added, pushing her wine glass away.

'You say that a lot, "joke", after making a comment. I do possess a sense of humour.'

'Nothing personal. I say it to others. It just pops out. I feel people might think I'm being serious and think me odd or worse, rude. Stop!' she suddenly yelled. 'You're going to accuse me of worrying what people think again.'

He smiled but made no comment. Emma picked up her glass.

'It's because I have no faith in people and the way they think. I feel I have to guide their understanding in a certain direction, otherwise they'd constantly get the wrong translation. Confusion would reign.'

'Sounds exhausting to me.'

'Oh it is,' she agreed , sipping her drink. 'Extremely.'

'And you think it works?'

'No. Not really.'

'People come to their own conclusions. They see what they want to see, hear what they want to hear. Sheer folly to try and change that. I used to for a while,' he said.

'*You?*'

He raised an eyebrow at her reaction. 'Yes, even me. But believe me, it's so much easier not giving a damn. I learnt that quite young, thank goodness.'

'Age two?'

'Don't tell me, "joke",' he said, a moment later

continuing, 'It's also quite patronising, to try and make a person think a certain way. Don't bother attempting it with me.'

'You're acting as though I practise some kind of mind control technique. It's nothing so calculating. I was just saying that I don't have faith in the way people interpret my actions . . . or anyone else's actions. That's all.'

Jack finished his last mussel. 'You must have the weight of the world on your shoulders. I'm surprised you don't topple over when you walk. Forgive me but you should lighten up.'

She glared at him, open-mouthed. 'I should lighten up, you say?'

He nodded.

'*I* should lighten up, you say?' she repeated, slightly louder.

Again he nodded. There was a slight, amused glint in his eye.

'*You* are saying that *I* should lighten up?'

'Are you going to keep repeating those words all night?'

She leant back in her chair and shook her head in comical disbelief. Jack sipped his drink.

Smiling broadly she said, 'If I need to lighten up, you need to defy gravity. Have you considered helium?' She let out a laugh but quickly stopped herself. His expression was initially blank but she felt she saw his eyes narrow slightly and sharpen their focus. Slowly the corners of his mouth started to turn upwards, but he fought it and pinched his lips together. Emma looked down at her empty soup bowl; her smiling, brimming eyes and the vibrations in her back were the only signs of the internal hysterics that she was desperately trying to hide. She pushed her wine glass away, deciding definitely this time, that she'd had enough. Luckily the waiter appeared.

'Excuse me, have you finished?'

They both nodded and thanked him as he cleared their plates away. He automatically filled up both their empty glasses.

Once alone again, Jack started to tap the table with his index finger. He was looking at her and still considering his response. Emma looked over at the pianist; glad there was something else to focus on.

The main course arrived, vegetarian lasagne for Jack, apparently he no longer ate red meat, and lemon sole with vegetables for Emma, allowed under the Hay system.

'How's the sole?' he asked, after she'd taken her first forkful.

'Good, very good,' she answered, suspicious of his sudden friendly approach.

'I'm pleased.'

'How's your lasagne?'

'Fine.'

'That's good,' she said.

They ate for a few minutes watching the pianist. She sang covers of well-known songs, pitch perfect. As she came to the end of 'The Way We Were', Emma said, 'She's excellent, isn't she,' her eyes still admiringly on the woman.

Jack had been staring at Emma, singing along under her breath. 'Yes, she's very good.'

She turned to him. 'I really admire people who've got the balls to get up and sing in front of people. Mind you, it would help having her voice.'

'So you're a frustrated cabaret singer, are you?'

She grinned. 'Yes, a frustrated singer, frustrated

nurse, vet, television presenter. You name it and I'm a frustrated one. Even a solicitor.'

'And you ended up as a legal secretary?'

'Don't like the phrase ended up. I'm only thirty-four, not that old.'

'For a vet or a nurse you are, Nurse Hughes.'

'Thanks.' Emma looked down at her plate. 'You sound like Tony. Maybe all men do it?'

'What?' he asked.

She looked back up at him. 'Reminding you all the time of practicalities. Limitations. Why is that? Maybe it's a male hormone. Boringosterone.' She picked up her glass again and took a sip, noticing him staring at her with a strange expression. 'You know, like testosterone. But . . .'

'Yes, I did get it, Emma.' He shook his head.

'You don't deny it?'

'Well . . . It's not just men. Women do it too. It's life. You do what you have to, to get by. That may mean playing safe, which could be viewed as boring.'

'Very. Playing by the rules all the time. Don't you ever get sick of it?'

'Actually yes,' he said.

'I do. I am.'

'Ah, but you can't blame anyone else. Everyone has choices. The old saying, "You make your bed, so lie in it", is very true.' He refilled his own glass and hers.

'And do you like the bed you've made, Jack?' She couldn't believe she had just asked him that.

He rolled his eyes. 'The bed I made fell apart two years ago. In fact,' he paused, his eyes focusing beyond her. 'In fact, someone else came and lay in it.'

Instant silence! Emma froze with shock, not even blinking. Her eyes were glued to his. She was unsure what to say or how to react. A moment later he shook his head, smiling oddly. He let out a couple of strange laughs. She put her hand to her mouth, still stunned and embarrassed by the personal comment from him. He was normally such a closed book. Anyone else but him!

After a moment he said, 'It's OK, Emma. Don't look so worried. I'm not going to cry into my lasagne.'

She smiled awkwardly.

'It was some time ago. Life moves on. It's all worked out for the best. In fact, they're getting married in May. Believe it or not, I'm invited to the wedding – not that I'll be going. Call me old-fashioned but that's a little too bizarre, I believe.' He added in a more serious tone, 'So you see, no one can say it's "a road going nowhere".'

Emma was watching Jack closely. She remembered her comment about Trish and Steve, and she glanced away.

Sometime later, the singer started another song. Emma watched and admired her dress, her hair, posture, voice, talent. Maybe it was Dublin or the alcohol, but she felt on a high and longed to get up and sing something. But it occurred to her that she never would; that was the difference, she told herself, between people like her and the singer. She just dreamt, while others *did*. A mild downer descended, she turned and looked at Jack to find him staring at her. His eyes seemed to penetrate people.

Lifting the empty bottle of wine he said, 'I'd offer to get another one, but we've got a lot of work to do tomorrow.'

'I've had my fill anyway. I don't usually drink that much,' she said quietly.

'A dessert?'

She shook her head. 'I'm stuffed. You have one.'

'No. But I'll get a coffee. I don't want a hangover.'

'I'd better have one too.'

'Boringosterone rules. Unfortunately, it pays the bills,' Jack said.

'The whole world has developed and evolved around paying bills. Survival of the fittest has become survival of the most creditworthy.'

'Would you really like to be a solicitor?'

Emma nodded.

'Why don't you then?'

She took a while to answer. 'For starters, I couldn't afford it.'

'There're evening courses. I'm sure Buckley & Dwyer would support you with time off for studying and exams. It's a long process though,' he said.

She stared slightly beyond him, deep in thought. Jack caught the attention of the waiter and ordered the coffee.

Within twenty minutes they had left the restaurant and had begun to retrace their steps back to Buswells Hotel. The streets seemed even busier than earlier; *doesn't anyone have work tomorrow?* wondered Emma. They headed back at a slower pace and this time briefly viewed and commented on the various landmarks.

Once inside the hotel, Jack stopped at the lift and pressed the button to call it.

'I'll walk,' said Emma. 'See you tomorrow morning.'

'I'll walk with you.' Jack followed her to the staircase.

They started to climb the steps and soon reached the fourth floor without having spoken. Emma would normally have felt embarrassed, but she was still a bit drunk and felt surprisingly comfortable in his presence. Nearing room number 43 she slowed and was about to say goodnight. But Jack carried on walking towards her room. On reaching 44, she stopped and took her key out.

'Well, goodnight then,' she said to him.

'Goodnight, Emma.' He turned, then stopped. 'If there's time tomorrow, I'll go with you to the galleries.'

'What, you don't trust me now?'

'Oh no, not that. I'd like to go. If there's time that is.'

She nodded and smiled.

'Goodnight then.'

'Goodnight.' Emma went into her room and shut the door. She sat on the bed thinking about the evening. She had to admit that she'd actually enjoyed Jack's company. Underneath that android exterior of his, he had quite a quirky sense of humour. He was human, after all. In fact, over the last six weeks she realised he'd been quite polite to her. But then she too had changed and was now deliberately assertive in her approach to him.

She smiled broadly to herself as she remembered some of their conversation that evening and even laughed aloud at her own helium joke. *Maybe being in Dublin is having a good effect on him.* She wondered what effect it was having on her?

## 13

'Thanks for coming in. The agency should be in touch next week to let you know either way,' said Emma, standing up and shaking the young woman's hand. She walked with her to the reception and watched her leave.

Back in the office, Emma slumped down on one of the boxes they'd been using as a chair; the furniture wasn't arriving until the next week. That was the last of the candidates. She felt she had been more nervous than they had, but luckily Jack wasn't sitting in on her interviews today. She decided that Rosemary was by far the best applicant and hoped she'd accept the position.

Jack was in the office next door interviewing a potential solicitor, Sean O'Brien. He was in his late twenties, tall with dark brown hair and a beautiful warm smile. Arriving too early for his interview, he'd chatted with Emma about the places she should visit both in and around Dublin; museums, parks, stately homes, plus beaches and towns, Brittas Bay, Kildare, Blarney Castle – he was like a walking tourist information office. She had enjoyed talking with him but had to cut it short when her own candidate arrived for interview.

Through the glass panel in the door of Jack's new office she could see them both chatting away. Checking her watch she saw it was nearly three o'clock. This was the first chance to pop out to the galleries. That morning, Jack had mentioned again that he'd like to go, so Emma decided to make herself some tea and wait another half hour in case he became free.

Sitting on another box in the kitchen, she drank the

tea and resumed eating the cheese and tomato sandwich that she'd started earlier but hadn't had a chance to finish. She took a huge bite out of it, only then realising how hungry she was.

'She's gone then?' Jack's voice came from the door.

Emma pointed to her mouth as she chewed vigorously to clear it. 'Yes. I was waiting for you. The gallery?' she eventually said, clearing her mouthful.

Jack glanced at his watch. 'Best go now then, there's still a lot to do.'

'Ten minutes?'

He nodded and flicked the kettle on. Emma moved to another box to get out of his way.

Swallowing another mouthful she asked, 'What was Sean like?'

'Impressive. Specialises in contracts. Fairly certain he'll be starting with us. And your people?'

'Not suitable.'

'So you think Rosemary?'

'Yes, definitely.'

Jack stood with his back to her, watching the kettle, waiting for it to re-boil. The tip of his right shoe was tapping the floor. Turning around he said, in a friendly manner, 'Just heard from an old client who's working over here. Arranged to meet up later.'

'That's nice.'

'Hardly. He's such a bore, but he's got a few contacts for me. It's expected.'

She felt obliged to give him a sympathetic look. He noted it with caution. 'What will you do?'

'Just relax in my room,' she replied. 'I'm quite tired.'

He looked back at the kettle and continued tapping the floor with his foot. 'You're welcome to . . . er, come along.'

'Oh, no,' she said, with some conviction, quickly

adding, 'That is, unless you want me there . . . as part of work.'

His eyes never left the kettle. He gave a quick, dismissive flick of his head which she guessed meant no. The kettle finally boiled and he made his tea. For a moment she thought he was going to sit on the box opposite her, but at the last minute he marched past it back to his office.

A few minutes later she put on her coat, knocked on his door and walked straight in. He was sitting behind a makeshift desk and looking through some documents.

Emma stood waiting for him to look up but he continued flicking through the various pieces of paper.

'Ready when you are,' she said finally.

He stopped and closed his eyes for a couple of seconds. Opening them, but without looking up, he said curtly, 'Something's come up, too busy. Expect you have things to do also.'

'Loads.'

'The paintings will have to wait. Hardly crucial.'

She glared at him. 'I agree.'

He was already shuffling through more papers as if oblivious to her presence. After watching him for a couple of moments, she turned sharply on the spot and made for the door, her teeth clenched. *Ignorant pig*! she thought.

'One moment,' he added.

She stopped, but didn't turn round.

'London have sent various faxes to the hotel. Could you collect them for me?'

There was a noticeable pause before she said, 'Of course, that's my job.' She shut the door and stormed down the stairs, fuming inside.

Jack's eyes gradually focused on the door. He stood

up slowly and walked over to the window. Standing a few feet back from it, he watched Emma leave the building and march across the street. Soon she was out of sight.

For the rest of the afternoon the atmosphere in the office was quite tense. Emma was relieved to have some time alone in her hotel room later, where she ate her dinner accompanied by a couple of glasses of wine. Yet within an hour she felt restless. There was so much to see, and here she was stuck inside because she didn't want to go out on her own. She sighed despondently. What a waste! It was only around eight. *Don't be such a wimp, Emma*, she scolded herself, and jumping up, she grabbed her coat and bag and headed out.

It was already dark and was colder than the night before but at least it wasn't raining. She found herself walking along the edge of St Stephen's Green, admiring the architecture of the buildings surrounding it. Soon she came across Grafton Street, one of the main shopping areas. The shops were shut but she looked in the windows intent on returning one weekend. It was fairly quiet apart from a handful of people wandering around.

Emma walked with no particular destination in mind, making mental notes of how to get back to the hotel. She found herself by the River Liffey; the slight stale aroma from the water merely added to the atmosphere of being somewhere else, somewhere new.

In the distance, she could see the famous Halfpenny Bridge and, feeling brave, she headed up towards it. There were so many people around this part that she felt safe. She stood in the middle of the bridge staring pensively upriver. Manchester seemed a long way away, which pleased her. I've seen so little of the world, she thought. Standing alone in the middle of Dublin, she became determined to travel more, to see more, to experience more.

After about ten minutes she started walking again and went through an alleyway into the cobbled streets of Temple Bar, packed with pubs and restaurants, music blaring out from every place, young people milling around, singing, some falling. Peering in the window of one pub, everyone was dancing and laughing – not a care in the world. She longed to go in and get madly drunk and dance all night. But she didn't. It was getting late and so she hurried back on foot to the hotel.

At just gone ten, she snuggled under the bed covers to watch *Last of the Mohicans* on the hotel video system. She'd seen it before, twice, but loved it, especially Daniel Day Lewis, with his bravery, passion and purpose. Hopefully Tony wouldn't ring half-way through it.

The following day at the office was even busier and at times quite fraught. Arriving by 8am, both Emma and Jack rushed to get everything done. There was paperwork, phone calls, deliveries, all Jack's typing and his constant requests to collect this, organise that, fax these, which meant Emma was running back and forth to the hotel on a regular basis; the fax machine was one of the deliveries which hadn't yet turned up. At twelve midday she took two paracetamol to head off an encroaching headache. Lunch was another sandwich that was eaten at various intervals throughout the day. There was certainly no time for paintings. *He* could buy the damn things.

Jack had two more interviews for the new solicitor and a meeting with a potential client that over-ran by nearly an hour. He snatched fifteen minutes to go and check on his new house in Ballsbridge that he had purchased the previous month. He returned most unhappy. Emma overheard him on the phone complaining to his builders about various items, the finish on the walls, wrong tiles and doors, the situation of power points. She kept out of his way.

By five, when the cab arrived to take them to the airport, they were both exhausted and they collapsed into the back seat. Emma closed her eyes and leant her head against the window, praying he wouldn't mention work any more. Unfortunately, owing to thick fog, the journey out to the airport was slow, with traffic jams quickly building up. Once there, they both dashed for their relevant check-in queues. As arranged they met up a little later at the entrance to the departure lounge, looking weary and forlorn.

Jack was already there, leaning against a wall. 'You've heard then?' he asked, as she approached.

She nodded despondently.

'I suggest we wait in the business lounge, more comfortable.'

Again she nodded.

He marched off through the crowded terminal and Emma hurried after him. After rushing needlessly, they finally entered the small corporate lounge that could cater for no more than thirty passengers. There was already twice that number squeezed in. The heavy, agitated atmosphere in the room hit them instantly. Smartly-dressed business people stood around, faces tense with impatience and frustration; delays were not acceptable in their tight schedules.

'I can't wait in here,' said Emma, determinedly.

Jack nodded. They left and walked a little further down the corridor until they came across some empty seats overlooking the aircraft docking bays. They sat down opposite each other next to the window.

'How long did they say to you?' she asked.

'An hour at least. That could mean two or three. This fog doesn't look like it's going anywhere.'

'I'd better phone Tony.'

She was gone ages. Every payphone she came across had at least three people queuing. Arriving back at her seat, she saw a selection of sandwiches and what she assumed was a gin and tonic spread out on the windowsill.

'Might as well make the most of it,' said Jack, sipping a pint of Guinness. The top button on his shirt was now undone, his jacket had been removed and his tie had been loosened. He was leaning back in his chair looking surprisingly relaxed.

Emma sat down, smiled and reached for her drink. 'Thanks. I could do with this.'

He raised his glass in acknowledgement. Emma gave a brief nod of her head and drank some of her gin and tonic. 'Hope we get home tonight.'

'Expect we will.'

'I've asked Tony to tape *Friends*.'

'You got through OK then?'

'Yes. He'd arranged to take me to dinner. First Friday night off in six months and I'm stuck at Dublin airport.'

Jack's eyes examined hers. He made no comment and eventually looked away.

They continued eating, chatting occasionally about something trivial. Work didn't enter the conversation.

An hour later, Jack had just returned from a visit to the Information Desk. 'Another hour at least,' he said.

Now resigned to a long wait, Emma nodded and closed her eyes. Her legs were neatly crossed in front of her. *Of all the days to wear a short skirt*, she thought.

Jack started to read a complimentary magazine about Irish business. Coming upon a crossword in it, he took out his pen to tackle it. Emma secretly watched him through slightly-opened eyes. His tranquil composure amazed her. She'd half expected him to be marching up and down clawing at the walls, but no, he appeared quite content, sitting doing his crossword as if he were relaxing on a sunny beach, instead of in an overcrowded airport. Looking up, he caught her eye. She glanced away.

'Another drink?' he said.

'I'll get them.'

'No, no. Wait there.' Before she could protest, he was up and out of his seat. He returned with the usual gin and tonic and pint of Guinness. They sat drinking and quietly gazing around at the hectic goings on in the building.

'Is that what you do on Friday nights, watch *Friends*?' he asked.

She looked across at him. 'Pretty much. Sad, isn't it? How do you spend your weekends?'

'Depends if I have my boys with me.'

'And if you do?'

'Could end up doing anything, mountain biking, hiking. Each time it's different, they choose. Fishing, orienteering,' he shrugged his shoulders. 'Like me, they love anything to do with the outdoors, especially my father's yacht. We sail around the Isle of Wight, usually with some bizarre music blaring out. Not that *I'd* call it music. Teenagers!' His face softened and he smiled, beaming proudly.

Emma smiled with him, but slowly her head lowered,

slightly shamed; it appeared that the Pilgrim Father of workaholics had a more interesting life than hers.

'How old are they now?' she asked.

'Daniel's fifteen, Thomas, seventeen.'

She raised her eyebrows. 'That's gone quick. Thought you were going to say twelve and thirteen.'

'Too quick. They're like a constant reminder of how it's all whizzing by.' He paused. 'And you? What do you usually do for the rest of the weekend?'

'Not as much as you, by the sounds of it.'

'Wasn't always like that. Just the last two years. I've made some changes.' His pensive gaze drifted beyond her, into the distance.

Intrigued about where Rachel might fit in, Emma asked, 'And when they're not around?'

'Probably the same, just at a slower pace, with more appropriate music.' Jack picked up his Guinness and drank some. 'Finding a secluded spot and mooring up the boat on a sunny day is pretty good. Have you sailed?'

She shook her head, after a moment asking, 'Does Rachel?'

'Yes. Proficiently.'

Of course, thought Emma, probably proficient at everything she does. The perfect woman! They should take some DNA samples and clone her.

'So when Emma Hughes isn't typing what does she do?' he persisted.

Emma studied his face, sceptical of the wording he'd chosen. She looked at the floor, considering her answer. Her trips to Tesco's, walks around the park that she'd been around a thousand times, television programmes she watched with Tony, the washing, ironing, cleaning and the occasional trip down the pub. 'We go walking in the Dales,' she stated, running her hand through her hair. They'd only been twice last year 'Family dinners, cinema, that sort of thing.'

'You like walking?' he asked.

'Very much.'

'County Wicklow has impressive walks; an intended pursuit of mine. You should stay in Dublin one weekend.'

She sipped her drink. 'I'll see if Tony can get some time off.'

There was a moment's pause before Jack slowly nodded then he resumed his crossword again.

Staring out of the window, Emma thought about all the activities he had mentioned. She found herself irritated by it. *It's all right for him, he has money.* Her eyes gazed into the heavy, grey darkness outside, a vast empty nothingness. An unpleasant feeling of being trapped, hemmed in by the unwelcome, almost suffocating fog started to develop within her. It was isolating her from her own world, which at that moment she longed to be back in. How long was she going to be stuck here? Stuck with Jack? She stood up and grabbed her handbag. 'Excuse me.' She walked off towards the ladies toilet.

Jack's eyes followed her until she turned the corner.

Over half an hour passed before she returned to her seat. Jack was standing up waiting for her.

'I wondered where you were,' he said.

'Just looking around, filling time.'

'The fog's lifting. Planes are going to London but not Manchester yet. Seems it's moved over there.'

'When are you off then?' she asked.

'Soon. They've called us to the gate.'

'Well, have a nice weekend. I'm sure you will.'

He stood still, hesitating to leave. He glanced down the passage then back at Emma and said, 'A wind's picking up so you should get home tonight.'

She nodded.

He continued to look at her. 'Presumably you'll be collected at Manchester?'

'I expect so. I'll call Tony later.'

Again he glanced down the corridor but didn't move. 'If there's any problem, just book into a hotel. Don't wait here all night.'

'I won't.'

He walked two paces away then turned. In a serious voice he said, 'Don't forget those paintings.'

She glared at him. He smiled and walked away.

## 14

It was a damp and foggy London evening as Julia looked out of the taxi window on her way to Jeremy's in Richmond. At her request, the driver took a route through Richmond Park; it felt good to feel like she was in the country for a few minutes, miles from the bustling city. The cab headed out of the park down an old lane running parallel with the River Thames. Large eighteenth-century houses set in their own grounds with gates fronting their drives lined each side of the road, a reminder of the quiet, wealthy village Richmond had once been before being swallowed up by the voracious appetite of London.

Reaching the town, they passed several bustling wine bars and restaurants, brimming with lively people, before taking the bridge over the Thames and eventually turning down a private street, which headed back along the river on the other side. Julia stared at all the beautiful houses, more modern on this side, their large, well-tended gardens, the expensive cars parked outside. How she would love to live in a place like this. She smiled – maybe one day.

At the end of the road, right beside the river they came across an imposing three-storey block of luxury apartments, each with an extensive balcony. It stood within its own grounds with mature trees and rolling lawns. Lights shone out across the river and a few boats were moored at a little pier beside the gardens.

Julia double-checked the address in her diary. This was it; Lake View Apartments. She knew Jeremy earned a good salary but even so, could it account for all this?

Within a couple of minutes she was in the lift travelling up to the third floor, most intrigued by what she would find. She and Jeremy had met a few times for drinks and dinners, and had become quite friendly, but this was the first time she'd been invited to his home. The lift doors opened and Jeremy stood there, wearing a bright orange shirt tucked into navy cords and a pair of brown furry, teddy-bear-faced slippers. As usual he was grinning broadly.

She frowned at the slippers. 'Hello, Jeremy.'

He ignored the insult and kissed her on both cheeks. 'Good evening, Madame, this way.' He took her hand and led her into his apartment, down a long hallway decorated in a red and gold patterned wallpaper – not for the faint-hearted. After passing numerous doors they eventually walked under an open archway that led into an incredibly large, split-level lounge with marble floors and light orange walls covered with the occasional spattering of red. Four steps led to the upper section where a grand oak dining table stood.

It was a spacious and contemporary design, yet Jeremy had it cluttered like an Aladdin's cave. There was an array of paintings, old and new, large and small, a few of them hanging crooked; several old mirrors in brass and copper frames; numerous clocks including two beautiful grandfather clocks, some ticking away, others stopped at different times. Bookcases as high as the ceiling covered what wall space was left, over-spilling with tatty old books. Right in the centre of the room, three full-length navy sofas surrounded a blazing open fire, with a funnel above it to capture the smoke. In the corner, next to the latest CD sound system, stood an old vinyl record player, which was blasting out 'Delilah' by Tom Jones.

Such a strange room, she thought; part of it ultra

modern yet at the same time it felt very traditional, almost conservative, as though it couldn't make up its mind which way to go.

Jeremy indicated to one of the sofas. 'Make yourself at home. What can I get you? I have some exquisite red wine opened.'

'A glass of white thanks.' She automatically handed him her full-length coat revealing a short, black lycra dress.

'Back in a moment,' he said, as he went out to the kitchen.

Julia casually walked around the room staring at all items. She picked up a silver cigarette case, inspecting it underneath before replacing it. Walking up the steps to the upper section she went straight past the table, which had three places set, and stood by the French windows overlooking the balcony. Her eyes stared thoughtfully out across the river. *What a great place to live*, she thought.

Jeremy returned with two glasses of wine and spotted her at the other side of the room. 'Oh, sit down here, it's much more homely.'

She turned, gave him an extra friendly smile and went over. Sitting down next to him on the sofa, she immediately felt the warmth of the fire against her legs.

Jeremy handed her a glass, which she took and held up towards him. 'To you,' she said.

He looked chuffed. 'How sweet. To tonight.'

They touched glasses and drank.

''Fraid Thomas is running late . . . work commitments. He said for us to start and promises to show as soon as he can.'

As he spoke, Julia stared at his chubby, smiling face, and thinning sandy-coloured hair.

'Should be ready in half an hour. I'm most impressed

with myself, really gone to town tonight. You like Thai food, yes? You'll like this. Hope Thomas hurries. You'll like him too,' he said. 'He's the guy I met at your club.'

Opening her bag, Julia took out a cigarette and lit up.

'Initially, he comes across like a bit of a square, but he's the complete opposite when you get to know him – most unconventional really, that's why I wanted you both to meet. Although I believe you may be at different ends of the scale. He wants to save the world, and you . . .?'

She raised an eyebrow in anticipation of his comment.

'Well, hopefully you'll click. He's very political so watch out. Can be a bit dogmatic at times . . . But he's kind of unusual too, I like that in a person. I have so many friends I want you to meet.'

Julia sat listening to Jeremy. All the while her eyes roved around the room. How could he afford such a place? The contents alone must have cost a fortune. She crossed her legs and sipped her wine, angling her head towards him. He was recalling one Sunday afternoon when he and Thomas had hired a boat and gone along the river. He was laughing his usual loud, exuberant laugh when explaining how Thomas had lost one of the oars.

'Took us over an hour to get back to the boathouse. Two beefy young men had to rescue us, towed us behind their cruiser. You can imagine our embarrassment.' He fell about laughing.

'Have you lived here long?' she asked, when he finally calmed down.

'Three years. It's great in summer, sitting on the balcony, sipping wine, cigar in hand, watching the boats go up and down. Idyllic.'

'Yes. Very impressive.' She uncrossed her legs, accidentally brushing one against his. 'Solicitors must be better paid than I thought.'

He gave her a more cautious, guarded smile. 'I've been quite fortunate in other areas. Inheritance . . . that sort of thing.'

She nodded and slowly sipped her wine.

He stood up. 'Come on, talk to me in the kitchen while I finish off a couple of dishes.'

Julia sat at the kitchen table chatting away to Jeremy who was randomly throwing ingredients into a very hot wok; herbs, oils, wine and seasonings. She watched him with increasing interest. He was a real dab hand – apparently the result of several years of evening cookery courses; he'd even passed his City and Guilds. After half an hour she helped him carry at least nine dishes from the kitchen into the dining area, laying them on the oak table.

Jeremy took the Tom Jones record off and put on an Elton John CD. Sitting down he said with a wink, 'We'll save Cliff for later.'

Julia smiled and started to fill her plate with spoonfuls of the various dishes. 'You're always so jolly,' she said.

'Life is for enjoying.'

'Don't you ever get down or fed-up?'

'Never.'

'Lonely?'

'No.'

'Horny?'

He frowned slightly at the sudden change of tack and in an exaggerated whisper said, 'Having an urge doesn't necessarily mean one should follow it.'

'One should follow everything.'

Jeremy screwed his face up, which made her laugh.

'Do you think you'll ever get married?'

He gasped and gulped at his wine. 'My God! What a thing to ask.'

'Just a question.'

'Marriage isn't for a person like me. Why would I want it? You said yourself, the motivation for you is money. I have money so why bother.'

'You're not a bad catch with all this. Surprised someone hasn't got their claws into you.'

'A few have tried all right.' He bit into some spicy bean curd, chewing it with pride. The next moment he stopped and glared at her, letting his fork drop out of his hand. 'Oh no!' he said, in a quiet yet worried voice.

'What?'

'Me being a good catch!'

'And?'

He eyed her suspiciously. 'This marriage for money thing?'

'Yes?'

He bit his lip. 'You wouldn't . . . well, you know . . . include me in your plans for that.'

She burst out laughing. 'Don't be ridiculous.'

'I had to ask.'

'Don't flatter yourself.'

'So you didn't even think about it?'

Julia sipped her wine, her narrowed eyes glancing around. Finishing off some rice, she finally said, in an easygoing manner, 'For a second you moved out of the "most definitely not" category into the "slight possibilities".'

He let out a loud, high-pitched scream, waving his hands frantically around. 'Shove me back with the "definitely nots", and never remove me again.' He shuddered and fanned himself with his napkin.

'It was just for a second, nothing more. The food is

lovely by the way.' She resumed eating, amused by his panicked state.

Jeremy continued to elaborately fan himself, remaining unusually silent, his mind ticking away. He sipped his wine then said excitedly, 'What about John Richards?'

Julia sneered. 'As a *husband*? He's gross. The manners of a pig. Hasn't heard of deodorant either.'

'David Chambers?'

'Too old, too boring and too poor since his divorce.'

Jeremy ate some rice, continuing to think. '*Of course!*' He banged his hands on the table. 'Jack!'

'He's not interested,' she said calmly.

'So you tried?'

'Gave out some subtle signs . . . but nothing. Anyway, Rachael's got her teeth firmly into him. She'll have him down the aisle within the year.'

'You think?'

'Definitely.'

At that moment the buzzer rang.

'That will be Thomas, and you can put him firmly with your "definitely nots". He lives on a basic monthly wage.' Jeremy grinned and headed towards the door.

'Might as well leave now then,' she shouted after him.

Julia continued eating and found herself on her own for several minutes; she wondered what was keeping them. Eventually, Jeremy burst back into the room, followed by a tall, slim young man with neat blond hair and studious glasses. He was wearing dark trousers, obviously part of a suit, but on top he wore a casual grey sweatshirt.

'This is my good friend Thomas,' said Jeremy, beaming proudly.

Thomas smiled, yet his eyes remained unchanged, serious and observant.

'Nice to meet you.' Julia confidently shook his hand.

'And you.'

'We've only just started. Sit yourself here.' Jeremy pulled back a chair and poured Thomas some wine. 'I'll fetch you a warm plate from the oven,' he said, as he hurried away.

Thomas looked around, then briefly back at Julia who was sitting opposite him, calmly staring back. He gave a shy sort of smile before looking down at his glass and sipping some wine.

'Don't think me rude if I continue to eat, I'm famished,' she said.

'Please do. It looks very good.'

'It is. I didn't realise what an amazing cook he is.' She took another bite of the fresh noodles. 'Just been hearing about your boating incident.'

'It wasn't half as dramatic as he makes out.'

Julia smiled. 'He rants on about you all the time.'

'You also.'

She raised an eyebrow and offered him a prawn cracker, which he took.

'You work at the BBC, don't you? Now that's what I call exciting. Seen anyone famous?'

'Just some newsreaders. I'm hidden away in the archives.'

'I'd love to work in television.' Her eyes glistened.

'What areas interest you?'

She thought for a moment. 'None! Whatever areas have the best parties. I'll work in that department.'

Thomas looked at her strangely, but said nothing.

Soon Jeremy walked back in, smiling at his two guests. He placed a plate in front of Thomas and proceeded to tell him what every dish was. 'A toast,' he said, sitting back down and lifting his glass.

Thomas and Julia raised theirs in response.

'To my dear friends.'

They clinked their glasses together and drank.

'Glad you weren't too late. Before you arrived we were just chatting about finding Julia a rich husband. Know any candidates?'

Julia frowned. '*Jeremy*! That sounds awful.'

'Don't worry about Thomas. He's very open-minded, aren't you?'

'Depends how you term open-mindedness. I admire your honesty yet I would question your motives,' he said.

'Motives aren't for questioning, they're for acting on,' Julia said.

Jeremy laughed. 'She even had me earmarked for a moment.'

'A mere second,' Julia added. 'Anyway this conversation is out of context. What will Thomas think of me?'

Thomas narrowed his eyes and took several moments to think. He appeared quite troubled by it. The other two in their flippant mood, aided by the wine, watched his serious manner with amusement. He finally leant forward, staring directly at her and asked, 'Does love feature in any of this?'

Julia sighed wearily. 'Love is too damned elusive. It's like an eclipse. Comes around every million, billion, trillion years, then it's too cloudy so you miss it. You can't rely on love.'

'She has a point,' said Jeremy, nodding despondently. 'And even when you do find "true love", it can be more of a burden than a pleasure.' A heavy sadness passed briefly over his eyes.

It didn't go unnoticed. Julia stared at him, intrigued.

'And you have experience of "true love".'

Jeremy looked at them both. They were eagerly awaiting his answer. An instant grin appeared on his face and he waved his hand dismissively. 'Absolutely none, thank goodness. I've managed to avoid such a debilitating state. I agree with Julia's philosophy – life should be arranged around practicalities and advancement . . . and fun, of course.' He laughed heartily.

Julia sipped her wine and eyed him suspiciously, unconvinced.

## 15

Emma's plane finally took off at 10.20 on its way to Manchester; a 737 with about ninety passengers. She was placed in a window seat at the front of a row and managed to stretch her legs out fully. Inside the galley section three young stewardesses were preparing the drinks and duty-free trolley; it was only a forty-minute flight so they worked rapidly.

Emma leant her head against the window. She felt exhausted and just wanted to get home and out of her formal clothes. Hopefully the man next to her wouldn't start talking again. He'd introduced himself as Derrick Watson, an insurance broker from Leeds, who reeked of BO. She had to breathe through her mouth and at times felt quite nauseous. Since sitting down, he had ranted on and on about the delays. 'All the advances in technology and a little bit of fog still cripples the place. I'm going to write to the head of the airline. We all should,' he said accusingly, staring at her.

Emma gave a brief, uncommitted nod of her head then turned away, breathing in deeply. Hopefully the people behind wouldn't think it was her who smelt. Outside, it was so dark and dense, it was as though they were travelling through a black hole in space. They had only just taken off, but no lights from the ground were visible.

About ten minutes into the journey the plane hit some turbulence and jolted, jerked and shook at intervals. Emma sat up straight and held on tightly to the armrests, her heartbeat quickening and becoming quite pronounced; she wasn't the best of flyers.

'Bloody bumpy. Who's flying this damn thing?' said Mr Watson.

She noted his already empty whiskey glass. 'Yes, very bumpy,' she said, looking back towards the window. She leant her head against the side panel again but the erratic movement of the plane meant her head kept banging off it. Closing her eyes, she started to do her yoga breathing, imagining she was at home in a warm bath and Tony was downstairs making dinner.

Her calm was again interrupted by her irritating neighbour who was now humming loudly – some inaudible melody. Next he started to quickly flick through the pages of a magazine. He continuously turned each page until he got to the end, then picked up another magazine and did the same. After flicking through the third and last magazine, he went back to the first and started again, this time mumbling something about plastic cups and single mums. She sighed quietly. *Why am I a magnate for weirdos? Buses, trains and planes – they always end up sitting next to me.*

The turbulence continued for most of the flight, so when the captain finally announced their descent, a sense of relief swept through the cabin.

'About bloody time. Only three hours late,' was the comment from her neighbour.

Emma ignored it and smiled; just relieved to be getting away from him, so she could breathe normally again. She was getting a headache through lack of oxygen.

Soon, two of the stewardesses strapped themselves in opposite her and although the approach was bumpy they continued chatting, occasionally laughing. Derrick Watson held on tightly to both armrests, so Emma laid one hand in her lap to avoid the close proximity. Looking out of the window, she still couldn't tell how close they were to the ground, as nothing was visible through the fog. At that moment the plane jolted, it bounced, jolted down again and finally touched. Thank God! She should be home within half an hour. A bath, a gin and tonic, then to bed.

The engines boomed loudly as they shot down the runway. The speed of the aircraft seemed much faster than usual, the force pinning the passengers back in their seats.

Suddenly, screams filled the cabin as the plane swerved sharply to the left, its engines shrieking awkwardly, desperately braking.

Emma was thrown hard against Mr Watson and her neck clicked with an almighty jerk. Her face pressed down into his armpit and she was unable to move against the thrust of the aircraft's forward movement. A threatening, unfamiliar noise vibrated through every surface, yet all she could think of was suffocating in his body odour. He smelt so awful that she dared not breathe. What a way to die! She could just imagine the autopsy report. In desperation she yanked her head around, sending a bolt of pain ripping through her neck. It was still preferable to having her nose buried in his armpit.

Still thrown up against him, she caught sight of the blonde stewardess. She looked terrified. The smile, previously set in concrete, had shattered. Her face was strangely contorted and she was clinging on for dear life, as the plane shot along at a strange angle, skidding sideways. A woman behind started to pray, 'Our Father, Who art in heaven, hallowed be Thy name. Our Father, Who art in heaven, hallowed be Thy name.'

Emma experienced the first tinges of fear. She shut her eyes tight.

Everything felt surreal – like a scene from *Airplane*.

She half expected to see a guitar-playing nun singing in the aisle, wanting them all to clap along. And then her thoughts began to slip away, deeper, deeper down they faded, a momentary vacuum, almost peaceful. Her breathing slowed. She sat, absorbed yet absent, in her coiled position against Derrick Watson – from a distance looking like two lovers entwined.

The next thing she knew, she was thrown forward then immediately back, as the plane jarred to a sudden halt. The seatbelt dug into her thighs and cases fell from the overhead lockers. An eerie silence descended and for a moment everything and everyone was completely still, motionless. The sound of a baby crying at the rear was like a signal for everything to begin again. Noises erupted all around, moans, cries, people moving. Over the tannoy, a voice started to speak.

'This is Captain Reeves.' He went on to reassure the passengers that they were perfectly safe. While he continued to speak, Mr Watson shoved Emma off him and jumped into the aisle.

Falling back in her seat, she instinctively grabbed hold of her neck as another jab of pain shot through it. She sat there, observing the frenzied scene, her expression blank, somehow removed from it all. They were down and safe, what was the big deal? Gazing out of the window, she could just about make out the dim haze of some approaching lights and the faint sound of sirens.

The hectic proceedings continued around her, frightened people pushing and shoving, worried that the plane might explode at any minute. Others were crying – two teenage boys were laughing excitedly, completely thrilled by the experience.

Eventually, the passengers started to get off and Emma watched everyone jumping barefoot into the fog and down the inflatable ramps. Mr Watson had jumped first, shouting back at the crew, 'You'll be hearing from my solicitor.' Then he slid away out of sight. *Good riddance*, she thought.

Emma took her place in the diminishing queue. Reaching the door, she stood for a moment, blinded by the glare of all the lights outside; red flashing lights, headlights and several spotlights were deliberately aimed at the entrances to the plane. Combined with the pale mist, they gave a radiant and strangely angelic illumination. Taking a deep breath that filled her lungs with the icy air, she leapt out into the light, the unknown, falling through the air with abandon.

'But why can't you pull out?' repeated Tony.

Emma stared blank-faced at him. He was sitting beside her hospital bed in Casualty, holding her hand and looking more distraught than her.

'You've done most of the planning, let someone else take over. You'll get some of the bonus, won't you?' he said.

With lips tightened together, her vacant eyes gazed beyond him.

'Jesus, Em. Surely you ain't just going to get on another plane. You'll be petrified. They'll understand.'

Her words were faint yet wilful. 'I'm going to Dublin, Tony.'

He shook his head and went off to get another coffee.

Mad rumours spread around the hospital that night about what had happened; everything from a bomb to a potential hijacking. Finally, representatives from the airport arrived to inform everyone that an unauthorised light aircraft had ventured on to the runway. The 737 had had to take evasive action to avoid collision and a full investigation was underway. Luckily, no one was badly hurt and they commended the pilot on his superb handling of the situation.

Returning from the coffee machine, Tony said enthusiastically, 'Em, I've just been talking to another passenger who mentioned compensation. Says we can claim for injury and distress, could be a few thousand in it! He's collecting telephone numbers, says it's better if we all stand together.' He sat back down beside her. 'Seems to know what he's talking about. He's an insurance broker from Leeds, Derrick Watson.'

For several moments Emma stared directly at Tony before her despondent gaze dropped to the floor. Exasperation kept her silent. At that moment she felt so distant to him, alien to his language and concept of life. All he was thinking of was an opportunity to make some money. *He hasn't a clue what goes on in my head, how I feel, who I really am. What I need as a person. What I need as a woman!*

After a long wait, X-rays and an examination, Emma was fitted with a neck collar for whiplash and given some strong painkillers. The doctor had mentioned the possibility of concussion and shock, and advised her not to be left alone for the next forty-eight hours. Apart from that, she was allowed to go home. It was after 3am when they finally left the hospital, a little late for that gin and tonic in the bath.

The next morning, Emma awoke at around eleven o'clock to find her neck more painful than she had expected – so last night had really happened then. She slowly and very carefully sat up. It felt strange waking up back in her bedroom; gone was the view over Dublin, gone too was room service, which had brought her breakfast every morning. She looked down at Tony, snoring next to her with his mouth wide open.

Cautiously standing up, she put on her dressing gown and went downstairs to take a painkiller and make her own breakfast.

Later that day, a white transit van pulled up outside their house, delivering her luggage and handbag. If she wanted her shoes she'd have to identify and collect them from Lost Property at the airport. Signing for a sealed envelope addressed to 'Flight MD313 Passenger', she sat down on the sofa next to Tony and opened it.

Inside was a joint letter from Midland Air and Manchester airport giving them a broad outline of what had happened the previous night. It apologised for the inconvenience, injury or any fright it may have caused. It offered passengers the chance to visit a trauma counsellor to discuss the incident and gave a telephone number to call and book an appointment.

'Trying to cover their arses against compensation claims,' said Tony.

Emma folded the letter and placed it on the armrest.

'You gonna go?' he asked.

Emma shrugged her shoulders and looked at the television.

'You have to. Otherwise they'll say they gave you the opportunity but you didn't take it. Could affect the compensation claim.'

Her critical eyes travelled over him, his two-day stubble, slightly greasy hair and torn T-shirt.

'I don't want to make a compensation claim,' she said firmly.

'Don't be ridiculous. It's easy money. Could get a new car out of this.'

'I'm fine though.'

'Your neck collar, the emotional distress.'

'It ran off the runway, *big deal*.'

'You ended up in a field. What if you start having nightmares about dying?'

Eyes closed, almost in a whisper to herself she said, 'It's living that worries me.'

Tony's face twisted and his eyes were full of anger. '*What*?' he cried.

'Oh nothing, ignore me.'

Snatching up the letter, he stormed out to the phone. She heard him chatting to someone, and after about ten minutes he came back in. 'Tuesday at two-thirty. One hour initially, but you can go back for more. It's a private practice, off Westgate in the centre. I've written it all down.' He dropped the letter into her lap. 'I'm making tea, want a cup?' He didn't wait for a reply.

That evening, Tony went off to work at seven. At his request, their neighbour, Mrs McDermott, came in to sit with Emma until he returned home. She was only too happy to oblige, especially after hearing what had happened. It was on the front page of the *Manchester Evening Post*, which she brought in for Emma to read. Feeling drowsy from the painkillers and lack of sleep, Emma took the paper and went upstairs to her bedroom. She sat on her bed while Mrs McDermott watched the television downstairs. Occasionally, she came up to offer tea and biscuits and check she was all right.

Emma started to read the article about the incident. It described in detail what had happened and the near collision with the light aircraft. The paper constantly emphasised the possible disaster and criticised safety standards. They made it sound like a scene out of *Die Hard II* and had statements from two passengers describing the five minutes of sheer terror as they contemplated death. It was like reading about something else, but she had actually been on that plane.

It just didn't feel real. She touched her neck collar, a

tangible reminder. *Maybe it was more serious than I thought. Maybe I could have died.* She sat contemplating it. *I could have died. Gone. No more. Dead.* 'What if' scenarios started whirling around her head.

One of the buttons she had been unconsciously tugging on her cardigan came away in her hand. It was thrown to the floor. She hated the cardigan anyway. Why had she ever worn it? It was pulled off and thrown to the floor also. *I could have died*, she thought again.

Mad images of her funeral came to mind and who would be there, not many; could be a bit embarrassing. She really must get out more and make some friends. Her mind turned to Tony. He'd probably marry again, a young girl like Rob's Rebecca. Of course he'd be sad, but he'd meet someone else, she was sure of that. He wouldn't live his life alone, he couldn't; a replacement would be found quite quickly. Hopefully, he'd at least wait until she was in the ground.

Was she mad to think like this? She was safe in bed – nothing had happened. Yet her imagination was racing off with alternative outcomes. No doubt she'd have a really big headstone, her parents would see to that, bought more to impress the neighbours and Vicar than as a tribute to her. Since her refusal to spend Christmas Day at their house, which meant the family spending it apart, her relationship with them had become very strained, especially as Emma wouldn't apologise. Why should she? In the past she would have said or done anything to patch things up, but not this time. She just couldn't. They still spoke but it was extremely tense.

'I could have died.' This time she said it aloud. Emma Hughes RIP! Just another statistic. What would have been the point of it all? *How has my life become so meaningless, pointless, so routine, and above all else boring; goddamn boring?*

She was filled with anger and threw the paper across the bedroom.

'I can't believe you're going in. Don't expect any thanks. Stay in bed and relax,' insisted Tony on Monday morning, as Emma got ready to go to work.

'I *can't!* Thanks for being concerned, but really, I'm absolutely fine. I need to go.' Emma closed the bedroom door leaving him in bed. The next minute it was flung open behind her and Tony stood there.

'Well, I'll drive you,' he said.

She smiled. 'Thanks.'

Emma spent most of the morning at the office answering everyone's persistent enquiries about the incident. They all gasped in horror and wanted to know every minute detail. She felt almost disappointed that it hadn't been as eventful and terrifying as they obviously wanted it to be. A few exaggerations started to creep into the story; it kept everyone happy. Soon the other branches were phoning her; she was quite the celebrity.

At ten past twelve a bouquet of flowers arrived. The card read:

> Darling Emma,
> The lengths women will go to for attention! And you call me the Drama Queen!
> Love, Jeremy.

She smiled broadly. The day before, she had telephoned Jeremy and told him all about it. Halfway through the conversation he dashed off to pour himself a whiskey – his nerves were getting the better of him, he said.

'They're obviously from Jeremy,' said Trish, seeing her reaction.

Emma showed her the card.

Trish smiled, but said in a concerned voice, 'You are OK, aren't you? Seem very blasé about it all.'

Emma hesitated. 'Yes and no. Part of it seems so unreal. After all, nothing really happened as such.'

'And the other part?'

Emma shrugged her shoulders. 'I don't know, see how it goes.'

'What don't you know?'

Emma considered the question for several moments, then said despondently, 'Anything.'

'Like what?'

'Like . . . what's it all about? What's the point of it all?'

Trish smiled. 'Oh, nothing serious then, just the meaning of life.'

Emma smiled too. 'Well, have you figured it out?'

'I don't want to . . . Have enough trouble deciding what to wear.'

'Why can't I be more like that?'

'Shallow and materialistic?'

Emma shook her head. 'No, just less . . . less, well . . . oh, I don't know.'

'Back at that again.' Trish had a puzzled look on her face and was biting the tip of her pen.

Emma gazed down at the pile of work she had to do.

'What's actually wrong? Thought your life was totally together,' said Trish.

'Neat and packaged were the words you used.'

'Ah! Sorry. Wasn't in the best of moods that night.'

'Doesn't matter,' said Emma, sighing wearily. 'I suppose I give off that impression.'

'*Is* everything OK?'

Emma shrugged her shoulders. 'Suppose . . . It's just . . . surely life should be more than just OK?'

'Of course it should. Have you discussed it with Tony?'

Emma stared at Trish, amused.

'What?' asked Trish, not knowing what was funny.

'Eight years of marriage. The only things discussed after that are what's for dinner and what to watch on telly.'

Trish looked horrified.

'I'm exaggerating. Ignore me, I'm just in a weird mood.'

'Look, I've got to finish this document, but then let's head off for lunch, have a proper chat, maybe hit the shops? Cheer you up.'

Emma nodded, staring out of the window; it was raining again.


On Tuesday morning, Emma went into work determined to get a lot done, but her mind was all over the place. She was trying to update the budgets, but events that had happened years ago drifted into her thoughts, college days, past boyfriends, holidays, instances with her parents. It was a losing battle trying to concentrate. She was also apprehensive about the appointment that afternoon with the trauma counsellor and considered cancelling it.

She was returning from yet another daydream, when Jackie the receptionist walked into their office and headed towards her. She was carrying a huge bouquet of flowers, white and gold chrysanthemums, white and yellow roses and orange tiger lilies, gift-wrapped with a large gold ribbon.

'My God, for me?' shrieked Emma, raising her hands to her mouth.

Jackie nodded, smiling broadly. 'Yep, that's what it says.' She handed them to her.

Trish leapt out from behind her desk and went over. 'Wow, they're lovely. I love tiger lilies. Think they're from Tony? Go on, open the card.' Both Trish and Jackie stood alert, eyes wide and eagerly waiting.

Emma laid the flowers gently on the table and pulled the envelope off the cellophane. They looked very expensive and she wondered how much Tony had spent. Removing the card, she read it. Her jaw dropped.

'What? What is it? Who are they from?' chirped Jackie and Trish, practically hopping on the spot.

Emma stared at the small piece of card in her hand. Her eyes slowly lifted to look at Trish as she gave a slightly awkward laugh. Biting her lip, she handed the card over.

Trish grabbed it and read aloud with Jackie peering over her shoulder: '"Just heard. Hope you're OK, Jack".' Trish squealed with laugher. Jackie looked disappointed and left the room.

Emma ran her hands through her hair. 'I can't believe it. Jack!'

'Neither can I,' said Trish, an edge to her voice.

'Flowers from *Jack*.'

'A bit thoughtful for him.'

Emma took the card back off Trish and read it again, twice, before holding up the bouquet in front of her and admiring them. 'Lovely choice.'

'Probably the shop's, not his,' added Trish.

'Must have cost a fortune.'

'He'll claim on expenses.'

'They smell amazing.'

Trish smelt them too before returning to her seat.

'Nice thought, though,' said Emma.

'Probably down to Julia. It's always us secretaries who think of things like that.'

'Doubt it. She wouldn't get me flowers.'

'Who cares anyway. They're lovely. They'll look great in your lounge, it'll smell like a florist shop.'

Emma smiled. But gradually the smile faded and her eyes narrowed, as if concerned. After several moments she said aloud, 'Think I'll keep them here, brighten up the office.' Maybe it was silly, but she didn't want Tony to see them.

'They're too good for here, it's a waste. Take them home,' said Trish.

'All my vases are full.'

'Borrow one from here.'

'No, really. They can stay here, cheer the place up.' Emma immediately stood up and walked out to the kitchen to put them in water.

A little while later she returned with the flowers nicely arranged in a large vase and placed them on the filing cabinet behind her. She typed an e-mail to Jack and after several different versions, settled on:

```
Jack,

Thank you for the flowers. They're
lovely.
Emma.
```

Within five minutes she received a reply.

```
Emma,

Don't wish to appear insensitive about
```

```
your near-death experience, but while
you're still breathing, could you inform
me when I can expect the revised
costings?
Jack.
```

Emma shook her head and quickly sent another message.

```
Jack,

Revised costings will be with you
Wednesday.

Don't worry, I'll try and stay alive
until the Dublin office is up and
running.
Emma.
```

A minute later her computer bleeped again.

```
Emma,

Good. I'd hate to have to alter the
business plan yet again.
Jack.
```

Emma smiled and logged off.

## 16

At around two-forty that afternoon, a cab pulled up outside a two-storey, red-brick building on Westgate Road. Emma got out and stood on the steps staring nervously at the entrance, unsure what to expect. Ironic, she thought, feeling more scared now than during the actual incident. Just to keep Tony happy and off her back, she walked up the five steps and rang the bell.

A friendly middle-aged lady answered it and led her straight into the ground-floor office of a Mr Philip Bruton. He immediately stood up, warmly shook her hand and welcomed her. His appearance surprised her, tall, blond and surprisingly young with compassionate yet inquisitive eyes.

'Sorry I'm late,' she said.

'You're here now. Please take a seat.' He smiled and indicated a two-seater settee behind her.

Emma sat down, kept her coat on and glanced around, heart racing. The room was more like a living room than an office, lemon walls, deep blue velvet curtains and polished wooden floors partially covered by a large Afghan rug. The counsellor sat opposite her in a large armchair and smiled again. 'From the incident, I presume,' he said, pointing to her neck collar.

'Unfortunately, yes.' Emma smiled briefly.

'It's probably best if I start by saying a few words.' His voice was deep and precise, yet calm and gentle. 'My two colleagues and I offer various types of counselling and psychoanalysis. However, in this instance, along with some other practices, we have been asked to offer trauma counselling, for those passengers who experienced the incident on Friday. We can offer anything from one session up to four. That is, if the individual wants to attend. You could of course have more sessions, but that would be at your own expense.' He paused then asked, 'Have you ever had any counselling before?'

'No, never.'

He regarded her for a moment before continuing. 'Basically, all that will happen is we'll talk. I'll ask various questions so you can hopefully get an insight into what you're feeling. After a traumatic episode people can experience different emotions. These sessions will be about reassuring you and helping you to work through any emotions, thoughts, feelings. I would add that anything you say is completely confidential, to everyone, including the airport authorities.' His words flowed like a well-versed song. He smiled again. 'Having heard all that, do you have any questions you'd like to ask at this stage?'

Emma shook her head.

'Unless you would prefer to start elsewhere, a good question would be, how have you been feeling about what happened?' He looked directly at her and waited.

Emma ran her hand through her hair. She glanced towards the bookshelf, then towards the floor. She was wearing her new knee-length, red fitted dress, bought during yesterday's lunch hour. Her layered hair, now with an auburn rinse, fell loosely around the neck collar. Her face was fully made up, including foundation. 'Um.' She coughed, then spoke very quietly. 'I'm not really sure why I came. I feel fine about what happened. In fact, it's like it didn't happen.'

Philip nodded, but said nothing.

'Maybe I should go. It wasn't such a big deal. My husband thinks we've only been offered counselling to avoid possible compensation claims.'

'Even if that is the case, it can still help. Could you explain further, "it's like it didn't happen".'

She took a deep breath. 'It was all so quick. No one died or was badly hurt. If it wasn't for this neck collar, I'd swear I dreamt it.'

A pause followed. Philip was holding his chin. 'Have you noticed any mood changes since the incident?'

Emma's face looked puzzled. Having read so many self-help books, she tried to guess where his question was leading. 'I suppose I've been a bit moody.'

'Why do you think that is?'

'Well . . . there was a slight possibility that I could have died, we all could have. I know we didn't and I'm not traumatised by that. But I do feel . . .' she screwed her face up, frustrated by the lack of an appropriate word. 'I feel . . . well, say I had died, I haven't done enough . . . anything in fact. But really that's for me to have a good think about. I've just been given a kick up the bum. It's not like I'm suffering sleepless nights or hot sweats so I feel a bit of a fraud being here.'

Philip said reassuringly, 'Everyone reacts differently. Your thoughts are certainly not uncommon. Stay the hour at least. See what develops. Of course you can leave at any time.'

Emma looked at the door but didn't move.

'Could we go back to the plane journey. How were you feeling just before landing?' he asked.

'Nervous. There was lots of turbulence. Plane kept dropping and climbing.'

'What was your main fear?'

She shrugged her shoulders. He waited for something else. Emma thought more.

'It wasn't dying. I suppose I was scared of . . . how I was feeling, fear of the fear, as they say.'

'Dying doesn't scare you?'

'Well it would, if I was dying, but I'm not . . . not yet, hopefully.'

'So you didn't think of death during the incident?'

Emma shook her head slowly, eyeing him cautiously. *He seems obsessed with death*, she thought. *So this was counselling! Feeling better already!*

'What *did* you think of?' he asked.

She glanced away. It might be best to keep suffocation by BO and the guitar-playing nun to herself. Philip waited for her answer, happy to sit in complete silence. She could hear the ticking of the carriage clock on the shelf behind. Feeling pressure to say something, she said, 'I wondered if it were real . . . kind of felt surreal.'

'When did you know something was wrong?'

'Well, the plane swerved and skidded. I was thrown out of my seat.' She added with a half smile, 'I suppose it was around that time.'

He nodded purposefully, oblivious to any humour. 'What happened next?'

'Some people screamed.'

'Did you?'

'No.'

'Did you feel like screaming?'

'Not at all,' she said, confused by his approach. It was as if he wanted her to be more traumatised than she actually was. *Maybe I'm a boring case*, she thought. It made her smile.

'So people screamed out – what did you notice next?' he asked.

'The blonde stewardess looked terrified.'

'Were you terrified?'

'No.'

'Were you scared at any point during the incident.'

'Nervous, not terrified.'

'Why do you think that is?' he asked.

She shrugged her shoulders and said, as a throw-away comment, 'Everyone else was freaking out. Didn't matter if I did.'

Philip stared straight at her, holding his chin again. Emma realised that must have sounded very odd. She spotted a flicker in his eyes but he was professional and kept a blank but warm expression. *He must think I'm mad*, she thought. *Jack will be most annoyed if I get sectioned before the Dublin office is up and running.* She fought the urge to laugh, covering her mouth with her hand.

Again, silence reigned. Emma stared at him sitting comfortably in his large armchair, watching her, as if determined for her to be the one to speak first. But Emma wasn't sure what else to say. A couple of minutes passed. Fed up of sitting in silence and wanting to appear helpful and explain her lack of trauma, she said, 'Have you seen the film *Plenty* with Meryl Streep?'

He shook his head.

'Well, in it she was this French Resistance worker. She helped numerous RAF pilots and other allied forces get back to England. She risked her life daily and fell in love with one of the men, a British Captain I think, something like that. Well, when the war ended, she married him and moved to England. But she couldn't cope with the banality of everyday life. It was so pointless after fighting for liberty and freedom. I can't remember it all but she went a little crazy for a while. Things got on top of her. She couldn't cope, started drinking. She sort of lost it.'

Philip nodded.

'Sometimes I feel like that. Not that I drink, only socially. I didn't mean that. I meant in the sense that little things can make me so nervous. I worry all the time about what could happen, losing my keys, not paying bills. When I'm two miles down the road I wonder if I turned the cooker off; sometimes I go back. Also the car breaking down, getting stuck in a lift, getting to the supermarket check-out and not having enough money.' She stopped suddenly, realising she'd probably gone overboard in making her point.

Philip was still silent, his expression unchanged.

'Anyway, sometimes I think maybe I'm like that. Little things can really throw me, but the big things don't worry me so much – you just have to get on with them. Like the incident with the plane. There was no time to worry about it. It happened! Sometimes I think that if I'd been born before the war, I could have been a resistance worker or even a spy. I probably would have been quite good at it. At least those things matter.' Her expression dropped as she looked away in horror. *Why am I saying all these things?* she thought. *I sound completely mad. He might think I'm suffering from insane delusions.* Her heart began to race again. She touched her bag beside her. 'As I said, I'm fine.'

Philip was stroking his eyebrow. Jack did that sometimes. It was an annoying habit. She could see Philip's mind ticking away and dreaded what he'd say next.

'Have you thought about attending counselling yourself, to explore some of—'

'No,' she interrupted, giving an awkward laugh. 'Why? My life's very straightforward, no great distress. I'm not depressed or anything.'

'Are you your life?'

She looked at him oddly. 'What do you mean?'

'Our lives don't always represent who we truly are. You said your life was straightforward. Are you happy with it being straightforward? From some of the things you've said, it seems deep down, you want more from your life.'

Emma shifted in her chair. Her face grew tense. Analysing her life right now was a road she'd rather not take. Where would it lead? Wanting more could be dangerous. She was momentarily silent, thinking of a reply. She appeared uneasy and felt his eyes examining every movement, every flicker and gesture of hers. She deliberately froze, totally motionless, even trying not to blink for fear of him reading something into it. *What's this got to do with the incident?* she wondered.

Philip Bruton seemed content to sit in silence until she answered. It was all beginning to annoy her. *How much does he get paid for this?* She'd had enough. She glanced at the door.

He noted it.

*Would it be rude to just get up and walk out? Then again, who cares? I could have died, I'm allowed to be rude*, she thought. *I can do what I want.*

She smiled at him. 'I think I'll go now.' She stood up.

He looked surprised. 'Won't you at least stay until the end of the session? It may help.'

Emma stared at him while she considered her response and how to convince him that she was all right and perfectly sane. She remembered. Did it matter what he thought? *Why should I convince him of anything?* She didn't plan to say her next comment; it just popped out. With a stern frown, and in a slow, serious manner, she said, 'No, I have to go. I'm being dropped behind enemy lines tonight. Late for my briefing already. *Lives depend on me.*'

Philip's composure disappeared. He glared at her. Emma winked at him, then bolted out the door.

## 17

The next two weeks dragged by. Each day seemed the same, work, cook dinner then sleep. Emma was surprised by how much she was looking forward to returning to Dublin, full-time for three months. It constantly occupied her thoughts. The impending flight scared her, but she felt desperate for a change of scene, to escape for a while, therefore the fear was conveniently put to the side.

She was spending money she and Tony didn't really have on new outfits for work, more stylish and a size smaller. She bought a light-blue tailored trouser suit and a plum-coloured short skirt and matching jacket, also accessories like scarves, belts and a couple of brooches. The Friday before she was due to leave, Emma visited the hospital again for a check-up. Thankfully the neck collar was removed.

On the afternoon of Sunday 5 March, Tony drove her to the airport along with her two suitcases and three large boxes containing various documents, files, reference books and also Jack's new portable laptop computer. Jack had asked her to take them over saying the excess baggage cost on the aeroplane would be cheaper than using a courier. Thankfully, he was collecting her at the airport. He had flown over to Dublin a few days before to move into his new house.

Tony and Emma stood for some moments staring at the entrance to the departure lounge. She was wearing her jeans and blue fleece jacket; at least if the plane crashed she'd be more appropriately dressed for sliding down the ramp.

'See you Friday then,' she said.

He nodded. He'd hardly spoken much all weekend, annoyed that she was still intending to go against his wishes. Emma leant over and pecked him on the cheek. He stood completely still. Her eyes continued past him and on detachedly in the direction of the departure gate. Tony suddenly grabbed her hand, pulling her towards him. He kissed her a couple of times. 'I'm gonna miss you,' he said.

After a moment's hesitation she replied, 'I'll miss you, too.'

She pulled free, presented a smile, turned and walked through the gate. She didn't look back.

As the plane sped down the runway on its take-off Emma clung on to the armrests. Her heart was pounding and her palms were sweaty but she was used to that. She hadn't slept much the night before but that wasn't unusual either. She was unconsciously holding her breath as the aeroplane lifted off the ground and climbed at a steep angle. Only when it levelled off did she begin to relax slightly.

Peering out of the window, Emma observed the shrinking ground, matchbox houses and farms, lakes like puddles, all of it diminishing before her eyes; so insignificant. Her little world departing behind her. Higher and higher they went above the greyness into a bright blue sky and blinding sunlight.

Up shot the stewardesses with the drinks and Emma ordered a gin and tonic. She drank it quickly and surprisingly found herself smiling.

Her heart pounded again on landing but it somehow no longer worried her. There were more important things to think of.

After some lengthy form-filling at Customs, she started to wheel the overladen trolley down the corridor towards the arrivals lounge. She was feeling a bit strange; unsettled, slightly anxious, but she wasn't sure why. Maybe the plane journey had affected her more than she realised. Just before the exit, she stood for several moments taking a few deep breaths. She hadn't eaten for a while, that might be it.

Looking through the glass panel she could see into the arrivals area, where eager relatives and friends were waiting for their loved ones. Her eyes scouted across each face, searching. They stopped. There he was. Just behind the rope section, dressed in jeans and a navy overcoat, stood Jack.

Emma drew back from the panel. She looked away. Other passengers walked past her, impatient to be on their way. She gathered herself together and followed the stream of people through the doors, into the arrivals area.

'Hello, Emma.' Jack was immediately by her side.

In a hurried voice, she said, 'Oh hello, Jack. Hope you haven't been waiting long. The luggage! Waited ages! Probably all these boxes, then Customs. Anyway, I'm here now. Dublin again. Lovely sunny day. Moved in OK?'

He nodded his head at each of her comments and automatically took the trolley from her. 'Bit of a walk, I'm afraid.'

She let him lead the way. They walked out of the busy terminal heading towards the car park signs.

Once in car park B, Jack approached the lifts. Emma felt her chest tighten. When Jack continued past them, she sighed with relief. Following him towards the car she asked, 'How's the house?'

'Still a lot of work to do on it.' Without looking at her he said, 'You'll have to come over one night.'

'Wouldn't mind having a look.'

They reached his new car, a white Audi Sport and

soon they were on their way towards the city centre, gliding along the short motorway section. Jack flicked on the CD player and Glenn Miller's 'Little Brown Jug' came on. She smiled at his choice. It didn't go unnoticed.

'There're some other CDs in the glove compartment,' he said.

'No, I'll listen to this. It's different.'

His eyes narrowed slightly.

After about twenty minutes they were nearing the city centre. Jack stopped at a red light. He started to tap the wheel with his fingers. 'What will you do tonight?' he asked.

'Nothing much. I bought a book to read.'

The light turned to green and they drove off. Within another five minutes Buswells Hotel appeared up ahead of them on the right, but they stopped at another red light. Jack continued to tap the wheel with his fingers. He quickly glanced at Emma then back to the road. 'Why not look tonight . . . at the house? It's only ten minutes away.'

Emma hesitated, intrigued yet surprised that she'd been invited into his home, a glimpse into Jack Tomkinson's private world. Her lips pressed hard against each other.

'It's still early. You won't want to be cooped up in your hotel room all night,' he added.

'All right. Why not?'

When the light turned green, Jack put his foot down and sped away. Fiddling with her bracelet, Emma watched in the side mirror as the hotel disappeared behind them.

The houses got larger as they drew nearer to Ballsbridge. It reminded her of parts of London, similar style with the same dark brickwork. They turned into a cul-de-sac and parked outside a three-storey, Victorian, freshly painted, white house. Steps ran up to a blue front door and a skip filled with wood and rubble stood outside.

'Looks massive. How many bedrooms?' she asked.

'Only four, two en-suite.'

'*Only*,' she repeated, under her breath.

He heard and shot an odd glance in her direction.

They walked up the steps and Jack took out his keys, opening the door. A strong smell of paint hit her. Her eyes widened as she noticed the size of the hall – larger than her lounge. The walls were painted in a green wash with gold and blue intermittent stencilled patterns. It was bright and modern, not as she had imagined. Plastic sheeting covered the floor.

'The floorboards are being varnished next week,' he said.

'Looks really good. Unusual.'

'I'll give you a tour.' He threw his coat over a chair by the phone and indicated for her to follow him.

She admired every room, from the white and stone-coloured, minimalist lounge, to the mad vibrant colours of the dining room, reds and golds, with wrought-iron fixtures. She loved the size of the rooms, so spacious and airy.

Hanging on the wall in the second lounge were two large abstract paintings. A mass of different coloured paint strokes cleverly portrayed the subtle outline of a naked man and woman embracing. The first painting had the couple standing, as if holding each other in a gentle clasp. In the second they were horizontal. The frantic strokes of the paint brilliantly captured the passion between them without showing too much detail, but it was very sensuous. Jack's contemporary taste amazed her.

Leaving the room she asked, 'Did you get a designer in?'

'No.'

'Who chose all this then?'

'I did.'

She stared at him in surprise. 'I'm impressed. Next you're going to tell me you painted those two paintings back there.'

He looked at her indulgently. 'They're Roberto Prendergast. Copies, of course.'

'Of course,' she repeated, comically rolling her eyes, not having a clue who that was. 'In fact, why don't you just order another two copies and we'll hang them in reception. Problem solved,' she said.

His doubtful eyes examined hers, trying to decide if she was being serious. 'And you think they're suitable, Emma, for an office environment?'

'Suitable, Jack? Wasn't it you who criticised me for being overly concerned by others' opinions?'

'In business, it's important to create the right impression.'

'Impressions, opinions, surely it's all the same. Maybe you're overly concerned too.'

His eyes sharpened their focus on her. 'Am I?'

She smiled and walked away.

He caught up with her and led her upstairs to the first floor and into an extensive, bright bedroom decorated in various shades of blue. It had a large balcony overlooking the rear garden and an en-suite bathroom, decked with delicately patterned marble. Two steps led up to a circular bath. His toiletries lay around, aftershave, deodorant, an electric razor. Only the one toothbrush, she noted.

The second master bedroom was decorated more traditionally with built-in wardrobes and a peach bathroom. Walking upstairs to the next floor Jack said, 'None of the other rooms are finished yet.' He opened various doors to reveal plastered walls and bare floorboards. 'Another three weeks,' he added.

'Won't you feel lost on your own in such a big house?'

'No, I'll love it. Shut the world out.'

She raised an eyebrow at the comment.

Back down in the spacious kitchen-cum-breakfast room, Jack walked over to the fridge and opened it. 'Would you like a glass of wine?'

There was a noticeable hesitation before she eventually said, 'Just one then,' and sat down at the kitchen table.

'There's gin and tonic if you'd prefer.'

'Wine's fine.'

He brought over two glasses and opened a bottle of Australian Chardonnay in front of her.

'Cheers. To Dublin,' he said.

They touched glasses and drank the toast.

Jack took off his Aran jumper to reveal a black, short-sleeved T-shirt that clung tightly to him. 'Heating's been on all day. Think I'll turn it off. Are you warm enough?'

'Yes, I'm fine.' She opened her fleece but kept it on. She watched him walk across the kitchen and raise his bare arm to flick a switch on the wall opposite. He turned. She glanced away. Sitting back down opposite her he asked, 'Any more plans on the new career? Have the BBC signed you up to read the news yet?'

She scowled at him.

'Well, ignore the BBC bit, but I'm interested to hear your plans,' he said.

'Maybe I should keep quiet. You are technically my boss.'

'I'll resign for the night. Consider me a painter and decorator.'

He did look different this evening, younger somehow. Probably the jeans and T-shirt. Also his hair wasn't cropped so short any more, the slightly longer layers suited him. She was beginning to see what other secretaries saw in him. He was quite nice-looking really.

Emma shrugged her shoulders. 'All I know is I just can't see myself going back to the Manchester office.'

Jack leant forward. His penetrating eyes fixed tightly on hers. In a serious, slow and intense manner, he said, 'Going back to anything is impossible. The place is the same, but the person is different. We have to keep moving forward, experience new things. Still waters poison.'

Emma was silent for a moment, sensing there was something more behind those words. 'The gospel according to Jack?'

He shook his head and looked away.

'For now I'm just going to concentrate on getting through the Dublin opening.'

Jack turned back to look at her. 'Don't look at it like that.'

'Like what?'

'Like it's a hassle. Enjoy it.' His eyes stayed on her for a couple of moments before travelling slowly downwards to his glass.

Emma sipped her wine and looked around again. 'Nice kitchen units,' she said, feeling a bit unsettled.

'They're units.'

'Nice colour.' She looked at the bare wooden dresser in the corner but felt he was watching her. After a few moments she braved a look. His gaze retreated to the wine bottle. He picked it up, examining the label.

'Nice wine.'

'It's wine,' she stated.

He smiled and slowly put the bottle back down. 'When did you get the neck collar off?'

'Only Friday.'

'Was it very frightening, the incident?'

'Happened so quickly.'

He went to speak, but seemed to hesitate, appearing for the first time slightly unsure of himself. 'I was concerned when I heard.'

She nodded awkwardly, then glanced away. He filled up their glasses again.

'Are you hungry?' he asked.

She was, but she felt she should go. 'I'm fine.'

'I'm going to order a pizza. Have some.' He stood up and went over to a drawer by the sink.

'I should get back.'

'Why?'

'Busy day tomorrow.'

'It's not even seven.'

She stared at her wine.

'Anyway,' he said. 'I'm the boss. I insist.'

'You resigned for the night. You're just the hired skivvy.'

'I lied.'

She narrowed her eyes. 'Typical.'

'Deep pan or thin'n'crispy?' He was leaning against the work surface holding the menu up in his left hand.

'Deep pan Meat-feast, then, with extra sweetcorn,' she said.

He nodded and walked into the lounge to use the phone.

Emma got up, walked over to the back window and gazed outside, deep in thought. It was completely dark now. How wonderful to have all this space, so much room to think and relax.

'Garden's a complete mess. I'm having a patio built.'

She turned. Jack was standing right next to her, a little too close. Maybe he sensed this as he walked away and leant against one of the kitchen units. After a few seconds Emma sat down at the table again. They both looked around the kitchen. She stood up. 'I'll just pop to the loo.'

He nodded.

'Which one should I use?'

'The closest is off the hall. I'll show you.'

'No. I'll find it.'

She walked out into the corridor, glad to be out of the room. She opened a couple of doors before finding the toilet.

Emma stared at herself in the mirror above the sink. She ran her hands through her hair puffing it up. There was a slight colour to her face, probably the wine. She should have gone straight to the hotel as planned. But sod it. It was only Jack, just a pizza. Enjoy it, she told herself.

Returning to the kitchen, classical music was playing in the background. Jack was still sitting on the work surface, glass in hand. She sat back down and took off her fleece, placing it on the back of her chair.

'Are you going to have a house-warming party?' she asked.

'Hardly know anyone in Dublin.' He paused then added, 'This is the house warming. You're the guest list.'

She smiled. 'Oh, I see. I'll try not to be too rowdy. Don't want the neighbours complaining.'

'Emma Hughes rowdy,' he said, sarcastically.

'It has been known.'

He looked amused and topped up her wine.

Eventually, the pizza arrived. Jack answered the door

and while running upstairs to get some Irish money, Emma heard the telephone ring in the lounge. She stood for several moments wondering if he had an extension upstairs and would answer it. When it continued to ring she went into the room and cautiously picked it up. 'Hello,' she said.

No one answered.

'Hello,' she said again.

'Who's that?' came the reply in a low, throaty voice.

'Oh. It's just Emma. Is that Rachel?'

'Working on a Sunday night? Committed of you.'

'Just having a look at the house. It's lovely,' she replied, in a friendly manner. 'Have you seen it yet?'

There was a lengthy pause. 'I've been all over the place, no time. In fact, I must come over soon. You and I should go out for a drink. I'm sure we have a lot to talk about.'

The invitation surprised Emma. What would they have in common? 'Yes, why not.'

'Good. Now, is he there?'

'I'll just get him, he's upstairs.'

Silence.

'Getting money,' added Emma, flustered. She didn't want Rachel getting the wrong idea. She hurried into the hall and found Jack paying the delivery man. 'Rachel's on the phone for you.' She thought he looked surprised, but he went and chatted to her with the door closed for about five minutes. He eventually joined Emma at the table and took a slice of pizza, saying nothing.

Halfway through eating she asked, 'Why don't you eat red meat?'

'People always ask this while they're eating it. I appear like some kill-joy when I answer their question.'

She nodded. 'True, but go on.'

'It's very unhealthy. Not just the fat but the chemicals they feed animals. We're the generation they're testing it on. Lots of unpaid guinea pigs. No thanks, I don't want it in my system.'

Emma's chewing slowed momentarily but then quickened and became quite exact.

'See, you've taken offence,' he said.

'No, I haven't.'

'You have. You're chewing like you're on display. Like some act of defiance.'

'No, I'm not.'

'It's true. You might not be aware of it. Body language never lies.'

She shifted in her chair. He noted her movements but refrained from saying anything.

'You're observing me now, double guessing what I'm thinking,' she said.

He shook his head, but couldn't help laughing a little. She laughed too. 'Is that how you knew about Trish and Steve? Body language?'

'Partly. Jeremy also mentioned it.'

'Jeremy?' she repeated, her smile diminishing. 'He shouldn't have told you that. Didn't think you spoke with Jeremy.'

'Of course we speak, usually have lunch a fair bit.'

'You and *Jeremy*?'

'Yes. Is that allowed?'

'Of course,' she said quietly, staring past him.

Jack took another slice of pizza. 'He's a lousy badminton player. Only goes for the beer afterwards.'

Emma's eyes narrowed and her voice hardened. 'You play badminton together?'

'With some persuasion. As I said, he mostly goes for the socialising afterwards.'

'Goes where?'

'We're members of the same club in Putney.'

She looked down at her pizza and was silent, unsure what to say. Jack stared at her, concerned and puzzled. 'Is something wrong?'

'No.'

He sipped his wine. 'Are you sure?'

'Just never knew you were that friendly.'

'Is that a problem?'

She sat back in her chair and slowly, unconvincingly, shook her head. Her thoughts were with Jeremy. He was the one who had named Jack the Pilgrim Father of Workaholics, plus a whole load of other names. Jeremy gave her the impression that at best, he and Jack barely tolerated each other. Why lie? An uneasy feeling started to descend on her. It made her wonder what Jeremy had been saying about her to Jack, and others. Maybe nothing, maybe everything. Jeremy knew the most intimate details about her and Tony. She cringed at the thought of Jack knowing her private business.

Jack eyed her suspiciously. There was an uneasy silence between them. She suddenly said, 'He doesn't talk about me, does he?'

'A bit paranoid, aren't you?'

She looked away towards the back window.

'I don't understand what's wrong. Jeremy's friends with everyone. He's out every night of the week. That's his personality. Are you claiming exclusivity?' he said.

She cast him an angry look.

'Look, we're not best buddies or anything. And we don't sit there conspiring against you. This is going over my head. Am I missing something?'

Emma continued to stare at him before slowly shaking her head. 'I'm sorry, you must think me very strange.'

Jack sipped his wine, saying nothing.

Emma tried to think of something to say to change the subject. She decided to finish her slice of pizza then politely make her excuses and leave. He went to top up her wine. 'No, I'm fine, thanks.'

He put the bottle back down and pushed his own glass away. She took a bite of her pizza and seemed to chew it for ages. 'I really like the house.'

He gave a nod of his head. The next moment he got up and flicked the kettle on. 'I'll have a coffee and drop you back. I believe you want to leave.'

She stared at him through puzzled eyes.

'Body language,' he stated.

## 18

Once in her hotel bedroom Emma made straight for the telephone and dialled Jeremy's number.

'Good evening, Jeremy speaking,' he answered, enthusiastically.

'Hi, it's me.'

'Emma darling, where are you?'

'Dublin, the hotel.'

'Bored, are you? Thought you'd give me a ring. Cheer you up.'

There was a moment of silence.

'No, Jeremy,' she replied, slightly distantly. Her tone wasn't lost on Jeremy.

'What's wrong?' he asked.

Emma bit her lip, unsure what to say.

'What's happened? Is everything OK?' he asked, sounding worried now.

'How friendly are you with Jack?'

'What? What do you mean?'

Her voice was calm, remaining distant. 'Just that. How friendly are you?'

'Not brilliantly. Tell me what's going on. This is weird. You sound really strange.'

'You have lunch together?'

'Occasionally.'

'You play badminton together. You're members of the same club.'

'I'm a member of a lot of clubs. Jesus, Emma, you're scaring me. What exactly has happened?'

Emma was feeling increasingly irritated. 'Over the years, we've had loads of conversations about Jack.'

'And?'

'I confided in you. You said lots yourself.'

'So?'

Her voice increased in pitch. 'Now I find out you and he are mates, drinking together, having a laugh at your club in Putney.'

'For God's sake, he's the London manager. I make sure I keep in with him. It could affect my career if I didn't. You know I've been wanting to become a partner for years.'

'But why didn't you tell me? That's what I don't understand. Why pretend? It's got me questioning things. At best you've misled me, at worse you've lied.'

'I never lied,' he stated. 'I just avoided telling you the details.'

'Same thing.'

'Look. I take the piss out of Jack, slag him off. Doesn't mean anything. He's all right really.'

'That's not the point,' she cried.

'Emma,' he said, with calm resolve. 'with the greatest respect, *get real*! We work in an office. Everyone slags everyone off. Bitching is the accepted pastime. It doesn't mean anything. Offices are more political than the House of Commons. It's a fact of life.'

Emma shook her head angrily. 'You're too flippant. All the things I've told you.'

'I'd never tell a soul about things that matter.'

'But that's it, Jeremy. Things *don't* matter with you. Everything's a joke. Nothing's real. My whole damn life, Tony, the lot. Like it's some episode out of a crummy soap opera.'

'It's just a bit of fun. Nothing more.'

She clenched her teeth. 'But why the pretence? I feel I can't trust you now.'

'Of course you can trust me. Why are we arguing over Jack Tomkinson?'

'Do you slag me off to him? Am I fair game?'

'Everybody's fair game. It's not personal, that's what I'm trying to say. What is up with you, Emma?' Jeremy started to sound annoyed himself. 'Can't you see you're really overreacting? Is there something else? You never get angry like this.'

That was it! The final straw. She screamed at the top of her voice, 'Jesus Christ! Will people stop telling me what I'm like. As if you all know me inside and out. Predictable Emma!'

Jeremy, for once, was silent. The only sound for several moments was Emma's heavy and stifled breathing.

'I'm sorry,' he said, sounding genuine. 'I'm sorry if you feel I've misled you.'

Emma closed her eyes, screwing her face up. Her head dropped forward into her hands, the phone still crooked between shoulder and chin.

'I have to go,' she said quietly. 'I have to go. I'll speak with you another time.'

She heard him protest at the other end, but she slowly replaced the receiver and fell back against her bed, lying flat out. She felt wound up but couldn't cry. In fact, a couple of minutes later she jumped up and marched over to the window. Opening it, she stuck her head out and breathed in deeply. Was she overreacting? She'd felt so irritable lately, against Tony, her parents and now Jeremy, suffocating and boxed in by their rigid, incorrect opinions of her. She gazed out across the city, relieved to be away from them all. *Is anyone as they seem?* Her thoughts turned to Jack. *Maybe he's more honest than all of us.*

Julia sat at her mahogany, oval dressing table thickly applying bright red lipstick. Once finished, she pressed her full lips against a tissue and stared pensively at her reflection in the mirror. Jeremy was pacing up and down her bedroom. 'I so hate it when we argue. Really disturbs me.'

She glanced over at him; his troubled face looked so sweet. 'Pour yourself a brandy or something – you'll wear holes in my new carpet.' Looking back at herself, she took a black eyeliner and continued to blatantly darken and define the outside of her eyes. 'Once the blinds are up, this room's done, although I'm not sure of the colour scheme any more. What do you think?'

He briefly looked around the large, L-shaped bedroom, with its selection of mahogany furniture, the blue carpet and peach walls. 'Yes, lovely Julia.' At that moment he didn't give a damn what it looked like. 'She takes things too seriously – overreacts. She's a goddamn walking conscience.'

'Why are you so upset?'

'Emma's my best friend. I hate letting her down. Says she can't trust me. That's *dreadful*.' Jeremy slumped down on the edge of the bed. It was a tall, deluxe king-size model and his feet barely touched the floor.

Julia swung around and stared at him. 'Jesus. What spell has she got you under?'

'I really care about her.'

'I can see . . . You're overreacting too, Jeremy. In a week it'll all be forgotten.'

He shook his head and sighed dramatically.

'Anyway, it's nearly time for me to leave,' she said.

'Can't you call in sick or something?'

'I need the money.'

'Oh go on, Julia. Wouldn't have come, but Thomas is away on some silly rally and so many of my other friends have gone and got themselves married, so

Sunday nights are out of bounds.' His shoulders drooped wearily.

Perplexed, Julia crossed her arms and frowned at him. 'I've never seen you like this. Where's the "life is for enjoying"? You said you never get down. Bloody *fraud*.'

'Don't *you* start on me. I'm upset because it's Emma. I've known her for years. We used to lodge together in Manchester before she married him, *Tony*.' He rolled his eyes. 'She's always been there for me. You don't know her – this could affect our relationship for ages. She's not flippant like us.'

'Speak for yourself.'

'You know what I mean.'

Julia stared back at her reflection. Her face was barely recognisable under the mass of make-up and her dark hair tied back in a tiny ponytail, ready to be covered with the blonde wig she wore when dancing at the club. Her eyes glanced downwards and she spotted a pack of cigarettes. She took one out and lit it. 'Thomas rang me, by the way.'

Jeremy looked up. 'When? Why?' he asked.

'Not sure. Persuaded me to meet up for a drink. I think he secretly wants to save my soul.' She grinned.

'I think saving the world would be easier.'

She jokingly glared at him, hands on hips. It made him smile, which pleased her.

'When are you meeting?' he asked.

'Thursday. Surprised he didn't mention it to you.'

He shrugged his shoulders. Julia took a couple more puffs of her cigarette then stubbed it out, wasting most of it. She stood up and picked up the large sports bag next to her bed. 'Sorry, but I really have to leave for work.'

'Take the night off. We'll go somewhere exciting and get drunk; my treat.'

'I told you, I need the money.'

He cradled his head in his hands. 'I could do with a friend right now.'

'But I'll get around two hundred tonight, probably more.'

'Oh, please, Julia?'

Slightly bewildered, she stood and stared at him. 'You really are upset about this, aren't you?'

He rolled his eyes again. 'That's what I've been trying to say.'

'You care about her a lot, don't you?'

As if suddenly shy, Jeremy just nodded then looked away.

Julia sighed and shook her head. 'OK. I'll call in sick.'

Jeremy smiled with relief. 'Thanks, Julia. Thanks.'

'I expect a very expensive dinner for this.'

'The very best, of course.'

She sat down at her dressing table and set about taking some make-up off. Looking at his reflection in the mirror, she said, 'Don't worry, I'll cheer you up in no time.' She winked. 'It's my forte, with men.'

They went for a late dinner to a new Italian restaurant in Clapham. As it turned out it wasn't that expensive, but they made up for it with the amount they drank, finishing off a bottle of wine each, followed by several liqueurs. Neither seemed to care that they had work tomorrow. Aided by the alcohol, they both spoke openly about their pasts and upbringings. Jeremy told her about his mother dying when he was eight and how he was sent to live with his spinster Aunt June. At first his father had visited at weekends, but when he remarried his visits became fewer and Jeremy rarely saw him now.

His Aunt June was eccentric to say the least. She was a committed member of the Salvation Army yet always had the company of different men in her bedroom.

'Maybe they were praying together,' laughed Julia.

'Extremely boisterous praying.'

It was gone one in the morning when they finally left the restaurant and headed back to Jeremy's apartment for a nightcap.

After several 'nightcaps', Julia held the Bailey's bottle upside down for several moments with a puzzled, absent look on her face. Eventually two tiny drops fell into her glass. She frowned and slowly managed to turn the bottle back upright, shaking it several times. 'Hey,' she shouted out indignantly.

'Hey what?' Jeremy slurred.

'Hey, you, you fool.' She started to giggle.

Jeremy casually lifted himself up on to his elbows. His bleary eyes inspected her. 'What are you "heying" about?'

'The Bailey's! There's none left.'

This new information took a few seconds to register with him. They had already finished his supplies of gin and vodka and were lying down on separate, adjacent blue couches, drinking and talking about the world, the universe and other small matters.

'Ouzo,' he shouted.

'Who's so what?'

'Ou-zo, you Philistine, from Greece. It's all that's left.'

Julia sat up excitedly. 'My glass is waiting.'

Jeremy slowly stumbled up and headed off in the direction of the kitchen, at one point holding on to the wall for support. He was gone for a good ten minutes. Julia, who was obviously better at holding her drink, got up and put on an old Cliff Richard LP. 'Devil Woman' came blaring out. She started to dance around his lounge singing along, 'Beware the devil woman, she's gonna get you.'

Jeremy returned carrying the bottle of ouzo and giggled at her exaggerated style of dancing. She was twirling around and around, waving her arms and swaying her hips like an Egyptian belly dancer. He slumped down on the sofa, watching her.

'Beware the devil woman, she's gonna get you, she's gonna get you.' She laughed loudly, unrestrained. 'That's me,' she yelled. 'I'm a devil woman!'

'No, you're not. Underneath that tough exterior, you're just a sweet little girl.'

Julia grinned, pulling a silly face at him. 'I'm the devil woman and I'm gonna get you,' she shouted, laughing boisterously, dancing wildly, making him the focus of her movements.

Jeremy poured two ouzos and sipped his own. He rubbed his head, which was beginning to ache.

As she sang, Julia pointed to him. 'I'm gonna get you.' Soon she fell into one of the dance routines from work, doing the steps she knew so well, pulling the provocative poses. She set off on another circular trip of his lounge. 'It's hot in here.' She tugged off her shirt, throwing it to the floor; underneath she wore only a black lace bra. Eventually she stood opposite him dancing on the spot.

Jeremy waved his hand dismissively. 'Cover up those things bouncing on your chest.'

She chanted, 'Beware the devil woman, I'm gonna get you, I'm gonna get you.'

He found himself caught up watching her – her every movement, every gesture and facial expression.

Knowing she had his complete attention, she smiled proudly, running her hands up the insides of her legs. 'See?' she shouted. 'Told you I'd cheer you up.'

He leant back on the sofa and smiled.

The song finished and uninspired by 'Living Doll',

which came on next, she flung herself down on the couch next to him, entwining one arm in his and giggling loudly. With the other hand she grabbed her glass of ouzo and sipped it several times. 'We can pretend we're in Greece on holiday. I'm dressed for the sun.'

'So I see. Just don't go for the all over body tan.'

'Maybe later.' She flashed him a wicked grin. 'We should go on holiday together. Should do lots of things together. We get on well.'

He nodded. She gazed up to the ceiling, sighing reflectively. The next moment she looked over at him. Her eyes stayed on him for some time. Sensing this he turned towards her and for a few seconds they just stared at each other. Everything stopped – even the drunken giggles and grins vanished under serious faces. Her questioning eyes examined his. He sat motionless, gazing back blank-faced. It was Julia who moved first. She slowly ran her index finger down the side of his round face and smiled. 'So, you're not going to marry me then?'

His only reaction was to raise one eyebrow. She laughed loudly. Jeremy smiled affectionately at her, dressed in her bra, messy, wild hair all over the place. Her bloodshot eyes still managed to sparkle. Very slowly he shook his head. 'Julia, if you were really out to marry someone for money, you would have done it by now. Face it, you're looking for love.'

She pulled a sulky face, nodded vaguely and gazed despondently off into the distance.

After several minutes of contemplative silence she turned back to him. 'Who have you loved, Jeremy?' she asked.

He shrugged his shoulders, but a shy, sort of half-smile appeared on his face.

'Who was it?' she persisted.

He looked away. 'No one. There's been no one.'

'You're lying. I can sense it.'

He grabbed his glass and took several gulps, screwing his face up. 'Not sure I even like this drink. Never tastes the same out of the country.'

'Who was it?' She put on a mocking German accent. 'Ve have vays of making you talk.'

Jeremy frowned and shifted uncomfortably on the sofa. 'How did we get on to this subject? It's extremely personal. I've never told a soul, not even the person.'

'So nothing happened?'

'Complications.'

'How can you love someone when nothing happened?'

'Well, that just shows how little you know of true love.'

Her eyes lit up. 'You're still in love, aren't you? And whoever it is doesn't even know. How sad! Oh who? Tell me. I won't tell anyone.' She was practically shaking him.

He rubbed his head again. He knew he should stop drinking, but instead topped up both their glasses. 'This will embarrass me dreadfully in the morning,' he mumbled.

'Why?' She frowned. 'So you're gay after all and it's Thomas. What's the big deal? Come out, there's no problem.'

'Come out! *Come out*?' He screwed his face up with genuine frustration, throwing his hands up in the air. 'Come out of what? I'm not bloody gay. Thomas is a dear friend but that's all. He's not gay either.'

Julia looked confused. 'It is a person, I presume, not some old family pet?' She laughed.

Jeremy gazed solemnly into the distance, gripping the glass in his hand tightly. 'Of course it's someone.'

'And they don't even know?'

'They must never know,' he said, glaring back at her. 'It would be awful. No future in it, you see.' He gulped at his drink, surprisingly sober all of a sudden.

'Why not?'

He shook his head. 'Just isn't.'

'Who the hell is it?' She grabbed her cigarettes and lit one.

Jeremy dropped his head into his hands, thinking, trying to decide. He rocked from side to side, his expression one of pain. Julia rolled her eyes; he was so over-dramatic at times.

'Why can't you tell me?' Her eyelids narrowed. 'Do I know them? Is that it?'

He stopped rocking, but said nothing.

'My *God*, I do, don't I! Who?' she squealed.

Again he didn't answer.

'If there's no future in it, she's probably married. If I know her, she must work for Buckley & Dwyer.' She drew hard on her cigarette, thinking. A bizarre grin started to emerge. She covered her mouth with her hand. 'Don't tell me it's bloody Emma.' She laughed, not really believing her own suggestion.

Jeremy stared ahead, looking faintly alarmed, but saying nothing.

'My God, it isn't, is it?' Again Julia laughed.

He glared at her. Her laughter stopped. He looked away, shoulders hanging heavily again, all the cheering up of the evening wasted.

Julia covered her mouth with her hand, completely shocked, part of her desperate to laugh. She shook her head slowly. 'Jeremy.' A burst of laughter threatened to erupt from her – yet seeing his sad, forlorn face, she calmed herself. She puffed on her cigarette, watching him, occasionally biting her lip. 'You're in love with Emma,' she stated loudly.

Jeremy shrugged his shoulders.

'How? I mean, you and . . . I can't believe it.'

'Your reaction says it all. It's a joke. Nothing will ever happen.' His eyes fixed on her and in a desperate, quite pathetic voice he said, 'Promise never to tell her. You do promise? . . . It would be *awful*.'

'Jesus, Jeremy . . . Look at you! You *should* tell her. I only laughed because . . . because,' she pulled an odd face, 'you don't seem that way. But if that's what you want, why not go for it?'

He slowly shook his head. 'She would never be happy with me. I could never make her happy. I'm just her odd, funny, flippant friend.' He sighed, eyes closing. 'Not that she'd ever leave Tony anyway. I just love her, OK? It's a feeling that will probably never be returned and nothing will ever happen. That's why she must never know. It would ruin everything. If she knew how I felt, our friendship would alter for ever. I've had to deliberately mislead her about not being interested in relationships full-stop, otherwise she'd never have let me get so close. She must *never* know. I wish I'd never said anything.' He leant back on the sofa gazing at the ceiling.

Julia took hold of his hand. 'Oh Jeremy.'

'Don't feel sorry for me.'

'But I do. How long have you loved her?'

'In a way, always.'

'That's sad.'

'Only sometimes. Most of the time I'm totally resigned to settling for a close friendship. Unfortunately, right now we don't seem to have even that.'

Julia cuddled him into her. He found his head resting against her bare chest, as she gently rocked him from side to side. 'Oh Jeremy,' she said. 'My poor Jeremy.'

## 19

'We've got to turn the power off for about forty minutes,' said one of the engineers installing the computer system the following morning in Dublin.

'Will it affect the phones?' asked Emma.

'Switch won't work. You could plug a handset into the fax line.'

Emma looked through the glass panel into Jack's office. He was talking on the phone and had been most of the morning.

'Can you hang on until Mr Tomkinson finishes his call?'

The engineer nodded.

As soon as Jack got off the phone Emma stood up and carefully picked her way over all the wires and boxes strewn across the floor. She knocked on Jack's door and waited.

'Come in,' he shouted.

She opened the door but deliberately didn't go in. 'Power's going off for forty minutes. We'll lose phones apart from the fax line.'

He nodded curtly. 'As long as it is only forty minutes. I need to make a number of calls this morning.'

'Should be.' She closed the door then returned to her desk. Picking up her pen, she sat biting the lid and gazing at her unconnected computer screen. Slowly her eyes travelled upwards to look through the glass panel of Jack's door again. His head was already back down in some papers. She sat for some time just staring at him, hoping she hadn't offended him last night.

Later that morning, Sean O'Brien turned up for another meeting with Jack. He'd accepted the job and was due to start the following Monday, but Jack had asked him in to discuss a few matters. He greeted Emma warmly as though they were old friends.

'So, where have you been in Dublin?' he enquired.

'Nowhere much. Just here and the hotel. Only flew over yesterday,' she replied.

'I'll have to change that,' he grinned and went into Jack's office.

At two o'clock, Teresa from the caterers arrived for her meeting with Emma concerning the launch party. She was a fairly plump, red-headed woman in her fifties with a smiley face and a broad Dublin accent. They chatted for nearly an hour about the arrangements and menu for the evening.

'Work on fifty guests,' said Emma. 'I'll confirm exact numbers a couple of days before the 23rd. Still waiting on some replies.'

'If it goes over fifty you'll need an additional waitress. I'll put that in a revised quotation.'

'If anything, it'll be less. Probably be some no shows on the night.'

'Don't bank on it over here. The Irish like a party. They'll show.'

Emma smiled and picked up her spreadsheet costing. After checking a couple of figures, she made an amendment in pen on the form. 'OK, add another one in.'

'You also need to increase the quantity on the drinks side.'

'Really? Surely that's plenty?'

Teresa raised an eyebrow and shook her head.

'It's supposed to be a relaxed drinks reception, not some wild party,' said Emma.

'I accept that,' Teresa replied, 'but if you don't want the evening to bomb, keep the alcohol flowing. On these amounts it could run out.'

Emma eyed her suspiciously. 'You really think so?'
'It's best to be safe.'

They discussed the issue at some length and eventually Emma agreed reluctantly to increase the order. She wondered how she was going to justify it to Jack.

With the computer system fully operational, late that afternoon Emma went to type an e-mail.

```
Dear Trish,

Hi. We have lift off! Dublin is On-line.

Missing me yet? So pleased you're coming
to help at the launch party - should be
fun. Just finished ordering the
champagne! We'll save a bottle for the
hotel afterwards.

I'm already missing our coffee breaks.
Rosemary doesn't start until next week.

Take care and e-mail me soon.
Emma.

PS See you in three weeks
```

At five-thirty, Jack's door opened. Emma looked up.

He was wearing a raincoat and carrying his briefcase. He walked over to her.

'There's a couple of lengthy documents on that,' he said, handing her a dictation tape. 'I'm afraid I need them ready for faxing by ten tomorrow morning. An urgent case has come up in London.'

Sounding polite, if a little unfriendly, Emma asked,

'Is plain paper OK? Letterheads won't be here until Wednesday.'

'Have to be.' He turned to leave but looked back at her and stated firmly, 'Don't think I'm swanning off somewhere, leaving you working away. I'm meeting that client who rang in earlier.'

She nodded, surprised he was accounting for his movements to her.

'See you tomorrow. Have a nice evening,' he said.

'Goodnight,' she said. 'And you.'

The following day, at the office, her computer bleeped indicating an incoming e-mail. She instantly recognised the sender ID; it was Jeremy's. Nervously she brought the message up.

```
Dear Emma,

Are you talking to me? I hope you are.
I'm sorry. (Times sorry by one million
times.) I suppose I did mislead you — I'm
not sure why.

It may have something to do with me being
a shallow, superficial, frivolous,
flippant, trite bastard at times.

I've been hard pushed to think of what
redeemable characteristics I have and
also what I value in this crazy world.
Your friendship is what I value.

Please forgive me,
Love Jeremy.
```

He'd addressed her 'Dear Emma.' He must be worried. She read it again, trying to work out how she felt and what, if anything, to write back. Right now she was busy. She'd have a think about it later.

On Wednesday afternoon at four, Emma picked up the working document plus some other files and got up from her desk. She approached Jack's office. His door was open and as she stood in the entrance he immediately looked up.

'That time already?' he asked.

"Fraid so.'

Jack set about clearing his desk. Emma went in and sat down opposite him, well-prepared for the latest update meeting. She watched him put all his papers neatly away in their folders, every page placed in the correct order. Two pencils were put back in his drawer. Even some loose paperclips got individually picked up and placed in their box. For some reason she found herself fighting a growing smile. He was quite comical at times.

He looked up at her. She quickly bit her lip and looked away.

'Shall we start?' he asked.

Emma handed him a copy of the latest budgets. She gave him a verbal summary of how each item was proceeding. Everything went well until they came to discuss the launch party. Seeing her order requisition for the drinks he exclaimed loudly, '*How much?*'

'Teresa says any less and we'll run short.'

Jack frowned and ran his finger down the list of items.

'Apparently that's how it is over here,' she added.

'Run short! They'll all be paralytic!'

Maybe it was the way he said it, or the odd mixture of shock and bafflement on his face, but it tickled her sense of humour and she found herself laughing out loud. She covered her mouth with her hand and tried to compose herself. Jack cocked his head at her before looking back down at the figures. He said in all seriousness, 'I've been on some mad rugby weekends and even we haven't drunk that much.'

Emma desperately tried to keep a straight face, but the thought of Jack on a mad rugby weekend started her off again. Her head dropped forward slightly and she was viciously biting her bottom lip. It was no good; a sudden burst of laughter erupted out of her. Jack eyed her dubiously.

'Sorry, not sure what's come over me,' she said, pulling a serious face again. 'I know it seems like a lot, but Teresa is convinced it's needed. It would be awful to run short.'

'Well, if Teresa is convinced, than make her agree, in writing I might add, to refund us full price for every unopened bottle that we return to them.'

'Already done.' Emma handed him a piece of paper.

While he read it, she couldn't help returning to the thought of Jack on a mad rugby weekend. All the rugby players she knew were totally wild, dropping their trousers for the least little dare. Maybe Jack was the referee? Again, she fought the urge to laugh.

They continued to discuss various other issues. Jack signed a couple of cheques she had prepared for suppliers and he approved her latest expense claim. She gave him a copy of the 'Training and Introduction Plan' she'd drawn up for Rosemary, which covered the first two weeks of her employment. Thinking they had finished she picked up her remaining files.

'One more thing,' he said.

She waited.

'Paintings,' he stated.

Emma sat back in her chair and smiled, wondering what he was going to say.

He seemed to hesitate then said in a matter-of-fact way, 'Decided the Prendergast paintings wouldn't look too bad in reception. I'll order a couple more copies tomorrow.'

She looked away. If her eyes met his she knew she would collapse in laughter. It took all her concentration to keep control. She managed to give one nod of her head and quickly stood up to leave. In a pathetic attempt to hide her laughter she pretended to cough. It was no good; she burst out laughing and held her stomach as if in pain. She looked back at him and shook her head, laughing even louder.

He sat staring at her, smiling broadly at the state she was in. 'By the way, keep tomorrow night free.'

Emma regained some control, intrigued by his comment.

He paused for several seconds. 'Sean's asked us to have dinner with him and his wife Kelly. Sort of a welcome to Ireland, show us the town.'

'That's nice of them.'

'Expect you'll like her. She's a legal secretary too.'

'Oh, *bound* to. We can talk about page margins and Post-It notes!'

He threw her a wry grin. 'Just up your street then.'

She glared at him. This time it was Jack who started to laugh, but he quickly stopped himself, looking back down into some papers with a muffled sort of throat-clearing sound.

## 20

'It's so quiet without you,' said Trish, eating a tuna sandwich.

Emma smiled and offered her a crisp.

'Looks like you're enjoying it here,' she added.

'I am,' said Emma firmly.

'You are coming back, aren't you?'

'To live I suppose, but I'm gonna leave Buckley & Dwyer once I get something else.'

'What does Tony think of that?'

Emma stopped chewing. 'I'll tell him when it's sorted.'

'Couldn't he come tonight? Thought partners were invited too,' Trish asked, changing tack.

'Didn't mention it. Not sure he would have anyhow.'

The two women sat on a bench in Pearse Square, a small rectangular green a short walk from the Dublin office. They were casually dressed in jeans and jumpers, as they had been setting up the rooms for the launch party that evening. It was an unusually sunny day for the end of March and they had decided to eat their lunch outside.

'After the plane incident, he wanted me to pull out,' continued Emma, 'as if I could at that stage.' She shook her head angrily. 'Last three weekends he's swung from being Mr Ideal Husband, doting on me, flowers at the airport, to being completely distant and moody, insisting I still pull out. It's doing my head in. I hardly saw him last weekend. He was out shooting most of Sunday, so I just did my washing and ironing . . . refused to do his. He left a big pile for me! Can you believe it? The house was in a right state. Like I'm gonna spend my weekends clearing up after him.' Emma sighed wearily. 'Don't know why I went back. I'm thinking of staying in Ireland the weekend after this.'

'Really? What will you do?'

'Lots. Walking in the Wicklow Mountains.'

'On your own.'

'I might go with Jack,' she answered, matter of factly.

Trish glanced sideways at her. 'You seem to be getting on well,' she observed.

Emma shrugged her shoulders, 'OK, I suppose.'

'I couldn't believe how you spoke to him this morning,' Trish continued. 'Then taking the piss out of his designer jeans.'

'He laughed, didn't he?'

'Exactly! What's happened to him?'

Remembering the incident that morning, Emma smiled broadly. She zipped up her fleece; it wasn't as warm as it had appeared. 'What about you? Anything exciting happening in Manchester?'

Trish seemed to hesitate before looking off into the distance. 'Just ticking along.'

Emma sensed that something was wrong. She'd felt it at the airport that morning. 'Is everything OK?' she asked, concerned.

Trish presented a smile. 'Of course.' She took another bite out of her sandwich. Her smooth complexion was flawless, yet even the concealer make-up couldn't fully hide the dark shadows under her eyes.

'If there was something wrong,' said Emma, 'please feel you could speak to me. I know . . .' She ran her hand through her hair, '. . . the Christmas party. I wasn't very . . . well, I said all the wrong things. I was a judgemental bitch.'

'You weren't.'

'I was,' Emma insisted, then added in a serious, sombre voice, 'I've been on the receiving end.'

'Tony?'

Emma shook her head. 'No, an old boyfriend. We went out for two years. Turns out he was seeing someone else for months. It felt like someone had gone through my whole body with a razor blade.' She shuddered at the memory.

'I'm sorry, that's awful. But you do know this is different, don't you?'

'That's what I'm saying. Every situation is. Who knows what will happen? It's no one's place to judge.' She beamed a warm, compassionate smile across at Trish.

'I'm pregnant,' stated Trish.

Emma's warm smile vanished. '*Pregnant!*'

Trish nodded.

'Shit! How?'

'It wasn't planned, if that's what you mean.'

Emma stared at Trish, totally stunned. 'You're quite sure?' she asked, finally.

'Yes,' Trish said quietly.

'How long?'

'Six weeks.'

Emma took a moment to digest it. 'What's going to happen?'

Trish stood up and threw the remains of her sandwich in the bin beside the bench. Sitting back down she replied, 'I'm booked in Monday.'

'Abortion?'

Trish screwed her face up. 'Hate that word.'

Emma bit her lip and sat silently for a moment. In a cautious, delicate voice she said, 'You've made your mind up then?'

Trish gave a slight nod of her head.

'You're quite sure?'

'Is anyone, ever?' Her young pretty face, usually so vibrant, in that moment was rather lifeless, anaesthetised. Footsteps came up behind them.

'Sorry to disturb you.'

Both women looked around and saw Rosemary, the new secretary, approaching.

'The caterers are here, setting up the tables . . . I think in the wrong place. I'm not sure. Jack said to get you.'

'I'll be back in five minutes,' said Emma.

Rosemary nodded and set off back down the path towards the office. As soon as she was out of earshot Emma asked, 'And Steve? What does he say?'

Trish's eyelids flickered. 'It's for the best, Emma. He can't leave Sarah right now, not with James so young. He says we've got to wait until he's older.'

Emma wanted to ask how much older but managed to restrain herself and instead nodded sympathetically. Both women sat there, gazing across the small green, quiet with their thoughts.

A little while later, Emma squeezed Trish's arm. 'Sorry, but we'd better get back. We'll talk later, after the party, in the hotel. It'll be all right . . . Whatever you decide, it'll be OK.'

Trish stood up and said firmly, 'I've already decided. I'm not a heartless bitch but I don't want a child right now, with or without Steve.' She sighed heavily and said in a softer voice, 'I shouldn't have told you. It's easier not to talk about it. It'll be over soon.'

Emma put an arm around her. 'Can I do anything? Anything at all?'

Trish shook her head and after a moment, pulled free. 'I'm not the little victim in this.'

'I know.'

'Do you?'

Emma stared at her, confused. Trish spoke defiantly. 'I made some choices, so I'll take what consequences there are. At least I take responsibility for my actions. I lied at the Christmas party, to myself also. It didn't "just happen" with Steve. Nothing *just* happens. People make things happen. I wanted Steve. I chased him, not the other way round.'

Emma's eyes widened.

'I wanted you to know that,' said Trish, in a calmer manner.

'I'm not sure what I'm supposed to say.'

'Say nothing. I just wanted you to know, that's all.' She looked down the path. 'Come on, we'd better get back.'

At first, they walked in silence, through the park and along the street. Emma was thinking about what she'd heard. She admitted to herself that she had seen Trish as a victim in this, but why? Because she was a woman? Deliberately to change the subject, Trish said in a cheerful voice, 'Rosemary seems nice.'

'Yes, she is.'

'And Sean. He seems nice too.'

'Yeah, he's lovely. We've all been out a few times, him, his wife Kelly, me, Jack and recently Rosemary.'

'Getting any work done over here?' Trish asked mock sarcastically.

Emma rolled her eyes. 'Loads! Jack and I are often in the office until eight.'

Trish smiled. A little further down the street she stopped to look into a shop window. It was as if the earlier conversation hadn't taken place.

Just after six, Emma and Trish were getting ready in the ladies toilet upstairs on the third floor. Trish had curled the ends of Emma's hair with her heated tongs and was admiring her work. 'You look quite glamorous.'

Emma laughed. She was wearing a long, clinging, blue knitted dress with her new Celtic design earrings and necklace. 'Come on, we'd better show our faces.'

The two women descended the stairs into the offices of Buckley & Dwyer and went and stood with Rosemary. The open-plan section, which included the reception area, had had all the tables and partitions removed. This was where the guests would stand and mingle and was surprisingly very spacious. The buffet spread was laid out in Jack's office and the other two glass-partitioned offices had been turned into a cloak-room and bar. Two waitresses and a waiter stood ready to offer the guests champagne on their arrival.

Jack, dressed in his business suit, walked over to the women. 'Just wanted to thank you three. All ready with an hour to spare.' He disappeared off to speak with Harold. Trish shot an odd glance in Emma's direction. 'He's even thanking us now. There must be something in the water over here.'

Various staff from Buckley & Dwyer were there to show support for the launch of the new branch, Harold and two other partners, Robert Middleton and Geoff Summers along with their respective spouses. Jeremy was also there. In the last two weeks he'd sent Emma a bunch of flowers, a box of chocolates and three e-mails, all stating how sorry he was. They'd spoken a couple of times, but she still felt uneasy towards him. Emma spotted him chatting to Sean and his wife, Kelly.

At that moment, Jeremy saw her and walked towards her, indicating that she should meet him halfway. She left her group and went over.

'You look amazing.'

'Thank you,' she said politely.

'You are talking to me then,' he said, in a soppy voice.

'You know I am.'

'Good, because I'm running out of ways to say sorry.'

'I thought we agreed to forget it.'

As if doing just that, his eyes suddenly lit up. Bursting with suppressed energy, his body was almost jumping on the spot. 'I have great news,' he said excitedly.

'If it's gossip, I don't want to know.'

'It isn't. It's about me. Fantastic news, the very best.'

Emma eyed him suspiciously.

He blurted the words out at speed, hands gesticulating wildly. 'Finally, and long overdue I might add, I've been asked to become a partner. Harold asked me last week. Richard Hayes also. Should all be arranged by the next partners' meeting. Jeremy Masters, a partner! I shall have to get a better car.'

'I'm pleased for you, Jeremy. You've worked hard for it.'

'That all you can say? No kiss and massive embrace?'

'Hardly appropriate here,' she said.

Jeremy was beaming proudly. His dancing eyes glistened victoriously. 'Now Henry's pretty much gone, Harold is starting to exert his own stamp on things. Winds of change are blowing. I've heard the practice might be totally restructured.'

Emma stood listening to the possible changes but wasn't interested in any of it. He could have been going on about a stamp collectors' club in Outer Mongolia for all the relevance she felt it had to her. *What's up with me*, she wondered.

'Sorry Jeremy, but I have to go and check on the food. Speak to you later,' she said, heading off towards Jack's office.

Jeremy stood and watched her walk away, crestfallen. When she was out of sight, his stare slowly drifted downwards. He eventually moved off to rejoin the others, immediately offering them all a broad smile.

On entering the office, Emma found Harold and Jack deep in conversation. She sensed a tension between them. Harold looked over at her. 'Would you mind leaving us, Emma? Shan't be long.'

She nodded and quickly exited the room, shutting the door behind her, wondering what was going on.

Inside the office, Jack stood by the buffet, one hand on the table, the other by his side. Harold stood a few feet from him. He was a well-built man, tall, in his mid-fifties, with a mass of brown curly hair – a man of consistency rather than being very dynamic. But he had waited, held back and allowed the others to run ahead and set the pace. And now, twenty years after joining the company, it was he who was finally out front.

'Impressive offices, but rather on the large side,' he said, frowning slightly, which made his thick eyebrows join in the middle.

Jack looked at him steadily. His mind was alert, equipped to catch anything Harold might throw his way. The two men had a certain respect for each other, mixed with a fair amount of distrust.

'Yes, impressive,' said Jack, refusing to justify the square footage.

Harold cleared his throat. 'I've been working on some ideas, changes, which—'

'Oh really?' Jack interjected.

'Hang fire, Jack, let me finish before you come storming in.' Harold put down his glass of champagne. 'I'm giving a presentation next Thursday at the partners' meeting. But I wanted to leave something with you first, let you mull it over. I'll warn you, you won't like it. But I have to put the best interest of the practice first. That's my job as head partner.'

Jack went to lean against the pillar by the table, arms

folded, staring directly at him, waiting. Harold glanced away, but spoke solidly, with conviction.

'Dublin was Henry's dream, never mine. We're here now and I think we should have representation here for our international clients. However, I see Dublin as being a small satellite office. Expansion is not an option. Two solicitors max and one admin person.' He shot a wary look across at Jack. 'I was surprised you accepted this position.'

'The position I wanted was gone. Henry asked me, I felt I owed it to him.' Jack stood up straight. 'So, is that it? Alter the business plan for Dublin and return to London? I couldn't go for at least three months.'

'No, I'm afraid that's not it.' Harold cleared his throat again. 'London generates the most income, it has the greatest client base, some exceptional solicitors and consultants, and yes, I know a lot of that is due to you.' He gave one nod of his head in Jack's direction. 'Seems obvious London should be the head office, expand it further. Manchester, Birmingham and now Dublin will just be satellite branches. We'll need to cut some costs, probably staff; it may involve moving Manchester to a smaller office. London will become the hub.'

Jack looked on suspiciously. 'And?'

'I, as head partner, should be based there.'

'You? London?'

'Yes.'

'Managing it?' Jack's tone adopted just a hint of mockery.

'Of course.' There were five seconds of silence, before Harold continued. 'The way I see it you have a number of choices . . .'

'Which are?' Jack asked.

'You could manage any of the other offices.'

Jack stood motionless, tall and proud, with an air of defiance.

'Or you could stay at London, working on cases and generating new business. You really are excellent in that area. But I would manage the branch, its staff, the business and control the direction of the practice.'

In a contemptuous yet controlled manner Jack said, 'I built London. I control it. It works. It doesn't need you.'

'I note your opinion, but it's not your decision.'

'The partners won't vote for this.'

Harold picked up his champagne glass and calmly took a sip. 'I don't anticipate a problem there.'

To the onlooker, Jack remained calm and composed, yet his eyes temporarily flickered with the realisation. 'So, you've already been campaigning.' He let out a dismissive laugh. 'Is it already in the bag or is it worth me launching a last-minute fight?'

'I'm hardly the person to advise you on that.'

'You want it all, Harold. How interesting! How times change. Inept of me not to keep my ear to the ground and watch my back. Must have been quite handy having me out of the way.'

'A bit over-dramatic. It's just business, Jack. You of all people should understand that,' said Harold.

Jack picked up his glass and raised it towards Harold. 'Forgive me. Obviously the gentlemanly thing to say is, "Let the best man win".' He gulped the remainder of his champagne down in one go. 'If you'll excuse me, I believe some guests may be arriving. Until next week.' He turned and walked out.

Emma was standing with Kelly and Rosemary, arranging to go to the theatre next week. A few guests arrived early but Sean and the partners were tending to them, doing their PR bit about the firm. Every so often, she glanced through the gaps between the plants and the people, trying to catch a glimpse of Jack and Harold in the office.

Suddenly, the door opened and Jack marched full speed across the room. Emma was in his path and quickly stepped to the side. His eyes, wild and incensed, met hers. He carried on past her, out the main reception door. She watched him go and fought the urge to go after him.

Kelly, oblivious to the little scene said, 'Supposed to be really funny, my brother saw it a couple of weeks ago.'

'Really?' said Emma, vaguely.

'Yes, Sean can organise the tickets.'

Emma nodded but kept one eye on Harold. He came out of the room and was immediately approached by Robert Middleton, the other senior partner. Both gentlemen spoke for several moments in close proximity to each other, their expressions stern and circumspect.

Jack was out of the room for twenty minutes. Emma knew this because she had checked her watch just before he returned. Displaying his usual confident manner he went and introduced himself to various people, chatting and smiling.

By eight o'clock nearly forty guests had arrived, slightly fewer than expected. It was just as well, as the room was full; any more and it would have been uncomfortable. The din of conversation drowned out the background music. Emma continued to observe Jack discreetly from a distance, suspicious that something was happening; not that his composure gave much away. The only clue was the amount of champagne he was drinking. When mixing with clients, he normally kept the consumption of alcohol to a minimum; it was an unwritten rule he impressed on all staff. Yet each time the waiter offered to top up his glass, he accepted without hesitation.

Rosemary approached Emma and asked to have a word. Emma followed her, weaving in and out of the guests, into Jack's office where the buffet was.

'Caterers want to know if they should take around the canapés?' she said.

Emma checked her watch. 'Tell them, yes. Get them to turn the music up a fraction too. And are you OK? I feel I've deserted you a bit.'

'No, I'm grand thanks.'

'Seems to be going well. Everyone is really friendly.'

Rosemary smiled. 'Free drink, why wouldn't they be?' She went off to find the head waitress.

Alone in the room, Emma spotted the mushroom vol-au-vents. She hadn't eaten since lunch. She went over, peeled back the cellophane slightly and quickly put a whole one in her mouth.

'Caught you.'

She turned. It was Jack. Her mouth was too full to speak. She chewed vigorously to clear it.

'Calm down, you'll choke yourself.' He went over to the vol-au-vents and took one himself, biting it in half.

'Starving,' Emma eventually said.

Jack half sat against the table, champagne in one hand, half-eaten vol-au-vent in the other. 'Same here. It's hungry work being sociable.'

'Don't you enjoy it?'

He grimaced, then ate the rest of the vol-au-vent. 'You seem to be enjoying yourself,' he said. 'One man mentioned what a charismatic secretary I had.'

'Who?'

'Daniel Flanagan.'

'He's not bad looking.'

Jack tutted, and took a sip of champagne. 'Don't you have a drink?'

'Don't want one.'

He looked at her. She faced him, staring back. Without embarrassment, Jack continued to hold her gaze. Emma dropped hers. She took a step forward and covered the vol-au-vents back up. 'Is everything OK?' she asked.

He didn't answer.

She stood back a couple of steps and said more cautiously, 'Just earlier, you looked kind of angry . . . something like that.'

His eyes slowly left her and gazed out through the glass panelling. 'No, everything isn't OK,' he said quietly.

Emma looked up at him.

'Actually it's pretty shit.' He finished off his champagne and took out a new bottle from a cooler box under the table. He set about opening it. 'Harold, friendly old Bagpuss, has turned into . . .' he paused, thinking of a person to compare him with. It suddenly came to him. '*Me!*'

'What's happened?'

Jack answered in an almost theatrical voice, his hands gesticulating in an exaggerated manner, more like Jeremy than himself. 'Demotion, Emma. Harold wants to run London. Wants it as the head office. I'm just an average Joe now. A well paid average Joe, of course, he can't touch that.'

Emma stood completely still, shocked by the news but also by his unusual manner. 'Can't you fight him?'

'My first reaction, of course. No doubt it will be my reaction tomorrow too, but right now . . .' He refilled his glass. 'I think "what the hell", he can have it; have it all. They can all have it, the lot, everything, wife, head partner and now,' he let out a contrived laugh, 'my job. My goddamn job.' His head dropped forward. After several moments of complete silence, he said quietly, despondently, 'I'm travelling backwards, Emma. Like a dream, running against an impossible wind, ending up back at the beginning. Jesus, I'm sick of running.'

Emma moved a step closer towards him, unsure what to say or do. He viewed her face fully, looking up at him, the concern in her eyes. He focused on the movement of her mouth as she spoke. 'I'm sorry, Jack. I really am. I know what it means to you. You must be feeling really shitty.'

He smiled warmly. 'Really shitty. I bet that's the worst word you've said in a long time, "shitty". I bet you never say "fuck".'

She withdrew, eyes wide, eyebrows raised in surprise.

'You're boxed in by constraints. We both are. Damn, fucking, shitty, go on. Surprise me. Say it,' he said.

Uncertain how to interpret him, she said guardedly, 'Damn fucking shitty. Does that make you feel better?'

He laughed aloud. 'Even your swearwords sound so polite.' He carried on laughing, only pausing to gulp some more champagne.

'If you're going to have a breakdown, should I run and get some valium, maybe a doctor? I've a first aid certificate, will that help?'

'No!' he bellowed, suddenly serious. 'Let me have my breakdown. Let me fall apart for a while and be goddamn reckless, fucking reckless. Let's not miss out that word. Maybe I'll do all the things I want to do. Take a gamble.' Lunging forward suddenly, he grabbed hold of both her shoulders, pulling her towards him. His face was barely two inches from hers. In a whisper he said, 'Be reckless with me . . . take a gamble too.'

Emma stood immobilised, gawping at him. Her mouth moved as if to speak. No words came. She probed his face for something more, another clue, confirmation. Jack's breathing was heavy. His pained eyes stared intensely back at her. He leant further forward. Emma's eyelids narrowed. Her legs stepped backwards of their own accord.

As if in slow motion his arms floated downwards, away, graceful in retreat. They looked at each other. Neither moved. Neither spoke.

The noise of the party swept in as the door opened to reveal Jeremy. Both their heads turned and gazed at him. The next moment Rachel stepped out from behind him.

'Here you are,' she said, in her distinctive voice. She breezed up to Jack and kissed him once on the lips.

Jack didn't move.

'A surprise, darling. I was able to come after all.' She turned and viewed Emma. 'Hello again.' She smiled, revealing the amazing white teeth. Emma stared at her. Her gaze travelled slowly and cautiously back to Jack. Their mutually disturbed eyes met. Rachel looked on, her full lips narrowing slightly.

'I'll check . . . the wine,' stammered Emma, as she turned stiffly and walked out.

Jeremy left Jack and Rachel alone in the office and went back out to the party. He stood for a moment, partly looking for Emma, but also trying to decide which group of people looked the most interesting, and therefore worth approaching. Harold appeared by his side. Jeremy smiled and said in a jovial manner, 'The Irish certainly know how to enjoy themselves.'

Harold frowned. 'One wonders how much actual business we'll get from this.'

In keeping with Harold, Jeremy's facial expression

grew more serious. 'Hmmm. Jack seems confident that all the right people are here.'

Harold suddenly smiled. 'I'm glad we're finally making you a partner . . . and Richard, of course. It's well deserved.'

'Thank you. We're certainly both pleased and honoured.'

Harold leant forward. 'As I mentioned before, there may be a number of issues which will be put to the partners over the next few weeks. I'm sure I can count on your vote.'

'Definitely. I'm sure it's in the best interests of the practice.'

'Of course.' Harold nodded and walked away before any further discussion followed.

Upstairs in the ladies toilet, Emma stood gazing at her reflection. The curl had already fallen out of her hair. She leant back against the tiled walls, closing her eyes and sighing heavily. After a moment she touched her left shoulder. Her eyes opened. *What the hell happened?* Surely Jack hadn't . . . ? Slowly her back slid down the wall, until she was crouching down. She buried her head in her knees. *Oh, God . . .*

Downstairs, Jeremy had finished off another glass of champagne and was standing at the side, still deciding which group of people to join. He wished he could have a laugh with Emma but she was nowhere to be seen. He also knew that she wouldn't be in the mood to laugh with him for a while yet. She was acting so strangely recently, extra touchy. It was a shame that Julia hadn't been asked to come over and help out. You could always rely on having a laugh with her. With Emma away he'd spent an increasing amount of time with both Julia and Thomas – even attending a few protest marches and fundraisers for some of Thomas' pressure groups. He and Julia only really went along as a favour, and of course for the pub afterwards.

After a few minutes, Jack left his office, followed by Rachel. Seeing Jeremy alone, they made straight for him. 'You look a bit lost, Jeremy.'

'Not at all. Just taking a breather.'

Rachel gave him one of her smiles.

Jack said, 'Wondered if you'd mind looking after Rachel this evening. You know what it's like, supposed to chat to everyone tonight. Won't have much time.'

'Ignore him, Jeremy. I'm hardly a social Neanderthal. I can mingle very successfully on my own.'

'Wouldn't hear of it,' said Jeremy. 'You would be doing *me* the pleasure.'

Jack nodded and walked away. Jeremy noticed Rachel's empty hand. 'My goodness! You don't even have a drink yet.'

Eyes narrowed, Rachel watched Jack disappear into the crowd. 'No, I'm feeling most ignored.'

'Wait there,' he said, and went off to find the nearest waitress.

After a noticeable absence, Emma returned. She immediately helped herself to a glass of champagne and spotted Jeremy and Rachel standing in the corner. Her eyes left them and travelled across the room. Trish smiled at her from the opposite corner. Emma smiled back at her but then caught sight of Jack, chatting to two women from Rancorn plc. She quickly looked away. On the spur of the moment, she made a beeline for Daniel Flanagan, the man who had called her charismatic. He was chatting to two other gentlemen, but all three warmly welcomed her approach.

As the evening progressed, Emma drank more champagne, yet felt annoyingly sober, and the onset of a nagging headache. Occasionally she dared a glance at

Jack or Rachel. They stood separately for a lot of the evening. Three times Emma's eyes met with Jack's. She immediately looked away, as did he. Each time she saw or heard Rachel laughing, a wave of anger swept over her. The men swooned around Rachel, waiting for any titbit of attention thrown their way, like scavenging seagulls. What the hell was Jack playing at? She found herself incensed with it all, furious with him. 'Be reckless with him. Take a gamble!' *Does he think I'm a fool?* she seethed.

A little while later, Emma helped herself to a coffee. Turning around, she found Rachel by her side, staring at her with an unusually serious expression.

'So how is Dublin agreeing with you?' Rachel asked.

'It's agreeing very much.'

'Strange thing, being away from home. Easy to forget . . .'

Emma eyed her suspiciously, unsure how to reply.

Rachel just smiled. 'You must be missing Tony terribly.'

'I see him at weekends. Why? Are you missing Jack?'

'Of course, but recently he's seemed so preoccupied with something. Do you know what?'

'He seems fine to me. There's been a lot of work on recently, maybe that's it.'

Rachel's eyes narrowed and focused sharply on Emma. In a grave manner she said, 'So there's nothing I need to concern myself with?'

'I wouldn't know. I just work for him.' Emma walked away.

The evening went slowly on. It was supposed to end at around ten-thirty, eleven at the very latest – the invitations had clearly stated 'drinks reception'. However by twelve o'clock, at least fifteen guests were still there, very drunk and loud. Daniel and the other two gentlemen Emma had talked to had left some time before. Since then, she had chatted mostly to Trish, either upstairs in the ladies or at the back of the temporary cloakroom. Tired and feeling redundant, they just wanted to head back to the hotel. Emma had let Rosemary leave half an hour before.

'Shame we can't go ourselves. Harold and Geoff are gone,' said Trish, sitting on the floor in between the coat rails.

'You can go . . . Expect I'm supposed to stay, though,' said Emma, sitting down beside her.

'No, I'll wait with you. Keep you company.'

At that moment, the door opened and underneath the row of coats they saw some legs glide in. They recognised the black stilettos, and nylon stockings as Rachel's. Emma and Trish shot an odd glance at each other, but neither got up. In fact, they were both hoping Rachel wouldn't see them down on the floor. They silently watched the legs walk up and down, twice. Trish fought a fit of the giggles.

'Oh, there you are,' said Rachel, parting the coats and peering down at them. 'You'll be glad to know that everyone is heading off now, some casino that Sean knows. We'll be out of your way in no time. Let you get on with the clearing up.' She graced them with one of her smiles.

Emma and Trish just stared up at her. Emma caught sight of another pair of legs in the doorway.

'Feel bad leaving you here while we're off having fun. Suppose it's your job as secretaries,' said Rachel, smiling again, so sweetly, so insincerely.

It was Trish who stood up first. 'Actually Rachel, we're bored shitless. Stuffing black rubbish bags will be a treat.'

As she started saying it, Jack walked in. Emma immediately got up.

'You're both invited of course,' he said, glancing disapprovingly at Rachel.

Defiantly, Emma shook her head. In a cold, inflexible voice she said, 'No thank you. Gambling doesn't appeal to me.'

Jack stood for a moment, regarding her. In the same pointed manner she'd used, he said, 'It does to me,' and turned and left.

## 21

'Kelly, the Roulette Queen!' exclaimed Jeremy. 'She won two hundred pounds! Sweetie bought the drinks after that. Even Sean came away sixty quid up.' Suddenly his face looked glum. 'Moi, lost ninety pounds.' He was sitting with Emma and Trish the next morning eating breakfast in the hotel restaurant.

'And Madame Rachel?' asked Trish.

'Never came. Jack didn't fancy it in the end. They both headed off to his place.'

Emma continued to butter her toast trying to ignore her colleagues' comments.

'Probably had a crazy night of passion,' he said, with a mischievous look in his eye. 'That woman has an intense personality. I doubt the missionary position would appeal to her.'

Trish laughed. Emma picked up the teapot and poured a cup of tea, trying to block her ears.' She didn't want to think of Jack and Rachel in bed together.

Jeremy continued in an ever-increasingly melo-dramatic fashion. 'Thought she was coming on to me at one point, scared me half to death! She'd probably have me hanging naked from the chandeliers, blind-folded with a feather up my bum.'

Trish laughed aloud, nodding in agreement. Emma bit into her toast and gazed pensively around the restaurant. The senior partners, Harold, Geoff and Robert, were at a separate table across the room engrossed in conver-sation. She guessed they were talking about business; it seemed to be the sum total of their existence. She'd be glad to be out of it. But maybe all companies were like this; inflated egos building little empires.

Within half an hour, Emma was waving them all off in the one taxi. She gave Trish a strong hug, said she'd be thinking of her and would telephone her on Monday night to see how she was. They arranged to have lunch in a couple of weekends' time.

She embraced Jeremy too and apologised if she had seemed a little distant. Pressures of work, she blamed it on. He said he understood and as the taxi pulled away he blew her a kiss through the rear window.

Using a different route than normal, Emma took a casual stroll towards the office – anything to delay going. Looking up at the sky, it was a brilliant blue; already the temperature was rising. She was sure she smelt the sea and had an overwhelming urge to catch a bus out to the seaside and walk aimlessly along a beach. She could walk for hours losing herself in daydreams, drink coffee in a small cafe, have a solo picnic high on the cliffs or paddle in a rock pool.

Instead, she carried on reluctantly, drawing nearer and nearer to the office. Her stomach turned over with the thought of seeing Jack. Her night had been restless. In the early hours her anxious mind involuntarily replayed those brief moments in his office, over and over again. Each time a different conclusion was formed and the resulting emotions drained her. He had made a pass at her, there was no denying that. Maybe he liked her. The thought of it terrified her. But there was also a part of her, hidden and locked away deep inside, a part she didn't even want to acknowledge, because she knew that part was actually pleased – more than that; it was excited. That terrified her even more.

She shook her head, refusing to think any more. He had been drunk, that was all. Longing to smell the sea again, she breathed in deeply, yet all she got was a mouthful of diesel fumes from a passing lorry.

She finally reached the building and went inside. With each stair she climbed, the trepidation grew, heavy and almost nauseating. She could have telephoned in sick, yet Harold and the others had all seen her at breakfast.

'Morning, Emma.' Her reverie interrupted, she glanced up. Rosemary was standing on the second-floor landing.

'Rosemary, hi. What are you doing out here?'

'No one's in.'

Emma checked her watch, nine forty-five. 'Sorry. Thought Jack or Sean would have been here.'

'Probably all hung-over.'

Emma nodded. 'I'll get that key cut for you today.' She opened up and they both went in. The office was a complete mess. The desks, partitions and computers were back in the room, yet they all needed repositioning and connecting again. Emma screwed her face up and let out a lethargic sigh.

'Cup of tea first, then we'll sort it,' said Rosemary, walking out to the kitchen.

Alone in the office and appearing in no immediate hurry, the women sat drinking their cup of tea, chatting about the party.

'Jeremy seems great fun,' said Rosemary. 'Some of the comments he comes out with . . . should be on the telly.'

Emma smiled. 'He has his moments all right.'

They heard the telephone ring in Jack's office, his external line. Emma got up and walked into his room. 'Good morning, Buckley & Dwyer,' she said.

There was a slight delay before she heard, in a cautious voice, 'Emma?'

She froze. Her heart instantly started pounding. When he heard no answer he said, 'It's me, Jack.'

Emma ran a hand through her hair, grabbing the back of her neck. 'Yes . . . Good morning.'

'I'm phoning from Heathrow.'

Confused and partly relieved, all she could say was 'Oh.'

'Spending a few days in the office here.' His manner became exact and businesslike. 'There are some things I need you to do. Do you have a pen?'

'One moment,' she replied, copying his professional approach. With her spare hand she grappled with the notepad on his desk, finally opening it to a blank page. 'Go ahead.'

'Ensure Rosemary gets the draft proposal out to Rancorn. Can you check it yourself and pp it?'

'Of course.'

'Tell Sean to go ahead and have the meeting with Tom Coughlan. I'll phone him tomorrow.'

'OK.'

'There're two cheques in my right-hand drawer. They need posting. I signed them earlier.'

'You were in?' she said, surprised.

'Yes, around seven. Any outstanding invoices have to be updated on Excel. There's a couple in my pending tray. Once done, fax copies to Julia.'

'PCs need setting up,' Emma reminded him.

'I know, I saw. Has to be today though,' he said.

'Fine.' She waited, pen at the ready, for the next instruction, but none came. All she could hear was the background noise of the airport, an inaudible announcement. She was unconsciously biting her lip.

When Jack spoke again, his voice sounded different, less formal. 'I've decided to see what I can do in London. Maybe put up a last-minute fight.'

'I'm glad. I think you should.'

'Not that hopeful; I've already spoken with a couple

of people. Seems over the years I've put a few noses out of joint.'

She was silent, knowing it to be true.

'Regardless, I'll be back in Dublin next Friday. E-mail or phone if you need me.'

'OK.'

He was quiet for a few moments.

'Good luck with it all,' Emma offered, uncomfortable in the silence.

There was another brief gap before he said, 'Emma.' It was spoken solidly, with purpose, as if it were a sentence on its own. She tensed, sensing something was coming, something she wasn't sure she wanted to hear. 'The party,' he said.

'Yes, I believe everyone enjoyed themselves. Just been discussing it with Rosemary.'

'Right . . .'

'Geoff and Harold are pleased about the Rancorn account. Hope to pick up the UK end . . . suppose you know that?' she said, flustered.

'It was mentioned.' He paused. 'I . . .'

Emma waited; scared at what might come.

'Rachel,' he said, with reticence. 'Complete surprise that she came. Mentioned the party weeks ago, hadn't seen her in ages.'

Emma glared into space, completely silent. What could she say? That he shouldn't be telling her this?

'We won't be seeing each other again,' he added.

Emma felt her hands trembling. Jack sighed, then suddenly reverted back into his matter-of-fact, speedy business voice. 'Make sure the Rancorn proposal is sent tonight.'

She hesitated. 'I will.'

'Registered post.'

'Of course.'

'Speak to you next week then,' he said.

'Yes . . . Goodbye.'

'Goodbye Emma.'

She heard him put down the phone. Her eyes stared ahead, unfocused, dazed-looking. Seconds grew into minutes. Maybe two passed before she slowly put the handset back on its base. Turning around, she leant against his desk, hugging herself. Her legs felt like jelly, her heart was racing. *Oh God!*

## 22

'Should we not wait for Tony, dear?' asked Charlotte, Emma's mother.

'He knew lunch was for two, it's now twenty past.' Emma put a plate down in front of her mother and handed another one to her father, before walking back out to the kitchen. Charlotte rolled her eyes disapprovingly towards her husband. William shook his head.

Emma returned with two serving bowls, green beans and new potatoes. She put them in the middle of the table and proceeded to sit down. 'Cheers.' She raised her wine glass and took a large gulp. 'Help yourself.'

Her mother offered a weak smile and with the serving spoon delicately put some potatoes on her husband's plate. She picked up the other serving spoon and placed a large portion of green beans on his plate too, before seeing to herself. 'Hope Tony won't be too offended that we've started without him,' she said.

'I doubt it,' said Emma.

'Any more news on a job?'

'He has a job, Mum.'

'Yes, but wasn't the pub going to be a temporary fill in? Thought he wanted to get something more . . . well, you know, dear.'

'You'll have to ask him later.'

'Unusual for a Sunday, isn't it?' said her father.

'What?' asked Emma.

He pointed to his plate. 'Salmon.'

'I'm cutting down on red meat,' she said, sipping her wine.

The three of them ate in silence for some moments.

Charlotte placed a portion of French bread on her husband's side plate, then slid the butter dish towards him.

'What's the food like in the hotel?' she asked Emma.

Emma stared across at her. 'Fine . . . nice.'

'And the staff?'

'Er . . . nice. Fine.' Emma finished her second glass of wine and filled it up again.

'You seem to be enjoying that wine,' stated William.

'It's really cheap at the airport. Do you want me to get you any?'

'No, no. We'll support Tom in our local off-licence. In fact, we didn't tell her, did we, Charlotte?' he said, turning towards his wife.

'Dreadful news,' said her mother, glaring at Emma. 'Everyone is up in arms. Tesco's want to build a superstore a couple of miles outside the village.' She had a look of abject horror on her face.

'Tell her the rest, dear.'

'Your father's been voted committee chairman.'

'On what?' asked Emma.

'The protest group.'

'Over two hundred signatures already,' said William proudly.

'It's only been going a week,' added Charlotte. 'Nearly everyone in the town has joined. Apart from a few on that new estate, Ellensborough. Not surprising. Town and city types mainly.'

'We're all marching to the council offices in about two weeks.'

Emma looked at her parents as they continued to elaborate about the protest group and their strategies to defy Tesco's ambitions. Her parents were at their most lively when they were complaining. They were avid contributors to *Points of View* and *Watchdog*; a couple of their letters had even been read out. It wasn't so much the complaining that irritated Emma. It was the issues they complained about: parking metres that only accepted silver coins and no copper; bad use of the English language on *EastEnders* and Des Lynam not wearing a tie one afternoon on *Grandstand*. Anything remotely important about life was never discussed. That was impolite, definitely taboo and possibly too unpleasant for their little world.

They all heard a key in the front door and a couple of moments later Tony walked in, soaking wet from the rain, carrying his rifle in its holder. The previous week he'd had his hair cropped really short. He told Emma that he'd joined a gym and wanted to get fit and back in shape, especially seeing how she'd done it. He nodded to the three of them sitting around the table.

'Hello, Tony,' said Charlotte. 'We've only just started . . . under protest I'll add.'

'That's OK.'

Emma carried on eating.

'I'll just change.' He left the room and ran upstairs. After a few moments, they heard him come down and go into the kitchen. He took his plate from the oven and joined them at the table.

'A good morning? Shoot much?' asked Emma's father.

Tony appeared uncomfortable and glanced over at Emma. 'Not much.'

'What was it? Birds, rabbits?'

'Er . . . don't really talk about it in front of Emma.'

Her father tutted. 'Salmon doesn't exactly grow on trees,' he laughed pointedly.

Charlotte smiled at him.

Shortly afterwards her parents began to tell Tony all about the campaign to stop the building of the local

Tesco's. Tony politely listened, occasionally nodding his head.

Over a dessert of ice cream and tinned fruit salad, her mother asked, 'So how are you coping on your own, Tony? How have you been filling your time?'

'I get by. Been working an extra night at the Swan.'

Charlotte turned to Emma. 'Are you cooking the week's meals and putting them in the freezer for him?'

Emma looked up and carefully shook her head, annoyed. 'No. Why? Tony's able to rustle up a dinner.'

Her mother continued, 'Not that it's the same but I suppose there're so many prepared meals you can buy nowadays. Packets and tins of everything.'

'Yes,' said Emma. 'Tesco's do a good range.'

Her mother stared at her, eyes unmoved. She smiled but said rather curtly, 'Not in *our* village.'

Fortunately Emma's parents didn't like staying away from home for too long so by four o'clock they had headed off. Without being asked, Tony washed up and a little later he entered the living room.

Emma was lying flat out across the sofa watching a re-run of *Hart to Hart*. He went to sit in the armchair but changed direction last minute and sat on the sofa so Emma's head was resting in his lap. She carried on watching the programme without saying anything. It was nearly over and Jonathan and Jennifer Hart were grappling with the murderer.

'Nice lunch,' said Tony, stroking her hair.

'Thanks.'

'Sorry I was a bit late.'

She answered calmly, without any real feeling, 'You're always late. It doesn't really matter.'

His hand stopped stroking her. After some moments it resumed. 'Everyone's going down the Swan tonight.

Shall we go? Should be a laugh. Everyone keeps asking where you've been lately.'

Emma closed her eyes. 'OK. If you want.'

'I'll phone Rob. We can meet up with Becky and Debra.'

'Who's Debra?'

'Becky's mate.'

'And how old is she?' she asked.

'What's it matter?'

'Should we really be hanging around with pubescent teenagers?'

'They're nineteen, Emma.'

'At least they've started their periods then.'

Tony deliberately bit his tongue. He closed his eyes for a moment and paused. 'Rob's the one going out with her. He's only twenty-nine, but we don't have to meet up with them if you don't want.'

Emma didn't respond.

*Hart to Hart* was nearing an end. Jonathan and Jennifer were kissing and saying how much they loved each other. Emma sat up. 'You're not going to be around much next weekend, are you?' she said.

'No, sorry. I'll be here Sunday night though. You could always come with me. There's no wildlife shot in competitions, only clay pigeons or target boards.'

'You know it's not my scene. Anyway, I was thinking . . .' She paused. 'As you won't be around, I might stay over in Dublin.'

He looked surprised, then concerned. 'But I won't see you for two whole weeks.'

'You won't see me much anyway. I just fancy staying there and looking around. I've hardly seen anywhere, only the city.'

'On your own?'

'Probably.'

'What about the hotel? Will you have to pay?'

'Some of it, yes.' She held his hand. 'I'd really like to do this. Have a break.'

'A break from me?' he asked quietly.

'A break from work, Manchester. It's just two days.'

He ran his fingers down the side of her face, resting his hand under her chin. His eyes stared off into a corner. He asked in a slow, serious voice, 'We are OK, aren't we? I don't need to worry about anything?'

'Tony,' she cried, 'don't say things like that!' She hugged him and kissed him on the cheek. Pulling back, she asked in a whisper, 'You think we're OK, don't you?'

'Of course. I love you, Emma.'

While staring at him yet speaking almost introspectively she said, 'I suppose we're OK then.'

## 23

'Hurry up, Em,' Tony shouted up from the hall.

Emma put on her jacket and came out of their bedroom. She didn't really want to spend an evening at the Swan but she had promised, so she'd go. Seeing Tony at the bottom of the stairs she put on a smile. As she came down and grabbed her bag from the lounge, the telephone rang. Tony answered it and after a moment he walked into the room saying quietly, 'It's Trish, sounds like she's been crying.'

Emma went straight to the phone and picked it up. 'Trish?' All Emma could hear was the sound of muffled crying.

Trish tried to speak but welled up with tears.

'Trish, what's wrong?'

'Can't believe . . . it,' she choked.

'What's happened? Are you OK?'

'No.'

'Why? Is it Steve?'

Trish didn't answer at first, just cried softly.

'Trish?'

'Can you come . . . come over.'

'Of course . . . I'll come right now. You'll be OK till I get there?'

'Yes.'

'I'll be there in ten minutes. See you then.'

Emma turned and saw Tony standing behind her. 'I'm sorry but I have to see Trish. She's in a right state.'

'What's happened?'

'Don't know. I'll take the car.'

Tony nodded reluctantly. She kissed him once on the lips and headed straight out.

Once in the car, Emma put her foot down and drove the five miles to Trish's in eight minutes. She knew something must have happened with Steve – maybe he had ended it, but surely he couldn't be so cruel, not with her abortion planned for the next day. Emma parked outside her block of flats and ran up to the second floor, pressing her bell several times. The door opened and Trish stood there, her swollen face looking like the result of several hours of crying.

'Sorry to call you, wasn't sure who else to contact,' she said, sounding calmer than she had on the phone.

Both women went and sat on the settee in her lounge.

'What's happened?' asked Emma, taking hold of her hand.

Trish leant back; her head lay limply to the side, like a wounded animal's. She was gazing into space through vacant, stunned eyes. She opened her mouth to speak but gradually closed it again, only managing to slowly shake her head.

'It's Steve, isn't it?' said Emma.

'I've been such a fool.' Trish bit her lip, desperately trying to keep control of herself.

'It's OK.'

'*It isn't.*' Her face contorted with pain. 'Sarah's pregnant.'

Emma gasped. 'No.'

Trish's head fell into her hands, but instead of more tears she let out a ferocious scream that echoed off every wall. She leapt up. '*Fucking bastard!* I hate him.' She was pacing up and down the room. 'Sleeping with her all the time! What a fool, fucking fool, bastard. She can keep hers, nice christening, celebrate the new family member. Me, get rid of it, inconvenient. Lucky dip, roll up, roll up. Sorry lady, you lose, pick again.'

Emma was perched on the edge of the sofa, shaking

her head in shared despair and anger. 'Did he tell you this? What's he said?'

'Hah! That would be *too* honest. Ann Ryan from Birmingham knew. Rang me last night.'

'How does she know? Is it true? You've spoken to Steve?'

'This morning.' Trish stopped dead and stood in the middle of the room, eyes closed, cradling her stomach. Tears fell from her eyes. 'It's true. Said he was going to tell me after tomorrow. Thoughtful bastard.'

'Oh Trish, I'm so sorry. Oh, shit. I'm *so* sorry.'

Trish slumped back down on the settee, gazing blank-faced into space.

Emma held her hand and both women sat for several moments in silence. Everything Emma thought of to say sounded insufficient and inappropriate. 'I'm really sorry . . . did he explain how, why, anything?'

'Said he only slept with her a handful of times. Said he had to, otherwise she'd get suspicious.'

'So she's definitely having it?'

Trish nodded.

'And Steve?'

Trish was silent for nearly a minute before saying, 'He can't leave her now. Checkmate.' Her hands started to tremble. Soon she was bent double, sobbing uncontrollably. Emma held her, letting her cry freely.

Nearly an hour passed; it was mostly filled with tears, but interspersed with sudden outbursts of anger and incoherent ramblings. Emma held her all the while, just listening. Her heart went out to her and at times she felt her own eyes glaze over with tears.

'Have you eaten today?' she asked, at one point.

Trish shook her head.

Emma went and put the kettle on and saw an empty bottle of Bacardi lying in the sink. She made a ham sandwich and two mugs of tea. Back in the lounge she handed them to Trish. 'You probably don't feel like this right now but just try. You should eat something.'

Trish drank the tea but left the sandwich. 'I will never find what I had with him.'

'You're hurting too much to think anything else. You'll feel different in the weeks to come. It'll get easier.'

She angrily shook her head. 'It won't. This was it for me. Maybe I'll keep his child, a reminder of him. Could be a son. I bet Sarah is so happy right now. Her life's so wonderful. She has her man and her children. One phone call could change all that.'

'*Trish!*'

'Why shouldn't she feel like I do: fucking shit?'

'That won't help anything. Please don't, you'd regret it straight away. You'll get through this. I'll help.'

'No one can help.' She leapt up, spilling the tea. 'Get some more Bacardi, will you?' She was pacing up and down again.

'Will that really help?' asked Emma.

'Yes it will. There's some money in that bag.'

Emma stood up. 'I'll pay.' On nearing the door she turned around. 'You won't phone her, will you?'

Trish shook her head.

'Promise.'

She nodded.

Emma went out and dashed down the street towards the off-licence. She ran in the door like a desperate alcoholic, grabbed a large bottle of Bacardi and threw down a £20 note. Almost snatching her change she ran from the shop and back up the street.

'You didn't phone, did you?' she asked, totally breathless, on her return.

Trish shook her head and took the bottle from her. 'Want one?'

'OK.'

For the rest of the evening they sat and drank, and talked. Trish cried more, yet the alcohol eased her pain, if only temporarily. Emma got the most intimate rendition of Trish and Steve's relationship, very passionate, very sexual. After three Bacardis she even had a twinge of envy at the obvious pleasure they shared with each other. She wondered what it would be like to feel like that – totally lost in another person. She tried telling herself that the pain and hurt weren't worth it. But nevertheless, her thoughts alarmed her. Why am I even thinking like this? She pushed her glass away, deciding instead to have a cup of tea.

Later that evening Emma said, 'Tomorrow?'

Now calmer, Trish replied, 'I'm still going. It's for the best.'

'Why not postpone it for a week?'

'No.'

'Then I'm staying the night and going with you,' Emma said firmly.

'What about Dublin and work?'

'I'll fly over Tuesday.'

Trish smiled. 'Thanks.'

'I'll just phone Tony. Don't drink any more, not if you're going ahead with it.'

The next morning, after telephoning Rosemary in Dublin, Emma drove Trish to the Altrincham Clinic. It was a large detached house, set in its own grounds, giving the impression of an exclusive country hotel; an expensive alternative but Steve was paying. Even the individual rooms were generously decorated and had en-suite bathrooms. Yet despite the effort, the atmosphere was still clinical and cold.

Emma sat in an armchair, next to Trish on the bed.

The television was on in the background; Richard and Judy were holding a phone-in on problem children.

The two women sat mostly in silence, partly watching, partly lost in their own thoughts. In fact, Emma was feeling quite nauseous. She hated any form of hospital, especially the disinfectant smell. Occasionally, young nurses came in and asked Trish some questions, took some basic tests.

'How come you and Tony don't have any children?' asked Trish, when alone again.

Emma was surprised by the question, especially in the current surroundings. 'It just never happened. I was supposed to go for tests but somehow didn't.'

'So you want them?'

'Yes . . . but the situation has to be right.'

'Does that mean it isn't?'

Emma stared her straight in the face but could only shrug her shoulders.

At eleven o'clock, Emma was asked to leave and told to phone back around five. If there were no complications Trish could go home that evening, although they'd prefer if she stayed the night. Of course, thought Emma, more money. However Trish said she'd like to go home if possible.

Emma bent down over Trish and kissed her on the cheek. 'Good luck.'

'Thanks, see you later,' Trish smiled wanly.

Emma was secretly relieved to get out of the place and stood by her car breathing in deeply. In that moment she hated Steve Ingrams. Maybe she should have let Trish telephone Sarah. She should find out what sort of a man she'd married.

When Emma arrived home, she found Tony still in bed. Feeling tired and drained she got in beside him, fully clothed. He woke and cuddled up to her.

'Trish all right?' he mumbled.

'Yeah. She'll be OK.'

Tony started placing some kisses along her neck.
Emma lay there gazing up at the ceiling. She felt his
hand across her chest, undoing the buttons on her shirt.

'Tony!'

'What's wrong?'

She sat up. 'I need some air. I'm going for a walk.'


When Emma telephoned the clinic that evening she was
told that everything had gone well with Trish. Relieved,
she went and collected her at six. The drive home was
mostly in silence but Trish assured her that she was
feeling OK, just sleepy and a bit tearful. She went
straight to bed while Emma sat watching the television,
planning to stay another night.

Halfway through *EastEnders*, the doorbell rang, so
Emma opened it. Steve stood there. He looked
surprised and somewhat ashamed when he saw her.

'Emma.'

'Steve,' she said coolly.

He hesitated. 'Is Trish in?'

'She's sleeping.'

'I need to see her.'

'Is that wise? She's very upset.'

'I have to see her.' He said it with determination and
took a step forward.

'Wait. I'll tell her you're here.'

Trish was awake in bed and said she wanted to see
him too. In fact, when Emma turned around, Steve was
already in the bedroom. He rushed over to her, taking
hold of her hand. Trish smiled at him; the first smile of
the day.

Emma left them alone in the room and sat in the

lounge staring at the television, her mind on Trish and Steve. She could hear them talking next door but couldn't make out any words. Within the hour, Steve came out saying Trish wanted to see her. Emma had a feeling about what she was going to hear. She went in and sat on the bed facing Trish.

'Emma, thanks for all your help. You've been brilliant.'

She smiled. 'That's OK.'

'I've had a long chat with Steve.'

Emma's heart fell.

'We've still got a lot more talking to do. He wants to stay and look after me tonight.'

'Is that what you want?' Emma queried.

Trish closed her eyes and was silent. Opening them she stared off into the distance, as if uncomfortable to meet Emma's eyes. 'Probably a bigger fool than I thought I was, but yes . . . I want him to stay.'

A long silence ensued. The only sound was from Steve who was making a phone call in the lounge. 'Yes, this damn meeting's run on. I'll grab a room at the Ramada and see you both tomorrow. Give James a kiss from me. Love you too.'

Emma pinched her lips together. 'It's OK,' she said. 'I'll leave you alone then, but I'm just a phone call away.'

'I can't help it,' whispered Trish, head hanging low. 'I just can't help it.'

## 24

Thursday evening and Emma was sitting on her bed watching television in her hotel room in Dublin. She couldn't concentrate. Her mind was trying to figure out how the vote had gone in London that day. Earlier she'd drawn a little diagram listing all the partners' names and placing a tick, cross or question mark against each one according to how they'd vote – Harold or Jack? It became overrun by question marks, so she ripped it up and threw it in the bin.

At seven, she left a message on Jeremy's answering machine asking him to call her immediately. He probably wouldn't be in until late, the partners usually went out to dinner after a board meeting. She flicked between the twelve TV channels, but nothing appealed to her. Jumping up, she made for the mini bar. A few gin and tonics might make the hours pass quicker.

Eventually, at half past ten, she rang Jeremy again.

'Hello,' he answered.

'You're in!' she said, in an accusing voice.

'Emma, hello. Just in this moment. Great to hear from you.'

She paused, thinking quickly. In a more friendly manner she asked, 'How have you been?'

'Fantastic. You're talking to a fully-fledged partner. Exciting, isn't it?'

'Yes . . . Congratulations.'

'Thank you. I'm so pleased you rang. I wish you were here so we could celebrate over some bubbly.'

'Another time.'

'Definitely.' Jeremy went on to elaborate about his new pay deal and increased profit share, also the sort of business Harold wanted the practice to concentrate on.

Emma listened impatiently, hoping to hear some news of Jack. After a considerable while, without even a mention of the vote, she politely interrupted him.

'So who will be managing London then?'

'Oh, you heard about that?' he said in a more serious voice. 'It was most unpleasant.'

'Why?'

'First task as a partner, first time I get to vote, and the motion was to place Harold as manager of London . . . make it the head office; in effect, oust Jack.'

'So what happened?'

'Difficult call. But what does one do?'

'Jesus. Just tell me who won?' Emma snapped.

Jeremy was slightly taken aback. 'Harold, of course,' he answered.

Emma was silent. She closed her eyes.

'It was always going to be Harold. He is head partner. He has some interesting plans for the future. Says I feature strongly in them.' Jeremy went on to describe some of those changes, insisting she keep them a secret. The other branches would be scaled down in a drive to save on overheads.

Emma didn't care about any of that. 'How was Jack? How did he take it?'

'Seemed OK. It was a private ballot. Geoff called both Harold and Jack into his office to inform them of the result first. By the time the rest of us were told, he appeared his usual composed, commanding self . . . didn't come out to dinner though. Who can blame him?'

'You voted against him, didn't you?' Emma's voice was quiet and full of disdain.

There was a moment of silence.

'It was a private ballot,' he said defiantly. 'No one reveals how they voted. It's just not done. Why are you suddenly so concerned for Jack? May I remind you that you delighted in the fact that he wasn't voted head partner. So don't try and make me feel bad. It's business, that's all. Jack understands that. Live by the sword, then be prepared to die by it.' Jeremy carried on justifying his actions.

Emma remembered how she had acted when Jack had lost out to Harold the year before; she had laughed. Jeremy was right. She frowned, feeling very guilty.

'I have to go,' she said suddenly, interrupting him again.

'Emma, what is up with you lately? You've been acting so weird, so touchy, so ready to pounce and start an argument for the least little thing.'

'I'm just a bit tired,' she mumbled.

'Is it Tony?'

'No.'

'Then what?'

'Nothing.'

'There is something. I've known you too long not to notice when something's wrong.'

'Length of time means nothing. You can know someone for years and still not really know them.'

'That's exactly what I mean,' said Jeremy. 'You keep coming out with weird little statements like that. What's going on?'

'Nothing!' she yelled. 'If anything, I'm pissed off with people questioning me, advising me, commenting on me, telling me what to do. It's bollocks, all of it.'

Her little outburst left both of them silent. Neither wished to argue further. Both were unsure what to say.

'You've shut me out, Emma,' he said in a sad, downhearted manner.

'There's nothing to tell. I'm just . . . just tired,' she said calmly.

'You know, if you ever need a break there's my cottage in Exmoor. In fact I'm down there this weekend with Julia and Thomas. I'd love you to come.'

'Thanks . . . but I can't.'

'Another time then. Go on your own if you need some space.'

'Maybe.'

'If I can do anything, I mean it, anything, just ask,' he said insistently.

'Thanks, I know you mean it. I really must go . . . I'm sorry. You know you mean a lot to me. As I said, I'm just tired. Bye.'

'Bye Emma, do take care. Call me soon.'

'Bye Jeremy.'

Emma replaced the receiver and slumped down on the bed. She lay for several minutes before jumping up and pacing the room. Up and down she marched, thinking, planning, worrying, totally confused. Those gin and tonics had made her head fuzzy, unclear, making her think things that she shouldn't; things that involved Jack. Her hands were gesticulating in short, awkward movements. Crashing down on the bed, she stared trance-like, up towards the ceiling. She closed her eyes as if that would shut it all out, yet the thoughts still came. Her heart pounded with fear. She bolted upright and switched the television back on.

The next morning Emma entered the office at 8.15. She had woken early from what little sleep she'd had and decided to get up and go to work. She made herself some tea and sat, gazing out of the window. At nine, she saw Rosemary cross the road and disappear into the entrance below. Emma went and sat at her desk and opened up a file.

'Morning,' said Rosemary, taking off her coat.

'Morning,' Emma replied.

'Gone cold again. Hope it brightens up for you tomorrow.'

'Hope so too.'

'Did you call that number?'

'Not yet. I'll see what the weather's like in the morning,' said Emma. Rosemary had given her a telephone number for an organised walk into the Wicklow Mountains.

By twelve, Jack still hadn't arrived; maybe there was a problem with flights. Sean and Rosemary worked away, seemingly unconcerned by his absence. Yet Emma was worried that he hadn't turned up. When his signature was required on an urgent cheque, it gave her the excuse of telephoning around to find him. She rang the London office, he wasn't there and no one had heard from him. She tried his mobile but that was diverted to the Dublin office. There was no answer from his house in London. When she phoned his Dublin home, his answering machine came on. She left a message. 'Hi Jack, this is Emma. It's just gone twelve on Friday 31st. Could you give me a call? There're a couple of queries I need to discuss with you. Also a cheque needs signing. Thanks.' She paused then added, 'Hope everything is OK. Talk to you later.'

At four o'clock, there still hadn't been any contact. Mad thoughts were entering Emma's head. She had to convince herself that Jack wasn't the type to do anything silly. It took her nearly all day to type just two documents. Most of the time she pretended to be working on the budgets and accounts, instead her mind was running wild; it was impossible to concentrate.

At five, when Sean and Rosemary were leaving, she almost considered catching a flight to Manchester. But why? Another walk in the park? She might as well stay in Dublin and have a proper look around. Once alone in the office, she stared down at her phone. Her eyes flickered. On the spur of the moment she picked it up and dialled his number. In a deliberately relaxed, matter-of-fact way she left another message: 'Hi Jack, this is Emma again. Thought I'd mention that I'm staying in Dublin this weekend. Expect you may have stayed in London. Anyway if you're at a loose end, give me a call.' She added in a more serious voice, 'I heard about the vote. I'm sorry. Bye.'

The phone was quickly put down. Part of her instantly regretted leaving the message. *What am I doing?* she wondered. She left the office and went back to the hotel.

## 25

The telephone was ringing in the background. Emma slowly opened her eyes. It stopped. She lay there, still half asleep. Had it rung? She squinted towards the clock on the bedside cabinet, quarter past seven. Snuggling her head into the pillow she closed her eyes again.

Almost immediately it rang again. She leant across, picked it up and said in a sleepy voice, 'Hello.'

'Don't tell me you're still asleep on such a beautiful morning.'

'Jack?'

'Yep. Get up. Get up. We're going walking up the mountains,' he enthused. 'Do you have a waterproof? I've a spare one if you want.'

Emma rubbed her eye with her spare hand and mumbled, 'Er . . . I don't think so.'

He was buzzing. 'Make sure you have a good breakfast. It's quite a trek. Collect you at half eight in reception.'

'OK.'

'See you then.' He put the phone down.

Emma lay back. Gradually, she replaced the receiver. After a few more dazed moments she sat up. That was Jack, she thought. We're going up the mountains. As if suddenly waking from a dream she leapt up and flung open her wardrobe, grabbing her jeans.

At twenty past eight, Emma was pacing around the reception area. She stood in a corner tapping the ground with her foot. Her stomach had anxious butter-flies, actually they felt more like attacking wasps. Best go to the loo again. She dashed off towards the ladies.

Emerging from the toilets a few minutes later, she spotted him. She stopped dead. Jack was standing by the reception desk, looking in the opposite direction. He was dressed casually in jeans and a yellow jumper with a pair of expensive-looking walking boots. She glanced down at her tatty trainers. He turned and smiled. She smiled back. He walked over towards her, a bounce in his step.

'Ready?' he asked.

She thought his eyes looked tired, slightly bloodshot. Apart from that though, he didn't appear to be the receiver of bad news. She nodded.

'Car's outside.' He turned and led the way.

Once in the car and driving out of Dublin, Emma thought about discussing the vote, but Jack seemed happy to talk about Wicklow and where they were going. He'd planned the whole day: a walk until lunchtime through part of the Wicklow Way; lunch in a village called Enniskerry and then a slow drive back down the coast road through Greystones, Bray, Dalkey and finally Blackrock. She delighted in his enthusiasm, smiling as she listened to him.

'Scenery's fantastic. And what a day! Should be able to see for miles,' he said.

She guessed he'd probably bring up the subject of the vote later.

Only three miles out of Dublin and they were driving down a country road, fields and trees on either side. The vast mountains and hills were visible up ahead. Emma opened her window and took a deep breath. 'I can smell the sea!' she exclaimed excitedly.

Jack opened his window. 'So can I.' They grinned like excitable children. Slightly embarrassed she quickly looked away.

The little village of Enniskerry stood six miles out of

Dublin. It reminded Emma of an English village, similar to one she used to visit as a child in the Cotswolds. All the shop and pub fronts were like something from the early part of the century, with hand-painted logos from the twenties and thirties. It had a small square on which a clock-tower stood. If you took the cars away, it would be like going back in time. The early hour added to its ambience and character.

They drove out the other side of the village and after about a mile, Jack took a left turn down a very narrow lane. It brought them to a large clearing surrounded by dense forest. Three other cars were already there. Jack parked up and they got out.

'How fit are you?' he asked, picking up a small rucksack from his boot.

'Don't worry, you won't have to carry me.'

Jack put the rucksack on.

'What's in there?' she asked.

'Bottle of water, couple of chocolate bars, plasters, waterproof.'

She smiled. 'Prepared for Everest.'

'Of course! This way.'

They followed the winding track through the pine forest, climbing steadily upwards. It must have rained that morning as drops of water occasionally fell on them from the branches overhead. The air was moist with a rich, sweet smell from the damp wood. Jack walked at quite a pace. After twenty minutes, Emma was surprised at how breathless she was. Soon they came to the end of the track where the forest met open fields. They carefully walked over a little makeshift wooden bridge that crossed a small stream.

After another mile they came across a circular cluster of large stones. Four stood upright and two appeared to have fallen on their sides. It was like a mini version of Stonehenge.

'What a strange place. Let's sit down for a moment, admire the view,' said Emma, needing a rest.

Jack came to sit next to her on the large stone boulder. They could see for miles, hills, valleys, the tops of the mountains with a light mist still hanging over them. A few cottages and farms were dotted around. To their left lay more cultivated land, sheep and cows grazing, behind them forest, but up ahead it appeared more barren, brownish instead of the lush green – heather, stone and the start of peat bogs. It was incredibly quiet. There was the occasional sound of a light breeze filtering through the trees behind, but apart from that, nothing. Silence.

Emma turned to Jack. 'Hope we don't get lost.'

He stared at her with a strange look in his eye, but didn't say anything.

'What?' she questioned.

He looked away, off into the distance and said in a dispirited voice, 'You're surrounded by beauty, nature in all its glory, and all you can say is "I hope we don't get lost".'

Emma's head dropped forward slightly.

'I didn't mean to attack you,' he added, looking back at her. 'You see, that's my reaction too. Sad, don't you think? What does that say about us? And what is lost anyway?' He stood up. 'Let's continue.'

She followed him, off in the direction of the bogs. They picked up another track that ran through the expanse of heather and other wild growth. A sweet earthy aroma filled the air. Underfoot was becoming muddy and Emma felt the wet seep through into her trainers. A mist had gathered around them and the distant mountains were no longer visible. She made a mental note of various landmarks, strange-looking rocks, the singular tree or bush that they came across. Anything that might assist them on their return journey.

Apart from casual bits of conversation and the exchange of chocolate, they mostly walked in silence. It wasn't an awkward silence. Both were just walking, observing, thinking and occasionally commenting. She looked at her watch, twenty-five past eleven. They'd been walking for two hours and she was tired, also worried about the two-hour trip back.

In a cautious voice she said, 'Maybe we should turn back now.'

He stopped to look at her. A strange smile appeared on his face. Emma took a step back. Out in the middle of nowhere, she was feeling quite vulnerable.

'We're not going back,' he stated.

She bit her bottom lip. 'I'm tired. I'll go back on my own, wait by the car.'

He walked towards her, frowning. Emma's heart was pounding.

'Please yourself. But I'll probably get there before you. Haven't you noticed we've been walking slightly to the right all the time?'

She shook her head.

'Well, we have. Soon we'll start to descend. If I'm right we'll eventually come on to the road about a mile from the car. About another hour.'

Emma sighed, relieved. She looked away, smiling to herself. After a moment she grinned at him and said jokingly, 'So you're not going to murder me and hide my body in the bog?'

Jack narrowed his eyes on her. 'I think part of you actually believed that. What? All men are murderers, as well as adulterers and bastards?'

Emma was embarrassed but amused. Jack opened his eyes wide, glaring oddly, pretending to appear mad and insane. In a scary, put-on voice he said, 'This way, little girl.' He turned and ran off into the mist.

Emma stood there alone. Suddenly she took off after him screaming, 'Wait for me!'

Jack continued running. At one point she lost sight of him, but she could hear him in the distance making weird ghostly noises. It was difficult to tell quite what direction they were coming from.

'Jack Tomkinson,' she shouted at the top of her voice, 'before you go completely deranged, could you please get me back to the car in one piece and buy me lunch.' She listened for a reply, nothing. The mist deadened any noise. 'I'm tired, hungry and I've got wet feet,' she yelled.

'OK,' he whispered.

She jumped violently. Jack was right behind her. He winked and carried on walking as if nothing had happened. Emma followed a few paces behind, still rather cautious of his strange behaviour.

Soon they started to descend and the land became more hospitable, grass and trees again. Emma started humming as they walked beside a large stream that was winding its way down the mountain, over rocks and fallen tree trunks. The mist had disappeared and apart from the odd white puffy cloud, the sky was a brilliant blue. They started to pass other walkers who were heading up the mountains. Everyone said hello and smiled.

Feeling more relaxed, Emma said in a friendly, supportive manner, 'You don't have to talk about this if you don't want to, but I was going to ask about . . . you know . . . the vote. How've you been?'

Jack glanced sideways at her and smiled. 'I don't mind. Rather boring though.'

He continued walking as if he'd answered her question and that was it.

'So? How are you?' she repeated in a more demanding voice.

'Truthfully? I'm unsure.' He screwed his face up trying to explain. 'Pissed off, yes. Angry, definitely. But at the same time . . . part of me feels that maybe I don't care as much as I think I should, or would have previously. Harold out-manoeuvred me. But I let him. Not just this week, but for the last six months. That's not like me.'

They climbed over a small gate. 'I came to a few decisions last night. I'm not one to mope around. When things happen, it's just best to deal with them and get on with it. Anyway . . . I decided to . . . oh, I should add, could you keep this to yourself?'

'Of course,' she said.

'I've decided to take some time out. Stay managing Dublin full time for the summer. The hell I'm going to continue building up London, working my arse off. No way. Sod them. I'll take my salary for the next six months and work nine to five. I intend to go sailing, walking, jogging, reading, *relaxing*.' Jack turned to see her reaction.

Emma smiled. 'Sounds wonderful. But then what?'

'Always so practical, Emma. You're worse than me.'

'Interested, that's all.'

He smiled. 'The idea is to take the summer to decide. Go work for another practice, set up on my own? Who knows? I'll just see how it all unfolds. I've always had this dream to take a year out and sail around the world – well, part of it.'

'You think you'd do it?'

'Not sure . . . who knows? Probably not. But for the

first time in my life I won't have such a definite plan. Or at least I'll try not to.'

'You're very fortunate you have choices,' she said.

'Everyone has choices.'

She shook her head. 'Not everyone.'

'That's ridiculous. Everyone has choices – it's just that people can't always see them because they don't look or they're too scared to follow through on them.'

His assured manner irritated her. 'That easy, eh?' she said.

'Yes. Absolutely.'

'No, it's not.'

'Why isn't it?'

'For a start you have money.'

'That helps, admittedly.'

'It's a major help, Jack, major.' She quickened her pace and walked in front of him. It was downhill and she felt like running. He quickened also. After a minute, she turned and shouted, 'See you at the bottom.' With that she took off, ignoring her soggy feet. She ran down the hill, at one point lifting both arms in the air and letting out a loud yell. She imagined herself as Julie Andrews in *The Sound of Music*. A handful of terrified sheep darted out of her way. She ran as fast as she could, nearly slipping on a muddy section. She let out a cry but managed to right herself. The racing of her heart and the aching in her lungs were telling her to stop, but her spirit urged her forward, as if she could take off and fly.

Finally, she reached the gate to the road, falling against it, bending double and gasping for air. Her legs felt wobbly, dormant muscles shocked by the exertion. Yet she laughed wildly, feeling alive, high on adrenaline. Glancing back she saw Jack jogging at a steady pace. Soon he was with her, not even out of breath.

'And here was me thinking I was going to have to carry you,' he said.

'You still might,' she panted, 'if the car's not down this road.'

He smiled, then continued on.

After another fifteen minutes they spotted it.

'Thank God, we're saved,' she joked.

'I've a spare pair of socks in the boot. Borrow them.'

'Why doesn't that surprise me? But thank you, I will.'

Soon they were driving back to Enniskerry. Once there, Jack parked on the edge of the village near the seventeenth-century church, which they planned to look in after eating. They walked the short distance to a small vegetarian cafe and restaurant situated in the main square, which was busy with tourists. They sat in the corner by the window.

Emma buttered the roll on her side plate and ate it. 'At last, *food*.'

Jack sliced open his roll also. 'Let's order. Where's that waitress gone?' He scanned the room.

Emma was facing the other way. 'Let's send telepathic hunger pains to her,' she said.

Jack laughed but gave it a go, before laughing again. Suddenly the waitress appeared and Emma nodded to Jack as if to say it had worked.

'You do seem remarkably calm about it all,' said Emma, returning to the subject again halfway through their lunch.

Jack shook his head. 'I'm livid. Furious, enraged, revengeful. But I'm also realistic. Murder is a messy business and you usually end up in jail.'

'You could lure Harold up to the mountains. Do the deed there. Never find his body. No body, no murder charge.' Her eyes glistened in mock mischief.

'I'd still need an alibi.'

'I'd give you one.'

Jack looked flattered. 'That's the nicest thing you've ever said to me. Thank you.'

Emma was smiling with him. They laughed at the absurdity of the conversation.

After a while they began to talk of Ireland and he told her places he'd visited as a child on holiday: Galway, Kinsale and most of Kerry. She learned more about his family, very conservative by all accounts, not too dissimilar from hers. They compared stories of who'd been the most rebellious teenager. Emma told him of the time she'd had a huge argument with her parents. At fifteen, she'd run away to London and had 'Boomtown Rats' tattooed on the top of her left shoulder.

'What!' Jack bellowed. 'Show me. I don't believe you.'

She delicately pulled her jumper down off her shoulder and showed him. He gasped with shock.

'*You have a tattoo!*'

Emma laughed. 'When I ran out of money and my anger subsided, I went home. Managed to keep my shoulder hidden for over a year. Mum caught sight of it one day – flipped big time.'

Jack laughed, shaking his head. After calming down he told her of the first and only time he'd dabbled with drugs. It was a tab of LSD, which had been brought into school by an older boy. 'I was fifteen too, at school in Religious Education. This real Hitler of a nun used to teach us, Sister Brooks. We were bored. It was a dare. No one refused a dare, it wasn't good for the image,' he said, rolling his eyes.

Emma was already laughing, eagerly waiting for the inevitable fall-out.

'I had this mad trip. Totally convinced Sister Brooks was an alien. In the middle of the lesson I stood up and screamed to everyone, telling them to run before she took over their bodies. The weird thing was, everybody did.'

Emma shook with laughter and wiped tears from her eyes.

He explained that his punishment was to attend extra RE lessons at lunchtimes for the rest of the year. They both laughed so loudly that the people at the surrounding tables looked over. Realising they were drawing attention to themselves, they immediately quietened down. Becoming aware of her actions, Emma appeared more reflective. 'Weird, isn't it?' she mused.

'What?' he asked, himself more serious.

'Well, look at us. Quietening down, in case we cause a scene. We spend our teenage years rebelling against everything, all our parents' values, the lot. It was all so black and white. Then as you get older you suddenly realise that somehow, over the years, without noticing it, you've become everything you hated. Guardians of and contributors to a society that once made you cringe. Bizarre.'

'Hopefully not everything we hated.'

'Maybe not.'

'You have choices, Emma.'

She leant forward. 'I know one choice.'

'Yes?' he said, as if waiting for a major revelation.

'I want a huge piece of that chocolate cake.'

He stared at her, eventually smiling. He turned and looked for the waitress.

On the slow drive back, they listened to a CD of Van Morrison as they made their way along the coast road. At the small seaside resort of Bray they parked and went for a stroll along the beach and wandered around a few of the local shops. They continued driving into the wealthy areas of Killiney and Dalkey, admiring what houses they could see from the road and guessing which famous pop star or racing driver lived there.

It was past five o'clock when they eventually entered the city of Dublin again. Jack made his way directly to her hotel. He pulled up across the road from it. Emma turned and smiled at him. 'I've had the most wonderful day. Really enjoyed it. Thank you.'

He gave a brief nod of his head.

Emma opened the car door but looked back at him. 'Do you want . . . a drink or something?'

Jack looked down at his steering wheel. Without staring at her he said, 'I'd like to cook you a meal. Can you come tonight? Eight o'clock?'

There was a noticeable pause where neither looked at each other. 'OK,' she said finally.

'I'll collect you at quarter to?'

'No. A taxi's fine.' She got out of the car and closed the door behind her. Going up in the lift to her room, her head was leaning against the side as she gazed into space. Part of her was telling herself not to go there tonight. *What are you playing at, Emma?* But deep inside, she knew she would go.

## 26

Emma spent nearly an hour in a steam-filled bathroom having a hot petunia and lavender oil bath, soothing her aching limbs. There was a constant smile on her face as she recounted little instances from their day together. Recalling Jack's LSD experience made her laugh aloud.

Tony had left a couple of messages at reception for her, yet she had opted to take her bath first. Clothed in only a towel, she picked up the telephone and dialled Trish for the second time that week.

'Hello.'

'Hi, it's me, Emma.'

'Hi. How are you? Did you stay in Dublin?'

'I'm here now, really enjoying it,' she enthused.

'Did you go walking?'

'I did. It was beautiful, scenery was amazing. Walked up a mountain, through streams, along a beach, threw pebbles into the sea. You should have seen it. Mind you, my legs are killing me.'

'Sounds great. Who'd you go with?'

Emma hesitated. 'Oh. Jack, in the end.'

'Really! I expect he talked about work all the way. Did he bring his laptop? I can just imagine him sitting on the top of a mountain tapping away.' Trish laughed.

'Of course he didn't. He's not like that really . . . anyway, how are you?'

'Actually I'm feeling fine, better than I thought I'd be.'

'Have you heard from Steve?'

'That's right,' she said, in an odd manner.

'What? He's there?'

'Yes. I believe so.'

'So you can't talk?'

'Yes. You're right there.'

A short silence ensued. Emma shook her head. In a cautious, pointed manner she said, 'Does this mean you're back together?'

'Er . . . can I call you early next week? I'm just on my way out.'

That was all the answer Emma needed.

'I'll definitely call next week – have a good chat then. Don't think me rude.'

'That's OK,' said Emma.

'Sorry to cut it short. Enjoy the rest of the weekend in Dublin. And thanks for everything.'

'I will. Bye.'

'Speak to you soon. Bye.'

Emma put the phone down. She couldn't help feeling angry – towards both of them. The strength of it surprised her. How could Trish put up with that?

It was just gone seven o'clock by the time she rang Tony, the time he usually left for work. Their answering machine came on so she left a message: 'Hi, it's me. Sorry I missed you. Hope you're OK. Expect you're at work. I'll call you first thing, around eight. I should catch you before you head off to the competition. Take care. Bye.' She replaced the receiver and stood biting her thumbnail.

Soon, her thoughts turned to the evening ahead and she wondered what to wear. After a lot of consideration she finally put on her black trousers and red, v-necked top: not too casual, not too dressy.

At five to eight, a taxi dropped Emma in the street outside Jack's house. She was carrying a bottle of wine and slowly climbed the five steps leading to his front door. Reaching it, she stood for several moments, hesitating. Her head lowered as a hundred thoughts pounced on her. What am I doing here? Almost panicking, she lunged for the doorbell, pressing it down firmly; it took away any option to flee. Within a few seconds the door opened and Jack stood there. He gave a brief nod of his head. He was wearing a pair of light brown jeans and a blue jumper. Thank goodness she hadn't worn a dress. Stepping back from the door and without looking at her, he said, 'Come in.'

She stepped into his house and he closed the door behind her.

Jack walked straight into the kitchen, so Emma followed him. The room smelt spicy like a Mexican restaurant. He indicated a chair by the table and she sat down.

'What would you like to drink?' he asked in a formal manner.

'I brought this.' She placed her bottle of wine on the table.

'Thanks. I've a bottle open already.'

'Drunk, are you? Have I some catching up to do?' she mocked.

He shook his head. 'Cooked with some.'

Emma thought him distant, unsettled. He'd been so relaxed and witty that afternoon. Sometimes it was like starting at the beginning all over again with him. She hoped tonight wasn't going to be like that. He poured her out a glass of wine and put it on the table in front of her.

'Smells interesting,' she said.

Jack was standing by the hob and stirring the contents of a large pot. 'Vegetarian chilli and rice. Unfortunately, I've put too much chilli powder in.' He looked quite disappointed.

She smiled reassuringly. 'I'm sure it'll be great. I'm

starving again, must be the fresh air.'

He tasted a small spoonful, immediately screwing his face up. He added some lemon juice and water to it.

Eventually he came and sat down opposite her. 'Another ten minutes.'

Emma refilled both their glasses. 'Cheers.'

'Cheers.'

She leant forward and whispered, 'Smile, Jack. I won't say it might never happen, because it already has. So you might as well smile anyway.'

'Thank you for those words of wisdom, Emma. I'm perfectly happy though. Just annoyed about the chilli.'

She eyed him dubiously. 'You're bizarre. All the things that have happened to you in the last two years and you've coped brilliantly. Make a chilli that's too hot and you fall apart.'

His eyes revealed that he saw the funny side.

A little while later, Jack dished up and carried both plates into the adjoining dining room. 'This way,' he said.

Emma followed him. It was a vibrant room, bright orange walls with gold and red stencilled patterns around the coving. It had a huge bay window with stone-coloured muslin curtains draped from an elaborate wrought-iron pole. A large oak table stood in the centre. On it were two wrought-iron candelabras, each holding three large candles. Two places had been set, opposite each other, widthways.

Jack put down the plates and lit the candles while Emma sat down and waited for him. He disappeared back into the kitchen and returned with her bottle of wine, already opened, then put on a CD of classical monastery music. Finally he took his seat.

'Feels like we're in some mediaeval church, especially with that music,' she said.

'As long as you don't start praying.'

Her eyebrows rose. 'Too late for that.' She smiled but soon her gaze fell downwards, suddenly realising that her comment could be misinterpreted. Jack was silent.

Emma took a large mouthful of the chilli. Instantly her mouth opened and she gasped aloud, waving her hand in front of it. She gulped at her wine, eyes watering.

Jack looked worried. 'Told you it's hot. Is it too much?'

'No, no. It's fine. Just took me by surprise.' She took a piece of French bread and buttered it, smiling. For some reason she found it quite amusing. Jack ate some chilli and deliberately tried to be more reserved in his reaction, with just a quick coughing fit.

Emma filled her fork mostly with rice, adding only a touch of chilli, yet she still felt a burning sensation in her mouth. They continued eating small mouthfuls, closely followed by some wine and bread. Each of them had broad smiles on their faces.

Emma asked him about his sailing and he told her of his numerous holidays sailing around Greece, Turkey, the whole of the Med, plus Bali and most of the Indian Ocean. He spoke passionately about it, saying it was a shame it was always only for a fortnight. All the while she listened intently to every word, her eyes reacting to each sentence he spoke.

As the meal progressed, they started to feel quite warm. Jack took off his jumper to reveal a light blue T-shirt. Emma rolled up the sleeves of her top. Yet still they grew hotter. Their faces were flushed and glowing, glazed by particles of sweat. They continued to drink the wine like water – anything to cool their mouths. Emma kept breaking into sporadic laughter.

'Well it's a good way to keep your heating bills

down,' she joked. 'Just make a hot chilli every night.'

Jack smiled and wiped his forehead with his napkin. 'I'm impressed you've eaten so much. You don't have to eat any more, I won't be offended.'

'In a strange way it's kind of addictive. Like when you've got toothache, you can't help pressing it.'

He glared at her. '*Thanks*!'

'Oh, sorry! Didn't mean . . .' She tried to look apologetic but instead couldn't help laughing a little.

Jack laughed too, but it was more at her. 'So my chilli's like a toothache. Goodness knows what you'll make of my curry!'

They both continued to laugh loudly, unrestrainedly. Their red and shiny faces beamed. After calming somewhat, Jack said, 'I even bought some red chilli peppers but didn't put them in.'

Emma's eyes lit up. 'I challenge you to a chilli tasting competition.'

'What?' he yelled. 'You're mad.'

'Totally. Go on, get them. I dare you.'

Jack stared at her and shook his head as if she were insane, but stood up and marched out to the kitchen. He returned with another bottle of wine and a small brown paper bag. Sitting back down opposite her, as if conducting some religious ceremony, he placed the paper bag strategically in the middle of the table. Very carefully he tore open the bag to reveal four small red chilli peppers.

'Small ones. They're the worst,' she blurted.

His eyes narrowed. 'Backing out, are you?'

'No! Why, are you?'

He shook his head very slowly, eyeing her reaction. The atmosphere became totally surreal with each of them acting like they were poker-faced gunmen in a saloon, psyching each other out.

'On the count of three,' Jack whispered, in a throaty Clint Eastwood take-off. 'We bite through half the chilli, chew both bits for another count of three, then swallow them.'

Emma nodded, suddenly appearing nervous.

'Ready?'

'Wait.' She gulped down some wine.

Jack gave a wry grin and in the same put-on voice said, 'That won't help you where we're going. Ready?'

She nodded.

'One, two, three.'

They each picked up one chilli. They bit it in two. Both their mouths moved in a chewing motion for a few moments. After they had both counted three in their heads, they stopped. In an instant of a second, they stared at each other. Jack swallowed hard, screwing up his face. At exactly the same time, Emma instinctively spat out the two halves into her hand. Jack glared at her, horrified. But before he could say anything, his mouth started to burn. He took a huge breath almost choking, as he spluttered, coughed and gasped. His face went completely red. His eyes stung from the inside.

Emma jumped up. She waved her hands and was practically hopping on the spot. 'Milk,' she screamed, and ran into the kitchen, yanking open the fridge and grabbing a carton. She turned. Jack stood behind her. He snatched the milk and guzzled it before coughing further. He gulped some more and it ran down his chin. He paced up and down the kitchen like a man possessed. Strange noises were coming from him, as if he was choking or suffocating. He kicked open the back door and stood on the newly built patio, desperately trying to breathe in the cool air.

Emma stood by the cooker, anxiously watching him

and worried by the severity of his reaction. She was relieved that she wasn't experiencing it herself but also felt ashamed for pulling out at the last minute.

It took at least ten minutes for Jack to start feeling more normal. His mouth and throat were still burning but he no longer felt like his whole body was going to explode. He was sitting on the steps of the patio, which ran down into his garden. He took another mouthful of milk and briefly glanced behind at Emma. He looked away.

'Are you OK?' she asked from the kitchen, her voice full of remorse and concern.

Jack closed his eyes. Emma went and sat on the step beside him. 'I'm so sorry, Jack. I feel awful. I just chickened out at the last minute. I didn't plan it like that.'

He looked at her and nodded. She bit her bottom lip and looked down.

They sat in silence for a few minutes, before Emma apologised a couple more times. She even considered going and eating a chilli herself, just to make it fair. Jack seemed to read her mind and told her not to bother. She sat with shoulders slightly bent, feeling completely annoyed with herself. Coward, she thought. Her eyes gazed out into the darkness. She didn't even want to look at him and considered going back to the hotel.

Jack eventually recovered and he began to see the funny side. He stared across at her and saw the distress on her face. In an odd way it made him smile. He edged slightly closer to her. She turned her head towards him, then away again, embarrassed.

'Emma,' he whispered.

For some reason she didn't answer. He continued to watch her. She was completely still, like a garden statue. She didn't even blink. As if in slow motion, he raised his hand and reached out towards her. It stopped, lingering just above her shoulder.

Emma saw it out of the corner of her eye. She stared ahead, her mind closed to thought.

'Emma,' he said again, still quietly.

Again she didn't answer or move. Jack edged his way closer. He gradually moved his hand and loosely took hold of her wrist. Her eyes focused down on it, touching her; he was touching her. He stared at it also, as though it wasn't his hand. It seemed to stay there for ages without anything else happening. Eyes and minds totally focused on it: his hand, her wrist. They sat and waited, confused, a state of innocent denial; a limbo from which to take stock, advance or retreat. Emma closed her eyes and breathed in deeply. Her heart was pounding. Jack felt her shaking . . . or was it him?

Emma's eyes opened and she gazed across at him. His eyelids slowly lifted and he stared directly back at her. The intensity in his eyes was totally hypnotic. Part of her fought to look away, run away, yet she couldn't move. She was overwhelmingly drawn to him, pulling, luring and reeling her closer and closer towards him. Thoughts tumbled away. She still tried to fight it, but a part of her urged him on. *Step further*, her soul whispered to her mind.

Jack's eyes focused down on her mouth. Emma felt his stare upon them and they parted, so very slightly, hardly noticeable. He slowly leant forward and gently pressed his lips against hers, barely touching, yet she felt the warmth of his breath brush across them. It sent a tingly sensation running through her. For an instant he drew back before leaning into her again, letting his lips meet and caress hers for longer. They felt so soft. His touch was so delicate and precise.

And she responded. It just happened. She found

herself kissing him back. In fact, within seconds she was kissing him as passionately, in a sense as desperately as he kissed her. Lips moving against lips, mouths open, moist and accepting. Jack's arms encased her holding her tight against him. She let out a loud murmur. For just an instant their eyes met and they stared deep within each other, seeing something, sensing something. It triggered another bout of frenzied kissing. His lips were fast and heavy on hers. She couldn't breathe. She didn't care.

She was actually kissing Jack Tomkinson! My God! She should stop and run. But she wanted more . . . more of this, more of him. His mouth was exploring her. His hands were exploring her. They found their way under her shirt and he was running his fingers up and down her back. And she wanted it, craving his touch all over. Every part of her body screamed to be discovered.

It was Emma who lay back guiding him on top of her. It was she who tugged his T-shirt from his jeans so she could feel his warm skin under her hands. And it was she who yanked the T-shirt over his head so she could see his naked, broad chest pressing down on her.

And soon Jack opened her top, pulling it to the side. Her bra was suddenly removed and she felt bare, exposed to him. But she wanted it that way, all the layers stripped away. She felt his hand caress her right breast with soft, circular movements. It sent little energy pulses shooting along each vein, pumping blood to every region of her body.

The next moment his mouth was there. He took her nipple fully into him, delicately sucking it. She instinctively arched her back and cradled the back of his head. His wet tongue teased her, sucking, licking, blowing softly. She let out a loud continuous moan.

The smell of him consumed her. She listened to the

sound of him at her. Emma wanted to see and brought her head up. It was at that moment that she would have done anything. She wanted and needed to do everything. And they did!

Secluded from the neighbouring houses by some fir trees, on a hastily arranged blanket, Emma felt a mild breeze brush against her naked legs. She felt her knickers being pulled down and away and Jack's hands part her thighs. She cried aloud as she felt his firm tongue there, exactly there . . . so perfectly there. Within a few minutes she cried even louder as she reached that moment when nothing else matters. And still he continued, she squealed with the sensitivity, but he carried on and soon she was shuddering again, her body overcome with sheer pleasure.

Jack eventually drew back and she watched him remove his jeans. She boldly continued to watch as he eased down his blue boxer shorts. And she stared on . . . biting her bottom lip.

While lying back on top of her and holding her like a precious gem, he entered her. They both let out sudden cries, breathing heavily, noisily. Yet they kissed so tenderly, with such meaning and feeling. And the intensity grew between them, hearts racing, bodies sweating, their smells working their native, primitive purpose. Emma felt him fully inside her and desperately wanted to scream loudly and endlessly, completely overcome with it all. It was one of the few times she had ever completely let go.

Just before it happened, before he cried again, he stared directly into her eyes, and held her so close, because it was her, it was all about her . . . being with her. She gazed back as he let out a mass of cries, his body jerking, gradually stopping. And they smiled as they lay clinging to each other, panting and exhausted.

## 27

Dressed only in a short, red silk dressing gown, Julia stood in the hallway, peering into the dining room where Jeremy was sleeping on a small camp bed, next to the window. He was lying outstretched under a single duvet with his bare leg sprawled over the side. It was fairly dark apart from a soft, hazy light that filtered in from the moon through the undrawn curtains.

Julia had been standing at the doorway for at least five minutes just watching him. Occasionally she glanced away, twice running her hand through her hair. It seemed like another couple of minutes passed before she finally took a deep breath and cautiously crept in, stopping barely a foot away from him.

Jeremy, Julia and Thomas had arrived late Friday night at his country cottage in Dulverton, Exmoor, ready for a weekend away from London. Jeremy had wanted to spend the Saturday driving them around the local villages and beauty spots, stopping to eat at a pub he knew. However on Thomas's suggestion they had spent the day pony-trekking across the moors. Jeremy went along under complete duress, considering it a torturous way to spend a day. How could it compare to a gentle drive followed by delicious food and exquisite wine? However, he didn't wish to appear a spoilsport; after all they were his guests.

Thomas and Julia could ride and happily cantered off with the experienced group. Unfortunately, never having sat on a horse, Jeremy had to remain with the other beginners, mostly noisy children. They kept secretly hitting the behind of his pony so it would trot off, leaving him clinging on for dear life and screaming loudly to the instructor to save him. After an hour and a half of this he'd had enough and in the middle of the moors, jumped off and refused to get back on. The instructor ended up having to lead his pony the four miles back with an exhausted and irritable Jeremy walking behind.

At the cottage that night, over dinner, he stated, 'Never again. My nerves are in tatters. My bones are wretched. Anything with four legs is not to be trusted.'

Thomas and Julia couldn't stop laughing. Recently they were always laughing together, thought Jeremy.

The cottage was small and very homely with two bedrooms upstairs and a lounge, dining room and kitchen downstairs. Being the perfect host, Jeremy politely offered the bedrooms to his guests, leaving him on the camp bed in the dining room. They were all tired from the day's activity and headed off to bed around eleven. However, half an hour later, having waited for the house to go quiet, Julia wandered back downstairs and now stood hovering over him.

As if sensing someone in the room, Jeremy opened his eyes and instinctively jumped. 'You scared me half to death,' he said in a melodramatic whisper.

Julia just smiled and knelt down on the floor beside him. 'Couldn't sleep. Fancy a night cap?'

'Not really. I'm was having no trouble sleeping until now.'

She looked concerned and said in a serious manner, 'I hope you didn't feel deserted today . . . with me and Thomas being in the other group.'

He leant forward, propping himself up on one elbow. The duvet slipped down revealing his plump chest, lightly covered with sandy brown hair. 'Story of my life,' he said despondently. 'Sticking with the beginners, the novice group, the un-athletic . . . In school, I was total crap at sport. Always last to be picked for any team;

considered a handicap to have me on your side.'

'Everyone's different. No doubt you excelled academically.'

'A bean bag with a brain!'

'Oh Jeremy,' she whispered sympathetically.

He frowned. 'I wish you wouldn't keep saying that. "*Oh Jeremy*." You've been saying it loads over the last few weeks. Makes me feel really pathetic. I never hear you say "*Oh, Thomas*".'

'He's not the sort of person you'd say it to. Not sweet like you.'

'Oh please. I'm sick of sweet. Women always see me as sweet and funny.'

'But you are.'

Jeremy cringed. 'Yes, everybody's best friend . . . but nothing more.' His gaze travelled past her and lingered in the distance.

Julia stared at him for some time; her eyes looked at his chest and down across the outline of his body. Biting her lip, she leant forward and gently squeezed his shoulder. In a quiet, fairly nervous voice she said, 'You could be more . . . with some people.'

His puzzled eyes settled back on her. Several moments passed where they just stared at each other, neither speaking.

Eventually she let go of his shoulder, letting her hand slide smoothly down his arm.

Jeremy lay watching her and the way she was staring at him.

Still no words were spoken. In fact, both in and out of the cottage there was complete silence – unsettling for those used to London with its constant background din.

Julia's hand started on the move again, retracing its steps back up his arm – so slowly, delicately. Once at the top, her index finger started to trace around his collarbone. Jeremy swallowed. Even the sound of that seemed to be magnified a hundred times. He looked away, unsure what was happening. Only when her hand started to travel downwards across his chest, slipping with ease under the duvet, and reaching his navel without showing any signs of stopping its descent, he suddenly grabbed it.

'*Julia!*' he squealed in a high-pitched panic before quietening down to a whisper in case Thomas heard. 'Is this some sort of pass?'

The corners of her mouth slowly turned upwards. 'Some sort of one . . . yes.'

His usual over-the-top reaction didn't materialise. Instead he just stared at her. His dazed eyes dilated. His lips parted slowly. All the while he held her hand locked against his lower stomach as if he'd trapped something that was too dangerous to let go.

A minute must have passed before he managed to say, 'Maybe you should go back upstairs.'

'I don't want to go upstairs,' she said calmly.

Jeremy shook his head, but a brief glimmer of a smile passed across his lips. 'I don't understand . . . you could have any man.'

'I don't care for many.' Her reply was forthright. 'I just thought it could be fun.'

'Until the morning, when we'd both die of shame.'

'I wasn't thinking of just one night.'

Jeremy gasped and eyed her suspiciously. 'Look, I'm not that wealthy.'

'That's not why I . . . oh, *God*! I don't care about that!'

He raised an eyebrow.

'I don't,' she protested with a mocking glint in her eye. 'Well I did, but not now. Thomas has been educating me on socialism and a caring, sharing world. I'm a changed woman. Even read the *Guardian* now.'

'How compassionate of you.'

'Well, maybe not totally changed . . . but I've genuinely grown really fond of you. We get on great. Can't you see that?'

'Yes, but . . .'

'You're just out of practice. I was right . . . .you do need to come out . . . *of bloody hibernation*!'

'Jesus . . . I'm not some squirrel.'

Julia started to giggle and even Jeremy was smiling broadly.

'Oh Jeremy,' she said.

He grunted loudly and fell back on the camp bed covering his face with both hands. 'Stop *saying* that!' he cried.

Julia lurched forward grabbing each of his hands in hers. She tugged them from his face, pinning them down on the pillow either side of his head. She was leaning over him with her face barely two inches from his. He stared up at her, wondering what the hell she was going to do next.

'Listen Jeremy,' she stated determinedly. 'I want you to know that although on the one hand you're a complete oddball, I also happen to think that you're the most witty, intelligent, interesting, sensitive and lovely man I've ever met.'

Jeremy bit his lip before cautiously mouthing, 'Thank you.' He could see out of the corner of his eye that her dressing gown had loosened and had come apart. He briefly glanced down, then back up at her. She wasn't wearing anything underneath.

'You can't put your life on hold for ever,' she said. 'Sometimes you should grab what's on offer.'

Again he glanced down seeing her near naked body towering above him. He breathed deeply. His eyes looked meekly into hers. After what seemed like the longest pause ever, Julia slowly leant further forward.

Jeremy waited, bracing himself. Her lips met his and she kissed him – just the once. Pulling back slightly, she smiled. Her eyes sparkled with intent. She kissed him again, this time for longer. She tried to open his lips with her tongue, yet they were pinched tightly together. Soon she felt his head turning away. Withdrawing back, she saw his face, which said it all; eyes closed, face twisted and distressed-looking.

She instantly let go of him, swinging her body around so she ended up sitting on the floor with her back leaning against the camp bed. Jeremy remained lying there for a moment. Eventually he opened his eyes and slowly sat up.

'I'm really fond of you,' he whispered cheerfully, 'I really am. But all that physical stuff doesn't do much for me. Unathletic, remember? You're not missing anything. It would all be terribly embarrassing in the morning. Mark my words . . . I'm no George Clooney.'

Julia raised her eyes heavenwards and shook her head. 'Funnily enough, I had gathered that.'

In a more serious manner he said, 'I suppose it's also because a part of me is still holding out for Emma. I think it would be different with her.' His gaze drifted downwards. 'I know I'm crazy, but maybe one day she'll leave Tony. She's not happy with him.'

Julia stood up, retying her robe. 'You're kidding yourself, Jeremy. Nothing's ever going to happen with her . . . and you know it. You can't keep your life on hold for some silly fantasy.'

'It's not a silly fantasy and my life's not on hold. I can't help loving her,' he said despondently.

Julia grunted angrily and stormed out of the room, leaving Jeremy gazing into space. *It's not a silly fantasy*, he told himself. *It's just a matter of time*.

## 28

Emma and Jack continued to lie in each other's arms for several minutes. The sweet smell of the fir trees that surrounded them filled the air. That smell would forever remind her of this night.

Occasionally they kissed but mostly they just lay there, holding each other, eyes gazing upwards into the clear night sky. It was fairly bright owing to a three-quarter moon and Emma counted at least fifteen stars. They could have been anywhere in the world. Under such a vast sky she felt small, insignificant. Maybe it was easier to think like that. After all, how important were her actions compared to those of all the rest of the world? She was just one of billions of people trying to find some happiness and purpose. Would anyone deny her that? Yet with each minute that passed she felt her body, so relaxed and serene earlier, stiffen slightly with an intrusive, unwelcome tension that gradually descended on her.

Sensing a change, Jack turned to face her. 'Are you OK?' he asked, in a whisper.

Emma stared into his blue eyes, but was silent, unsure how to answer. Looking worried he kissed her softly on the lips and held her securely, gently stroking her back. Closing her eyes she clung even more tightly to him.

'It's all right, Emma,' he said reassuringly. 'It's all right. Everything's going to be fine,' he repeated over and over.

Listening to his softly-spoken, soothing words, she gradually began to relax, drifting away under his attentive hands. After a few minutes she opened her eyes; two tears ran down her cheek. Slowly she eased herself on top of him bringing her face right up next to his. Jack smiled at her. She traced around the outside of his lips with her finger, then up to his eyes. He watched her, watching him.

'Your eyes are so intense,' she said.

He appeared concerned.

'No, that's good,' she added hastily. 'Things matter to you.'

'And you,' he replied.

Coming from the garden next door they suddenly heard, 'Rosie! Rosie! Come on, Rosie.'

They lay completely still, staring at each other.

'Rosie, where are you?' It was the neighbour calling her cat. Outside and naked, Emma felt vulnerable. Jack sat up.

'Let's go inside,' he whispered, jumping up and quickly grabbing both sets of clothes.

Emma stood up and picked up her court shoes, holding them tight against her. She was nervously looking around hoping nobody had seen them; the thought of it disturbed her greatly.

Jack took her hand and led her inside. They ran naked through his house and up the stairs. With each stair she climbed her body seemed to tense a little. When finally in his bedroom, Jack threw their clothes in a pile on the floor and sat down on the bed lifting his arm towards her.

Maybe it was the break in their passion, or the neighbour, or the double bed that Emma now stared at, but her eyes opened wide, only now taking things in. The reality of the situation came crashing down on her. She looked at Jack Tomkinson sitting naked on the bed waiting for her to join him. She looked down at herself, completely naked standing in front of him. She glared ahead of her and thought of all they had just done.

Jack instantly noticed the change in her eyes and his head dropped forward into his hands. For a moment neither of them moved.

Gripped by a sudden panic, Emma darted to the pile of clothes. She dropped to her knees and desperately began to separate her own from his. She made for his bathroom, locking the door behind her. Within a couple of minutes she emerged fully clothed, apart from her knickers, which she guessed were still outside. Seeing Jack, she instantly stopped in her tracks and stared at him. He was bare-chested, but had put on his jeans and was sitting, shoulders bent, silent, motion-less, gazing trance-like towards the floor. He looked sad, as if defeated. Part of her desperately wanted to hug him and be with him again. Yet she felt desperate to get away too. Tony's image refused to leave her mind.

Jack's dispirited eyes gradually looked up at her. In a quiet, almost timid voice, he said, 'Please don't go, Emma . . . not like this.'

Tears sprang to her eyes. She looked in pain. She *was* in pain, a deep cutting pain that was tearing through every limb of her body. Hugging herself with both arms she cried, 'I'm so sorry . . . *So sorry*! I . . . I . . . Tony . . . have to think. Give me some time.' Turning sharply she ran from the room, down the stairs and into the kitchen. She grabbed her bag and jacket. For an instant, she looked out to the garden then she fled from the house, down his street and finally on to the main road heading back to the hotel. She slowed to a hurried walk, gasping for breath. What had she done? She knew nothing would ever be the same again.

At three o'clock in the morning, Emma was still wide awake, lying fully clothed on her hotel bed. The television was quietly on in the background. She hadn't even attempted to sleep; her mind wouldn't rest or shut down, not tonight anyway. She didn't try to calm herself, but instead allowed every emotion, good and bad, to possess and swamp her, letting them run their course before the next feeling took its place. At times she sobbed uncontrollably, cradling herself like a child. At other times there were no tears, just a paralysing fear. But occasionally, within the maelstrom of emotions, there was a mere glimmer of a smile that surfaced on her lips as she remembered the incredible pleasure and feelings she had experienced that evening. Exhausted by it all, she welcomed the numb, anaesthetised state that eventually descended on her.

By eight o'clock the following morning, feeling nauseous and depleted, she ordered a continental breakfast from room service. She sat up in bed and tried to swallow a piece of toast but it just wouldn't go down. Pushing the breakfast tray to the side, Emma stood up. She walked into the bathroom and turned on the shower. She undressed and when the water ran hot, too hot, she stepped in. Leaning against the wall, she lowered her head as she allowed the force of the water to run over her. Steam filled the glass cubicle. She stood there for some time, not moving an inch. Slowly her eyes focused down on her naked body. She ran her fingers softly over her breasts, her stomach and down to the tops of her legs. Closing her eyes, she held herself and imagined Jack was with her. She wondered how he was? How he felt about her? Yet from nowhere, the image of Tony appeared again. Tears filled her eyes.

Suddenly her sight became blurred. Her head felt heavy, as though it had been injected with lead. Her legs started to collapse beneath her. Her body slowly slid down the tiled wall. She tried to hold on, balance herself, but her hands couldn't stop her descent. Soon she was lying sideways on the shower floor, semi-aware, yet unable to move.

The cubicle was completely filled with steam as the hot water pounded down on her. A thought occurred – *maybe I'm dying right here, right now.* Emma closed her eyes as if accepting it; she would just drift away to whatever came next. At least that way she wouldn't hurt anyone. But it was in that moment she felt some feeling return to her limbs. Her eyes opened and began to focus again. Within another minute she had managed to sit up against the wall. She continued to sit there, thinking, shaking her head as she continually changed her mind. Only when the steam from the shower made her breathing too difficult did she stumble up and turn the torrent of hot water off.

Wrapping herself in a towel, wet and with red, crinkled skin, Emma went and lay on the bed, arms outstretched like a crucifix. And she prayed! She prayed for the first time in ages. At first she wasn't exactly sure what to pray for – certainly not forgiveness. She prayed no one would be hurt, but she knew life wasn't like that, people always got hurt. She prayed that she would do the right thing, but decided that she had spent her whole life trying to do the right thing. That had got her nowhere and she was sick of it. Lying completely still, pausing mid-sentence with God, she couldn't think of anything else to say. It eventually came to her, 'I pray to have the courage to truly be me and live the life I want.' She continued to lie there, closing her eyes and eventually drifting off into a light sleep.

It was nearly two o'clock in the afternoon when she woke fully. She rubbed her eyes. They were itchy from all the crying and the remains of last night's make-up, which she hadn't taken off. Feeling chilly she stood up, dropped the towel and wrapped herself in her dressing gown. It could have been any lazy Sunday, but of course it wasn't. Her eyes were drawn towards the telephone. There was only one thing to do. Walking over to it, she proceeded to dial Jack's number. Her heart was racing and her legs felt weak again. Fearing a repeat of the earlier fainting incident, Emma sat down on the edge of the bed and waited, biting her lip.

His answering machine came on. Even hearing his voice on the outgoing message sent a wave of anxiety through her. It was a struggle not to put the phone down. After hearing the tone she managed to speak. 'Jack, this is Emma.' She waited, thinking he might be there and would pick up. Nothing happened. Screwing up her face in frustration all she managed to say was, 'Please call.' Slamming down the receiver, she fell back on the bed and curled herself up in a ball.

Ten minutes later, Emma was still curled up on the bed, gazing into space when the phone rang. She jumped, her whole body instantly tense. It continued to ring. She sat up cautiously and stared at it, mentally and emotionally preparing herself. Slowly she picked up the receiver. 'Hello?' she said, tentatively.

'Em?'

She wasn't expecting that voice and she panicked. Taken off guard, no words came to her.

'Em, it's me. You there?' asked Tony.

Emma's stomach was knotted in two. She deliberately tried to compose herself and finally replied, 'Yes. I'm here.'

'You OK?'

'Yes, of course.'

'How was yesterday then?' he asked.

'Fine, nothing great.' She clutched the receiver more tightly.

'That's a shame. What did you do in the end?'

'Walked around the city and its parks . . . a bit of shopping too,' she lied.

'Buy anything?'

'Nothing.'

'Sure you're OK? You sound a bit irritable,' he said.

'A headache, I woke up with it.'

'Don't talk to me about headaches. Had the mother of all of them this morning myself. That's why I'm here, I didn't go.'

Emma was silent.

'You know . . . the competition.'

'Yeah, of course, the competition,' she said, closing her eyes and holding her stomach with her left hand.

'So what are you up to today?' he asked.

'I don't know yet.'

'You could have travelled back in the end. Sounds like we're both fed up and on our own. We could have gone walking in the Dales. Must sort that out,' he said. 'Suppose I'll head off to the Swan later. Meet up with Rob and Becky.'

It was strange, but in that moment she felt a sudden and overwhelming anger towards him, towards it all. She felt and saw it in her mind's eye, hopes and dreams blown away, ashes in the wind. It was all such a waste.

Rage welled within her. It came out of the blue, gripping her violently. Confused and threatened by the strength of her feelings, she remained silent, desperately fighting to hide and suppress the scream that wanted to erupt.

Tony didn't really notice the long drawn-out silence, as he had carried the phone into their sitting room. He slumped down on the sofa, picked up the remote and flicked the television on in the background. Italian football came on.

'You gonna stay in your room all day then?' he asked.

In the distant background she heard his voice but was somehow detached from it. His words just blurred together.

'Emma?'

She was remembering the last time they had gone to the Dales. Tony had hardly spoken to her all day. When she'd asked if anything was wrong, he said it was nothing, as usual. He had looked like he would have preferred to have been anywhere other than there with her that day. He was so obviously bored. She hadn't enjoyed it either, not with him that way. How could she?

Tony shouted. '*Emma!* Can you hear me?'

'Yes,' she answered, calmly.

'I said, are you staying in your room all day? Sounds boring.'

'I don't know.' She swallowed hard. 'I don't know what to do . . . a bit of a quandary.'

'Well whatever, just enjoy.'

'You never went to the shooting competition,' she stated.

'I told you, bastard headache.'

'You mean bastard hangover.'

He hesitated before saying, 'Same thing.'

In a weary, resigned voice, she said, 'We would never have got to the Dales, you do realise that.'

In the background Juventus had just scored. 'What are you going on about?' he asked, bewildered.

'It never happens,' she said in a whisper down the phone. Her eyes glazed over with tears. She was shaking her head. 'It never happens . . . none of it . . . all the plans, ideas, arrangements. They never actually happen.'

Tony frowned. 'I didn't realise it meant that much to you. We'll go next weekend, make a day of it.'

Emma stared in front of her. He continued talking but she was thinking of other things. Everything started to make more sense. How she had managed to find herself in this situation suddenly became clearer. It had only been a matter of time. She considered how easily she had lied to him. She thought of Steve Ingrams lying to his wife, Sarah, so he could grab a few moments with Trish. I am no Steve Ingrams, she told herself. There will be no more lies. This will be sorted.

'Tony, I have to go,' she interrupted.

'Why? You said you weren't doing anything.'

'I have some things to deal with. I will talk with you soon, maybe in a couple of days, but right now I have to go.'

'*Is* everything OK? Why are—'

'I suppose so. Take care and look after yourself . . . bye.' She put down the phone before he could ask her anything else. Two minutes later it rang again. Guessing it to be Tony, she didn't answer it.


Emma sat on the stool staring into the dressing-table mirror. She ran her fingers over her slightly swollen and puffy face. After taking off yesterday's make-up, she set about freshly applying some more. She put on foundation, blue eye-shadow, black eyeliner and mascara. The eyeliner was used to really define and exaggerate the outline of her eyes, much more than usual. A deep red lipstick was chosen to add to the effect. Her layered auburn hair was scrunched up with hair mousse.

She stared at her reflection in the mirror. She looked so different and it wasn't just the make-up. There was a strange presence about her. Her eyes, although tired and slightly bloodshot, had an added quality to them, an extra depth and intensity.

She was pleased she looked different. 'I am different,' she said aloud. 'I *am* different.'

Emma put on some black knickers and a new black bra, over which she pulled the long blue knitted dress that she'd worn for the launch party. She slipped on her black court shoes and grabbing her handbag, left her room and walked along the hotel corridor. Up ahead were the lifts. She stopped abruptly, pressing the button several times to call it. When the doors opened, revealing no one inside, she stepped in and pressed floor six; the top floor. The lift doors slowly closed, encasing her inside, and the car started to move.

Emma stared, transfixed by her reflection in the mirrored walls; a strange smile gradually appearing on her face. She looked up at the ceiling of the lift and around at its four walls. She gave a wiggle of her hips. Soon she did a little dance, bopping side to side, waving her hands in the air. On reaching the top floor the doors opened, nobody was there. She pressed the ground-floor button and the lift started its descent. Again she wiggled her hips and turned sharply as if doing the Tango. As the lift continued on its journey she danced, turned and posed. Her long clinging dress emphasised her shape.

The lift came to a stop and Emma stood up straight, head up, shoulders back. The doors opened and she gracefully and confidently walked out and across the lobby. A number of heads, both men and women, turned and glanced at her as she glided through the reception area as if she owned the world.

Nearing the entrance, she stopped sharply as she caught sight of the doors to the hotel bar. For about ten seconds she stared at it through pensive eyes. With a sudden look of determination, she marched towards it and once inside, headed straight for the counter. The place was fairly busy with a good mix of people, mostly residents. Seeing an empty stool by the bar, she sat down and waited to be served.

A barman approached her and smiled. 'What would you like?'

'Gin and tonic,' she replied.

He nodded and went to prepare it.

Emma looked around. There were a number of men sitting alone, some reading newspapers. A few stared directly at her. The rest of the people sat in small groups chatting away and barely noticed her.

'There you go. Three pounds seventy,' said the barman, placing a glass on the counter.

She paid him and sipped her drink, preparing herself for her next destination and what was going to happen. Maybe it was just her imagination but she felt the eyes of a number of people on her. She didn't care. She was happy to be seated there totally alone; it was like another little challenge, a statement to herself. People could think what they liked. Emma took another sip of her drink and ate some peanuts that were laid out in little dishes on the bar.

A tall, plump gentleman in his early forties, with thinning, brown wavy hair and a full moustache, stood up and approached the bar. He was well dressed in casual brown trousers and a blue patterned jumper. He stood at the counter a little way down from her. Emma was aware that he had been watching her. She looked over at him. He smiled. She looked away.

As soon as the barman took his order, the man walked towards her and coming across an empty stool near hers, sat down. Several moments passed before he said, 'On your own?'

She nodded slowly.

'Can I buy you a drink?' he asked, in what she guessed was a Canadian accent.

She glanced sideways at him then back at her half-empty glass. 'Thank you, but no. I'm not staying.'

'That's a shame. The name's David Bryant.'

Emma sipped her drink. 'Emma.'

'Pleased to meet you, Emma.'

The barman brought the gentleman's drink over.

'Whatever the lady's having too.' He stared back at her and smiled. 'Like me, you sound as if you're a stranger to these shores.'

She nodded.

When she added nothing else, he said, 'Toronto, Canada. Over on business at the trade show . . . Telecommunications. What about you?'

'England, business, secretary, new office.' She ticked off each word like they were items on a shopping list. The barman brought her drink but she ignored it. David Bryant ate some peanuts, watching her. His eyes travelled across her. Emma kept staring at her glass, hoping he'd go away.

'So how long are you in Dublin for?' he asked.

'Another month maybe.'

'I'm here for two weeks. Perhaps we can meet up. Travelling's damn lonely, don't you find?'

'Too busy.'

'Everyone has to relax, let off steam. You look like the sort of girl who knows how to have a good time.' He was leaning forward into her; she could smell the whiskey on his breath. Inside she cringed, wanting to leave. But then she stopped herself. *What am I doing?* She stared directly at him for a few moments then looked away. Her eyelids lowered and she slowly shook her head, emitting a strange laugh.

'Hey, what's so funny?' he asked.

'Everything! Everything is so funny. One can hardly take it all so seriously. It's all a joke.'

'Exactly,' he said, with a reassured smile. 'It's about enjoying yourself.'

Again she glanced at him then away.

'So how shall we enjoy ourselves, alone in this country together?'

'But we aren't together,' she said.

'We could be,' he smirked.

'I don't think so. You see, I have a husband . . . and, I think, a lover. It's confusing enough.'

His eyes lit up. He laid his hand on hers and whispered into her ear. 'I'm married too. I'm not talking long term here.'

She stared at him through narrowed eyes. He winked and ran his index finger slowly across her hand, heading up along her arm. 'Let me buy you dinner,' he suggested.

Clenching her fists, Emma jerked her hand away. He was a large man and though seated, he towered above her, oozing confidence, with an insincere, smug smile.

It suddenly hit her – it was that same look as the creep on the train had had. She remembered how intimidated she had felt and of course the anger afterwards. Damn that man! Damn this man! She recalled Jeremy's comments – '*You've got* I don't want to make a fuss *written all over your forehead.*' Well not any more, she thought. I want to make a fuss, a fucking big fuss!

Her face slowly grew cold. Her eyes glared at him with an inner fury. He withdrew slightly. Gulping down the last of her own drink, Emma leapt up. With an air of defiance and in a deliberately loud yet controlled voice she said, 'If you want a fuck . . .'

At the word 'fuck' a number of people looked over at them. Even both barmen stopped what they were doing. Knowing she had everyone's attention she continued in the same determined voice, 'If you want a fuck, I *suggest* you hire a prostitute.' Emma turned and started to walk calmly out of the bar. She felt everyone's eyes on her. It made her walk with extra confidence, feeling strangely euphoric after her outburst. She stopped for a moment, looking around at everyone, staring back at her. God it felt good not giving a shit! Amazed by the little scene, several people passed comment to each other as she went by. *So what*, she thought. *I'm different now.*

David Bryant smiled uncomfortably at the barman and sheepishly returned to his seat. Feeling everyone's continued stare, he shortly left for another bar – maybe better luck there.

Once outside, Emma laughed aloud and went on her way with a smile. Coming across a newsagents, she went in and bought a family-size bar of Cadbury's Dairy Milk. She opened it and ate chunk after chunk while she walked. On her nearly empty stomach it tasted wonderful. In the last few months she'd hardly eaten any chocolate and right now she was going to make up for it. She wanted to make up for a lot of things.

She walked for miles around the city of Dublin, all along the River Liffey, through every park she came across, sitting on a bench for ages in St Stephen's Green, dreaming.

Eventually she found herself on the main road heading towards Ballsbridge, but coming across a pub by the canal, she stopped for another drink. She sat on her own, gazing out of the window.

Looking at a clock on the pub wall, she saw it was

nearly eight o'clock. Somehow the whole afternoon and early evening had disappeared. It was time to go. She stood up and continued on her journey. Her pace quickened all the time and within twenty minutes she was finally there. She stood at the bottom of the steps to Jack's house, staring at his blue door.

## 29

Jack's car was parked outside. Emma slowly walked up the steps to his front door. She pressed the bell. Footsteps could be heard inside. The door was unlocked. It opened . . . and there he was.

Jack stood tall in the middle of the doorway; his proud and reserved stance had returned. Unshaven and wearing last night's clothes, blue T-shirt and brown jeans, he stared down at her. His tired, guarded eyes examined her.

Emma stared back, noting his distant manner. Neither of them moved or gave any sign of acknowledgement.

Eventually, Emma's eyes slowly drifted downwards and beyond him. Jack stood aside from the door. She stepped closer and went inside. Shutting the door, he walked straight into the kitchen and pulled a chair away from the table. He stood back against the kitchen units while Emma nervously sat down. This wasn't what she had expected.

Looking up at him, nothing was given away in his aloof, stern expression. She bit her lip and shook her head. Maybe last night had meant nothing to him. *I could just be one of many*, she thought. *Maybe he's still seeing Rachel!*

Jack's eyes narrowed as he watched the emotions flickering across her features. Emma brought both hands up to her face, breathing loudly.

'*So!*' she suddenly exclaimed, sitting back and smiling awkwardly. 'Last night?' She glanced at him then away, waiting for something, anything from him. But he was silent. Why wasn't he saying anything? Her gaze slowly returned to him.

'So,' she said again, this time sounding annoyed. 'We've had sex, Jack.' Hopefully that would provoke a response.

Jack looked on tentatively. He stepped forward and sat down at the table, his eyes fixed tightly on to hers. When he spoke his voice had a hint of annoyance also. 'What exactly are you trying to say, Emma?'

Her eyes shut as if trying to escape his penetrating stare.

'You regret it?' he asked, accusingly. 'Is that what you came to tell me? Want to pretend it never happened? Want to return to the Manchester office right away . . . run away back?'

'Figured me all out, have you?' she replied bitterly.

'I don't know . . . *have* I?'

Emma gave a loud, irritated sigh. 'What it is about you? Jesus, you know how to wind me up.'

'You have a similar effect on me,' he retorted.

They both glared at each other. A heavy silence descended. With each moment that passed, Jack's distant manner infuriated her more, as if confirming her worst fears.

After several moments she asked, 'Is that what *you* want? To forget it?' She waited anxiously.

Jack closed his eyes and shook his head. Practically in a whisper he said, 'Most definitely not.'

Emma eyes flew open.

'Do you want to forget it?' he asked.

After a lengthy pause she also shook her head.

'What do you want to do then?'

There was so much she wanted to say, but it was as if she'd suddenly lost the power to speak. Her mouth was open yet no words came out. Tears came to her eyes. Jack reached across and coupled her hand in his. He squeezed it reassuringly. A well of emotion rose up in her; all she could do was smile at him. He carried on holding her hand and smiled back. They remained sitting there for a few minutes.

'I'm not the sort to have an affair,' she said determinedly.

'I know. I don't want an affair.'

'What *do* you want?'

'I want it all.' His eyes lowered as if he was embarrassed to speak so openly. 'To get to know you better, all of you, have a proper relationship . . . I'd like to promise a happy ever after, but I can't. Maybe that's life's cynicism in me.'

'No one can,' Emma said.

'But I'd really like . . .' he paused and breathed heavily. 'I'm forty-three, Emma. So-called middle-aged.' He smiled. 'Life's short enough, why pussyfoot around. I just want to . . . to try.'

'Do you know what you're asking me?'

He stared directly at her and nodded.

She stood up and walked over to the back door, gazing outside at the patio. She could see the beautiful array of early flowers and shrubs in his garden, starting to blossom with the spring.

'It's going to happen anyway, Emma. Maybe I'm being selfish but you're not happy with Tony. I know you're not.'

Emma turned towards him. 'Let's not go to work tomorrow.'

Jack looked surprised but slowly nodded. 'What do you want to do?'

'Anything, nothing, everything, go somewhere, stay here.' Her face grew intensely serious. 'I want another day of this, where none of it matters. It can stay out there, outside.' She stretched out her arm as if pushing something away from her. 'Where it can't touch me.

You know, all the decisions, the fall-out. I want a day to do whatever.'

'Then what?'

Her head lowered. 'I won't think about that now. I won't think, I'll just do.'

'You won't run off again, will you?'

'No, Jack. I want to be here.'

Jack continued to look at her, slightly perplexed and concerned.

That evening, they drank large amounts of expensive wine; it added to her sense of abandonment. After dinner they moved into his lounge where Jack lit an open fire and they danced freely to his Glenn Miller CD, imitating the forties' style while laughing loudly. Next came Elvis, and Jack taught Emma how to jive. While trying to swing her high over his hip he pulled something in his back.

'You really are middle-aged,' she teased. He chased her around the settee, bombarding her with cushions.

Whenever Elvis sang a love song they embraced and slow-danced, kissing tenderly. It was as though neither of them had a care in the world – each moment was extremely precious, elevating and heightening every emotion.

After nearly two hours of the energetic mayhem, they both fell back on the couch, giggling and drinking more wine. Jack clutched his back while screwing his face up.

Now serious, she asked, 'Is that really aching?'

'A bit, not too bad.'

'I'll massage you.' She didn't wait for a reply and jumped up. 'Do you have any oils or creams?'

'A muscle rub lotion for sports injuries.'

'That'll do, plus a sheet and a towel. I'll do it in here, it's nice and warm.'

Jack disappeared upstairs and returned with a blue

bottle, a towel and a sheet off his bed. Emma had prepared the lounge. The only source of light was from the fire and the lit candelabras that she had fetched from the dining room and strategically placed on two side tables. An instrumental classical CD was quietly playing in the background.

She took the sheet from him and laid it flat out on the floor in front of the fire. She looked up at him.

'Clothes off,' she ordered with a smile.

'That's rather one-sided, don't you think? Maybe you should undress too.'

She glared at him, narrowing her eyes. 'Off with them.'

Of course he gave in and was soon lying naked, face down on the sheet, with a towel over his lower back and legs to keep them warm. She rubbed the citrus-smelling lotion into her hands and started to massage the top of his back with strong circular movements. She worked on his neck, his shoulders, moving downwards towards his waist. He lay there silently, listening to the light crackle from the fire, the soothing music in the background and the sound of her hands working over him.

'Just relax, Jack, let all the stress drift away.'

Emma enjoyed the feel of him, getting to know all the contours of his body. She couldn't help placing some kisses along his spine and running her fingers sensuously up and down. Her hands occasionally slipped under the towel and were brought back up with a smile.

It was when she started to massage the tops of his legs that he suddenly turned over and grabbed her, pulling her to the floor and getting on top of her.

'I'm supposed to be massaging you,' she protested.

'And now I'm going to massage you.' He tugged her dress up to her waist.

It was an unusual massage, thought Emma – the

detail he paid to such a small area! In fact, far from initially releasing tension his touch gradually built it up and up in her. 'Jack . . .' she mouthed incoherently.

He continued with the so-called massage until she screamed loudly, almost violently, as her whole body shuddered, finally releasing the pent-up tension. A little while later he pulled her on top of him. She was sitting up facing him and cried aloud as she felt him inside her. With his guidance and her own desire, she moved in ways she hadn't before; at times she was almost disorientated, losing herself, yielding yet demanding, chaotic yet controlled, moaning, crying, loving, touching and screaming – screaming so the world would hear and know.

And later they bathed together.

'A bit decadent, isn't it?' said Emma.

'What?'

'A circular bath.'

'Only if it were filled with champagne. Maybe we'll try that tomorrow.'

She stared at him, her eyes alarmed; the word 'tomorrow' like a swearword. This was her twenty-four hours of living only in the moment, doing whatever she wanted to.

'Sorry,' he said, understanding.

She smiled and flicked some water at him. He flicked some back, which was enough to start a fully-fledged water fight; the bathroom came off worse.

Later that night they slept coiled and entwined together in his bed. Exhausted, Emma drifted off quite easily. Jack watched her for ages, tuning each breath in with hers, looking at her eyebrows, her eyelashes, nose, mouth, every part of her face. He kissed her gently on her lips before nuzzling even closer and gradually slipping off into sleep.

## 30

'Hi Rosemary, it's me, Emma,' she said the next morning while telephoning the office.

'Hi, wondered where you were. Are you OK?'

'Actually I'm not feeling well,' Emma lied.

'Nothing serious, I hope.'

'No, just a cold. Feeling really achy, you know. I'll just rest up.'

'Your mother, Charlotte, just called. She said it wasn't anything serious but can you call her back.'

'Thanks, I'll speak to her later . . . Is Jack in yet?' asked Emma.

'Rang and spoke with Sean earlier, apparently he's working from home today.'

'Oh I see. Well, can you let Sean know I rang?'

'Sure. I hope you're feeling better tomorrow. Do you need anything?' Rosemary sounded concerned.

'No, no. I'm sure I'll be fine tomorrow. I'd better go.'

'Take care, if you do need anything, let me know. I'll run it around for you.'

'Thanks a lot. Bye then.'

'Bye.'

Emma replaced the receiver. She turned over in the bed and saw Jack smiling at her.

'Very convincing. Emma, I shall have to watch that.'

After a light breakfast, Jack drove Emma back to the hotel so she could change her clothes and waited in the car while she ran in. The receptionist handed her a message saying Tony had rung twice, last night and that morning. Going up in the lift she scrunched up the piece of paper in her hand and let it drop to the floor; another few hours, she promised herself. Within ten minutes she was seated back in Jack's car wearing jeans and a jumper.

They headed out of Dublin, deep into County Wicklow towards a place called Glendalough, about an hour away. It was a fairly overcast day but was brightening up the further they travelled. By twelve o'clock they had pulled up in a car park and instantly noticed how fresh the air was. They stood and breathed deeply for several moments, admiring the surroundings, mostly trees, hills and mountains; it felt like the middle of nowhere – it was.

Jack took Emma's hand and they casually followed the path into the grounds of St Kevin's Monastery, with its ancient stone buildings, small chapel and graveyard; its foundations dated back to the sixth century. They looked at the names and dates on most of the gravestones, wondering what it must have been like to live in those times. The site stood near two immense lakes bordered by mountains and dense forest. They walked slowly, hand in hand, around the lower lake.

'What a beautiful and tranquil place,' said Emma.

'Isn't it.'

Being a Monday, the only people they came across were a group of American tourists who thankfully kept to the path, while Emma and Jack wandered off the track into the forest.

'Look! A *deer*!' Emma suddenly exclaimed.

Up ahead, deeper into the trees stood a fully-grown deer staring straight at them. Emma and Jack stood completely still, not even breathing for fear of scaring it. For a moment the whole world seemed to stop, nothing moved – even the swaying of the branches seemed to cease. Suddenly the deer took off, bolting back into the forest. Jack and Emma smiled at each other, feeling privileged to have seen it. They walked on.

Coming across a waterfall, they sat down on a fallen tree trunk, watching and listening to the sound of the rushing water falling over the rocks, descending down the valley. It was like another world, far removed from everything. All thoughts trickled away, deeper down, washed and cleansed. Jack put his arm around her and Emma leant her head on his shoulder. They sat silently gazing into the water, as if in some deep meditation that they didn't want to wake up from.

It was Jack who finally moved, squeezing her hand. She smiled and kissed him gently on the lips. After another two hours of sitting and walking, plus a cup of tea in the visitors' centre, they headed back to Dublin taking a long scenic route. Eventually they arrived back in the outskirts of the city and seeing a Tesco Jack stopped to pick up some shopping. Emma felt like she'd been in two completely different worlds today; the past, and now very definitely back in the present.

The Tesco immediately reminded her of her parents' protest against the building of the superstore. That one thought proved to be an open door leading to an onslaught of others: Manchester, Tony, work, Jack, everything! She remained in the car biting her thumb-nail, wishing Jack would hurry up. In that moment she longed to telephone Jeremy and tell him everything. He'd die of shock but would at least be supportive. She realised his friendship meant a great deal to her. She could really do with his company and advice right now. Jack returned with the shopping and they drove back to his house.

Emma didn't speak much on the drive back, nor while Jack cooked, and now over dinner she was pushing the pasta around on her plate without actually eating.

'Would that go down better with a glass of wine?' Jack asked.

'Not this evening.'

'Aren't you hungry?'

'I thought I was.'

He continued to eat his own, watching her. It was several minutes later she said in a quiet, introspective voice, 'My day is nearing to a close.'

Jack stared at her through narrowed eyes. 'Why just one day?'

'Because . . . because reality always rears its head.'

'Meaning?'

'Meaning, I have some decisions to make.'

He was silent and put down his fork.

Emma sighed wearily, her eyelids lowered. 'I can't just go back, Jack,' she bit her lip, 'just pretend that nothing happened . . . it's not me. The minute I see Tony I feel I'm going to crumble. How can I carry on just as before? Why would I want to? Not after this, after you.' Her head fell forward.

Jack took her hand in his.

'I feel . . .' she paused. 'I don't know what I feel, just that I can't go back and carry on with the pretence.' She frowned. 'I've pretended for too long. What else was I supposed to do? I can't be with him any longer, whatever happens with us. I'm so hemmed in, squashed, limited, frustrated, angry. Angry for living my life as a compromise, in every way. I'm too young to be put out to grass, like that's it, now and for ever, the end . . . typing, cooking and watching telly.' Her voice was becoming louder. 'There has to be more, there *is* more! I know that now. I need to live, I need to be me, find out who "me" really is. I want to talk. I want to learn, to see, to feel, to enjoy. That's not too much, is it?'

Jack shook his head.

'I want to be with you,' she said.

He smiled.

'As you said, let's try. Things would never have happened with you if I was happy with Tony. Deep down I haven't been in ages. I don't love him. I do care for him, I really do. He's not a bastard, just . . . well.' She buried her face in her hands and sat with hunched shoulders. After a couple of minutes she sat back up and stared at him. Her eyes were filled with fear. 'He does love me . . . I don't know how I'm going to tell him, what he'll do, where I'll go.'

'Stay here,' said Jack.

Emma shook her head. 'How can I?'

'I told you, why pussyfoot around. Let's go for it.'

'It's too soon. A step at a time . . . I don't want your name coming up in this. Tony would go crazy, make it a million times worse.' She sat there contemplating her options.

'You are intending to stay in Dublin for a while, aren't you?'

'Will that be OK? I mean, continuing to work at the Dublin office? I'll need money.'

'Of course. If you won't stay here, I'll find you an apartment nearby. It'll be cheaper than the hotel. I'll put it through expenses. Plus you'll have your bonus.'

'The apartment would just be for a few months, till the end of summer, let everything settle. I need time to think, get my head together.'

'We can start looking right away.'

'No,' she said firmly. 'I have to talk with Tony. Have to sort things, fly over there.'

'When?'

'Straight away. I have to.'

'What will you say?'

Feeling instantly nauseous, she buried her face in her hands. Her eyes gradually glazed over with tears. Jack held on to her arm. She bit her lip, desperately trying not to cry. 'I can't believe this is happening. This isn't like me. Jesus, what am I going to say?'

Within a short while, they abandoned their dinner and sat down on the sofa in the lounge with some coffee. Jack put his arm around her. Emma stared into the unlit fireplace, now filled with last night's grey, cold ashes. They sat in silence in the darkened room, with only a side lamp switched on. This time tomorrow night she would have told Tony. Her stomach turned over each time she thought about it. *How can I do this?*

'How did you meet Tony?' asked Jack a little later.

She raised an eyebrow. 'At a pub, where else?'

'So how come you got together? You seem so different.'

'He was different then, I think. I suppose I was too. He was still in the army, the life and soul of the party, full of dreams, places he wanted to see, things he wanted to do. He always wanted to get to Canada. He'd been there a couple of times and loved it.' She sighed and paused. 'He was a bit wild, always getting into little scrapes – adventures he'd call them. It seemed really exciting at the time. And of course my parents disapproved which I took as a blessing.'

Jack smiled. Emma was silent for a moment remembering how it was.

'But,' said Jack.

'But.' Her expression grew intense and downhearted. 'He left the army and never really settled into anything, six months here, six months there. We tried to emigrate to Canada but were refused – Tony's got a record, GBH. He's not violent, it was a long, long time ago, but it was enough to be turned down.'

'So that's why you never went.'

'I could hardly tell you that.' She shook her head and continued to speak with long reflective pauses between each sentence. 'He still spoke about various other dreams, but that's all he did, speak. Nothing ever happened. I tried to encourage him, he just interpreted it as nagging. Eventually I stopped. He was only the life and soul of the party when he was drinking, the next day he was always down and moody. It's like he lost all hope. I'm only just realising that somehow he drained me of my hope too. I can't explain, there're many reasons. We don't connect any more, not sure if we ever did . . . no, that's unfair, we did at the beginning.'

'You never had children,' he said.

'Just never happened. At this moment that's quite a blessing.'

They sat for a while, deep in thought, before Jack spoke.

'I was completely devastated when Miranda left me. I should say, when she asked me to leave. But now I look back, I think it was the best thing that could have happened. We weren't happy, Jesus no. Hadn't been for ages. Not that we were *un*happy together. We just existed side by side, playing our roles in life. The love had gone years before, but we both accepted it, like it was normal. It didn't help that I was always working. Then Miranda found someone who in her own words, "brought her back to life". Made her feel alive again.'

'She actually told you that?' said Emma, shocked at the cruelty.

'Not at the time, but we've discussed it since, several times. Anyway she was right to grab at it. You only get one life.'

'I doubt Tony will ever think that way. He'll hate me until I die.' She quivered at the thought.

That night they lay in bed. Emma couldn't sleep. Jack kept awake with her and occasionally they chatted about what was going to happen. At two in the morning he suddenly announced, 'I'm going with you.'

'You can't, no way!' she told him, horrified.

'Listen, I want to be nearby. We can drive over, arrange to meet up later. You can pack your things in my boot. I want to be there for you.'

'You couldn't come anywhere near the house.'

'I wouldn't want to. I agree we should keep "us" a secret from Tony.'

'Definitely. Tony would flip,' she said.

'Fine. I'll make the arrangements in the morning.' He pulled her closer into him, but she was rigid as a plank of wood. She started to shake, her heart was pounding. Jack kissed her gently on the forehead. 'It's OK,' he whispered.

Suddenly she pulled away, sitting bolt upright. '*Jesus*, what am I doing? How can I do this? I can't!' Tears streamed from her eyes.

Jack sat up too and placed his arm around her. She was shaking her head and eventually turned to him. In a panicky, breathless manner she said, 'I need more time, Jack. Everything's so blurry.'

He nodded reassuringly.

'I'll go to Jeremy's. He'll know what to do. Stay a few days there. He always knows what to do.'

'If that's what you want.'

She nodded several times. 'Yes. I really need to be with Jeremy right now. I'll go tomorrow.' She instantly felt a sense of relief at the thought of seeing her friend.

## 31

Emma's plane landed at Heathrow airport at 4pm and by 4.30 she was sitting in the back of a taxi on her way to Jeremy's. After telephoning him early that morning from Jack's, they had arranged to meet at his apartment that evening.

'Is everything OK?' he had asked, after learning that she wanted to stay with him for a few days.

'Yes, fine,' she said, trying to sound as relaxed as she could.

'Will you be working at the London office? Is that it?'

'Yes . . . work . . . that's right.' She couldn't tell him anything over the phone. She had to tell him face to face.

Emma stared out of the taxi window, deep in thought. Now back in England, away from Dublin and Jack, part of her was questioning if the last few days had actually happened. It couldn't have happened – not to her. *Nothing like this happens to me*, she thought.

Had she really made love with Jack Tomkinson – several times? Was she really going to leave Tony, her husband of eight years? Could she really hurt him like that, just walk away from their marriage? Her stomach churned and she felt a hot sweat rush over her. Her legs felt shaky as if they mightn't carry her. Winding down the window, she breathed deeply, calming herself.

At least she'd be at Jeremy's soon. She couldn't wait to see him so she could pour it all out, every last detail. He could scoop it up and make some sense of it all. Underneath his flippant, carefree exterior, she knew he was more sensible and sensitive than most. Thank God she had Jeremy.

Jeremy anxiously stood by his French windows, peering down into the car park, waiting for Emma's taxi to appear. He checked his watch: five to five. She'd be here any minute. He could hardly believe it. Her phone call this morning was a complete surprise. He hadn't expected to see her for some time. Instead she was coming to stay for a few days. *Hooray! There is a God after all*, he thought.

Strangely, Julia hadn't known anything about Emma working in the London office. She'd seemed a bit put out when he told her, wondering why Jack hadn't asked her to do whatever it was. She was hardly rushed off her feet these days. Jeremy was just relieved that Julia seemed so relaxed about the incident at the weekend. They'd spoken about it at length on the Sunday. 'I just think you have to tell Emma how you feel about her,' she had said. 'Until you do you'll be stuck in limbo. Your life's on hold, whether you realise that or not. Right now you're in denial.'

The thought of telling Emma terrified him. He'd spent over eight years desperately hiding his feelings from her, even deliberately misleading her about his views on love and relationships. He knew that if she had found out, she would have pulled away from him and he might even have lost her friendship totally.

However, he assured Julia that he'd give it a lot of thought and maybe he would tell her. In fact, back home in Richmond on the Monday night, he had really considered it. He finally admitted that he wasn't that happy alone. In fact going out every night was becoming quite tiresome. Whatever the outcome, he should be truthful and tell Emma. But now that she was actually coming around, the thought of it terrified him again.

He looked around his lounge, which he'd quickly

tidied. He'd taken the afternoon off work, buying some champagne on the way home, which was now chilling in the fridge. They could celebrate his partnership with the firm. Also, maybe, if she got a little drunk she might open up and tell him what'd been going on with her lately. He was sure something wasn't quite right. And if *he* got drunk, maybe he could pluck up the courage to confess his feelings. But then it occurred to him yet again. *Why* tell her? What was the point? She would never leave Tony and it would ruin their friendship. Stalemate! But then again, maybe . . . just maybe?

At that moment, his buzzer sounded. He jumped and his heartbeat raced. He literally ran into the hall to press the entry button on the intercom without even checking it was her. Opening the door to his apartment, he leapt out on to the landing and stared down the staircase, while nervously tapping the banister with his fingers.

After the expected time, he still couldn't see her. Yet a moment later the lift doors opened and out she stepped.

'Emma!' he exclaimed loudly, pointing to the lift.

She looked behind, wondering if she'd forgotten something.

'The lift!' he gesticulated.

Emma nodded. 'More important things to worry about.'

It was at that moment that he noticed the strange look she had. Although fully made up with bronze-reddish lips, she looked troubled and at the same time energised, eyes gleaming, if a little bewildered-looking. Wearing jeans and a clinging blue top, she made straight for him, dropping her small case and throwing her arms around him.

'It's so good to see you,' she said, as a well of tears

rose up in her, yet she managed to hold them in.

Jeremy stood gently holding her back. He was smiling broadly and gazing into space. When she eventually let go he examined her face more closely, narrowing his eyes. 'Are you OK?' he asked, looking worried and intrigued.

She let out a burst of uneasy laughter. It was either that or cry. 'I don't know.'

With a supportive smile he picked up her case and taking her by the hand led her inside.

'Drink?' he asked, a few minutes later, as they sat in his lounge.

'Oh Jeremy,' she said, biting her lip. 'I so need to talk with you.' She jumped up. 'Let's go out. Get some air. The river . . . We'll talk then,' she added.

Jeremy shrugged his shoulders, then nodded, before grabbing his keys.

Within ten minutes they were walking along the river path heading away from Richmond towards Kingston. On either side of the river were parks, playing fields and clusters of trees, filled with young, bored teenagers and people walking their dogs in the early evening sunshine.

Emma inspected the manicured environment, frowning. The setting gave the impression of a country walk, yet the path was paved in concrete, slightly angled for good drainage, neat and exact – not even one weed growing through. With each breath, you could taste the mild presence of exhaust fumes. The mountains in Wicklow came to mind, with the abundance of fresh air and the muddy dirt tracks and fields that she and Jack had walked over. She had felt such a sense of freedom there, with its wild, unspoilt lands where foliage, bushes and trees were left to grow on their own terms, allowed to *overgrow*, without being chopped down so as to fit in and appear like something they were not.

*I need to be left to overgrow! I can't fit in any longer*, she thought.

Up ahead was a wooden bench next to a large weeping willow tree, its sprawling branches hanging down into the water. Sitting down, Jeremy said in a flustered voice, 'Jesus, the intrigue is killing me. In heaven's name, *what is it*? I love a bit of drama, but this is getting my blood pressure up.' He perched, leaning forward on the bench anxiously waiting.

Emma wondered how to begin to tell him – even little things sent him into a self-inflicted theatrical frenzy. *What about when he hears this?* she wondered. Sir Laurence Olivier on speed! Looking away and breathing deeply she said in a nervous whisper, 'I think I might . . .' She bit her lip and paused for several seconds. 'I might . . . leave Tony.'

Silence.

She looked up at him.

Jeremy hadn't moved, not even blinked. He sat glued to the spot as if he hadn't heard. Yet his mouth slowly opened and she thought his bottom lip quivered slightly.

'A piss-take, right?' he said.

She didn't answer.

'A joke? Yes?'

Emma gazed blank-faced at him.

His eyes narrowed. 'Did you say . . .'

She nodded.

'No joke?'

She shook her head.

For a couple more moments Jeremy remained completely still, continuing to stare at her. It was his eyes that reacted first, gradually opening wider and wider, dazed and vacant – totally stunned, like an animal caught in a car's headlights. Next, and almost in slow motion, he started to shake his head. Then, as if her words had finally registered with him, he screamed at the top of his voice, '*You're leaving Tony?*'

Even from across the river you could have heard him. His expressive hands finally came alive, waving around frantically. 'You're really doing it?'

Emma was digging her nails into her hands. 'That's why I'm here . . . to have a bit of space to think, to talk with you about it. To really decide.'

'*Jesus!* You're serious.'

Her head fell forward – was this so unbelievable?

Jeremy stood up as if to address a large audience in front of him, yet there was only a small group of ducks, which had gathered, expecting to be fed. '*My God!* This is huge! I can't believe it.' He was right at the water's edge shaking his head, hands sporadically waving like a mad conductor. 'You're leaving Tony.' He breathed deeply, staring down into the water. Suddenly he turned and sat back down. In a desperate-sounding voice, he said, 'Tell me it's true . . . Tell me it's really true.'

She just nodded, bewildered at his reaction.

He kept asking her again and again if she was really serious, still not believing it. Emma looked at him strangely. She had a confused, unsettled feeling inside. Yet she was awash with so many emotions she couldn't pinpoint what it was.

Jeremy was saying something in the background but she wasn't really listening. At that moment her thoughts were with Tony. His face embedded itself within her mind's eye. Tears burst out of her as the enormity of what she was proposing to do rampaged through her. 'This is the worst thing I have ever had to do . . . *ever.*' She wiped her eyes. 'I'm dreading telling him. Can't bear to hurt him. I feel so sick.'

Jeremy looked at her and only then realised the state she was in; he'd been so caught up with his own emotions. He grabbed hold of her hand, squeezing it firmly. He couldn't say he'd ever liked Tony that much, but he understood how hard it was for her to hurt him. Hurting anyone was awful. He hated seeing her this way. 'It's OK, Emma. It'll be OK.'

'Will it?' she asked, disbelief in her voice.

He nodded. 'Everything will work out in the end. You have to be true to yourself.'

'Do I?'

'Yes . . . I know how awful it must be right now. I'll help in any way I can. You're so brave. Thought you were with him for life. I didn't even know you were considering it. Is that why you've been a bit . . . you know, different?'

Her eyes closed and she shrugged her shoulders.

'Why now though? Has anything happened? *My God*.' He suddenly looked angry, ready to pounce. 'He's not been unfaithful to you?'

Her stomach tightened but she managed to shake her head.

'Thank God for small mercies. I always dreaded that he'd wander.'

It was she who now looked angry. 'Well he hasn't, OK? *Fuck it*, he's a decent person. It's just . . . It's just . . . I need *more*. I want *more*. Is that so wrong?'

'Of course not. I understand, I really do. I take it Tony knows nothing of your intentions?'

She shook her head.

'Of course, he'll be hurt . . . but in time you'll both be happier. You know you can always stay with me . . . for as long as you want.'

She didn't answer. He knew he was being selfish but

he had a sudden urge to run up and down the path shouting, 'Alleluia, she's seen the light.' *Stop it*, he told himself. *Emma's hurting.* 'It'll be OK, Emma. It really will. You'll easily find a job in London. We'll commute together. It's the right thing to do – just never thought you'd ever do it. Can't believe it! My God. You're so brave, Emma. Did it all just get too much?'

Her eyelids slowly lowered and she nervously bit her lip again. Gazing down at the ground, images of the last few days with Jack came to mind. Her whole body seemed to tingle of its own accord. She felt she could smell him next to her, on her – in her. She let out a confused sigh. 'There's something else.'

Jeremy was silent.

'You won't believe this next bit . . . Not sure *I* believe it.' She looked back at him.

He stared deep into her eyes, sensing something. He let her hand slip from his.

'Something's happened, Jeremy.'

He looked away, not wanting to hear. He'd heard enough. She was leaving Tony. Leave it at that. He could sleep tonight with renewed hope, dreams and thoughts. Nothing else had happened. There was nothing else to know.

'It wasn't supposed to,' she said.

At that, he stood up and walked over to the river, gazing into the murky waters. The ducks had disappeared, and in their place litter was floating on the surface, crisp packets, old cans; he hadn't noticed it before. Emma watched him. When he showed no signs of sitting back down, she got up and followed him over. Standing right beside him she looked out across the water towards two beautiful swans a little way downriver.

'I can hardly believe it myself. I didn't mean for

anything to happen. It just did.' She turned towards him. 'I'm so scared, Jeremy, terrified. We haven't been having an affair, it just came about all at once.'

Jeremy started to shake his head in complete disbelief, face contorted. He turned and glared at her, his eyes penetrating hers. 'No,' he said loudly. 'It can't be . . . Not you. Not Emma.'

'Yes, me,' she said, emphatically.

'But that's not Emma.'

'It wasn't planned, Jeremy. It's not an affair. It just happened. But I don't regret it.'

'No! It's not right this way.'

'Don't go all moral on me. You're the last person I expected that from.'

He glanced away. 'Sorry,' he said, trying to compose himself. But the next moment shouted, '*Shit!* Who, for God's sake?'

A woman walked past pushing a pram. It gave Emma the chance to take a few deep breaths. This wasn't going how she had thought it would. Jeremy was acting like her disapproving mother.

'*Who?*' He practically yelled it this time.

Emma swallowed and cleared her throat. 'It's Jack.'

They were just two words, two small words, yet they changed everything – sweeping down like a tidal wave, destroying all in its path. Jeremy couldn't look at her. In an eerie and unnaturally calm whisper he said, '*Jack?* Jack Tomkinson . . .? You and *Jack!*'

'Crazy I know. But I have to pursue it. I can't walk away.'

'You and Jack? Him. Jack. Emma and Jack.' He was slowly shaking his head, repeating their names over and over. His eyes dilated and became unfocused. Strange noises came from him, a mixture of gasping, sighing and swallowed, hidden cries. His head fell forward and his usually exuberant hands lay limply at his sides. His whole body seemed to deflate as if his energy and life were leaking from him, punctured deep inside. He stood there on the edge of the river, now totally silent, motionless, empty – momentarily reinstated dreams crushed in seconds, sinking down and away. A few pent-up tears glazed his eyes. The rest would have to wait until later.

'*Jeremy*?' Emma squeezed his shoulder. 'It isn't that unbelievable. You were right, all those months back. Saying fate was dealing me a card but would I take it. Well it has, and fuck it, I'm taking it. Wherever it leads.' She waited for a reply, a comment from him, his opinion, a piss-take, anything! None came. Where was his melodramatic and histrionic reaction? The screaming? The gesturing?

She stared at him, confused. 'Are you OK?' she asked, finally.

He didn't move or respond.

'What is it?' she said. 'Say something. You're acting so strangely. Tell me I'm not mad.'

He slowly stared across at her. After what seemed like ages he said, 'You're one of the sanest people I know.'

She smiled. 'We didn't mean to fall in love.'

Another small singular word! Yet it tore through him like a razor blade, severing any last remaining hope.

'Love,' he repeated, barely audible.

She nodded, eyes filled with tears. 'I think so. Maybe we're just mad.'

He didn't plan to say the next thing, it just came out. '*I* love you, Emma.' How he'd wanted to say those words for years and now he finally had. '*I* love you,' he said again, grabbing her hand in his. How easy to say they had turned out to be.

She reached out and hugged him. 'And I love you, Jeremy. You're the best friend in the world.'

He pulled away, eyes open yet seeing nothing – hearing nothing apart from the word 'friend'. A wave of anger swept over him.

'I'm not leaving Tony for Jack. This has just made me realise a few things. I feel so alive . . . scared shitless, confused, guilty, everything . . . yet very alive. Oh, Jeremy. I really don't know if I can go through with this.'

He reached out and held her face firmly in both his hands. He was pressing so hard he was almost hurting her. In an intensely serious and fervent manner he said, 'You must, Emma. If you think there's some happiness out there, you have to chase after it. Only fools like me let it drift on by.'

'But hurting Tony. Can I really do that?'

'The world is full of hurt people. More than you'd think. Maybe it's meant to be that way so they can move on. Too many people have their lives on hold.'

She planted a kiss on his unsuspecting lips. 'You're brilliant, Jeremy. The very best.'

'Let's go back,' he said. 'I don't feel like walking any more.'

## 32

At just gone three, on Wednesday afternoon, Jack parked some streets away from Emma's house in Manchester. He switched off the engine and turned to face her.

She sat motionless, gazing out of the window: at this moment, everything was still in place.

Earlier, as arranged, he had met her off the London train; he'd been insistent that he wanted to be here with her. She had only spent the one night at Jeremy's, having decided to just tell Tony and get it over with. No matter where she was, she wouldn't be able to relax again until the situation was sorted.

Jeremy had been sweet to her the previous night, making her dinner and listening to her going on until the early hours about Tony, Jack and her life. However, this morning he had complained of feeling unwell and after taking a cup of tea to him, she left him in bed, saying she'd call in a few days.

'Are you going to be all right with this?' Jack asked.

She turned towards him, but stared out the other window. She gave a couple of nods of her head.

'Can't I drop you a bit closer?'

She shook her head.

'At least phone me as soon as you can.'

She nodded.

'Sure you're OK? Do you need more time?'

'No.' She picked her handbag up off the floor and opened the car door. Within a second she was out.

Jack shouted, 'Phone me on the mobile. I won't leave the hotel.'

Emma was about to slam the door shut but stopped

and poked her head back in. She managed to raise a small smile for him. 'Sorry. Thanks. You know.'

'I know.'

She closed the door and headed off across the park towards the house. It was a dull, grey and drizzly day and within a few minutes her hair felt limp and wet. She'd taken the path a thousand times, yet everything felt alien to her, the trees and terraced houses that bordered it, even the people that shot past her, miserable with the cold, desperate to be on their way. Everything seemed different.

Within twenty-five minutes she was standing at the gate to the front garden. She stared at the little two-bedroom house with its shabby windows and tired-looking exterior; paint peeling off the front door. She had meant to paint it numerous times but never really felt the inclination to actually get up and do it. Tony was always somehow too busy. Nervously, she put her key in the door.

Once inside, she listened for signs of life. Her heart was thumping. She heard nothing. Clearing her throat she shouted feebly, 'Tony?'

Silence.

She tiptoed into the lounge and glared at the cluttered, untidy room. There was a strong smell of stale tobacco, four empty beer cans lying around the floor, newspapers strewn across the table and a discarded Pizza Hut box on the couch. She felt an automatic instinct to clean the place, polish the coffee table, open the windows to let some air in. But then the realisation dawned on her – there was no point, it wasn't her business any more; she was leaving him. Never again would she sleep in this house. It suddenly felt so real, the enormity of it swamped her. She pushed the pizza box to the floor and slumped down on the sofa. Leaving him had seemed easier in Ireland, but here, now, back in her home. Her eyes closed. *Shit!*

It was some minutes later before she ventured to open them. She gazed around the little room – all the evenings spent here. The ashtray was full of fag butts. Rob must have been here, but then again it could have been anyone. Her eyes lifted up to the ceiling. Maybe Tony was still in bed. He could have decided to take a day off. She sat upright. Maybe he was with someone.

As if on a mad fantasy adventure, she crept up the stairs, slowly, silently. The usual floorboard on the landing creaked. Emma stood still and waited. Nothing. She leapt at the bedroom door, pushing it open with all her force and jumped in the room. Empty. She hung her head. Ridiculous! What had she really expected to find, an easy way out? Tony in bed with someone? She could have played the injured party, gaining pity from friends and family, instead of condemnation. She sat on the end of the unmade bed, holding her head in her hands, rocking backwards and forwards.

Half an hour must have passed before Emma stood up. Soon the practicalities took over. She packed her clothes into a suitcase; they all fitted into one because she was leaving so many behind. She wouldn't wear most of the clothes hanging up, they no longer fitted her and weren't how she wanted to look any more, belonging to the old Emma. She was quite good at separating the old and the new her; it somehow made everything easier. The new her, she could define with qualities she always wanted, maybe even possessed but had never managed to realise within the confines of the old life.

Emma took out an empty cardboard box from under the stairs. She was very selective in what was placed inside; two silver candlesticks that Jeremy had given her on her thirtieth birthday; personal papers such as passport and birth certificate, plus a small hand-painted china bowl. She went from room to room checking what else she wanted, but whether it was just the way she was feeling right now, she couldn't generate any great desire for anything else. She suddenly realised how unimportant all her possessions were. She liked the cut-glass decanter that was a wedding present from her Aunt Lillian, but for that very reason she wouldn't take it. It was the old life and would only remind her of the old self, the part that was now dead – or soon would be.

The box and case were placed under the stairs.

By 4.30 she was perched on a chair at the dining table, waiting, dreaming, wishing it was already a year from now and everything was settled. Tony would be with someone else, she and Jack would be blissfully happy and doing whatever took their fancy. Maybe they'd have a child – if she could. Her eyes suddenly widened. *Am I mad?* she thought. *Is this real? Can I really go through with this?* The awful nausea returned.

By quarter to five, Tony still hadn't shown. He could come home at any time depending on how busy the couriers were. She could have telephoned the company and checked, but she didn't bother. Instead, she went out to the hall and dialled Jack's mobile number. Without it even ringing she heard in an abrupt voice, 'Yes?'

'It's me.'

He sounded anxious. 'You OK?'

'Yes.'

'Have you seen him?'

'No. He's not come back yet.'

'Jesus, Emma. Why didn't you ring earlier? I've been

going out of my mind. Worried sick. Nearly rang myself.'

'*No!* Don't ring here.'

'I didn't. I won't. I'm just saying, waiting's been torture.'

'For me too.'

Jack rubbed his forehead and spoke in a less aggressive manner. 'Sorry. Shit. Just really on edge. Worried for you, that's all.'

'I know.' Emma's voice lightened up also. 'I'm OK . . . just about.'

'Are you packed?'

'The few bits I'm taking, yes.'

'I've checked in, room 202.'

'I'm not sure what time I'll get there,' she said.

'I'm not going anywhere. But *please*, just keep me informed. Phone me again.'

'I'll try, depends what happens.' As if speaking to herself she said, 'I hope I can go through with this.'

Outside, some footsteps approached the door. Her heart stopped. Jack was saying something in the background. She could only hear the key in the door. 'Thank you. Goodbye,' she said in her professional office voice.

'*Emma*,' cried Jack.

She put down the phone. The door opened. It was Tony.

On seeing her Tony stopped dead and pulled a look of surprise. 'What you doing here?' He was wearing his jeans and hunting jacket, carrying his rifle in its holder under his arm.

For a split second she froze. She glared at him. Her legs felt weak. This was too much. She looked away. 'They don't need me in Dublin today.'

He closed the door behind him. 'You back all week then?'

Slowly, so very slowly, she shook her head.

'Why didn't you call? Didn't you get my messages?'

'No.'

'Damn receptionist, I rang twice.'

Emma retreated into the kitchen.

Tony placed the holder against the hall table and followed her. 'You got the day off then?'

'Yes.'

'You should have rung, I would have stayed in.'

She automatically started filling up the kettle. 'I wasn't sure.'

'Doesn't sound very organised.'

Emma didn't look at him, couldn't. She just stared at the kettle, waiting for it to boil.

'So how long you back for?' he asked.

'Not sure.'

'Why not?'

'Have to speak to the office.'

'What? They just expect you to run at a moment's notice. Seems like when they say "Jump", you just say "How high?"'

She didn't answer.

'I'm going for a shower. Covered in mud. I threw a sicky and went hunting.' He walked over to her.

She stood frozen, almost cowering. He kissed her once on the lips. 'I'm glad you're back. I've really missed you.' He smiled before turning and walking out. Emma touched her lips and slowly closed her eyes.

She went and sat down at the dining table. The sound of the shower could be heard from upstairs. Her head hung low and heavy over rounded shoulders. *How can I do this? How can I stay? I can't.*

Sitting at the table she didn't move a muscle, apart from her eyes, which darted nervously around the room. After fifteen minutes, she heard Tony's heavy footsteps coming down the stairs. Her heart banged in time with each step. It had to be now.

Tony stood in the doorway and stared at her. She had her back to him. 'Are you all right, Em?'

She took a deep breath. Without turning she said in a serious voice, 'Could you come and sit down for a moment.'

Tony hesitated, he wanted something to eat, but he gathered he should probably do as she said. He sat in the chair beside her. Eventually her eyes lifted to meet his, but she couldn't look at him.

He frowned. 'What is it?'

She managed to raise her eyes to the neckline of his jumper, but no further. She tried to swallow, but couldn't, her throat was too dry and tense. She coughed uncomfortably. What to say? In the early hours of that morning she'd gone over and over it, planning a little speech. But now her mind was blank.

Tony said again, 'Look, what is it? Is it work? You seemed really fed up the other day.' He went to take her hand in his. She pulled it away. He glared at her, increasingly irritated by the little scene. He was wondering what he might have done to cause her mood. Glancing around at the messy room he said defensively, 'I didn't know you were coming home today or I would have cleaned up. Can't blame me for that.'

'It isn't about the house, Tony.' She shook her head, adding in a whisper, 'I wish it were only that simple.'

'*What* then?'

Emma bit her bottom lip. 'I haven't been happy for a while, some time actually.'

'Could've fooled me. Looks like you're having a great time at the moment, living it up in Dublin. It's me who's stuck here.'

She shook her head again. 'I don't mean work. I mean,' there was no other way to say it. 'I mean *us*.'

He was silent, eyes brooding. Emma quickly continued before she changed her mind. 'This is probably going to come as a huge shock to you, and believe me, the last thing I wanted to do was hurt you.' Her voice became more high-pitched with each sentence. 'Maybe that's why I let things continue as they were, I don't know. I just know that I'm not happy and I have to do something about that. It's gone on too long. I have to do it now or I'll die inside. I can't let that happen.'

Tony's face hardened.

Emma rambled on with increasing speed; a few tears were falling down her face. 'I have to leave. You have the house, the lot. I don't want it, none of it. Not much equity in it but you could get a lodger in, might be able to keep hold of it then, not sell it. I'll stay in Dublin for three months, maybe four, not really sure. I haven't really planned anything. Kind of taken me by surprise too, this, you know. Not like—'

'*Emma*,' he yelled, interrupting her. 'What the *fuck* are you going on about? Selling the house? Working in Dublin?'

She stared at him. He glared back, frowning, baffled. He didn't get it. Her mouth opened. She saw his heavy and fearful eyes waiting on her words. He had nice eyes when he smiled. He used to smile a lot. They both had.

A surge of emotion swept up within her. She let out a long whine like a wounded animal. It took all her energy to suppress the overwhelming urge to fall and keep falling, downwards and away from all this.

'*Damn you! What?*' he screamed.

She screamed back at the top of her voice, '*I'm leaving you.*'

Then silence. She added in a whisper, 'Today.'

There were several lengthy seconds of silence, no response, no movement. Tony started to shake his head. Soon it was moving in vigorous, erratic jerks. 'You're leaving me,' he repeated in disbelief. 'What do you mean? As in divorce?'

The word tore through her like a knife. She opened her mouth to speak, but just nodded.

He let out a strange strangled noise, half laughter, half gasp. He was moving jerkily around on his chair. Again he almost laughed, but saw Emma motionless, head hanging low.

'Em. Tell me this is some fucking lousy joke. Has someone been saying something about me?'

With tears streaming down her face, she shook her head.

'Fuck it, Em. Have you gone insane?' His voice had become uneasy, distressed. He leapt up and marched over to the front window. 'You're leaving me?' he cried out again, practically dancing on the spot. He turned towards her, total shock across his face. 'Why? What's happened?' He was making odd noises that weren't really words. 'Us? I . . . You haven't . . .'

Tony stopped. He stood still. His face fell serious as he asked in a slow and hostile voice, 'Someone else?' His eyes conveyed a warning.

Emma glanced away.

His eyes widened.

Suddenly she looked back at him and screamed, 'Of course not. This isn't about anyone else.'

'*Fuck's sake, why then?*' he shouted aggressively, at the top of his voice.

She had prepared herself that he might lose his temper. In fact she had secretly hoped it would be that way. She couldn't stand it if he broke down in front of her, crying. How could she walk out of the door and leave him like that?

She looked him straight in the face but could only offer in a timid voice, 'It's not working. Hasn't for ages. I'm not happy. I can't be with you any longer. I'm so sorry.' She sobbed, tears flowing freely. 'I'm so sorry. I still care about you. I do. I'm sorry. It's not your fault – no one's fault. I can't explain it right now. We want different things. We're living separate lives anyway. I still care, but I have to go. No choice.'

He took a step closer to her. 'If you care, why then? I don't understand. Jesus, what's happened?'

She closed her eyes and swallowed. 'I'm sorry. It's over. I need more.'

Suddenly, his face contorted with rage. He stormed over to her, towering high above her. She closed her eyes, waiting. She could feel his exaggerated and furious breath against her. It made her cower beneath him. She opened her eyes. Both his hands hovered a few inches from her face, stationary apart from a little trembling. She stared at them. Gradually she raised her eyes up towards his face. As her eyes met his, his aggressive expression diminished and softened. His whole posture seemed to deflate, shrinking in size, his face appeared disfigured with pain. His hands floated down to his sides, his wounded, broken eyes searched her for something, pleading, almost begging.

Emma screwed her face up, sick inside. She looked away, crying loudly. Tony stood over her for what must have been another minute. Neither of them spoke or moved. Emma tried to think of what else to say to take some of his pain away, but there was nothing.

'*I don't understand!*' he screamed, abruptly filling the whole house with his roar. All of a sudden, he turned and bolted out the door.

'Tony,' she shouted, jumping up herself. 'Wait. *Please!*'

By the time she reached the hall, he was already out of the house.

'Wait!'

Tony sprinted down the cul-de-sac, across the road and into the park opposite. He ran, totally breathless. His heart raced. He carried on running, further and further, out the other gate and across the main road. He darted down a side road nearly crashing into an elderly lady. She jumped. He leapt sideways and continued. His lungs screamed for air, his whole body hurt.

Soon he had no choice but to slow down. Bent double, he stumbled along an overgrown alleyway, eventually falling against a garage. He slipped down the rusty door, gasping for breath. He lay huddled in a ball, rocking back and forth, banging his head against the entrance.

## 33

Emma sat on the bottom stair gazing solemnly into space, motionless, as if deeply tranquillised. Stagnant and numb – like a spectator with no personal involvement.

It was done, no turning back, no rewind. The telephone started to ring beside her.

Picking it up, she said in a dazed voice, 'Hello?'

'Thank God! You all right?'

She took a moment to answer.

'*Emma?*'

'I'm here, Jack and yes I'm OK.'

'What happened?'

'I did it,' she whispered, closing her eyes. 'He took it bad, ran off somewhere.'

'I know.'

'I hope he's OK.'

Jack deliberately calmed and slowed his voice. 'He'll be OK, Emma. He's hurting but he'll deal with it. Everyone does. You're hurting *too*.'

'Am I?'

He didn't respond.

'No choice in the end, I have to leave now,' she said, sighing wearily.

'Listen, I was worried when you hung up. I'm parked round the corner. That's how I saw him.'

Suddenly alarmed, she shouted, 'He could have *seen* you.'

'He didn't. Calm down. He didn't. Ran into the park. I'm coming round.'

'*No!* Keep away!' she begged.

'Why? I won't stop. Come back to the hotel and talk.'

'Maybe I should wait here. See how he is,' she said.

Jack was silent for a moment. He gathered his thoughts and said, 'You have to do what you feel is best. But take it from me, at this point there isn't anything you can do . . . unless you've changed your mind?'

'No. I know I'm going.'

'I'll be around in a minute. Get your things ready.' He put down the phone.

Jack turned his Audi into the narrow cul-de-sac. He parked a couple of houses away from hers and immediately saw Emma standing by the door. He hurried to her but once there, they didn't touch, only stood and exchanged supportive smiles. She stepped back allowing him into the cramped hall. They embraced only briefly, both uncomfortable in the surroundings.

Almost immediately she opened the door under the stairs and pulled her case out. Jack took it from her. She lifted the cardboard box herself.

'Ready?' asked Jack.

'My coat.' Putting down the box, she ran upstairs and into her bedroom. She grabbed her coat off the mattress and was about to leave when she suddenly thought of her books holding up the bed; she wanted to take them with her.

Kneeling down, Emma managed to lift the side of the bed up while her other hand quickly pulled the books away. With one leg missing the bed continued to stand but wobbled and slanted sideways. *Tony can prop it up with his* Rifle *magazines*, she thought.

As she sorted out the books, something caught her eye – on the floor, underneath the head of the bed was a small red, shiny piece of paper. She picked it up. It was like a corner of something, made of hard paper foil, with the letters, 'rex', on the piece that was left.

Oh my God! It couldn't be. She glared at it, before wincing repulsively at the unmade bed. She cradled herself as if she'd been hit in the stomach. Could it be true? She closed her eyes and shook her head erratically. It was from a Durex packet.

Downstairs, Jack was becoming impatient. Tony could come back any moment and that was a scene he'd rather miss, especially seeing the rifle lying against the hall table.

'Emma.'

No reply.

'Emma, we need to be going.'

Outside, approaching footsteps could be heard getting louder. Jack peered through the side window; luckily it was only a woman, who went in next door.

'Emma,' he shouted again, this time starting up the stairs.

Emma stood up defiantly and composed herself. She deliberately dragged the quilt off the bed and laid a single pillow in the middle of the mattress; on the top she placed in full view the torn-off condom cover. Her fierce eyes travelled around the little room, imagining, picturing, wondering, questioning. Turning sharply on the spot she grabbed her coat and books and marched out.

'There you are,' said Jack, meeting on the landing. He took the books from her hand. 'We have to go, Tony could come back any minute.' He led her down the stairs.

'I have to go to Rob's,' she stated.

'Who's Rob?'

'His brother.'

Jack looked back at her. 'Why?'

'I need to get something confirmed by him.'

Jack narrowed his eyes but didn't say anything. He grabbed the box and case and they left. Emma posted her key back through the letterbox.

'Was that wise? You still own half,' said Jack.

In a strong, determined voice she said, 'It's all his now. I'll *never* come back.' She walked past him towards the car.

The white Audi turned out of the cul-de-sac and headed towards central Manchester. Apart from giving Jack directions, she didn't speak, but instead gazed out of the window deep in thought. Their progress towards Salford was slow as it was rush hour and Manchester United were playing at home.

Stuck in a long queue at some traffic lights, Jack asked, 'What is it you need confirmed?'

Emma looked over at him. 'I'll tell you later, if that's OK . . . might not be anything to tell.'

Although intrigued, he just nodded. She reached over and laid her hand on his thigh in a supportive, affectionate manner. With a smile she said, 'Thanks for being here . . . I'm really glad you were.'

'So am I.' He covered her hand with his own, squeezing it slightly.

About half an hour later Emma said, 'That's his flat there. Carry on round the block and I'll walk back.'

'You will be all right, won't you? Is this a good idea?'

'I have to talk with him.' Emma got out of the car, crossed the road and walked up the four flights of steps to Rob's one-bedroom council flat. The staircase always smelt of urine; no wonder he spent so much time at their house. She rang the bell and waited apprehensively, preparing herself for whatever she heard.

'Who is it?' Rob shouted from behind the door.

'Emma.'

The next moment, she heard several locks being undone and the door opened to reveal Rob, dressed in jeans and T-shirt. His expression was one of shock.

'Thought you were in Paddy land.'

'Can I come in?'

'Is everything OK?' he asked, standing back from the door.

'I just need to talk with you.' She followed him into the small lounge which, surprisingly, had been decorated. The walls were painted a fresh peach colour, even the old brown sofa and chair had ivory throws over them. It was impressively tidy as well, probably Becky's influence.

'Want some tea?' Rob asked.

'No thanks.' Emma sat on the edge of the armchair.

Rob sat on the sofa, and glanced around uncomfortably. Emma took a deep breath. Fearing Tony would eventually make for the flat, she launched in straight away. 'There is something you should know.'

He quickly lit up a fag.

'Me and Tony have separated.'

'*What?*' His face registered disbelief. 'You can't!'

'He's been seeing someone, hasn't he?'

Rob glared at her, looking horrified. He took a large drag of his cigarette.

'It's OK. Tony's told me all about it,' she said.

He continued to stare at her but said and did nothing.

'I know you know, Rob, there's nothing you two don't know about each other,' she said bitterly.

'Why are you here?' he asked, narrowing his eyes.

'He's in a bit of a state, ran off somewhere. If he doesn't turn up here, I want you to find him and stay with him for a few days, as long as it takes.'

'This is madness,' Rob shouted, jumping up and walking over to the window. 'You can't split up.'

'We are, we have.'

'Tony wouldn't want this, *fucking hell*! He loves you!'

Her eyes lowered. 'It's over, Rob, nothing can change that.'

He was shaking his head, suddenly angry. 'I never understood you. It didn't have to be like this. You were never around, never made the effort. Were we beneath you? Is the Swan too lowly?'

'I can't apologise for not wanting to spend my life in a pub.'

'Didn't even try. He was always out on his own; everyone had partners, but not Tony. Tony's wife didn't give a damn.'

'Is that how you see it?' She was standing up too. 'He didn't have to fucking go out so much, could have stayed in.'

Rob stubbed out his fag. 'Where is he?'

She shrugged her shoulders. 'He just ran off.'

'He could have slept with loads of girls but he turned them down.'

'Except one,' she stated.

'He loves you, doesn't that mean anything?'

'I don't know. Does it?'

Rob grabbed his jacket. 'What did you expect?'

'Was it one of Becky's friends?'

His face closed up. 'I want to know,' she said.

'Why you asking me? And why now?'

'He didn't tell me the name, just what happened.'

'What's it matter and why now? It was six months ago,' he said.

Emma felt her whole body shudder. So it was true.

She slumped back down on the chair, covering her face with her hands. Rob studied her from a distance. 'You didn't know, you fucking bitch. You tricked me . . . *You fucking bitch*,' he shrieked. He continued screaming abuse at her.

Bizarrely, Emma let out a little laugh. She started swaying side to side, eyes glazed, laughing menacingly. In the next instant she let out the most ferocious scream that thundered around and off every wall in the small room.

Rob recoiled backwards. When she ran out of breath she looked up at him, strangely calm and composed again. 'So Tony had an affair.'

'No,' he protested.

'What then?'

'You're a fucking cow. Tony'll kill me . . . Wasn't even an affair, started and ended within a couple of months because he didn't want to lose you. He loves you. It was a mistake that he really regrets.'

'Who was she?'

'Nobody, doesn't matter. She's long gone and I ain't saying another word,' he said.

Emma sat silently, eyes lowered. Rob lit another cigarette. 'He'll kill me for this. You said he told you. Fucking bitch for dragging me in.' He was pacing up and down. 'He'll kill me.' He stopped dead. 'How'd you know then?'

'Condom packet under my bed . . . rather careless of him, then again he never was one for details.'

'He never took her there, only . . .' he trailed off.

'Here?' she said, as if reading his mind.

Rob was silent.

Emma closed her eyes. She'd heard enough.

'Condoms were mine,' he added. 'Me and Becky have been staying over a bit.'

As if oblivious to his last comment she stood up and said in a serious, yet fragile manner, 'Look after Tony, he'll be hurting more than me.'

'You cow, Emma.'

She let herself out.

'What's happened?' asked Jack, as she got into the car.

Emma was pale and had a strange vacant expression. She looked at Jack but was initially quiet.

'What? Tell me,' he urged.

In a nonchalant manner she said, 'Tony had an affair, about six months ago.' She went on to explain about the condom packet and her conversation with Rob.

Jack gave no reaction of his own, just stared at her, gauging her response.

She ran her hand through her hair and sat quietly for a few moments. 'I can't believe it,' she eventually said.

'It doesn't change anything, does it?'

She shook her head and sighed wearily. 'I suppose it makes it easier, less guilt to feel.' Her head dropped forward. 'It doesn't take the anger away. Maybe I'm a hypocritical bitch, but at least I dealt with things quickly . . . Tony would have been screwing this woman and sharing a bed with me at night. How could he do that? Bastard.' She cringed all over, clenching her fists. Her eyes filled with tears. 'I can't believe he did that to me.'

Jack took hold of her hand. 'I know how that feels.'

With a sudden sense of urgency she pleaded, 'Let's get out of this place.'

'We'll talk more in the hotel,' he agreed.

'No, I mean here, Manchester. Let's go back to Dublin tonight. There's a sailing at nine, we'll be back at yours by twelve.'

Jack checked his watch. It occurred to her that he'd lost his habit of checking it every few minutes. She smiled as she thought of them as a couple – it felt good.

'Should make it if I put my foot down,' he said.

'Let's get going then.'

'Next stop Dublin.' He winked at her and started the engine.

## 34

'I've been buzzing for ages. Didn't you hear me?' asked Julia, walking down Jeremy's hall.

He followed her into his lounge without answering. Once inside, she turned and inspected him.

Although it was 6pm on Friday evening, he was still in his dressing gown, barefoot and probably hadn't shaved for a couple of days, if the short, sandy-coloured growth was anything to go by. He slumped down on one of the sofas.

Julia stood, regarding him critically. 'People at work have been asking where you are.'

He shrugged his shoulders.

'I told Harold you had the flu.'

Again, he just shrugged his shoulders.

She sat down on the sofa opposite and looked around at the messy room – old beer bottles and chocolate wrappers were lying everywhere.

'Feeling any better today?' she said with a sympathetic smile.

He shot her a look of annoyance. 'Oh super duper. Couldn't be better.'

'Don't be sarky with me. I just thought you might be coming to terms with it today.'

Jeremy glanced away. Last night, when Julia had rung to enquire why he hadn't gone to work, he had told her all about Emma and Jack. Once she'd got over her own shock and bemusement about the two, she had listened intently and tried to be supportive. They'd chatted for over an hour and a half yet he seemed more miserable at the end of the conversation than at the beginning.

'Will you be in on Monday?' she asked.

'Depends.'

'On?'

'If I haven't thrown myself in the Thames over the weekend.'

'Don't joke about things like that.'

He leant back on the sofa gazing up at the ceiling.

Julia opened her bag and lit a cigarette. Smelling the stuffiness of the room she walked across to the upper section of the lounge and opened the French windows wide to let some air in. Sitting back down opposite him she asked, 'Have you eaten?'

'Chocolate and ice-cream – fuels to mend a broken heart.'

'Thomas is worried about you. Says you haven't even taken his calls.'

Jeremy dropped his head forward into both hands. 'I just need some time. I've been doing a lot of thinking about my life and where it's going.'

'Come to any conclusions?'

'None worth mentioning.'

Julia drew hard on her cigarette. After a moment she got up and went and sat beside him. 'Don't think too much right now. You've had a knock. Get yourself back into circulation and take your mind off it. Too much thinking isn't good. Maybe you should go away for a week's holiday.'

Jeremy sat up straight and briefly squeezed her hand. 'I was thinking about that. You'd come too, wouldn't you? My treat . . . somewhere warm. How about the week after next? Sod work.'

Her gaze fell downwards and she paused for several seconds. 'Sorry, I can't.'

'Why not? Said it's my treat.'

'I'll be in the Lake District.'

'*Lake District*? You! Why?'

'A conservation week, planting trees and things.'

Jeremy laughed. It was the first laugh in days for him. '*You* on a conservation week?'

Her eyes glinted. 'I told you, I'm changing. I've even left the club, although I said I'd help out the odd night.'

Jeremy huffed. 'This is Thomas, isn't it? His missionary zeal in saving the world is becoming quite tiresome.'

'Not to me.'

'Obviously not.' He crossed his legs over and looked away. 'So, he's going too?'

There was a noticeable hesitation. 'Yes. Come if you want.'

'No thanks. A week planting trees with a load of New Age warriors . . . think I'd prefer a week stuck in quicksand.' He had a sad and sulky look on his face as he wondered who else he could ask to go on holiday with him. So many of his other friends had settled down with partners and wouldn't go alone. He couldn't even invite Thomas now, as he was obviously busy with Julia. A strange thought occurred to him. He stared oddly at her. 'Is anything going on between you two?'

Julia took a final draw on her cigarette before stubbing it out. 'Why are you asking?'

'That's not an answer.'

She hesitated and shifted uncomfortably on the sofa. 'Maybe,' she said finally.

He glared at her. 'What do you mean, "*maybe*"?'

'Well, it's early days.'

'How early? Last weekend you were coming on to me.'

She tutted. 'Look, I've been aware that he's liked me for a while. However, after last Saturday night when I thought that nothing would ever happen with you. I . . . I . . .'

Jeremy smirked. 'Don't tell me you went straight into his bedroom after leaving me.'

'Not that night, no. But we've met up a couple of times since. Let's just say our relationship is about to move on.'

'Julia, you're unbelievable.'

'Just because you put *your* life on hold, doesn't mean that *I* should. You wouldn't catch me waiting eight years.'

'Eight seconds would be too much for you.' He jumped up and marched over to the window, his mouth pinched and twisted. His pulse was racing and for the second time that week a wave of anger swept over him.

Julia remained seated gazing downwards, looking annoyed herself but also a little guilty. Finally glancing up she said, 'Sorry . . . I probably shouldn't have told you all this tonight.'

'Kick a man while he's down, why don't you?'

'I'm sorry. But I didn't want to lie . . . It won't change our friendship. Nothing will change with the three of us. Thomas agrees. We've discussed it.'

Jeremy let his head fall against the window pane. In a quiet, despondent voice he said, 'Everything has already changed.'

Julia went to take out another fag but stopped. 'Maybe I should go,' she said.

He gave a shrug of his shoulders. She stood up and walked over to him. When he didn't turn around to face her, she just leant over and kissed him on his cheek. 'I'll call you tomorrow. Maybe the three of us can go out?'

He nodded briefly.

She slowly walked away but on reaching the door,

turned and stared at his back for several moments. In a sincere, heartfelt manner she said, 'You'd still be my first choice, Jeremy.'

He didn't respond, just continued to stare out of the window.

Julia turned and quickly left.

Jeremy watched her walk across the car park and down the road, until she was eventually out of sight. *Crazy woman*, he thought. *And shallow. And more flippant than me – that's saying something. Saying I'm first choice.*

For what seemed an age he just stood, head leaning against the glass, not sure what to do. *So that's it*, he thought. *Emma's with Jack. Julia's with Thomas. And as usual, I'm alone.*

He surprised himself by thinking of Tony and wondering how he was coping. For a mad moment he imagined drinking away his sorrows with him – the perfect companion right now, united in abandonment and self-pity.

*Everyone's moving on*, he thought. *Nothing will be the same again.*

Over half an hour passed before he moved away from the window and eventually wandered into the kitchen, opening the fridge. There it was, still unopened – the champagne to celebrate becoming a partner. He might be a partner in the firm, but would he ever be a partner in his personal life? Did he truly want to be?

He grabbed the bottle and a glass and marched out on to his balcony. Once there, he quickly opened it and poured himself some, gulping it down in one go. Life always appears better after champagne. Filling up the glass again, he continued to take large mouthfuls. Sacrilege to gulp such a fine vintage, but right now who cared?

His thoughts turned to Julia. She was probably on her way to Thomas. *We do get on really well. Is this another chance I'm letting go?* He couldn't help but wonder. His head sagged downwards and at the same time the glass slipped from his hand, smashing on the floor into little pieces all around him. He sneered at the mess then took a large swig directly from the bottle. The champagne fizzed up and spurted out all over his face. Wiping himself with the corner of his dressing gown, he soon realised the champagne was mixed with his tears. He slumped down on to the balcony railings, grabbing hold of them for support.

'Oh, Emma,' he whispered under his breath. Part of him couldn't believe she was actually with Jack. His Emma with Jack. A jabbing pain cut through his chest. Maybe it wouldn't last – it couldn't last. He stood up straight. That was it. Of course it wouldn't last. Then she'd be single, he thought. Jack could be like some stalking horse, his role merely to free her from Tony. Maybe it was all meant to be this way. There was still some hope – maybe even more hope, not less. He gave Emma and Jack a year, nothing more. He smiled. Another year wasn't too long to wait.

And then . . .?

## 35

On Monday morning, Emma put on Jack's robe and wandered downstairs into his kitchen. As she opened the blinds, the sun instantly shone in; it was going to be a beautiful day. She planned to sit in the garden for a couple of hours. Putting on the kettle, she decided to make herself a late breakfast of Spanish omelette.

The routine of the last few mornings had been the same, except that Jack had been with her on those. They'd both decided to take the remainder of the week off and had been inseparable – walking, talking, eating, intimate moments shared and enjoyed. Neither of them had mentioned looking for an apartment for her.

Unfortunately, on Sunday afternoon, Harold had telephoned Jack and asked him to attend an urgent partners' meeting early the next morning. Jack had flown over to London late on Sunday night arranging to be home with her by eight o'clock that Monday night.

Emma was supposed to return to work today but, at the last minute, she hadn't gone. She thought it would be good to spend a day on her own.

After finishing her breakfast, she ran back upstairs and dressed quickly. She had planned a special meal for that evening and wanted to get to the shops and start preparing it. She was missing Jack already. Seeing her clothes hanging up next to his in the wardrobe brought a smile to her face, yet of course, she immediately thought of Tony.

Emma sat down on the edge of the bed and turned her thoughts to him again. The night before, she'd almost telephoned him, just to see how he was, but then guessed he had already transformed any hurt into a deep hatred against her; it would remain that way always. It would be how he'd cope, burying it deep down, kept hidden at all costs with all the other crap – stewing inside, growing, manifesting, fuelling demons. She pitied his next relationship. She knew him better than she knew herself. If she had rung, he'd probably just have told her to fuck off. She considered telephoning Rob, but decided his response would probably be the same.

Instead, she had written Tony a long letter, trying to explain her feelings and at the same time trying not to attack him, or blame him for his own affair. After she'd written ten A4 sides, she read them back to herself. It was a complete rambling mess, yet she'd gone out that night and posted it in the nearest letter box. She could hardly remember what she'd written now. Hopefully it would bring him some comfort. Probably not!

She was still worried about him. Hopefully he wouldn't drink himself silly – another of his coping mechanisms.

But there was no going back. It was done. That was it. *Eight years*, she thought. Eight years neatly tucked away in the bottom drawer. Maybe she should be more upset, but she wouldn't lie to herself. She felt relieved, happy and excited. Guilt was tugging at the back of her mind, yet she couldn't let it rise up in case it destroyed any future chance of happiness.

Guilt had been a constant companion throughout her life, drummed into her from early childhood. Everything she ever said, did or even thought would be checked against her internal guilt monitor, so expertly installed by her parents. It was probably guilt, or fear of it, that had kept her stuck in her old life for so long. That's why she wouldn't let it descend on her now.

Maybe in the months to come it would affect her more, but right now she wanted to live life to the full and do everything that she had been too nervous to do before. She felt intoxicated with the freedom – unburdened and liberated. So many thrilling possibilities were lined up ahead of her. Jumping up, she grabbed her bag and left the house. There was a real skip to her step as she headed along the road, breathing deeply, smiling broadly.

At five past eight, Emma was pacing up and down the lounge, sporadically looking out of the window for Jack's car. He'd rung from Dublin airport to say he was on time and she felt like an excited six-year-old eagerly waiting for Christmas. Her stomach was filled with butterflies, pleasant, dancing ones, happy with their new-found wings.

Dinner would be served around nine, stuffed tomatoes, followed by vegetarian moussaka and finally chocolate fudge cake, all hand-made by herself. Her mother would be proud. *My God! What will they* think *of all this? Not that it matters.* In a weird way her parents would almost be pleased – a wealthy solicitor, sounds good. And appearances are what counts. Not that there were any plans for them to meet him, no way! Absolutely *not*! Jack would be kept safely hidden away for many months.

She continued pacing up and down, occasionally sipping her wine.

Ten minutes later, Jack's car pulled up outside. She ran to the front door but deliberately didn't open it – she didn't want to appear too desperate. Then *sod it*: she undid the lock and bolted down the steps to greet him.

'Hello,' he said with a smile, lifting his case out of the boot.

It was strange seeing him back in his suit. He was still technically her manager. She remained a few feet back, suddenly shy. He locked the boot and walked over to her. With one arm around her he led her back into the house and once in the hall he embraced her fully, hugging her for a considerable while as if it were a relief to see her still there. She clung to him tightly and they kissed several times, smiling in between.

Then Jack pulled back and stared at her. Emma couldn't quite work out his expression but it unsettled her. 'I need a two-minute shower, then I have something major to tell you,' he said.

She looked worried. 'Good or bad?'

'Both. The outcome, I believe, will be good.'

'The meeting?'

'Partly.'

'What is it?'

With an odd, mysterious smile he said, 'Just prepare yourself for a major life change.'

'Another one. Not sure I can take any more right now.'

'Of course you can, we're on a roll.' He turned and ran up the stairs.

The two minutes he promised felt like two long drawn-out hours. She finished her glass of wine and poured herself another. Anxiously walking around the kitchen she hadn't a clue what he was going to say. It had been such a crazy week that anything was possible. *Maybe he's going back to his ex-wife? Ridiculous! He's probably just being posted elsewhere. Dear Lord, don't let it be Manchester. I've only just escaped!* Could life really be so cruel?

She marched over to the back door and opened it, refusing to think any more.

'That's better.'

She turned and saw Jack standing in the doorway.

She eyed him cautiously. Helping himself to a glass of wine, in a serious voice he said, 'You'd better come and sit down.'

Nervously she obeyed. They sat opposite each other at the kitchen table sipping their wine in silence for a moment.

'The meeting,' he began.

Emma's eyes slowly travelled up to meet his.

'You won't believe Harold. He's changing everything.' Jack shook his head angrily. 'Wants to halve Manchester in size. Staff can have positions at London if they want, otherwise they're out of a job.'

Emma thought of Trish.

'To top it all, guess what? Dublin's closing.'

'*Dublin*! Why?'

'Says he doesn't see it within the long-term strategy of the company. Says it won't generate the level of profits needed to justify its existence.'

'But all the money spent, all the work?'

'I know. It's crazy, the man's crazy. It'll all be written off.'

'What about you? Back to London? When?'

Jack shook his head slowly and narrowed his eyes. The previous mysterious smile appeared again. Taking a deep breath he said, 'I've resigned.'

Emma gasped.

'Had to, Emma. I can't work for Harold, he'd drive me mad. The man has as much business acumen as Noddy or Big Ears. I disagree with everything he's doing, and anyway . . .'

'What?' Emma waited for the next bombshell.

'I called him a fucking jerk.'

She covered her mouth with her hand, eyes gleaming brightly.

'A fucking *useless* jerk to be precise.'

Gradually both of them began to laugh.

'Well he is,' said Jack. 'And I'm too old to start kissing people's arses.'

She raised her glass up. 'Good for you! Cheers!'

He lifted his. 'Cheers.'

'So we're both unemployed,' she said with a strange smile.

He was grinning oddly too. 'Seems that way.'

Unexpectedly, they both laughed aloud at the situation.

'So what happens Monday?' she asked, after calming down. 'Do we go to work?'

'You'll be asked to return to Manchester.'

'I'm not going.'

'You'd better not,' he said. 'I'm supposed to give a month's notice but they won't want that. Probably removing my signature from all the bank accounts right away.'

'My bonus?'

'I have a three thousand pound cheque in my case for you.'

She sighed with relief. 'Thanks. Looks like I'm going to need it.'

Jack stood up and took the bottle of wine from the fridge before returning to the table.

With that same strange look he said, 'That's only half of it.'

Emma buried her face in her hands before sitting back up. 'My heart can't take much more. For eight years nothing has changed, not even the milkman. Now, every time I blink, something major happens.'

'This is the good bit.' Jack took Emma's hand in his. His stare penetrated deeply into her. 'You may think me completely insane for what I'm about to suggest, maybe I am. But let's face it, why not? We're both unemployed, nothing to lose.'

She stared on nervously.

'I've had a dream for ages . . . not that I ever thought I'd do it. Dreams are for dreaming, not actually doing. But you've brought something out in me. Now with the way things are, it's ideal.'

Her eyes narrowed.

'What is six months, Emma, six months of a person's life? It's nothing.' He paused, then said determinedly, 'Let's sail my father's yacht around the Indian Ocean for the summer, you and me. It would be wonderful. Just think of it, doing exactly what we want, mooring up at the most beautiful beaches, the sun, the sea, the food. *Paradise*!'

Emma held her heart as if supporting it. She opened her mouth wide but closed it again. She gasped then coughed a couple of times.

'Well?' he asked, squeezing her hand tightly.

She wanted to speak, but couldn't.

'It would be an amazing experience,' he added. 'We both need to broaden our horizons. Take some time out, decide what we want next. My father's already said yes. He thinks I'm having a mid-life crisis. Hell! Maybe I am. Some guys buy flash cars, but I never do things by half.'

In a quiet, timid voice she said, 'I've never been on a yacht.'

'You'll love it: thirty feet, a good size, two bedrooms, sleeps six. My boys will probably fly out and meet us occasionally.'

'What about money?' she asked.

'Forget money. I'll pay. Won't cost much, fuel and food. You'll be my guest.'

Emma was still clutching at her heart. 'When would this happen?'

'Two weeks' time, maybe four. By the start of June definitely.' He watched her eyes dilating, mind ticking over. For once it was her expression giving nothing away.

'Please Emma, say you'll come.'

Out of nowhere she suddenly squealed, '*Yes*! Yes, yes, yes. Let's do it. Let's *really* do it!'

'You mean it?' Jack's eyes lit up with relief.

'I'm shaking like a leaf, terrified, but yes, I mean it. I'm going to go. Damn it, how can I not?'

Jack laughed and grabbed both her hands in his. She laughed with him. Tears were falling from her eyes. 'This is mad,' she yelled.

'Absolutely,' he shouted.

'We're *insane*.'

'Potty,' he agreed, grinning.

'What if we don't get on?'

'You're thrown overboard.'

She leapt up and practically jumped on the spot a few times. 'Don't let me change my mind. Make me go. I have to go. I'm going.'

He was laughing at her behaviour. She sat down on his lap.

'Tell me I'm not dreaming.'

'Maybe we both are.'

He embraced her and soon the laughter and smiles disappeared.

Suddenly serious, they stared into each other's eyes. It was a couple of minutes before he leant forward and pressed his lips against hers, delicately kissing her.

'Oh, and by the way,' he said calmly, 'I love you.'